The Afflicted Saga

Deception

Tale of the Fallen: Book II

Katika Schneider

For my husband
Without you, I'd have never set foot in Abaeloth.
Your support means the world to me.

ACKNOWLEDGMENTS

Forever and always, my eternal gratitude goes to my cover artist, Sarah Anderson. Thank you for your patience, your skill, and your ability to bring my vision to life.

Much thanks also to the amazing Lacey Sutton. May I someday understand formatting half as well as you do.

To my lovely beta readers, thank you for your endless enthusiasm and for not laughing at me (too hard) for calling Veed a door.

Michael, Sammy, Honey, and Judy, you not only gave me delicious food, but let me stay to work in your inspiring atmospheres. About half of Deception was composed and polished in your establishments. Thank you for the havens.

And a special thank you to my readers and fans for your patience, support, and unrivaled faith while life tried to keep me from finishing this book. I hope it's everything you dreamed it would be.

ONE

Commander Brant Maliroch burned with rage so hot it drove his tensed muscles to quiver. When his cousin and general, Nessix, stormed off to sputter her frustrations elsewhere, Brant had leapt at the chance to knock Mathias Sagewind down a peg. Or completely to the ground. As usual, Brant's scrutiny and ultimatums barely even fazed the pretentious paladin, and when Mathias went as far as to run from their confrontation astride Nessix's mount, Brant lost the ability to care about the image he displayed to the army surrounding him.

Despite the blessings Mathias had brought to Elidae, Brant had fermented a rich loathing toward him over the past several months. The paladin's bold move of acting behind Nes's back infuriated Brant. Discovering her stumbling out of Mathias's bed chamber snapped the final thread of patience the commander had left. He'd warned Mathias to stay out of his cousin's life and fully intended to use whatever force was necessary to ensure as much today. The only misgiving tugging at Brant now was Logan's peculiar behavior immediately before Mathias vaulted onto his back. The warhorse allowing that blasted human in the saddle was a miracle in itself.

Nervous eyes from sheepish soldiers studied Brant in ginger anticipation of his inevitable response to their current position. Even under Nes's guidance, Brant had gained the reputation of

1

being a bit of a wild card, and it never took much to rile up the commander. Guilt of sneaking off without their rightful general's knowledge settled over the army, and the smartest of the nearby soldiers must have known how Brant looked down on them. Reactivity aside, Brant was but a one-man force in the midst of an abundance of well-armed and skilled men who clearly loved Mathias. Hissing his condemnations, Brant spun to follow the path Logan's massive body had crashed through the timber.

"Commander Maliroch, where are you going?"

Brant clenched his fists at his sides, brown eyes smoldering with the caustic remarks respect held at bay. Peer by rank, but subordinate by age, protocol insisted Brant at least respond to Sulik. Jaw aching, he shuffled to a stop and turned. This quarrel wasn't meant to be with Sulik, but if he wanted to intervene, Brant would extend the courtesy. "I am going to track down my general, Commander Vakharan."

Sulik halted his advance a safe dozen paces from his indignant comrade. He couldn't fault Brant for his conduct and had warned Mathias against acting outside of Nes's consent. Sulik was equally aware that he was the only candidate calm enough to take control over this upset. "I think it would be wisest to let Sir Sagewind—"

"Would you quit with that bullshit already!"

A strict frown pressed patience into the wiser of the two officers. "Son, you are acting out of the chain of command."

Brant spat. "The chain of command? *Your* general, that foreign piece of shit, violated Nessix and—"

Sulik crossed his arms. "Violated her."

"Yes."

Sulik coughed out an abrupt laugh at the absurdity of Brant's claim. There was no way a man of Mathias's integrity would stoop so low as to take advantage of a woman, but given the severity of Nes's reaction, the thought of the two generals sharing an intimate encounter prior to this movement wasn't an impossibility. It was a shame Mathias hadn't listened to Sulik's advice; the paladin would have been good for Nes, good for the nation of Elidae as a whole. Sulik rubbed his forehead and met Brant's feverish eyes.

"I'm not sure our definitions of that word are the same. And you're speaking as though *you* can judge a man for sleeping with a woman."

"I can when that woman's Nes."

Sulik rolled his eyes. Staying the course of Brant's debates, especially those involving Nessix, seldom ended without headache. "Nessix wanted a break. She *needed* one. Sir Sagewind knew the war wouldn't wait—"

"And so he just snuck off without a word?" Brant flung an accusing hand at the soldiers who kept their heads shamefully ducked as they continued with camp preparations. "This is Nes's army. Sagewind has no say over its movement or management."

"It is Nes's army," Sulik agreed, praying for his patience to hold out, "and she's done a fine job managing it so far, but this is a war against demons."

"A war that would have been over months ago if your damned paladin wasn't here enticing the beasts."

"The only way it would have ended without his help is through our deaths or submission. Please tell me you haven't forgotten how Nessix was nearly killed in the beginning?"

Brant sucked his teeth and speared his seething glare aside. He remembered, alright, and it was the only time he'd found a positive side to Mathias. Nessix, as she stood today, had all the necessary skills to wrap up this war, but Brant rejected the notion that she only got this far because of Mathias's guidance.

"You can take your doughy-eyed commitment to that—"

Sulik pinched the bridge of his nose. "Brant—"

"—son of a bitch and shove it up your ass." Brant sneered at Sulik's labored sigh and perturbed glance to the heavens. "*I* will not stand for this sort of insubordination to our general, to our ancestors. Even if Nes and I have to defend her position by ourselves, we will not let this filthy human take it from us."

"Sir Sagewind has no desire to take Nes's position or loyalties from her." Sulik squared his stance, the cold veil of logic settling across his face.

Brant narrowed his eyes, sweeping his silent criticism across the subdued troops around them. "He ordered all of these men, yourself included, to act outside of Nes's knowledge and consent, and they did. If that's not a grab for power, I don't know what is."

Sulik looked away. From the start, Brant had brandished wary skepticism against Mathias's faith in the Mother Goddess, Etha, and the divine abilities he wielded in her name. Nobody faulted Brant for that, considering the bitter void left when the island's own god, Inwan, had abandoned them, but Brant remained one of only two people Sulik counted who discredited the paladin's positive influence on this war. Even Nessix, in all her stubbornness, had learned to rely on Mathias's judgement, whether or not she agreed with his actions. Sulik sighed.

"I will admit he should have gone about this differently."

"He shouldn't have gone about it at all," Brant snapped. "Open your eyes, Sulik. That man's conduct and lack of respect is tearing our army apart."

The older of the two commanders worked his jaw slowly and rubbed the back of his neck. There was no talking this through with Brant—the younger man had made up his mind long ago and Sulik knew better than to expect him to change. "So what is your plan? Are you going to just stand here and whine about your perceived injustices?"

Brant scowled. "I'm going to track that fucker down and put him where he belongs. That's what I'm going to do. When Nes and I get back here, we will expect this army's obedience."

As far as Brant was concerned, this camp and the subversive soldiers posted in it deserved an ambush, and Sulik had earned the right to be the one to manage it. Once this war found its end and Mathias ceased to serve a purpose, Brant would rid Elidae of the paladin with a clear conscience. The chastened troops hustled to part for Brant as he shoved his way past Sulik to storm off in the direction which Logan had disappeared.

Sulik shook his head and blew out a deep breath. "All will be well," he told the speechless men around him, wondering where he found such a lie. "We'll proceed setting camp as Sir Sagewind instructed."

The flimsy reassurance of Sulik's words trickled motivation back into the army, and the commander cast his apprehensive gaze toward the timber. It was too late to influence any of the decisions that had already been made, so damage control was the only option left for him. Sulik cleared his throat, blinked clarity into his mind, and busied himself with coordinating the camp's construction. After all, Mathias had earned his trust.

* * * * *

The warmth tapered from Nes's arms and cheeks, despite Mathias's most impassioned efforts to will otherwise, and he was thankful he'd thought to close her eyes. He squinted through pooling tears to track the demons' departure, the trees obstructing his view of the horizon and any impulse that might drive him to give chase.

Mathias had missed reaching Nessix in time to stop the fatal blow by mere heartbeats, and he'd rescued far less important people much further gone than this in the past. What spun his mind into turmoil now was how the oraku who called himself the Spirit Binder had extracted Nes's soul as it unshackled from her body and sealed her away in his wicked hands. Instinct urged Mathias to turn to Etha for help, but the thought of hearing her confirm Nessix was gone made him want to fall back to a time when hiding beneath the covers could chase his terrors away. A body without a soul was nothing more than a corpse, and on any other day, Mathias hated the blasphemy of necromancy even more than he hated demons. No spiritual trace remained in Nes's body. Mathias had thought he'd felt helpless when the demons' curses blocked him from Etha's blessing, but none of those recent struggles had prepared him for this.

Experience scolded him of the stupidity of sitting in a known zone of combat, but the strength to hold himself upright abandoned Mathias in a rapid whirl of numbness. He searched for the tiniest glimmer of something to restore until a sharp ache began to drive into his temple. The measly twenty-two years Mathias lived before Etha resurrected him had been the only time he lacked the ability to feel the souls of mortals, but nothing remained of Nessix for him to find. Neither in the physical world, nor the divine realm. Nothing in her, nothing pending entry to the heavens, just a haunting scrap of the beautiful warmth Mathias coveted. The only force capable of removing his goddess-given ability to reach another's soul existed in the darkest corners of the hells. Mathias couldn't remember the last time he cried.

* * * * *

Brant stalked through the forest, no longer caring how much noise he made. He had neither the need nor desire to hide from what he tracked. The path of snapped branches and trampled underbrush cleared by Logan's hectic strides led Brant down a clear path to his destination. When the sound of the great horse's frantic screams interrupted the bitterness of his internal ranting, Brant hastened his pace. Logan had picked Mathias up with some amount of urgency, and Brant doubted the paladin meant Logan any harm to merit calls of distress. That left one other source for the stoic warhorse's agitation.

Bursting through the timber's clearing, Brant stumbled onto the road and narrowly dodged Logan's senseless frenzy. Logan nickered a trembling greeting and lowered his head into Brant's familiar hands. Hot breath bellowed from the horse's flared nostrils as he tried to convey what happened to Nessix, but without sharing the sacred bond which bound fecklan and rider, those forlorn thoughts escaped Brant's comprehension. Logan did manage to convey that Nessix had found trouble, and Brant needed no other information. The horse popped up onto his hind legs, spun, and bolted back down the road.

Even wearied and taxed for breath, Logan outpaced the commander with ease, but Brant chased after him hard. He rounded a bend to discover Logan stopped beside Mathias, who sat at the side of the road. Emptiness consumed the horse's eyes, muscles twitching in preparation to flee from terror, all attention focused on the paladin. Agonizing clarity ran Brant through, confirming facts his leaping heart screamed to deny. He slammed to a stop and stared, panting from exertion.

Normally, Mathias jumped at the chance to spurt his snide remarks when he thought he could flaunt about his divine gifts, especially if he could tie it to some lesson he hoped to beat into Nessix. This time, Mathias stayed silent. Brant had been everything but discreet upon his arrival and had a difficult time believing Mathias hadn't heard him.

The paladin always approached Brant with a grating arrogance, throwing about that cocky calm to try to belittle him. Ignoring Brant's presence completely, though, was a new level of disrespect. Brant grit his teeth and clenched his fists, inflating himself with the brashness to charge ahead and demand the paladin's submission, until he registered the disturbing way in which Mathias hunched his shoulders forward, sturdy frame shaking in a weakness he'd never before shown to the flemans.

Drawn forward by Mathias's vulnerability, Brant skidded to a stop once again when he saw legs peek through the undergrowth. His heart caught in his throat and even agape, his mouth couldn't draw air. For the briefest moment, Brant's mind went blank.

"What did you do?" Hostility never made it past the tremor in Brant's voice, and a shrill ringing flooded his ears. Then, silence.

Silence as he watched Mathias's shoulders tremble. Silence as his body refused all commands to rush forward to confirm the only true fear he'd ever carried. Silence, and then a sharp pop. Brant's vision blurred.

A familiar giggle, long ago stifled by the weight of duty and honor, danced through the denial vying for purchase in Brant's mind. *He didn't do a thing, silly.*

Mathias ducked his head toward his shoulder. The emotional battering rendered the paladin's eyes red and quiet sobs escaped through an open mouth. All of Mathias's characteristic whimsy and impulsiveness drowned beneath an oppressive swell of despair and uncertainty.

"Commander, I..." Grief devoured the rest of his words.

Reality swept over Brant on a cold wave. He choked on his devastation and rushed ahead, crashing to the ground beside Mathias. The paladin made no attempt to stop Brant from snatching Nessix away from him. "Don't you do this to me!"

Brant shook Nes's body once by the shoulders, stopping to study her face and chest critically before he dropped her to the ground to search for her pulse. The last of her life's essence painted half of her neck and chin, the grass and her blouse soaking up the rest. Several chaotic breaths passed in silence and a strangled gasp snuck past Brant's barricades. Tears flooded down his cheeks and he shook Nessix again, even ventured to slap her. Sucking in breath so rapidly it numbed his face, Brant pressed his fingers against the wound at his cousin's throat, as if stopping what no longer flowed would do him any good.

"Get back here," he gasped. "We can't do this without you…."

Adrenaline exhausted, helplessness claimed Brant and he fell across Nes's chest with ugly sobs. The hand at her throat tangled in her hair, the other clenching fistfuls of earth. Stones bit into Brant's palm in an attempt to battle his fleeing sanity.

Still too stunned to begin grasping at answers, Mathias watched the haughty commander crumble through defeated eyes. The handful of scouts Sulik sent to safeguard his agitated comrade stumbled onto the scene, the scuffs of their boots severing the stuffy haze in the paladin's mind.

Mathias seldom mourned death, well aware of the limitless nature of spiritual life, but he had never been subjected to loss like this before. His position in the divine realm had spoiled him, allowing him to stay connected with those dear ones who passed from the physical world. He had loved Nessix and would have had endless days to catch up with her in the afterlife, but the demons had torn that chance from him.

Frightened of what tortures awaited in Nes's eternity, Mathias held his misgivings to himself. If he wanted to save Brant—and he needed to—it was imperative for him to push his heartache aside. Besides, Affliction would never let him succumb to something as simple as a broken heart.

Mathias pressed his fingers against his eyes and cleared his throat. "She's gone, Commander." Even as the gruff words formed the indisputable truth, the depth of their meaning danced fingerbreadths from comprehension.

Silence broken by intermittent gasps and muted weeping pulsed between the two men as Brant's hyperventilation gave way to a vivid clarity. *Nessix was gone.* He'd wrapped his entire life around protecting his cousin, leaving him with no set direction to press toward. Instinct kicked in and Brant roared in senseless retaliation to Mathias's words. He pushed himself up from Nes's still form, ineffectively fumbling with his sword. Mathias's weakened hands caught Brant by the shoulders and eased him back to the ground. Emotionally drained, Brant gave up on his will to fight Mathias for the first time in their turbulent history.

"Why didn't you heal her?" The timbre of Brant's tears nearly rendered his words unintelligible.

"There was nothing left for me to heal."

Not ten minutes ago, Brant had stood smug witness to the fall of Nes's relationship with Mathias. She'd been so passionate, so alive! Fury wrapped itself around Brant's sorrow, strangling his senses. *I never should have let her come after him....*

"They took her soul someplace out of my reach." The more Mathias repeated this fact, trying to make sense of it, the stronger those claws of despair dug into his heart.

I never should have woken her....

"Brant, I'm—"

The commander moaned an agonized lament and crawled his way back to Nes's body, collapsing across her chest in a fresh fit of sobs.

Mathias hid his discomfort at the brash man's weakness behind a hand to his mouth and looked up to the soldiers clustered around them. Eyes wide and tainted with disbelief, none of them fully processed the scene before them, much less grabbed words to express their thoughts. That was their general. Their *leader.* Nobody wanted to betray their loyalty to Mathias, but they hadn't been willing to pay this price. Repulsion would replace their grief once shock wore off, and Mathias let his hand flop back to his side. He scowled at his own limitations and looked away.

"There's nothing to see here," he told the scouts.

Nervous shuffles answered Mathias, but none of the scouts complied with his directions to move away. Brant's erratic sobs and incoherent blubbering hadn't yet convinced their stunned minds that this lifeless woman truly was Nessix Teradhel. War saw people cut down daily, but not their general! She'd been the only reason the army had managed to accept losing Laes and now she'd been torn from them just the same. Aching to reject the realizations of their splintering hearts, the soldiers soaked up Brant's cascade of emotion, succumbing to the bleak reality of a future without Nessix.

Accusing eyes seared into Mathias's back, blaming him for standing by while this tragedy struck, and he accepted their scorn without flinching. The restrictions of his capabilities aside, Mathias owed the fleman people so much more than an apology, more than something simple explanations failed to justify. Their charismatic and dramatic leader had made a clear effort to display the dispute which pushed her from their recent confrontation, and Mathias knew plenty of witnesses had watched him relieve Nessix of her sword. Even adequately armed, against the number of demons she'd faced on her own, Mathias suspected Nessix would have found a similar fate. But what if she'd been able to hold on one minute longer?

"Brant, we need to get back to camp."

The commander lifted his head slowly from where he'd buried it in the crook of Nes's neck, blood painting a crescent across his chin. "Unless you can fix this, you will not speak to me."

Mathias pinched his eyes shut, too spent to deal with the belligerent side of Brant, but equally aware of the likelihood of demon stragglers lurking about. It was imperative that he scraped Brant together long enough for them to reach the army's safety.

"She went with a fight," Mathias said, a heated lump swelling in his throat. "It was the sort of death she prayed for."

"But this wasn't supposed to happen!" Brant's pupils restricted and he clutched Nessix tighter against his chest. "None of this was supposed to happen!"

Plans already dashed terribly awry, Mathias couldn't help but think this was a much worse outcome than even Etha's warnings had meant to convey. At present, the army stood dangerously close to the remaining cavern which the demons used to access the surface of Elidae. The fact that they sprung such a quick attack on Nessix and disappeared just as fast suggested their acute awareness of the fleman army's current position. Mathias could resume wallowing in guilt and grief after he saw the troops out of harm's way, but right now, he focused on his obligation to protect these people. Whether or not the army still wanted his service, Mathias would not tolerate one more defeat.

Etha, find her for me, Mathias begged. His body ached with the aftereffects of his earnest rush, and his knees creaked as he hauled himself to his feet. He turned his eyes from the cousins. "We need to get back to camp."

Repeating the order didn't yield a different reaction from those around him. Brant's weeping and the hushed accusations passed between the scouts behind him were the only answers Mathias received. The entirety of his senses strived to their fullest to erect protective barricades, and while they held in this moment, he knew the fragility of the foundation supporting them. Somebody needed to maintain their head and right now, and Mathias seemed the only one capable of standing a chance. He'd allow himself to mourn in time, but the army had marched out here for a reason, one Mathias now struggled to convince himself was right.

"The demons won't leave us alone for long, not with us in shambles," he said, his voice devoid of its usual gusto. "We are vulnerable out here."

"No shit!" Brant wailed, wiping his nose on his shoulder.

Brant, this is nobody's fault.

Nes's voice clenched around Brant's throat and he gasped, disoriented eyes scouring her dead face. Adrenaline muted all but his most basic functions, limiting common sense to a bleak whisper.

Right now, you need *to trust him. Do it for me.*

No! This wasn't happening. It couldn't be happening. Brant's shoulders slumped forward.

Oh, it's very real, Nessix said to him, her voice ticking with tension Brant had never grown accustomed to. *Just like the danger of the demons coming back here. Get to the army. They need you.*

Brant squeezed his eyes shut and shook his head fiercely, rasping his voice against its limits. Watching Brant fall apart struck Mathias another blow, threatening to send him back to the ground. He was thankful the commander no longer looked his direction.

11

Brant wasn't the type to take well to pity. Logan bumped Brant's shoulder with his muzzle, trying to coax him back to sanity. Brant glanced over at the great horse to meet a gaze tainted with dullness more appropriate for a lesser beast. This wasn't happening.

You'll take care of him for me, right? You'll take care of each other?

Blinking past the echo of Nes's chipper voice, still unable to comprehend how those words hadn't left her lips, Brant's thoughts screamed defiance against her placid expression. He longed to respond to her, to ask her if she was actually there or if he was going mad, but the scraps of battle sense that pulsed on high alert reminded Brant of the audience surrounding him. Unable to stare at Nessix any longer, Brant scooped her close.

"Gather her possessions," he told the six men who had followed him. Stupefied minds grounded them in unintentional disobedience, and Brant roared his reprimand. "Get them!"

Mathias winced at Brant's harsh tone, but refrained from correcting any part of it. The soldiers staggered into motion, retrieving the pieces of armor strewn about the bloodied road. Brant pulled himself to his feet. His legs threatened to buckle beneath the added weight of Nes's body, but holding her took priority over his own stability. His head swam.

Are you alright? Nes's voice creaked with worry.

"No," he whispered.

I'm scared you're gonna drop me.

A new wave of tears rolled past their boundaries at the playful goading that had comprised Nes's youth. Brant knew she was dead. He held her lifeless body. He'd searched for a pulse and breath that weren't there. He'd seen Mathias cry. But her voice, the innocent, sprightly one that disappeared the same time Inwan had, was so real.

What are you talking about? she scoffed. *Of course I'm real.*

Brant approached life with bold enthusiasm, but this wasn't a day he wanted to live through. Barely grasping the coherence to realize this was all in his head, Brant withered to Nes's bubbly quips. His chest heaved at his last efforts to cling to sanity and he reeled over the concept of holding himself together. Mathias's hand grasped Brant's shoulder.

Brant hated this man. If valid reason had escaped him before, it was clear and indisputable now.

Please don't, Nes murmured. *We still need him to reach the end of this war.*

Brant's arms shook and he latched them tighter around Nessix. She didn't want him to drop her, and he didn't know how much longer his strength would allow him to support himself.

You don't have to do any of this on your own.

Of course he didn't. As Mathias's gentle guidance steered him to Logan, the vulnerable side of Brant surrendered to the fact that Mathias would still cleanse Elidae. He had someone to do the heavy lifting for him. Logan could carry Nessix back to the camp, back home, allowing Brant to fall into the dirt and cry until his heart stopped beating. He had Sulik. He had the army. If he could open his mind to the idea, he'd been assured he had a goddess.

Now you're getting carried away. You have me. We're all we ever needed.

Brant choked on an audible sob, a shrill growl accompanying the clench of his jaw as he fought off the instinct to respond to this torment. Complicating his ability to press on, Brant didn't even know if he wanted to tell Nes's voice to get away from him or break down in agreement. He didn't want her to disappear any more than she already had, but the depth which his reliance on Nessix had infiltrated his psyche terrified him. Mathias reached an arm across Brant's shoulders and steadied him before he collapsed.

With the support of the man he'd loathed for so long, Brant reached Logan's side. In silence, the two men lifted Nes's body into the saddle, laying her forward against the great horse's level neck. Booted feet were slid into stirrups she'd known so well, and Mathias stationed himself on the opposite shoulder from Brant.

"We need to get her back to the army." Brant's murmur beat Nessix to the same sentiment. "They need to know."

The soldiers clutched the pieces of armor possessively, their attention darting between their two living officers. Mathias suspected even the most devout of his advocates would have grudging fingers shoved his direction when it came time to place blame, but he had neither the time nor the mental fortitude to worry over that right now. There would never be an explanation worthy or passionate enough to compensate for Nes's death, and he wouldn't insult these people by trying to find one. He cleared his throat, placed a hand on Nes's knee, and averted his eyes.

Broken, the party set off through the woods to deliver the news to the army.

* * * * *

Rigid pacing carried Shand back and forth through the musty chamber. Crystalline orbs imbedded within stone walls cast a dreary light across the room, and she curled her lip at the filth around her in the depths of the demons' realm. Residue from the clay floor stained the hem of the goddess's robe and she sneered at the sniveling demon intended to serve as her host. Ever since last night when she'd instructed her fleman pawn to find a way to dispose of Nessix, thoughts of the young general's demise filled every free crevice of Shand's mind. Removing the inconvenient girl from Elidae would snatch away the island's greatest influence, not to mention the torture it would bring to Mathias. Shand blew out a forced sigh, mouth twisting in disgust.

"How do you vermin tell time down here?" she muttered.

The demon kept his head lowered as he glanced at his escape route. "Time isn't one of our greatest motivating factors, my lady."

Shand hissed her dissatisfaction and the demon cringed. On second thought, even if he tried to run, she'd catch him with little effort. He continued to watch Shand's repetitive path, fretting over how the irritable wrinkles in her scowl etched deeper with each step. Confident strides whispered down the hall, and the demon sighed. Moments later, Kol and his massive oraku companion rounded the corner. Dwarfing this host with the presence of his wings, Kol allowed the other demon to slip from the scene with minimal attention. The alar bowed.

"Is it done?" Shand breathed, jarring herself to an abrupt halt.

"It is." Nessix's blood still covered Kol's hands.

Shand drew a great breath through parted lips, her relieved grin brightening the light in her eyes. If this first attempt on Nes's life would have failed, Shand suspected Mathias's meddlesome nature would have found a bounty of methods to safeguard the girl. This fate Shand ordered, however, had succeeded in tearing Nessix from the world and Mathias both, alleviating the goddess's worries over the inconveniences Nessix provided. Unless...

A frown flawed Shand's face, chilling the mood in an instant. "What did you do to ensure Mathias won't just fix her?" She inclined her chin and narrowed her eyes as she appraised the two demons, trying to gauge how cunning she thought they were. "Did you take her head?"

Kol smiled—a wicked expression that would have daunted the mortal version of Shand—and extended a hand to his companion. "Much better than that, my lady. We took her soul."

His answer tickled Shand's heart and snatched at her breath. The concept of soul extraction had never occurred to her, seeming an impossibility, given Etha's original design for her mortal creations. If anyone could come up with a method to part a soul from eternity, it would be the creatures who Etha had abandoned. Shand wrung her hands in excitement. This limited Mathias's ability to tamper with her agenda beautifully. "May I see it?"

Annin the Spirit Binder strode up beside Kol and held up a fist sized glass flask topped with a blood red seal and etched with a script Shand didn't bother to decipher. Inside swarmed a milky haze, sparking with livid red bolts of energy which struck the walls of its confines. Awed, having never seen such a specimen before, Shand crept closer and watched as Nessix's soul swirled about in dismal frustration.

Shand laughed heartily and clasped her hands beneath her chin. "Much better, indeed! Kol, my dear, you have served me beautifully. I will be in touch with your lord in regards to your superior performance."

Kol lowered his head to hide the twitch of his lip. "Thank you, my lady."

"And I trust whatever you've done to her will keep her securely contained?"

"She will never again be in Etha's reach," Kol assured.

A second peal of laughter streamed from Shand. The mechanics of what Kol had executed escaped her, but she didn't particularly care about that. All that mattered was that the permanency of his method promised devastating impacts to Elidae and Mathias both, and should something go awry, Shand knew exactly which demon to hold accountable.

"Go and do whatever it is you do with souls," she said. "I've got some business to attend to upstairs."

Kol bowed once more and by the time he'd straightened, Shand was gone.

* * * * *

Sharp whistles from scouts detailed on the fringes of the camp announced the solemn procession, granting them clearance before anyone realized what marched toward the army. Clumsy crashes from watch posts ushered Logan and the men back to the makeshift establishment as anxious soldiers rushed forward to insist answers for their torrent of questions.

Mind still shuttered to any of Etha's reprimands, insight, or even consolation, Mathias's stony expression repelled the troops who had grown accustomed to his infallible warmth. It took long moments of Mathias gritting his teeth through the confused cacophony before the first of the soldiers noted Nes's unnatural posture. Not long after, the tremble of Brant's lower jaw disclosed the truth.

An eerie hush smothered the army, Logan's hooves and the dragging steps of those with him drumming through stilled hearts. Whispers of Nes's condition preceded the label of death, and a steady eruption of disbelief fought against even the most intense hopes. As soldiers packed around to peer on in horror, the formation was forced to a halt. Heartbeats later, after word trickled far enough through the camp, Sulik shoved his way through the gathering mass, soaking in Brant's aimless movement and the dejected vacancy spinning through his eyes. Sucking in a sharp gasp of revelation, Sulik cast his stunned gaze to Mathias.

"Sir Sage—"

"Deliver orders to pack up camp." Mathias refused to meet the commander's eyes. "We cannot fight like this."

Sulik's discipline forbid him to declare any sort of hostility or disobedience toward Mathias, but as his mind processed Nes's pale face and lack of breathing, he demanded a logical explanation. "What happened? Why didn't you—"

"He couldn't."

Brant's voice cut through the multitude of despondent moans. He made no attempt to shield his bitter interjection from those around him. If Mathias considered it just to abandon Nessix, it was fair for the army to soak in this valid reason to reject him at last. For the first time, Mathias let his head hang at Brant's stifled aggression without throwing about any confident excuses. Brant's thoughts raced out of control as he snatched at some amount of sense, and it occurred to him that Mathias could have been telling the truth.

That's because he is.

Brant pinched his eyes shut and turned his face against Logan's shoulder.

With Brant's burgeoning instability and Mathias well aware of his deficit of time before accusations began to fly, the paladin tore his hand from Nes's leg and forged his way toward the command tent. Stunned soldiers not yet knowing what to make of the situation parted to allow him passage, and Sulik left the solemn crowd to chase after his friend.

"Commander Vakharan," Mathias growled, keeping his head low. "You will distance yourself from me."

"But, sir—"

Mathias dug his heels into the ground and spun on the gentle soul. "Do not think it a request!"

As if this avalanche of insanity—something which Mathias had initiated last night when he first suggested this attack—hadn't floored the weathered commander on its own, the harsh reprimand bit hard. Sulik parked himself with no further objections and choked on the torn halves of his heart as Mathias stalked past the growing assault of bitter ridicule until it grew to a mutinous roar. The paladin remained stoic and unresponsive to their scorn.

Each of the cruel words and hasty threats struck Mathias on a superficial level, compounding his guilt for speaking so harshly to

Sulik and pricking holes in the thin film that held his composure together. He pressed through this consumptive anger, owing as much to the flemans, and stomached their due hatred. Too numb to care about himself, the only person Mathias felt sorry for was Sulik, who watched the army's cohesion collapse around him, trust locked against loyalty. Mathias needed to distance himself from the commander if he hoped to keep Etha's influence alive in the flemans' hearts. Let them hate him, but let them believe in Sulik's faith.

Mathias made it halfway to his destination before shame overtook him. This time, he couldn't blame his faults on curses or tainted blood. This time, he'd simply been too slow, thought too long. This was the preventable loss Etha had warned him about in the beginning, and he'd walked right into it. He should have told Nessix about this movement—he knew it then and, Etha, he knew it now. Infuriating her would have been laughable over this. A swell of remorse shook him and Mathias spun back to face the troops. He unsheathed his blade and threw it to the ground, kicking it out of reach and holding his arms wide. The flemans deserved their retribution, and he welcomed them to come.

Eager to release their sorrow and frustration through a physical outlet, the boldest soldiers needed no further enticement to charge their tarnished savior. The closest of the men made it only two strides before startled cries shot up from the northwest border of camp. Thoroughly battered and emotionally absent, their close proximity to the final road connecting Elidae to the hells had escaped even Mathias. But their opponents remembered just fine.

Though he knew better than to expect anyone to listen, orders flew to the tip of Mathias's tongue as a fierce regiment of demons pushed into the disorganized army. The flemans claimed no fear of death, but Mathias would personally stand in the way of them confirming that truth. The demons had told him months ago that they aimed to make him suffer, and they'd succeeded. With a bitter curse, Mathias dashed forward to retrieve his sword and charged toward the first ripples of combat. If he could protect anyone else, by Etha, he would.

The demons pressed through the fleman ranks like a flooding

river, mocking the memories of the effort meant to oppose them. Once Mathias reached the point of engagement, the demons' gleeful ferocity assured him they knew Nessix was dead. Not wounded, but dead. They'd planned on this all along, and Mathias sucked down that knowledge to fuel every blow. He hadn't fought demons with this depth of sheer abhorrence in quite some time, and as his focus slipped into the dark realms of his fury, Mathias caught the sound of Sulik's hoarse shout to provide support.

TWO

There wasn't a fleman alive who wanted Etha's guidance more than Sulik did right now. After the broken army limped back home in the darkness following their brisk and brutal engagement, Mathias hastened to seclude himself to tend to Nes's remains, and Brant darted off before anyone had the chance to assess his state of mind. That left Sulik alone in the grand entry, surrounded by weeping veterans and wailing civilians. The only senior officer with half a mind, duty and necessity robbed him of the chance to mourn. Hand pressed against his temple, Sulik scanned the dismay around him, helplessness gaining on him with each heavy breath.

Suppressing his vein of guilt for failing at the task he'd sworn to uphold in Nes's youth, Sulik invested his all in tending to the present demands of the wounded. Emotional outbursts from his would-be patients hindered his efforts, distress masquerading as injury. It didn't take Sulik long to realize how much he had yet to learn, and his heart fretted over whether or not his fledgling capabilities stood a chance at mending this fractured army. Overwhelmed and seizing a death grip on a responsibility he couldn't quite claim, outside stimuli shot straight past Sulik until spindly fingers tugged at his arm.

"*Hey!*" A little girl's peevish voice scolded him with the effort it took to gain his attention. "I *said* you're going to need to do something to pull these people back together. Mathias is not of capable mind right now, Sulik."

The child's words cut through the clamor of disorder and in this crushing tension, commanded the entirety of Sulik's threadbare focus. Teetering on the cusp of breaking, the girl's casual approach and disregard to his title snapped at his calm demeanor and Sulik spun around.

"Little girl..." He closed his eyes through the span of a pleading sigh. "I don't have time to—"

A flawless face, smooth and soft and innocent of anything harsher than bathing, beamed up at him. The girl stood just as high as his elbow and wore caramel colored braids on either side of her head. Her brows were set with authority, but not the stubborn sort most children attempted when trying to get their way. No, this child commanded authority from an innate expectation which Sulik couldn't begin to fathom, and when his brown eyes ventured to meet her amber ones, instinct screamed its justifications. His mouth sagged.

"Go on," Etha said. "You don't have time to what? Deal with my childish antics?"

Sulik's eyes widened, grief obscured by shock and shame and awe. He shook his head and backed two steps away, jaw flapping with broken syllables meant to reply. Etha let go of his arm.

"First thing's first. You keep your mouth shut about this," she said, her tone strict despite sympathetic eyes. "And stop with your groveling. There's no time for that."

He wobbled a mute nod and cleared his throat. "Of—of course, my, um..."

Etha held up a finger to demand his obedient silence. "I said none of that. This is a secret, remember?"

Sulik struggled to make sense of Etha's physical presence and what it meant. Mathias claimed to speak with the Mother Goddess on such an intimate level, and Sulik had personally known Inwan before the god lost his decency and abandoned Elidae. But he'd never expected Etha, in all her power, to manifest on the mortal plane, least of all as a little girl.

"Does my form offend you?"

He blanched, also having never imagined her to be so forward.

"Mathias must have told you some rotten lies, then."

Sulik crossed his arms and quickly ceased his speculations.

"Very good." Etha delivered a curt nod, her eyes growing sadder. "Now, dear commander. You go see to the tattered bodies as Mathias taught you, and let me see what I can do for the broken hearts."

Still silent, Sulik's head bobbed in assent. Etha smiled tightly at him, squeezed his hand, and flit deeper into the crowd. The last thing Sulik heard from her was a compassionate little voice coaxing condolences into rattled warriors and lost civilians. With the burden of managing the grief-stricken masses passed along to someone much more qualified for the job, a constricting lump gummed up Sulik's throat and he felt his nose start to run. Coughing down the sensation, he brushed a hand across his eyes and turned to the mess hall. All this time, Mathias had been right. Etha was with him.

* * * * *

Brant staggered through the halls of the fortress, sapped of the ability to keep crying. Too wrapped up in their own lamenting, nobody but Mathias had even bothered to extend concern toward him. No matter. The rush of blood pounding through Brant's head prevented him from discerning the sounds around him with any degree of accuracy, and the heavy tingling in his limbs made his movement erratic at best. There were no actions or words capable of changing what happened, so any well-wishers might as well save themselves the effort and Brant the awkward acceptance of words he didn't care to hear.

Brant, tell me what's going on. Please!

And then, there was that. Brant wasn't a stupid man. He knew the ins and outs of war well enough to understand death, he'd just never imagined Nessix finding it before him. He'd walked beside Logan, clutching his cousin's cold hand, over the entire trek back to the fortress. Every last miserable part of him understood that Nessix was dead. But it seemed as though a substantial part of him longed to believe otherwise.

Spirituality had been an easy concept to grasp before Inwan left them, but Brant found very little use for such virtues these days. Whatever fragment of Nessix that still existed tagged along with him, rattling off questions as if he stood an honest chance of delivering answers. Her voice had shed the worry which plagued her of late, and in death, she seemed to reclaim the innocence she'd lost along the way. Brant's boots clicked to a stop as a frustrated growl raked free from his throat. He pulled at his hair and shook his head. Nessix hadn't reclaimed anything. Nessix was dead.

Now, stop it. I haven't gone anywhere.

"Shut up…" he begged.

Don't be so—

"I said shut up!"

Brant's voice rebounded back at him from stone walls, emphasizing the indisputable fact that Nessix was not there. Heart racing, he raised his head, bleary eyes scanning the passage for anyone who might have witnessed his humiliating outburst. Besides his mind's badgering, Brant stood alone in the hallway, and he blew out a ragged breath. His sundered heart begged him to clutch at this echo of his beloved cousin, to never let her go, but in this brief glimpse of clarity, he knew the safest path required him to purge every last tangible aspect of Nessix from his life. He didn't remember a time without her, and he didn't want to envision such an empty future.

All of this fell back on him. Discrediting Mathias had become such an obsession for Brant that he'd jumped at the first available chance to do so, encouraging Nes to recklessness. He never should have riled her up. He shouldn't have even woken her when he found Mathias missing. This fatal error rested fully on Brant's shoulders. It pushed down on him, buckling his legs beneath the crush of its weight and promising to claim him before the demons had the opportunity to. Knees quaking, Brant clenched his teeth and set his eyes against a fresh flood of tears as snappy strides dragged him down the hall.

Where are we going?

Brant shook his head, refusing to acknowledge the chirp that

23

wasn't there. True to life, Nes's memory bristled at his neglect and spoke louder.

I said, where are we going!

Brant muttered a vague response under his breath, words which escaped his full comprehension. He knew exactly where they were going and no version of Nessix would appreciate it. If the dead truly could interact with him the way Nes's persistence now suggested, there was only one destination left for Brant to go. The longer he attempted to ignore the lively questions battering his distraught mind, the faster he walked, until an ache in his side begged him to slow down. If he could ignore Nessix, he could ignore something as petty as physical discomfort, and Brant maintained his resolute pace until he stopped in front of Laes's chamber door.

For several moments, the only sound came from Brant's labored breathing and the dull thud of his heart.

What are—What are you doing, Brant?

He swallowed hard and put his hand on the door.

It won't work. That door's been locked since... since...

As much as this very accurate likeness of Nessix wanted to seal away her father's tangible memories, Brant's determination to preserve his mental integrity begged him to treat her the same. An unseen force had guided him to Laes's quarters, and though his faith was less than limited now, Brant trusted this same force sent him there with some greater objective.

Unknown to the vibrant, living version of Nessix, Brant had tried more than a few times in the past to access his late uncle's quarters. As Nes's voice insisted, a locked door had met him each time. He lowered his hand to the handle, drew in a deep breath, and pushed forward. The door creaked open on neglected hinges.

Brant recoiled his hand with a startled gasp as the door swung open the rest of the way, and stared silently into the chamber's entryway. With the curtains still drawn across the windows, it took several slow blinks for Brant's eyes to adjust to the darkness. Dust had settled in a substantial carpet across the floor and film on the furnishings, but the room radiated a warm serenity, not at all eerie as he'd always imagined. A chair had been pulled back from the receiving room's central table and stood waiting to accept him, neither trails from the legs nor footprints left in the dust on the floor. The stale air inside didn't linger with the scents of sweat and the battlefield, and the immediate need to immerse himself in a way to forget struck Brant like a lance.

Close the door, Nes's voice begged.

He blinked once, eyes refocusing from where his staggering thoughts led him.

Brant, we can't go in there.

He frowned. "Then don't." Before whatever part of Nes that haunted him protested further, Brant stepped forward and into the peaceful solitude of Laes's chamber.

Soaking in the memories of how he'd bypassed mourning his uncle to preserve Nes's will, Brant faced the bleak fact that no one would be strong for him. He stopped three paces inside then turned to look back at the door. Delusion gaining on him like a ravenous wolf, he half expected to see Nessix fuming from the doorway, arms crossed and eyes alight with anger. The more pathetic side of him contemplated why she wasn't screaming at his insubordination. Reality prevented such hallucinations from taking hold, and Brant's breathing steadied. He turned away from the door and sank into the chair.

All his life, Brant had considered himself and Nessix protected from the world—vulnerable to life, but ever rising from its challenges. Nessix had proven her strength by persevering through the loss of her father, Veed's hasty departure, Inwan's betrayal, and most recently, the death of her grandfather. History had marked her untouchable. She'd not only filled the role of Brant's best friend, but the entire nation's golden child, their banner of hope and the will of the nation. The blood in her veins traced back to the first nobility to step off the ships that had carried refugees from Drailged. She'd never wasted her time on courtship, left behind no progeny, and the sacred line had been snuffed to ashes after twenty-one generations.

Brant's head sank into his hands. "Sir, what am I supposed to do?" he asked the much more reserved memory of Nes's father.

Of course Laes never answered; he hadn't been a deep enough

fixture in Brant's life to merit outbursts from the other side. Instead, the question launched the distraught young man down a frightening path. He could follow Nessix's lead and suck it up to accept his duty, or resort to relying on Mathias—as Laes had intended and Nessix had finally managed. These sorts of decisions were meant for much sharper, more stable minds than his own.

A tremor shook Brant's core and he abandoned his resolve once more. Tears assaulted him as twisted demands of why worked their way through his mind and, as he lost control, out loud. The people needed their leader, but she was gone. To try to take her place would be as much of a mockery as standing idle as the demons ravaged Elidae.

Brant's tears cleansed his mind, comfort wrapping its arms around him as he rejected his strength. Life on the battlefield had routinely denied him of expressing such emotions and today, all of those years of witnessing death caught up to him. Frustration and agony untied themselves from the snarls in Brant's heart as he faced aspects of life he'd never had the luxury to experience. So much had been wrapped up in war, and for what?

Despair slowly tooled itself into an insatiable need for vengeance. Duty no longer provided an accurate description for Brant's motivation. From now on, he welcomed madness and retribution to guide his sword arm. Inwan was no longer there to grant his strength, and Nessix was no longer there to obey. If Mathias wanted to try to stand in his way, Brant would sort matters out with him or gladly die trying.

The tears stopped as Brant leaned back into the seat, body surrendering to the need for recovery. Nessix would have been furious if they lost the war on account of her. Brant didn't owe this to the soldiers or civilians, he owed it to his general. The days of childhood innocence were far gone, and with them, the last bit of Brant's sanity. He'd never escape the sting in his eyes or the knife in his heart, but maybe that was the point. He would never forget this insult, and if he picked up only one thing fromNessix, it was to never forgive.

If Brant could trust Mathias's words, not even death would allow him to find Nessix again, so that held less for him than life.

He'd find no peace, no manner of rest, until every last demon writhed to a torturous end. Brant's eyes darkened with resolve and a shell encased his heart. He stood up.

"Do not resent me, Uncle, for failing you," he murmured, head bowed. "If you're with me now, know that I will not let the demons go unpunished."

Brant stood in the silence, waiting for a response he didn't expect. He stared out the open door a heartbeat longer, both dreading and longing his return to Nes's haunting. Drawing a steady breath, he strode from the room and pulled the door shut behind him.

So, are we gonna do this?
"Yeah," he said. "We are."

* * * * *

Mathias had taken up apprenticeship under Sir Markus Vogan at the age of nine. He saw his first dead body at ten and dealt the same not long after. Though he never delighted in death, he'd grown accustomed to it, but no amount of experience or desensitization prepared him for coping with losing Nessix.

Given the full spectrum of Mathias's capabilities, the act of preserving a corpse was one of the simplest divine tasks in his repertoire. It took little more effort than putting someone out, and the fact that the subject's welfare no longer needed consideration made it exceptionally easier than healing wounds. Logic defied why it took him five minutes to carry out the procedure, ten more to pray a blessing over her, yet he still didn't consider his service through. How could he?

Warmth radiated against Mathias's back as he sat facing Nes's bed and his hands tightened their hold on hers. He pinched his eyes shut and blew out his distress, lowering his head as he soaked in Etha's comfort.

"You were right," he murmured. "I should have told her."

With the silence broken, Etha curled her lips between her teeth and approached him. She laid a soothing touch on her child's shoulders, imparting what peace he was willing to accept.

"Mathias, not even I saw this coming. You had no way of knowing."

He leaned back in the chair, muscles rippling free of their tension beneath Etha's warmth. "I should have told her. She'd have ridden alongside me and not one of those cursed abominations would have touched her."

Mathias was the only creation alive that truly tortured Etha to disappoint, and the longer she left her hands on him, the more overwhelming the emotion pressed down on her. She recoiled timid fingers from his back and stepped around the chair to stand beside him. Etha had hoped to raise Mathias's spirit by commenting on Nes's peace, but she knew he was far too clever to believe it. Wherever the demons had stowed her soul, Nessix was far from at ease. Even in death, the late general's brows appeared drawn too close, her lips tucked in the slightest frown. Etha lowered her eyes.

"You did all you could," she said instead. "Whatever the demons did was something neither of us have seen before. We never could have expected it."

Mathias jerked his head away from his goddess. "That doesn't change that it happened."

"You've admitted yourself that time is something you can't undo. Dwelling on—"

"Etha, I have no other choice!" Mathias's words erupted from him in an aggressive burst, driving the petite goddess a step away from him. "Nes being their target was a deliberate jab at me, but the demons are stealing *souls* from you. How am I not supposed to dwell on that?"

With his bout of boldness through, Mathias slammed back into his chair, staring at the ceiling. He'd never felt as helpless as he did now. Every living being on Abaeloth contained a soul destined for the afterlife, an essence Mathias could track and find. Something for him to hold on to and keep safe and warm. The thought of demons gaining possession of such sacred energy terrified and enraged him. The fact that his dear Nessix was among those souls only made matters worse. Mathias clenched his jaw until tears seeped from his eyes.

28

Etha recognized the perverse tenacity which bore down across Mathias's brows and glanced down at her folded hands. "My dear, the time will come to sort this all out, but right now, we must protect the living, lest they are given the same fate."

Mathias's chest heaved with great breaths as his seasoned mind wielded common sense against raw desire. No matter how strong the urge to abandon his sworn mission to tend to this disgusting breach of nature, leaving the flemans, especially in the perilous state they now scrambled in, would do nothing to honor Nes's memory. Etha inched closer to Mathias as his expression settled away from the frightening glow of hysteria.

"Did I lead her to this fate?"

Mathias's question caught Etha off-guard. "What do you mean?"

"I was meant to be devoted to you. You are quite literally the only reason my heart is still beating."

The conviction in Mathias's voice alarmed Etha, and his loyalty to her made her tremble with guilt. All mothers wished nothing but happiness for their children, and Mathias had earned that right several times over. She brushed her fingers across his cheek.

"I cannot deny that you might have prolonged her life by taking a different path, but your affection for her had nothing to do with that."

He turned his gaze to Etha at last, allowing her to take in the extent of his distress for the first time. The fire in his eyes had dulled to a haunting glow, fueled by a distinct disregard for his own well-being. Etha couldn't tell by this one assessment whether the decay of his resolve came from his fear of losing her, his agony of losing Nessix, or his regret and shame of having failed his quest. Her tender eyes gazed back at him, further muddling his mind with confusion amidst the doubt.

"Why did she even bother to visit me last night?" Mathias muttered. Maybe this wouldn't have hurt so much if she'd never reciprocated his affection.

Etha chewed over the impact her honesty would have on Mathias before tucking her lips in a frown. "I think you know the answer to that."

The stubborn part of Mathias's mind that wailed over how he could have done things differently insisted Nessix had only been after a good time, but his memory was too sharp to believe it. When Nessix had come to him, she'd displayed herself vulnerably, anticipating his rejection. Her hands had been timid, her lips longing, and her sweet voice had gasped words only his most delicate fantasies had imagined to hear from her. Mathias glanced away from Etha.

"Whether or not she loved me, she's dead, and even her soul is—" He choked on the statement and rubbed his eyes with one hand. "Mother, please tell me you know where she is."

Etha's eyes drifted back toward her hands. "The demons no doubt have her tucked far away, to places you know I can't reach. She won't be easily found—"

Mathias spun to face Etha with such force his chair threatened to tip over. "It doesn't matter if it's easy!"

"Math—"

He fell to his knees, fingers grasping Etha's hands. "Great Mother, do not let my body come to rest until I have set Nessix free from the demons."

A gutted breath fled Etha. "You cannot be asking this with a clear mind." She followed Mathias's gaze to where it locked on Nes's solemn expression. "You've felt the consequences of such restlessness before and have too much knowledge of what the demons of the inner realms are capable of."

He shook his head fiercely. "Do not make me face eternity knowing she's nothing more than a puppet for the fallen."

Etha's shoulders slumped, her hands trembling in Mathias's grasp. "Do not ask me to allow your vengeance."

The gentle plea soaked through the pounding in Mathias's head. Weariness scratched at him, reminding him that even the mighty White Paladin had physical limits. He looked up at Nes's still face, longing for all of those things he'd never hear her say. When he'd first set out for Elidae, he'd never expected to develop a fondness for Nessix, and upon their initial pleasantries, he'd found her more obnoxious than charming. Somehow, though, she'd

30

wriggled her way into his life and he'd never intended to let her go.

Over the centuries which Etha had wielded Mathias against the demons, he'd developed a unique regard for them. He'd forged coarse relationships with some, and rid more than his fair share from Abaeloth. In the end, though, he never lost sight of the distorted souls cast aside from the Divine Battle. Fighting the fallen, pushing them to exile, was exactly what had launched this ceaseless war between demons and mortals in the first place. Mathias knew better than to hope for the two sides to ever unite, but he dreamed that maybe one day the suffering could end.

But here he was now, as tortured as the demons could ever hope to make him. Nes's chest still refrained from rising with breath, despite Mathias's most fervent wishes. He pressed his tongue against the roof of his dry mouth and frowned. He was the only real advocate the demons had in the upper realms, and they'd thrown it away, degrading themselves to filth in his eyes. Mathias had no more excuses for their conduct, and he wouldn't try to make any. With or without Etha's grace, he'd see vengeance for Nessix, carrying no regret for whatever measures he deemed necessary to find it. It had taken them ages, but the demons had finally pushed his placid mind too far.

"Will I ever see her again?" The question snuck past Mathias's ambitions to hoard his fears, but he didn't hide from it.

Etha ducked her head from Mathias and gnawed the inside of her cheek. When she'd said Nes's soul was beyond her reach, she'd meant it. "Nightly, in your dreams. Beyond that, I can't be sure, not without knowing more about the demons' intentions."

Mathias needed more than dreams and dismal prospects. Of all the brutalities he'd faced in his past—townships burned to the ground, children claimed by the atrocities of war—he'd never survived something half this painful. He needed Nessix, her charisma, her temper. He'd grown so fond of her that he no longer knew how to deal with those around him without wondering grimly or mischievously or anywhere in between what Nessix thought of his actions. Her voice had been so terribly sweet…

"And speaking of sleep…"

Mathias blinked at Etha's words, shaking his head as if a

stubborn child posed with the same suggestion. "Etha, I can't—"

Her gaze hardened against his weary rebuttal and her hands clamped down around his. "What can your worry do for you now?"

If Mathias had been of present enough mind to form a sound stance against the torment of these dreams Etha promised him, he suspected he'd flow with no end of excuses. As it was, his body and mind ached from the past day's rigors, and the only thing keeping him from passing out was the ridiculous notion that he still had some way to bring Nessix back to life, to save her soul at the very least.

Etha took in her servant's exhaustion. His reddened eyes and the creases across his forehead betrayed any sense of resolve. Even without the ability to hop into his mind to unearth his most sincere hidden thoughts, Etha saw how close Mathias tipped on the edge of collapsing. Besides, she needed to get back to Sulik.

Mathias was as strong willed as they came; he and Nessix had been meant for each other in every conceivable way. Etha disliked forcing her will on her dear disciple, but the fleman army required him sharp and able for when the demons struck next. She twisted a hand free from his and reached two fingers forward. Before Mathias could even begin his hasty objection, Etha swept her gentle touch across his forehead and his eyes fluttered closed. The tiny goddess caught her paladin as his shoulders slumped forward and with the tenderness of the most devoted mother, she lowered him to the floor beside Nes's bed. Rising briefly to locate a blanket, Etha knelt to kiss Mathias's cheek and tuck him in deceptive comfort.

"Worry no more, my love."

THREE

Since the day Etha first brought him back to life, Mathias often dreamt with lucid tendencies, and as raw as his thoughts of Nessix burned in his heart, he indulged himself the glimpses of happiness these dreams of a future he'd never have might offer. He could keep hurting when he woke.

One of the best things to come from Nes's obstinate move of harboring her citizens in the fortress was the number of vacant inns in faraway towns. Even Mathias doubted their ability to keep knowledge of their trysts a secret, and Nessix had quit fearing his teleportation quite some time ago. With nothing to worry about, they were free to enjoy each other's company in any capacity they desired whenever the demons had the decency to give them time.

As Nes's gasps tapered to heavy breathing, Mathias couldn't help but smile. He'd often insisted to himself that he still felt youthful, but being caught up with Nessix made him feel alive in a way he thought he'd lost long ago. With her, he truly felt peace. Looking down into deep blue eyes, he leaned forward to kiss her lower lip. Moments later, her legs relaxed their hold around him and allowed him to lay beside her to catch his breath.

"We need to quit doing this." Nes's words rushed out on a single breath.

The corner of Mathias's mouth twitched. She'd made the same

declaration every time they'd shared company in this manner over the past few months. "What's the reason this time?" Her answers often flirted with an endearing absurdity.

"'Cause." Nessix flailed an arm toward the night stand, grabbing aimlessly for her water skin. Mathias leaned across her, kissing her shoulder as he retrieved it for her. She took a drink before continuing her explanation. "This isn't the way generals in the middle of war should behave."

Mathias grinned. "We're well past the middle of it."

The Nessix who still clung to her stubborn inhibitions would have sputtered frustrations at his quip, but this delectable version of her smirked. "If the demons were to show up..."

"I'd take care of them." Mathias's answer danced with jest, immediately followed by him burying his lips into the crook of her jaw.

Nessix stifled a giggle that encouraged Mathias to redirect his attention to her collarbones and slide an arm around her. "I'm serious!" Her laughter insisted she was anything but. "They could have this inn surrounded right now, and all you want to do is—"

He planted a quick trail of kisses between her breasts and down toward her navel, glancing up at her with mischievous eyes. "You want it, too."

Nessix reinforced his statement by making no effort to discourage his attention. As his lips traced across her belly, he glowed at the sound of his name just slightly less than he had a few minutes prior. Nessix squirmed at his touch in that delightful way of hers and in that instant, Mathias realized they weren't alone in the room. He lifted his lips from her trembling flesh, arm growing tense around her as he redirected his focus.

"M-Mathias?"

He didn't respond to her, wrapping his concentration around the identity and nature of this intruder. The soul beat with little more than a whisper, quite possibly the only way Mathias's distracted mind had overlooked it in the first place. He sat up slowly to survey the room, the soul's impact growing fainter the farther he distanced himself from Nes's abdomen. A jolt of dizziness struck Mathias between the eyes. The sharpness of his gasp struck down the final glimmers of Nes's euphoria and she pushed herself upright, quickly scanning the room for where she'd dropped her sword belt.

"Brant's… going to have to find out," Mathias murmured. "About us."

Nessix's legs shoved Mathias off of her and she snatched the sheet around her body. "He's *here*?" she breathed, sending a fleeting glance at the window.

Mathias grabbed her arm in case she planned to launch herself away from the perceived threat of her cousin's judgement. "No," he said, voice unusually subdued and solemn. "But this isn't a secret we can keep much longer."

Nessix made no effort to pull her arm from Mathias's hold, but her brows furrowed. "What in Inwan's name are you talking about?"

Swallowing his guilt and his fear and the slightest tremor of excitement, Mathias grasped her hands. "Nes, you're…" The words caught in his throat and he coughed, heart racing as he met Nes's eyes. "You're with child."

Color drained from Nes's face, her mouth sagging open. A pair of soft gasps suggested she had an opinion to share, but her efforts to express herself were limited to a feeble shake of her head.

"It'll be okay," Mathias said, mind racing with the explanation he'd prepare to deliver the flemans and, Etha help him, the officials back home in Zeal.

Nessix shook her head harder, reservations humming against closed lips.

"We'll figure this out."

Her eyes brimmed with tears, and Mathias spotted something deeper than the embarrassment he'd assumed she suffered from behind them.

"Nes, what's wrong?" he begged. "Please tell me."

A ragged breath trembled Nes's frame. After all of the secrets she'd already shared with Mathias, delivering this one should have come easily. But it didn't. "My mother…"

Those two hushed words explained the entirety of Nes's confession and thrust forward an abrupt reminder of the past

Mathias never got to know. Nes's mother died in childbirth and she'd grown up silently blaming herself for it. No matter how big she wanted to talk about bravery and not fearing death, Nessix quaked with terror at the thought of following in her late mother's footsteps.

"Do you really think I'd—" Mathias's lucid mind snagged on his words. He cleared his throat. "You think I'd let you die?"

Those beautiful, frightened eyes, painfully ignorant of reality, bled with hope as Nessix sorted out the extent of her paladin's miracles. "No," she said. "You'd never let me get hurt."

Mathias's heart tore at her innocent confirmation, launching a rush of tears to the corners of his eyes. He fought to keep the ugly frown from his lips, but his efforts threatened to fail him. This is what should have waited for him a few months down the road. He should have had Nes's gentle faith, been on the cusp of fatherhood! He should have been leading these patient and courageous people into a brighter future. In front of him, Nes's expression fell as his anguish coiled tighter.

"Mathias, what's the matter?"

His fingers clenched up locks of her hair and he leaned forward and kissed her. Nessix accepted the gesture, but gingerly, and when Mathias pulled away, trouble cast a veil over her clear eyes.

"Nessix, don't leave me," he whispered.

Her brows furrowed. "I'm not going anywhere."

Overcome and heart racing, Mathias choked on the saliva he inhaled with his gasp, shooting upright from his place on the floor. He panted for breath, frenzied eyes sprinting across Nes's quiet chamber. His knuckles ached from how firmly he clutched the blanket at his sides, and his eyes fell on Nes's still form. He fought to hold his breath to keep the heaving of his chest from giving her body the illusion of movement. As his adrenaline settled and his mind wrapped around reality, Mathias unlocked his fingers and covered his eyes.

If this was what seeing Nessix in his dreams meant, he didn't have the strength to handle it.

* * * * *

Kol pressed his cheek against the cool stone of the tabletop, watching as Nessix's soul swirled about in its despair. She'd quit trying to fight her way out of confinement for the time being, and the muddy green of her misery soothed the alar's demented mind. Footsteps clomped down the hall and Kol lifted his head to rest his chin on the table's surface. Moments passed and an imposing air rushed ahead of those steps, jerking Kol upright. Suppressing a scowl, he cleared his throat and stood, laying a protective hand on the lid of Nessix's glass cell.

Not all inoga were equipped with wings, but Grell was. A beast even for a demon, Grell hunched his shoulders forward and twisted his body sideways to clear the doorway, though Kol knew his lord could just as easily crash his way through the walls. A quick assessment of Grell's scowl, enhanced by a scar stretching from eye to lip, confirmed a preexisting irritation. Kol swallowed hard and waited for whatever the inoga's temper sought.

Grell spared Kol little more than a glance, choosing instead to snatch the jar from under his subordinate's hand. He tilted it roughly, raising it up to eye level, and a bolt of red agitation crackled through the confines. Kol would have corrected anyone else, even some other inoga, but not Grell. He frowned.

"This is your Nessix?" Grell's voice boomed loud enough for dust to sift from the crevices of the walls. He continued to focus his scrutiny on Nes's soul.

"I harvested her myself, my lord."

Grell curled his lip at the clip of Kol's reply and tipped the jar the other way, enticing a greater flood of red from Nessix. "What did you tell Shand?"

"Exactly what we'd discussed."

"And she believed you?"

"She was too delirious not to." Kol wound his fingers into fists of restraint as the red haze warped into an insecure yellow. Nessix was meant to be his masterpiece, and it took the entirety of his will and common sense to hold himself back from snatching the jar away. The days when he'd have survived such a bold action rested well in the past.

"Good." Grell plunked the jar back on the table. "Keep things that way and notify me when you move forward with her. I trust it won't take you long."

The only thing that truly frightened Kol was Grell investing faith in him. Even demons feared the right kind of pain. "We will work as quickly as conditions allow."

Grell still wore the same unimpressed frown he arrived with, but nodded in refined satisfaction. Acutely aware of how little Kol wanted to disappoint him, Grell left to entertain himself in the holding cells. Once the inoga's massive frame vacated the room and his shadow disappeared down the hall, Kol sank to his seat.

Pulling Nessix back in front of him, he lowered his chin on the tabletop once more. She swirled about in a fiery confusion, reds of anger, yellows of fear, reeling through a plague of worry. Kol wrapped his hands around the jar, darkening its interior until Nessix's foggy mass stabilized and settled to the floor of her prison.

"That's a good girl," Kol murmured. Pressing Grell's insistence on hastening to the next phase of Nes's transformation aside, Kol sighed and let himself get lost in his delight of Nes's increasing gloom.

* * * * *

Etha played the part of Sulik's diligent assistant a bit too well for the commander's comfort. In more youthful, less trying times, he'd been familiar with Inwan, but the departed deity never generated half the awe of Etha's aura. She guided Sulik with the same patience Mathias used, and her support drove him to persist past both physical and emotional fatigue. Halfway through the first full day since Nes's death, Sulik finally settled into his role, fulfilling the clerical duties in Mathias's stead until it became apparent that Etha invested more concern in something outside the mess hall than the patients within.

Tiny shoulders drawn back, Etha's spine held her posture rigid. Her eyes still glittered, but no longer with that boundless warmth Sulik had found peace in. She shook her head in the most insignificant bobble he'd ever seen. Having left his sword and armor by the door, Sulik rose and glanced around for the most feasible makeshift weapon.

"Oh no..." Etha breathed. She murmured the second word several more times, increasing pitch with each repetition.

Sulik braced himself for the unknown, mind racing over how to rally adequate heart to lead the army into combat, investing his utmost to believe he'd stand a chance delivering successful orders. He was a mere breath from requesting Etha's insight when the goddess popped to her feet and gasped. Veed strode through the door.

As usual, he carried himself with self-assured arrogance, a malicious glint in his eyes. Veed cast a casual survey through the room, smirking at Sulik before his eyes snagged on Etha. His smile faltered for a heartbeat as he worked an appraisal over her mortal form. Sulik frowned and took a step in front of the little goddess.

Veed blinked at the commander's action, his grin returning. "What's with the dismal air? Nessix screw this one up?"

The handful of wounded soldiers awake and coherent gasped, choking on weak sobs at Veed's callous assumption. Sulik's frown deepened and his eyes burned. He still hadn't found the opportunity to mourn. Etha's hand gripped the back of Sulik's arm, loaning an artificial strength to the tense commander. Sulik cleared his throat.

"General Astaldt, this is a bad time."

Veed rolled his eyes. "You think I care? I need to have a chat with Nes. Where is she?"

Sulik's clamped jaw prevented his tongue from working around the truth.

"Fine then," Veed muttered, scouring the room with a more thorough glance. "I suppose I can take my business up with your wretched Sagewind."

"Sir Sagewind is busy."

A flare of annoyance tugged at Veed's amusement. Opposing authority was not in the realm of Sulik's character. "Busy with what?" As soon as he'd voiced the question, Veed derived the answer from recollection of past events and the tattered state of

Nes's army. He belted out a noxious laugh that sprung tears in Etha's eyes. "So Nes *did* screw up." He turned to leave for her chamber, where Mathias must have been doctoring her.

Sulik could hate Veed for the foul beast he was all he wanted, but no man deserved to stumble upon this sort of revelation.

"General Astaldt," Sulik hailed sharply.

Veed was unaccustomed to the firmness in Sulik's voice—the second unusual display from him in this single encounter—and stopped at the commander's address. He turned to face empty eyes and a mouth that hung open, words blocked by palpable reservations. Veed's brows furrowed at Sulik's atypical behavior, but before he could demand clarification, the sobs around them pierced through to Veed's logic. These men weren't crying over pain of a physical nature, nor blows done to their pride. They were in mourning.

Features sagging on his aging face, Veed's eyes drained of their cold arrogance, replaced with a foreign, forlorn glint. He stared at Sulik, silently pleading for the answer he never wanted to hear. The commander's downturned mouth closed to stifle his surge of emotions and he lowered his head. Veed's legs buckled beneath him.

Bereaved moans echoed in ears unable to clearly decipher outside stimulus, rendering any further explanation Sulik might have given him useless. Veed's heart pelted his ribcage in disbelief and his mouth went dry as he failed to convince himself that this was a cruel joke. Mathias would have been in the infirmary if Nessix was well, and the infirmary wouldn't be wailing in devastation if she was merely injured.

"Where is—?" Repressed tears lodged the remainder of the question in Veed's throat.

Sulik lowered his gaze. Of all the unpleasant tasks he was trained to deal with, aiding Veed was among his least preferred, but there had been a time when Veed served a warmer role in Nessix's life. The commander cleared his throat and murmured, "He's… He has her in her chamber."

There was only one thing that meant more to Veed Astaldt than pride. Crying out a garbled lament, he spun and ordered his legs to race him up to Nes's room.

* * * * *

After waking from the bittersweet lies of his psyche, the last thing Mathias wanted to hear was Etha's announcement of Veed's imminent arrival. The thought of that beast soured Mathias's mouth and turned his stomach atop the twists already ailing him.

In her last few months, Nessix had rightfully gone out of her way to avoid interactions with Veed. Always one for a challenge, the foul man took Nes's avoidance as an invitation, making a game of seeking her attention. Veed had flaunted his perceived ownership and domination of Nessix at every available opportunity, stooping as low as to threaten blackmail if necessary. Afraid of caving from insecurity, Nessix had remedied these situations by diverting their conversations to one of her officers or busying herself with any available task to put her far away or make her unavailable. Among her inner circle, Nes's aversion to Veed had been no great secret.

Mathias's desire to protect Nessix from Veed beat as strong as ever, but in his fragile state, he doubted his ability to muster the drive to chase the other man off. Besides, if Mathias wanted to believe accounts of the past, Nessix and Veed once shared a much more wholesome relationship, one which he had no justifiable reason to interfere with.

Veed pounded on the door, and Mathias didn't move to answer it.

"You will let me in," Veed insisted, "or so help me…"

It was the manner in which Veed left the threat hanging and the sharp upswing in the pitch of his voice which caught Mathias's attention, and he glanced up at the closed door. From the first time Mathias saw Veed and Nessix interact with each other, Veed had made his fondness for her blatantly obvious. Mathias's perception of Veed's motives skewed even further after the villain's lewd manipulation of her, and Mathias had assumed psychological control was the awful man's objective all along until this exact moment. Mathias had never hated any individual the way he hated

41

Veed Astaldt, but it wasn't his place to forbid his opponent the right to closure. He stood and kissed Nes's temple.

"I'm sorry for this."

It took the remainder of Mathias's will to trudge over to the door and pull it open, and for several piercing heartbeats, he didn't recognize the man on the other side. Veed was arrogant and selfish. He'd proven his cruelty several times over. That destructive monster familiar to Mathias was not the same man who waited in the hushed hallway. Confidence lost within despondent lines across his forehead, Veed's haughty air was snuffed into feeble vapors of a different kind of pride. His sharp eyes glistened with a purity Mathias never dreamed to see in Veed, and the paladin couldn't find the nerve to tell him to make this visit quick.

They stood locked in this awkward stalemate for several harsh breaths, both struggling to feign command and stare the other down until remorse got the better of Veed. His eyes darted from Mathias's stubborn hold, catching a glimpse of Nes's body. He fumbled over his composure, but his grief screamed too loudly for him to care about dignity. A gasp strangled Veed and he shoved his way past Mathias.

Veed ventured to guess that he accepted death better than any fleman alive, but beholding Nes's pale complexion, the lack of vibrancy glowing from her, he wished he didn't understand it so well. Questions and demands tumbled over one another in his mind, but his heart ached too painfully with the truth for him to speak them. Nessix looked more at ease than her father had. Veed braced his stance against the bedpost and hung his head.

Over the past year, Veed had disturbed Mathias on a regular basis, enraged him through the use of foul conduct as no mortal man ever had, but Mathias had never been uncomfortable in Veed's presence until now. Emotions Mathias loathed to name warred inside Veed as his sturdy arms trembled to support him and his bold chest heaved. Veed had mocked Nessix every time she sustained injury in the past, but fate sapped the humor from him now. If Veed wouldn't have been so repulsive, Mathias would have been inclined to comfort him.

As if aware of Mathias's moral dilemma, the haunting sound

of Nes's siege bells tolled from the watch towers, slower than usual, but alerting the army to danger per their stoic duty. Veed didn't respond to their song and Mathias wouldn't have, if not for Etha's gentle reminder.

Use your anger if you must, but you need to take the field.

Had there been anything left of Mathias to tear down, confirmation of the enemy's approach would have disheartened him. Body weary and mind prepared to resign his impressive record to failure, Mathias's heart whispered a valiant petition for the good he could still get done, of how innocents depended on his strength. That tiny internal plea threw its might against his burdens and tugged him into motion. He would do this for Nessix. He had to.

Veed was a disgusting man, worthy of every last critical accusation made against him, but Mathias banked on a vague concept akin to faith that Veed possessed enough decency to behave in a respectful manner toward Nessix at last. The empty void of the vile man's eyes suggested it would take actions much more drastic than Mathias leaving the room to spur a response of any sort from Veed, and Mathias would not demand his participation in the coming fight. Mathias still hadn't recovered in full from the explosion of power he'd used to collapse the first tunnel, but he had plenty of raw skill and unique talents at his disposal to stand against the demons. Leaving Veed in silence, Mathias strode out into the hallway as it buzzed with an eerie intensity.

Mathias shouldered his way through the halls, grimacing against the afterthoughts of his dream and the foul misgivings which came with leaving Veed so close to Nessix. He pressed on past his guilt and remorse, descending the stairs into chaos. Edgy soldiers attempted to organize through the tangle of confusion, and Mathias's innate abilities identified Etha among them. Before he could contemplate objecting to her physical presence, Etha glanced over her shoulder and gave him a resolute nod. Refreshed by her ceaseless conviction in him despite his obvious failures, Mathias breathed in a deep calm, squared his shoulders, and turned to find Sulik.

The commander hadn't made it far from the mess hall,

struggling to establish control of the masses.

"Do we know what's coming for us?" Mathias asked.

Face worn weary from the responsibility thrust upon him, the tension fell from Sulik's entire body as Mathias's voice reached him through the commotion. He pressed his fingertips to his temples and closed his eyes. A brief wave of sorrow swept over Sulik, but he swallowed it down in light of his duty. "It's hard to say." His hand flopped back to his side and he looked up to his trusted savior with eyes pretending to have direction. "Initial reports suggest a solid force, but it doesn't seem as though they're organized."

Mathias frowned and nodded. It wouldn't be unlike the demons for a band of skirmishers to strike out amidst their opponents' disorder. "Whoever has the heart and mind to fight will take the field," he said, uncertain if that would limit his command to himself or the entire army. "I won't require anyone to come with me, but won't turn away assistance."

Reason wriggled itself free from where Mathias usually cultivated it with such care. He made no effort to keep it rooted, but that served him just fine. He didn't want to think. Etha had sent him Sulik to act as his compassion in this dark time, unshackling him from the rational disposition he preferred to hide behind. The demons chose Nessix over the army. If they'd taken the army first, she'd have handed herself over with little fight. They must have overlooked the power which rage drew from Mathias.

"Sir, you aren't thinking about engaging right now?"

Wild embers scattered about Mathias's eyes, brows hooding them in a darkness Sulik balked at. "There is no other option."

Sulik had grown to know Mathias rather well over the past several months, well enough to know the paladin was not of clear mind. Too many mistakes had already come from Sulik holding his tongue due to respect, but the ruthless aberrance lurking in Mathias's eyes and the sharpness of his actions warned Sulik against picking this fight. "You're not even in your armor," Sulik tried, voice cracking in unintentional weakness.

It was an accurate observation, one which adrenaline prevented Mathias from considering. He blinked, knowing discretion ought to scream about his stupidity, but he shrugged instead. "No time for it."

Sulik grimaced and sent a hasty glance in Etha's direction, but found the goddess unconcerned and wrapped up in her work. She wouldn't *possibly* allow Mathias to traipse out to real harm, would she? Exhausted on every level, Sulik's brain pawed through valid debates against Mathias's disregard but failed to latch on to any of them. He wrung his hands, an ache creeping across his forehead.

"I'll um… I'll see who I can rally," Sulik murmured.

"Good man." Mathias clapped Sulik on the shoulder, holding him there a moment longer. "See if you can find Brant. We'll need that bastard's lack of rationale."

Sulik suppressed both his gasp and abrupt argument that Mathias's clear lack of judgement seemed to surpass the needs of one battle. Neither the immediate circumstances nor the relationship between the two of them permitted such a reprimand. "No one's seen him in hours," Sulik said. "I'll task those who don't ride out with you to find him."

"Good. Have whoever finds him get him angry. Tell him the demons broke into the stables or something."

"Sir!" Sulik was through with this recklessness. The army had already lost one general. "Where have your morals gone?"

"They are very much here," Mathias assured through a wicked grin. "Just a little masked right now."

Realizing Sulik's lack of enthusiasm for his unconventional orders, Mathias turned on a heel and left the commander to sort through these decisions on his own. Mathias knew he flirted with madness, and if he stayed much longer, he'd either succeed in shaming himself completely or risk Sulik coaxing him to a calmer state of mind. Neither option sounded beneficial for the fight to come, and so he left his friend gaping at his conduct.

Mathias strode toward the massive fortress doors, gaining momentum until he ran down the stairs. He didn't turn to look back, but the violent and vengeful energy flowing from the flood of reinforcements rushing behind him was an attractive match for his own. On any brighter day, it would have disturbed Mathias to soak in such anger from so many, but this anger—this intrinsic compulsion to survive if only to see the demons punished—ensured they'd all keep their lives. Scowls were unbecoming of Mathias and he'd abandoned the ugliness of hatred long ago, but he rode this coarse emotion hard. Though his raging heart begged him to obliterate the demons before him with one massive pulse of the divine energy he'd recovered, he refrained from stealing the opportunity to seek retribution from the flemans who craved it with such passion. Mathias gave no orders, relying on the soldiers to execute the job they'd vowed to do.

Tragedy hadn't dulled the flemans' drive half as much as the demons had hoped or expected, and the first few lines of the fallen crumbled against the shock of the impact. The demons who kept their heads through the flemans' wrath recovered quickly, embracing the exciting challenge ahead of them. Orders spoken within individual minds and beyond the control of any commanding officer drove the flemans, a madness their opponents understood well.

Mathias had no desire to hinder their crusade, and even if he wanted to coax compassion from his army, he doubted the soldiers had the heart to obey him. The demons served but a temporary focus for the army's rage, and when this battle resolved, accusing sneers would once again fling his way. Mathias saved his breath for combat, fueling his efforts with experience and repressed fury. He threw himself into a disgusting routine of methodical slaughter, blade sweeping a pattern consistent enough to relieve him from the hassle of thinking but with a calculated variety to avoid predictability. His blessed weapon twisted and contorted to his whims, reaching every vile face that ventured within reach, and for the first time in ages, Mathias enjoyed the surge of might brought on from cutting down demons. Limbs exposed to the hazards of the battlefield, Mathias relied on the bitter pound of resentment to defy any pain that tried to slow him.

Etha wouldn't let him die. She couldn't.

The first whisper of reality hit Mathias as powerful silver haunches driven by a brutal roar thundered past him. Mathias didn't acknowledge Brant's arrival. He didn't have to. Always a loose cannon, the violent beast named vengeance drove Brant past any inkling of restraint.

Armina had nothing on Logan as far as combat was concerned, but she fed off her rider's vigor. She'd been among the lucky few fit with armor before the rush to arms; Brant might have lost the sense to protect himself, but he wouldn't risk losing his most treasured mount. Brant drove Armina into depths her instincts hummed warnings about, but she obeyed his orders faithfully. They plunged into the demon force, trampling over top their enemies until Brant threw himself from the saddle to intercept an axe aimed at his horse's legs.

Madness spewed from Brant's eyes as he slammed the hilt of his sword into the demon's forehead and pummeled it to the ground. He pressed the length of his blade against his foe's neck. The butt of the offending axe struck Brant in the side, attempting to repel the troublesome commander, but Brant absorbed the blow and repurposed his pain into motivation. Leaning low, Brant stared into the demon's eyes, a pitiless savagery burrowing deep into the beast until a spark of apprehension surfaced. It wasn't the terror Brant lusted after, but it was a close second.

"You don't even deserve the hells."

With a fluid motion, Brant slammed the cutting edge of his sword toward the ground, severing the cartilage of the demon's throat and the tendons of its neck. He watched apathetically as its life flowed away with slowing pulses of blood. Dizziness swept through Brant as the demon's body shivered in one final memory. There, for the fraction of a breath, the body beneath Brant was Nessix, her throat slit, unable to sustain her life any longer. Frightened eyes gazed up at him, screaming with the realization that she truly did fear death. What a fragile thing life was!

One blink and Brant once again straddled the cold beast beneath him. A disturbing reason insisted on this violence, and Brant shoved himself up from his defeated target to spring after the next one. He had no idea how many more he'd have to punish before he felt justified, but he'd charge down this path without fail until he felt satiated. Some things were worth that much.

Demon horns pled for a retreat as the flemans' resolve and refusal to accept their defeat overwhelmed the beasts' expectations.

Those trapped too deep within the fleman ranks found themselves facing passionate monsters in their own rights and were left with nowhere to run. All they could do was turn and embrace their ends.

Across the field, the calls for retreat processed slowly in Mathias's mind, sensitizing him once again to the world around him and the concept of morals. Panting from the strain of pushing himself so hard, the sting of wounds nagged at Mathias at last. He stopped to watch the turmoil around him, an agony that was all his fault. Blood coursed down his arms. His left eye had nearly swollen shut, and a sharp, pulsing ache promised to seize his lower back once adrenaline abandoned him. The demons scattered from the merciless torture chasing after them. As much as Mathias's need for justice thrived at their panic, his old heart wept in a quiet corner, appalled by his lapse of compassion.

Everything happened for a reason and, for now, Mathias was tired of battling fate.

FOUR

The demons limped their way back to the safety of their realm. Based on the intelligence Shand and her pawn had provided, they hadn't anticipated the Teradhel army to pull together the strength to offer any sort of challenge. Nobody had prepared them for the danger which lurked in the opposing force. Weariness slowed the flemans and they abandoned their pursuit as the demons slinked back into their tunnel, allowing them a seamless retreat. Seamless, that was, until Shand and her heated opinions intercepted their return.

Those lacking the rank and strength that went along with it skittered away from the goddess's ire before she decided to lay into them. They'd already danced too close to fate once today. After a brief squabble between the active inoga, Grell was selected to deal with Shand's fit. Grumbling his dissatisfaction, detesting how it felt to stroke this spoiled child's ego, Grell trudged his way to the chamber Shand had selected for their meeting.

"You work for *me*!" she demanded of Grell before he'd even squeezed through the doorway. "Your men do not engage unless I clear it first. Do you understand?"

Grell frowned, his scar tugging against the gesture. He hated taking demands from anyone, especially Shand, but it had been declared vital to their objective to play her game as long as she continued to prove useful. "We never sent them."

Shand hissed between bared teeth. Grell didn't frighten her—if only because of her untouchable station—and the fact that she had yet to find a way to intimidate him frustrated her to no end. "They very well didn't send themselves." Her fist clenched at the sound of Grell's deep rumble of a laugh.

"I can assure you they did," he said. "As smart as you are, revered lady, you must have caught on that the chain of command down here is shaky at best."

If any lesser demon had stated as much to Shand, she'd have already terminated its pathetic life. Instead, she flung her glare aside. "The chain of command is that you do what I tell you to. Nothing more, and absolutely nothing less."

He raised a brow and retained his smirk. "You expect the small percentage of my class to control the masses of all the others?" Of course, that was exactly how hierarchy in the hells worked, but Grell banked his faith on Shand's ignorance in regards to this particular matter.

Shand hesitated. All she knew was that when she first forged her agreement with the demons several years ago, permission for them to act on their own accord had never been among the terms of their deal. She closed her eyes and discovered her regulated breaths hadn't calmed her. "Were you, inoga, ever mortal?" she asked instead.

Grell cocked his head. Was she really looking to travel down this road? "Yes."

A light of shock flashed through her violet eyes at this beast's confession. Shand knew the demons' origins as well as anyone else who had spent any amount of time in Zeal, and certainly as well as anyone who had ascended into the divine realm, but she hadn't fathomed the possibility of any of the original demons still breathing.

"Well," she snipped, snatching a quick save to redirect her motives. Demons were laced with divine essence, and if this creature had truly witnessed the Divine Battle with his own eyes, there was a very real possibility of him posing some amount of a threat to her. Needlessly angering him may not be in her best interest. "It's clearly been some time since you've had to think like one."

"You are a whelp of a goddess, I suppose," Grell agreed.

She frowned, infuriated at the manner which her fingers twisted around each other beneath Grell's scathing appraisal. "Which suggests I am much more in tune with the way mortals work than you are."

"Your point?"

"Right now, those wretches don't care about survival." She blew out her knot of nerves as quietly as possible. "All they want is vengeance, and your stupid soldiers rushed right into that. They'll destroy us if we attack now."

Grell grunted, still unconcerned. "I can assure you that we outnumber them."

Shand shook her head. "Mathias is unshackled again, and you don't want to face his wrath right now, do you? You *are* aware he and that girl were lovers?"

This piqued Grell's interest. He'd make sure to convey the report to Kol. Either way, Shand's terse statement held a firm degree of merit. If Mathias had any sort of bond with Nessix, he would be most unpleasant to deal with.

"Give them time to stew in their misery and for their morale to dwindle away," Shand said, misreading Grell's lack of debate for compliance. "Once their wills are gone, that's when we'll take them. The hurt hasn't festered enough. Give it time."

The thought of submitting to Shand disgusted Grell, but he held his tongue regarding that matter. After all, he hadn't survived this long by being a fool. "My men will grow restless."

"Then let them have at the minotaur and ogres. They don't have the brain power to be a danger to me, anyway."

Grell assumed Shand had slipped in her indirect admission of the flemans posing a threat to her, and as he was keen to do, squirrelled the information away to exploit in the future. If Shand feared the flemans, she must be afraid of the demons on some level. Her use of the demons and curses as a buffer against Mathias confirmed her reservations about him, as well. But to think mortals—backed by Mathias or otherwise—frightened her? Grell flashed a toothy smile.

"I will pass that along," he said, not divulging to her the insight he considered most valuable.

"See to it you do." Shand curled her lip at the filth which soiled her shoes and met Grell's eyes. "You will not disappoint me again."

The problem with Shand was that she believed the demons feared—or at least respected—her. Individuals might, and they all understood her capacity to render damage to those unfortunate enough to stumble into her path, but she had no idea that as a whole, the demons simply didn't care. Grell would mention this tantrum to his peers, and they'd comply with her desires until her purpose was served. Waiting this out could prove beneficial in the end, especially with Kol needing time to finalize his plans for Nessix. Shand vanished from sight, and Grell chuckled and shook his head. Turning his brutish mass, he wedged his way through the door and went to go talk to Kol.

* * * * *

When Mathias arrived back at Nes's chamber, Veed still sat beside her, face pale and sweat glistening at his temples. Relief of a post-battle homecoming tarnished, Mathias stood in the doorway and stared at the other man's rigid back while impulse and guilt scuffled over what to do next. The paladin couldn't recover Nessix, and the only other thing he wanted to do was beat Veed to a brutal death. Veed had no right to be here, no right to his mourning. He'd claimed himself that he saw Nessix as little more than a possession, but as the arrogant man sat clutching one of her cold hands, head bowed and shoulders slumped forward, the compassionate side of Mathias, the faintest sliver able to distance itself from his urge to protect Nessix from Veed, understood that she'd meant more to Veed than Mathias wanted to admit.

Whether or not he'd accept that fact, this tiny part of Mathias understood. All that Nessix worked toward to hold her country together was far too important to risk offense at such a delicate time.

Mathias swallowed against a dry throat and coughed, just in case Veed had been unaware of his presence, and walked into the chamber. Let Veed pitch a fit about it. This room was not only within the fortress Mathias now managed, but it was where he'd taken up temporary residence. Veed could order him away all he wanted, and if Mathias's bloodied state failed to attest his ability to handle hostility, the paladin would tend to any objections as they came. Instead, Veed answered with a single sniff, not raising his eyes from the floor.

The sun cast a line from beneath the curtains, light growing dimmer as the day pushed toward retirement. Mathias glanced at the candles burning throughout the room, noting that he'd soon need to send for more. Walking past Veed to Nes's desk, he laid down the weapons that had accompanied him to battle and flexed his fingers against the scabs which flawed his knuckles. He scratched an itch behind his ear, grimacing as he pulled open a fresh clot.

Please tend to your wounds.

Mathias heard Etha's gentle guidance, but hated the idea of heeding it. These wounds lent him a feeling much more real than the trouble in his mind. They stood testament to the fact that though he carried a blessing nobody else on Abaeloth possessed, he was still of mortal creation. The channel Affliction opened between his body and Etha's grace would ensure a brisker recovery than anyone else in the army, and if his racing thoughts would clear his mind, he'd have wondered if maybe that was the only reason he was still alive. No, he'd keep these wounds for a bit longer.

With Veed offering no indication of leaving, Mathias pulled back the desk chair and stared at the collection of opened scrolls and half penned thoughts written in Nes's hand that sat on top. He saw where the cloak she'd worn that last night lay crumbled on the floor by her armor stand, how her armoire door hung open and the blouses nearest the one she'd yanked down before chasing after him drooped halfway off their hangers. An open bottle of wine sat close to the corner of the desk and he eyed the remaining volume, wondering how much of it was responsible for loosening her tongue to address him.

Mathias wanted to disregard each of these reminders, but if he turned away from them, he'd face Veed and Nes's body. There was no escape from this as long as he stayed in the room. His tolerance stretched just shy of snapping, but too much flit through his mind to allow him rest. His arms and legs ached from the pinch of lacerations stitching back together, from the hasty rush to battle, and the release of his stoic facade. Duty tugged at him, begging him to find Sulik and his students to instruct them in tending to those who brought injuries home, but those damages Mathias would never manage to mend held his sense of obligation captive.

Those last thoughts Nessix must have faced as she fought in her final desperate struggle gnawed at Mathias and he pressed his fingers to his eyes. She'd burned with such anger toward him, filled with well-deserved hatred he hadn't seen in her until then. His recollection of the scene of her death assured Nessix had put up a valiant fight for her survival, one Mathias would have been proud of, but something greater bothered him.

Nessix hadn't been slain by the demons in a brutal fashion— no horrendous wounds or poisons. Instead, they'd taken an unusually clean approach, bleeding her out until her body lost the strength to keep hold of her soul. Mathias wished he understood the significance of that action, but the longer he tried to sort out a reason, the harder common sense shook its head, warning him that this path led to darker truths better left unknown. He needed answers, answers Etha couldn't give him because they didn't exist. At least not yet.

Mathias, please stop this.

He curled his lips between his teeth and dragged his eyes back to Veed.

The rest of the army, he was sure, slept after the recent battle. Between the cascade of events over the past day, if exhaustion had evaded them before, it must have caught them by now. Sleep, quality sleep, was a seductive thought, but each time Mathias so much as blinked, images he preferred to not dream about flashed to life. If it wasn't of his last conscious memories of Nessix, it was those terribly sweet promises he'd never see fulfilled.

Silence built a stifling prison, chirping insects from outside and the occasional footsteps in the hall the only auditory stimulus. As the second candle flickered out, Veed gently raised Nes's hand to his lips then placed it back on her chest.

Veed rose and seared Mathias with scornful eyes, ravaging him with the blame and disgust the paladin felt he deserved. Mathias registered the unspoken criticism, but left it unacknowledged. It wasn't as though Veed was innocent of his own streak of faulty conduct. As it stood, Mathias preferred to avoid further exposure to the perversions dwelling in Veed's tainted mind. Before Mathias had the chance to convey as much, Veed lowered his head and turned to the door.

One step and then another. In just a few more, Veed would be gone, allowing Mathias to hole himself up alone with Nessix, but duty forbid him to let Veed go quite yet. Gathering up the last of his nerves, Mathias opened his mouth for a parting address. His words hung at the back of his throat, culminating in a pathetic squeak, just enough to merit Veed's hesitation. He didn't turn back to Mathias, but tilted his chin toward his shoulder.

"I need to report this to my army." Sorrow raked the words from Veed.

Mathias kept his head bowed. He wasn't ready to let go of Nessix, but then again, he never would be. The flemans had to move forward if they hoped to survive. "We'll bury her tomorrow." Extending a formal invitation seemed like too much of a betrayal, but Mathias considered this notification as permission for Veed to attend.

A sweltering sigh filled Veed's lungs as he failed to muster the grit to respond. Pride whispered that he'd shamed himself enough for one day and, before his frown began to tremble, Veed left Nessix to Mathias's prayers.

FIVE

Mathias watched in repentant silence as the selected members of the honor guard escorted Nessix to her final resting place. Eyes locked on her delicate face, relieved at last of the stress of her station, Mathias struggled to see past the trouble that claimed her in death. After living lifetimes on the battlefield, he'd seen his share of fear in the deceased, but never this sense of oppressive dread. With or without her soul, Nessix did not rest well.

Pinching his eyes shut against the tears he worked hard to dam up, Mathias's mind wandered down the road of what Nessix meant to him. A proud girl, a powerful general in her own right, she'd loved to claim she maintained the respect of her men through charm. Had grief not stripped Mathias bare, he'd have smiled. It wouldn't have surprised him if that was precisely what had kept the troops in line. Her brilliant eyes had snared him from the start, and on the rare occasions he'd gained access to a smile…

Mathias slammed this door closed before longing for the impossible pulled him through it, determined to keep his focus on his present burdens. Even if he'd failed to protect Nessix, he still had to see the flemans to the end of this war—a hefty responsibility, considering where they now stood. Nessix was the last of the nation's revered line, nearly survived by her grandfather. These people had followed her blood longer than Mathias had been alive, and that thought daunted him. Some bastard child of a noble must have run around somewhere in the general population, but that seemed unlikely to present a worthy candidate to fill Nes's role.

When Mathias first received the assignment to safeguard Elidae from the demons, he'd promised Laes only to guide the active general, but this last breath of Nes's memory urged him to challenge any who tried to replace her. Sulik stood as the most appropriate option, but Mathias doubted the affable commander's air of authority in that regard. Hasty decisions plagued Brant's demeanor, though such tactics had fared well for his cousin until so very recently. Mathias's eyes tracked to Veed as he tramped his way to his position, and the paladin frowned. Veed was bound to make a grab for Nes's territory once his grief passed, and Mathias would blaze through the hells to prevent it. The paladin would continue to act as the flemans' guide and cleric until this war saw its end. After that, he'd devote himself to uncovering Nes's true fate.

Mathias worked his tongue in a dry mouth. He'd conducted hundreds of funerals from renowned kings to unknown beggars discarded by society, but it hadn't been since burying his own lord centuries ago that the loss of a single warrior had crushed him so thoroughly. As he looked at Nes's still frame, displayed for the public, all of his mental preparation and experience slipped from his grasp. For a long moment, nobody else stood in the solemn field; no sobbing soldiers or townsfolk, no fellow officers gnawing through the insides of their cheeks to keep their sanity. All that existed was his immortal life and Nes's lack of one, obstructed by a sticky haze between them.

The honor guard positioned Nessix on the catafalque and Logan stumbled up to his rider's remains. With the line of vision intercepted by the great horse's movement, motion rippled through the crowd as those present began to process the beginning of a legacy's end. Some remained standing in mute silence, while others genuflected on reverent knees. Mathias allowed the people time to settle, savoring any excuse to delay the inevitable. He heaved a weary sigh, troubled by false memories of a future which was no longer his, and stepped forward at last.

Mathias cleared his throat, the sound grating against the thick silence of the field. He trained his broken gaze on the ground and drew a shuddering breath. "I don't have any words worthy of describing what we've lost. Rather, we're left with this memory." His voice didn't carry half as far as he'd intended. What did he think he was doing? He didn't know what to say to these people, to Nessix. He didn't even know what to say to himself. Mind scattering far from his prepared address, a frown creased his lips. "I've never been part of one of your promotional ceremonies, only departures. But to my understanding, your people do not fear death. You accept it as part of battle, part of life. Your Nessix—" His voice cracked and he choked on suppressed remorse. After failing these people in so many ways, revealing this weakness now did little to redeem him. Mathias closed his eyes.

Mother, help me…

Mathias's heart rate slowed on cue and the warmth of an invisible embrace wrapped around him from behind. *You are not alone in your sorrow. You will find your answers, and I won't make you seek them on your own.*

Etha's words drew tears in Mathias's eyes. He coughed and looked up at the disheveled crowd at last. "Your Nessix lived for the fight," he continued, voice gruff but still travelling. "If I knew nothing else about her, it would be that. Even the most proud and beloved must meet their end, and while Nessix would be the first to correct me for saying so, Etha will grant her rest from the burdens her life taxed her with."

He sucked in a sharp breath at the last statement, unsure of why he spoke such a lie. Sulik was the only one who knew and understood the implications involved with Nessix losing her soul, and even he struggled to grasp the concept. Shame on Mathias for delivering this hope!

Love, this hope is what will keep you pushing forward. I will not let this go unsolved. Trust in me, please.

Mathias lowered his gaze, the tightness in his chest restricting his ability to catch his breath.

Do not be ashamed. Use this, Mathias. Use this and save these people. Save your Nessix.

Lips pressed together, Mathias nodded. He'd already started

down this path of deceit and might as well finish. "Know that she can be at ease, at last," he said. This time, some amount of conviction backed his words. After all, anything was possible with Etha. "If Inwan still graces Abaeloth, Nessix will find him, urge him to return to you. Keep your strength, children of war! You know she would never forgive herself for being the reason this war was lost. I beg of you, fight for your Nessix, if not for yourselves."

Mathias stopped his address before he began gushing his apologies and regret. Plenty of the flemans openly blamed him for Nes's death, and such a lapse in composure would only hinder his ability to repair the broken trust between them.

If he opened his mouth again, he'd explain the truth of Nes's dismal fate, that there had been no way to heal her. With no soul, there was no life. Where he went wrong wasn't even as direct as taking her sword or chasing her off from his protection. It all boiled down to his doubt in her. He'd seen the way out of this war and he'd been too afraid her stubbornness would bar her from listening. It would have taken him two minutes, a few enraged insults, binding and gagging at the very worst, to have changed this fate, but he'd chosen to rely on himself instead. That was his secret. That was what tore him up inside.

The silence pressed on, and when Sulik realized Mathias intended to say nothing more, he stepped forward and approached Nessix. Looking down at her, a sad smile wished itself to his face. As a newly promoted captain, he'd been tasked with serving as Nes's personal guard, and he thought he'd done a fair job keeping up with her until Mathias came along. He sighed and drew on the strength he'd conditioned into himself and unclasped the cape worn over her left shoulder. Indulging tradition, the fallen general's cape would be passed on to the rising one. The fabric's weight pulled at Sulik's strong arms. Hefting it reverently between open palms, Sulik turned back to the somber gathering to approach Brant.

The young commander cast his dejected gaze at the ground, unresponsive as Sulik walked toward him. Sulik ached to reach out to Brant in some way, but hesitated in an attempt to preserve what remained of his comrade's pride. As fond as Sulik had been of

Nessix, she and Brant had spent nearly every waking moment together, constructing a foundation on which Brant had built his life. This was neither the time nor place to stir up the regrets stewing in his mind, but Sulik yearned for a way to pull the commander back to himself. Little more than a pathetic beast existed behind those deep, dulled eyes, one bent on senseless destruction and one which Sulik was reluctant to engage. Brant put up a valiant effort to forbid himself tears in public, and both Mathias and Sulik knew better than to bring up those they'd seen shed in private. Sulik's boots scuffed in the dirt as he stopped in front of Brant and beside Mathias. The cape remained draped across his hands, held in the space between them.

"Sagewind." Brant's absent address startled both of the other men. "I cannot do this."

Mathias swallowed his opinion on the matter. He'd feared it might come to this. "I know you don't care for me, but know that I will help you in any way I can."

Reddened eyes swept to Mathias's, but no further moves of aggression followed. "I cannot lead these people!" Brant insisted in a harsh whisper. "This army cannot be forced to rely on me."

Sulik averted his eyes, but Mathias held Brant's gaze with strict patience, demanding obedience. Mathias hadn't thought the phenomenon of surrender was possible for one in this line, but Brant had been related to the Teradhel family through marriage, not blood. Nevertheless, the bond shared between the cousins had never been a secret and everyone expected Brant to carry the people forward. A general in his own right, Mathias took the cape from Sulik and stepped behind Brant.

"You are the next in line for power," he murmured, fastening the cape to a trembling shoulder. "The people need their leader."

Brant pinched his eyes shut and jerked his arm back to shove Mathias away.

Nes's memory disapproved. *Don't do that! You look absolutely dashing.*

He froze and a pathetic whimper balled up in his throat.

Brant was not the person to lead these people. Their leader was gone, and it was shameful to imagine a pitiful hack like him to prove even half her peer. Nothing remained of him now, and while his head insisted how his position bound him to the people, his heart protested that his only obligation had been to Nessix.

You're overreacting.

No, he wasn't, and these constant reflections from the cousin who wasn't there only better proved his point. He was too unstable to take this station. They still had Mathias, even if Brant's stubborn mind rooted itself in the fact that Nes's death was due largely in part to Mathias's incompetence. Without Nessix, where would this war go?

I told you, this isn't his fault. And this war is going to press along just fine. Those colors look good on you.

Brant grit his teeth and his eyes slipped out of focus. "Then I relinquish my station."

The words came as little more than a whisper, but Mathias caught them. He sighed and walked back in front of Brant, resting a hand on Sulik's shoulder to dismiss him. Bitter, shameful tears fought to seep from Brant's eyes, and Mathias didn't even pretend to imagine what internal struggles the commander trudged through. Brant's eyes were blank, his grimace feral, and Mathias's heart fell. The commander had no intention of changing his mind. Whatever made him decline—whether pain or fear or self-loathing—Mathias retained his objections. If Brant carried this much doubt in himself, he'd never manage to serve the people the way they deserved or needed.

Mathias nodded and placed a hand on Brant's shoulder. "I will not impose such a burden on you again, Commander," he said gently. "But you will keep her cape and come to me if you have a change of heart."

You're being silly, Nes said. *You'll make a fine general.*

"But not today."

Blissfully unaware of Brant's internal struggle, Mathias delivered a sad smile at last. "Of course not, Commander."

See? Simple as that!

Brant sucked back his tears and recoiled into the mute shell he'd clung to over the past few days. He kept his eyes away from the catafalque and the people gathered around them. Mathias watched Brant a moment longer, regretful that he didn't know what else to say. Any further attempts to console or embolden the grief-stricken commander carried the risk of deepening the gouges already taken. Brant's palpable reluctance stemmed from a force far greater than self-doubt. Suppressing his own emotions as thoroughly as possible, Mathias sighed and faced the crowd.

He left Brant, walking down to the catafalque. Regardless of any of Logan's predisposed notions, Mathias laid a hand on his shoulder as he passed by to stare down at Nes's beautiful face. It was time to let her escape the horror of this world. Prolonging these final rights would only drag Mathias's heart to those grim places which provoked the darkest sides of him.

Over the past few days, Mathias had practically lived in the room with Nes's body, but he continued to stare at her, afraid to forget the small details. He'd left her hair brushed down and at ease, hoping his effort would allow her some sort of peace. The wind hung still and her loose locks didn't stir to give the illusion of a fleeting breath of life remaining in her. As his emotions threatened to vanquish him, Mathias shifted his gaze to the massive sapphire pendant clasped around her neck.

Pride had never been a foreign concept to Nessix, and she'd found particular delight in that ridiculous bauble, one of a complementary set which Veed had used to leverage an alliance between the three of them. Mathias had misplaced his, but even after her foul encounter with Veed, Nessix was seldom seen without hers. Knowing what the silly trinket had meant to Nessix made it one of the few material items Mathias coveted. He'd lay her to rest with her sword and armor, but he needed this last tangible memory.

Silently, Mathias worked the clasp from where it hid in Nes's hair. Nothing besides a direct order from Etha herself would stop him from claiming it, and nothing tried to as he freed the chain from her neck. He held the gem in his hand, grasp clenched around the massive stone, and his tears leaked out at last. He'd never wear the pendant with half the grace Nessix had, but he'd keep it close as a reminder of what never was.

Pulling his lips between his teeth, Mathias chanced a final gaze at Nes's face. There was no fixing this. Time was one of the few things beyond his control. With no more excuses left to torture himself with, Mathias shut out the somber buzz of his surroundings, only partly aware of the public around him. He bent forward and pressed a kiss on Nes's cold forehead. Pausing there, an inch from her silent face, he entwined his fingers in her hair.

"You were a beautiful general," he murmured. So many other thoughts jumbled in his mind, but failed to make it out. Gratitude for her love of her people. Admiration of her spirit. Awe of her determination. Pride to see what she'd become. His entire face fell, aging him in ways his immortality often hid. "I love you."

She never acknowledged him—she couldn't have—and Mathias straightened before dwelling on that fact claimed him. Drawing upon his lifetimes of experience, Mathias forced his sorrow into the depths of his heart for the benefit of the army and civilians and, for the love of Etha, Brant. He gave himself the span of a slow breath to restore some semblance of composure, sniffing back the most resilient of his tears, and nodded to the honor guard who had escorted Nessix this far.

Mathias gave Logan a hearty pat once more, trying to invigorate them both. A feeble effort. "It's time to let her go."

Logan remained stationary and unblinking as the soldiers took their stations around the catafalque, until Brant moved up beside him and worked a hand beneath his mane. Scattered chokes and sobs now interrupted the persistent silence as Nessix was reverently moved onto the network of ropes that would bear her into the ground.

Nes's descent passed in delayed motion, each count to lower her body more reluctant than the previous. When Laes had been buried, the nation quaked with sorrow, but also a sense of hope. This time, there was no new era to anticipate and the future's bleakness exceeded any dreams of a brighter tomorrow.

Never more thankful for Logan, Brant tucked himself from the public behind the great horse. He didn't have the mind to care if Mathias or Sulik—even Veed or Renigan—saw him crumble, but he had enough of Nes's pride to instinctively try to hide his pain from the masses. As pathetic as a lost child, his lower lip quivered, mouth turning down into an ugly frown as he tried to hold back the assault poised to rush his defenses. With the final count, Nessix was laid on the floor of her grave, and the soldiers tossed the ends of their ropes in after their defeated general. Mathias turned to Brant and his own tears sprang to the forefront. Nothing should have been able to hurt such a man, but his love of his cousin had proven his only weakness. Mathias lowered his head and stepped aside.

Dignity urged Brant to find an escape, to hide himself deep in this loneliness and let the world forget about him. Against his better judgment, he was thankful Mathias delivered the eulogy; Brant couldn't form words in his mind, much less on his tongue. It took a dozen beats of his racing heart to accept that it was his turn to actively participate in the service. Tradition required the most applicable next of kin to initiate the burial, and Brant forbid his heartache to give Veed the opportunity to claim the wretched honor.

Each step forward ripped at the integrity of Brant's soul, legs aching in protest of the actions to come. Standing beside Mathias, exposed so clearly to the public, dimmed his bleak outlook to the eerie twilight which lurked just before darkness fell. Brant stared down into the hole, scouring Nes's face as carefully as he had through the past few days, begging for her to wake up. It was far too easy for him to see the girl she'd been, the beloved family and playmate and leader. In his mind, her eyes still glittered above a radiant smile.

You can still hear me, too, right?

A broken sob crumpled Brant's torso. Few living people ever knew the Nessix Brant had, and now it was all he could see. Mathias's steady hand on his forearm tugged Brant back to the present, exposing the truth behind Nes's cold corpse and preventing him from jumping in after her.

That touch jarred awake a new, frightening swell of emotion within Brant, and he plunged his hands into the mound of loose earth piled beside the grave. He couldn't ask how Nessix could abandon them like this, neither wanting to hear her laughing voice answer him, nor believing she'd ever planned her inevitable fate.

Such simple wants couldn't stop the twisted anger whirling about in his chest. The sensation threatened to suffocate him, prodding his heart with rods of searing steel, but that anger was the only thing that allowed him to release his handful of dirt. It spattered across Nes's cheeks and rained gently atop her breastplate. The stimulation of his senses awoke Brant to the fact that this was more than some routine duty—it was his dismal reality—and as quickly as the anger had flared, it flashed away. Brant stood there, his dirtied hands open and frozen in place before him, face pale. Mathias and Sulik followed his actions, and as Veed stepped forward to do the same, Brant felt gentle pressure close around his shoulders and encourage life back into him.

He couldn't be sure what words Mathias's lips formed, but through the blur of his tunnel vision, confirmed he was being spoken to. The ringing in his ears muted all other sounds as he turned his gaze back to where Nessix slowly disappeared from the world, her face consumed by the land she'd died for. As the last corner between her eye and cheekbone was masked from mortal view, Brant snapped at last.

He'd held back his pain too long and had expended the strength to care about anyone's opinions or criticism. A shattered moan escaped Brant as he flung himself from Mathias's grasp and threw his arms around Logan's neck. Burying his face into the fecklan's mane, he cried wildly, coarse hair soaking up the first few rounds of tears.

Logan's body obstructed the crowd's view of Brant, but the officers bore full witness to the commander's surrender and exchanged troubled glances. Even Veed was forced to shift his eyes away from uncomfortable respect. Neither Brant nor Logan moved from where they mourned, nursing off each other's sorrow, but Mathias was ready to end this chapter in fleman history. Meeting Sulik's eyes, he guided his friend toward Brant, knowing Sulik was the last mode of comfort Brant would accept. As directed, Sulik laid a strong hand on the young man's shoulder.

The six soldiers appointed to the task of filling in the remainder of Nes's grave grimaced their way past tears and regret, the rhythm of their shovels sinking into the dirt preventing them from brooding over any single thought for too long. Mathias hadn't watched Nes disappear, not the way Brant had, and he was glad for it. All that remained of her now existed in the facets of a cold pendant and the memories engraved in tortured minds, and a thick ceiling of earth would forever protect her from Abaeloth's cruelties. This war would end, Mathias knew, and when that day came, he'd spend all of his effort sorting through the known details with Etha. A spirit could not simply disappear; he would find Nessix and set her free when the world was once again safe.

"Go and rest," Mathias told the crowd, his words penetrating little more than a few lines deep. "Mourn if you must, but remember our battle is far from over."

Mathias nodded in satisfaction of the obedience given to his order and turned to look over the officers, Veed included, to gauge their conditions. No matter what feuds existed between them, the flemans depended on these men regaining their strength. The demons were still a valid and vicious threat and no one could handle them on their own.

Renigan rode off to gather those of Veed's forces in attendance, leaving his general standing beside the grave, fists clenched as he stared at the increasingly shallow hole. Brant's sobs persisted and Sulik peeled him away from Logan to remove him from the scene. It was no easy feat to battle Brant's need for comfort, and as Sulik coaxed him free of Logan, Brant clung to him like a lost child. Cramming that sour lump back down his throat, Sulik wrapped an arm around the younger man's shoulders and led him back toward the fortress.

The field vacated rapidly—after witnessing Brant's distressing breakdown, no one knew how to handle their own grief—until the only beings who remained were the two surviving generals and Logan. The great horse made no sign of moving, even when jostled by Sulik's efforts to unlatch Brant's arms from him, and neither Mathias nor Veed objected to his position. A suffocating solemnity surrounded the trio until whispers of madness dared the silence to break.

"You feel guilty, don't you?" Veed's voice rasped against suppressed tears and he glared up at Mathias from across Nes's grave. "She was a beautiful woman and a fine general. It's a pity you couldn't curb your tongue enough to keep her alive."

Mathias had anticipated such affronts out of Veed eventually, and was prepared to explain whatever details of his deception he considered appropriate. "You know nothing of what happened. It was my curbed tongue that caused this."

"That's not what the rumors say." Veed would have found humor in the stunned expression that crossed Mathias's battered face if not for the nature of the circumstances which had brought them together. "Nobody wants to betray you, but they're not happy."

"No one is happy!" Mathias roared, heart skipping against the control he sought to take over his pain. "No one!"

Veed scowled. "You ought to be. Isn't this what you and your goddess wanted? Order? Control?"

Mathias returned the sneer, his hurt only enhancing the anger festering inside of him. He'd hoped Veed would have chosen a more civil route for such a formal setting, but Mathias never held high expectations of this particular knave.

"I have never wanted power, Veed, and you are well aware of that." Mathias stared Veed down, trembling with the urge to order him away from ground as sacred as this. "You are a horrible creature to feed off your people the way you do, all for some ungodly power trip."

Veed shook his head, no longer looking at Mathias, but the grave instead. "And because of *your* power trip, god-blessed or otherwise, we've lost the most valuable part of this entire nation." Dark eyes found their way back to Mathias's, anger clashing in the thick air between them. "I will never forgive you for this."

Mathias frowned. "Then don't. There's no more time for hateful words or bickering. This blow was too deep and the demons know of our weakness."

"And we have you to thank for showing it to them." Veed scoured this opponent of his for guilt, no less disgusted by Mathias as Mathias was with him. "Nes didn't want anyone to know, but I'd known her all her life and could read her plainly. For whatever reason, she trusted you."

The accusation jumbled Mathias's stomach and scratched at the back of his throat. He wasn't too proud to cry in front of others, but forbid Veed that pleasure. He'd wanted to spend so much more time with Nessix, getting to know her outside of war and hear about what her life had held in happier times. He'd wanted to learn why she relied so heavily on herself and try to teach her to depend on others in a way more intimate than the simple love between general and army. Nessix had shown him fleeting moments of this trust, but always with a reluctance in her eyes to contradict her willingness, as though she expected to get hurt. Mathias had invested tireless hours trying to convince Nessix to put her fears and need for control aside. As much as it disgusted Mathias to admit it, Veed was right about this. Somehow, he had earned Nes's trust.

"I know," he murmured. "But when I needed her faith the most, I didn't have it. That's where this tragedy came from. I'm aware of my actions, and I accept responsibility for what they caused, but I stand by them still. There is no changing the past. We have to move on."

Veed crossed his arms and coughed on his disgust. "It won't be as easy for some of us as it is for you."

Mathias's eyes flashed as he met Veed's condemning glare. If he allowed it, this argument would continue until Veed pushed him to fatal violence, and right now, the flemans needed all of the strength they could get. "Do not goad me further. I asked you to leave. You should not think it a request."

"This is neutral land," Veed sneered. "You have no jurisdiction over me here. If I want to pay Nessix my final respects, you cannot deny me that right. I'd hate for her to be gone without knowing what she meant to me."

Mathias's lip curled as he bristled, discipline barely containing the instinct to draw his sword. "She was nothing to you but an object to covet," Mathias spat. Veed's frown deepened into a snarl, one which Mathias disregarded. "Her title, her power, her beauty. Things you attempted to own with your foul magic and money." Drawing on his sense of justice, Mathias borrowed calm from the only source he could cling to. "Etha cannot save the damned, and I will not pray she tries."

Veed's lips pursed with politically shielded rage, and Mathias doubted his ability to control his anger any longer. He'd already exhausted himself holding back his desire to wring Veed's neck for past transgressions, and he spun from Nes's grave, leaving Logan and Veed behind. Veed looked over the fecklan as Mathias trudged back to the fortress, frowning at the extinguished fire in the bold horse's eyes. A ragged sigh shook Veed and his shoulders dropped, torso slouching forward. He sank to the ground, hiding his head in his hands.

SIX

Twelve years ago, Veed had considered himself an honest man. Flawed, but honest. He'd spent months failing to convince himself of how faulty his unsavory plague of thoughts were before surrendering to the fact that he could do nothing about them. Another two weeks passed while the bold commander scratched up the courage to properly tend to his predicament. He stood outside the war chamber door, scolded harshly by the shameful part of his mind. Good sense warned him of a devastating response to his pending actions, but he needed to get this off his chest before it killed him. Veed held a deep breath and pushed his way into the chamber.

"Sir, we need to talk."

The words left Veed's mouth before he had the opportunity to take in the room's current occupants in full. Laes looked up at his friend's sudden address, letting the scroll in his hands flutter down to the table. At the opposite end, Inwan lounged in his chair, one foot propped up on the corner of the table as he thumbed through a tome. The god did not falter from his business, but that didn't ease any of Veed's anxiety.

As color drained from Veed's cheeks and his eyes brandished an apprehensive tinge seldom seen past his robust confidence, Laes pushed his chair back and stood. "Sir?" he asked, unable to produce the laugh this question deserved in light of Veed's twitchy demeanor. "I'm hurt, Veed. What's on your mind?"

Veed glanced at Inwan as the god continued his reading. To stand the chance at resuming normal function, Veed needed these answers. He'd gone to the war chamber with the sole purpose of addressing the concerns that had ridden him lame for so long, but as he stood there now—facing Inwan no less—his courage threatened to take its leave. Veed choked down those lingering reservations and secured the door shut behind himself. Nerves firing in rapid succession, Veed braced himself through the past several months' worth of this arduous burden, amazed his tension held out this long.

He cleared his throat. *Why* did Inwan have to be here? "I'm uh… not sure how to tell you what's on my mind."

Laes bellowed a hearty laugh at Veed's abnormal conduct, approaching his friend to clasp him on the shoulder. "My daring Commander Astaldt is out of words to speak to me?" When Veed's distressed frown met the general's gusto, Laes blunted his approach. "Alright, alright. Sit, and let's talk about what's got you bothered."

Subdued, Veed allowed Laes to guide him to the table, and Inwan raised his gaze at last, golden eyes as cunning as ever as he tracked their movement without a word. Veed lowered his head and darted his eyes away, hating the fact that his usual seat would position the god on the very fringes of his peripheral vision. Laes forced Veed down into the chair with firm hands pressed on his shoulders and turned to prepare them both a light drink. Veed didn't move, even after Laes returned to the table to deliver them each a chalice of wine and one of water.

The general took his seat, pushed his work aside and smiled at his friend. "Now, what's on your mind."

"Well…" Veed took two gulps from the more potent of the two drinks. "I've been watching Nes lately."

Inwan flipped to the next page in the tome, the parchment snapping sharply.

Laes nodded and leaned back in his chair, a satisfied grin lighting his face. "She's getting vicious out there, don't you think?"

71

Veed studied the trail of bubbles at the surface of his drink. "She is."

When no elaboration followed Veed's response, Laes furrowed his brows and leaned over the table to peer a closer look at Veed. "What in the world has gotten into you?"

Any other man would have seen the intended direction of this conversation by now, and Veed couldn't quite decide whether Laes's simplicity made him feel lucky or cursed. There was no tactful way to express the thoughts trapped in his mind. Veed's silence persisted, and Inwan began to hum a quiet tune.

Laes frowned and sat up again. "Has Nes been up to something I need to know about?"

Veed's eyes flashed up to read the concern on his friend's face. "Not that I'm aware of." But his own mind had ventured to more than a few scandalous places...

"Forgive me, Veed, but I must be growing dull with age." Laes's chuckle reinforced Veed's suspicion of his ignorance to the current objective. "Please share with me your concerns. If you expect me to guess, we'll be at this all day."

Veed closed his eyes, Inwan's humming burrowing deeper and deeper into his sanity, before gathering his resolve to look up at Laes. This man had been his best friend since the day they met. He'd taken him into his troops, into his home, and into his heart. They'd ceased considering each other mere friends or comrades in arms to the point of embracing each other as brothers. Veed would throw his life down willingly for the sake of Laes, and he knew without a doubt that the favor would be returned. He'd been there when Nessix was born and soothed Laes after Cora died. Veed had taken it upon himself to watch over Nessix when duty called Laes away, watched her grow, and developed an increasing fondness for her as the years progressed. The pressure of looking at Laes overwhelmed Veed, and he returned his focus to his drink.

"Laes." Veed swallowed hard to clear the roughness from his throat, heart threatening to pound its way to an early death. "I love your daughter."

Laes's silence provided a more powerful response than any angry fit would have, and all the while, Inwan continued humming.

Chair creaking in question, Laes straightened and laid his hands flat on the tabletop to convey his intention of not bringing harm to his best friend. At least not yet. Veed's breath raced shallow and quick, and he watched his most trusted comrade for tells of danger. Not even in the thick of battle had he ever felt more endangered or vulnerable than he did right now.

"And you should." Laes's words clipped a firm warning. "As her heritage demands it."

A sickening vise clamped around Veed's insides. Laes was a genius with tactics and combat, but was known for his lack of attention spent on matters outside the battlefield. Nessix was his world, and Veed suspected the general had already begun preparations to engage him as an opponent. Inwan quit humming and Veed clenched a fist. He was willing to get hurt over this.

"Sir, I am asking your permission to court her."

Laes leapt from his chair with such force that he shoved the entire table, impelling Veed to his feet as well. Inwan's foot clomped to the ground and he sat up straight with an inconvenienced sigh.

"You are her *uncle*, Veed!"

Committed too deep to pull back now, Veed met Laes on the terms of his argument. "Not by blood."

"You're only three years younger than me!"

Veed supported himself with arms braced against the table and hung his head. Did Laes honestly think those thoughts hadn't already occurred to him? Could he possibly imagine Veed hadn't tried to control it? That he'd *intended* for Nessix to allure him in the worst ways? The commander's breath heaved heavier now as he fought to settle the rapid thump of his heart. It would do him no good to react with force.

"You are a good man, Veed." Laes picked through his words with a disciplined tact foreign to Veed. "But I am uncertain if you are an appropriate match for my only daughter."

Inwan snorted, drawing the attention of both men. "Just who would you have court her? Brant?" He casually linked a leg over the arm of his chair. "There *is* blood there, Laes, and it's not as though there's a lengthy list of men suitable for her station."

Veed's eyes widened at the unexpected support, a source even Laes balked at. Any single man in the kingdom would willingly take Nes's hand if politics allowed such informal arrangements, and now Inwan himself had declared the average man unworthy.

"If Veed's an inappropriate candidate for her, tell me who holds the standards you've set."

Laes took his time to look up at Inwan, a blustery storm chained behind the clench of his jaw. "I haven't put any thought into such matters. She's still a child."

Inwan's laughter grated on the smallest hint of calm left in Veed. At least someone found this entertaining. "If she was a commoner, she'd have been wed by now."

"Her station merits prior obligations."

A scalding heat backed Laes's voice, warning Veed to take every necessary measure to cleanse his mind from the undoubtedly salacious thoughts he had about the general's little girl, but Inwan's golden eyes remained undaunted. The god sighed and stood at last, walking over to stand beside Veed. The commander ducked his head lower.

"Laes, if you don't let her leave your safety, your family will die out and with it, the flemans. Do you really think Veed—of all people!—would ever lead Nes to harm?" Inwan slapped Veed between the shoulder blades, drawing a nervous cough from the commander. "Now, would you?"

Veed glanced up into the stern eyes of his best friend. "I swear to you, I would never let harm come to her. I would sooner die."

Aware of the friction in the room, but well above caring about it, Inwan chuckled. "And there you have it."

Laes pinched his eyes shut and blew a slow breath through pursed lips, unwilling to dispute his god's contribution to this trying dilemma. "In the end, this isn't my decision or even Inwan's." His voice rumbled a low growl, one Inwan cocked his head at and Veed cringed from.

"Of course, sir."

The general blinked again at the unaccustomed formality and a small fire stirred itself up in his eyes. "The two of you haven't arranged something without my consent, have you?"

Veed choked on the assumption and Inwan raised his brows. "Of course not!" The clever side of Laes had arrived at last, and that worked Veed's last nerve one notch closer to snapping. He'd known from the start that this would not pan out smoothly—it was why he fought it for so long—but he'd hoped to avoid making an enemy out of Laes. Veed didn't know how far his general intended to go to make this drop, but he stayed his course. Today, determination demanded he win his battle. He trained his eyes on Laes's hands, watching carefully for signs of a pending attack. "If I disrespected you so much as to sneak around with Nessix behind your back, do you really think I'd be asking your permission now?"

Laes chewed over this thought, searching every crevice for a flaw in Veed's ambitions. As none became apparent, the general sighed, shoulders slumping in surrender. "You must forgive my harshness," he said, though he kept his gaze from both of the other two men in the room. "Nessix is the only child I have, and this is not a scenario I'd been prepared to face. Veed, you are her..." Laes ground his teeth and turned from the table. "This idea will take some time to acclimate to."

Pride stifled Veed's gasp as he shot a hasty glance to Inwan. The god shrugged, a slight smile toying at his lips. Had Veed heard right? Had Laes just given him some form of consent? Heart pounding so hard it threatened to pull his legs out from beneath him, Veed straightened and kept his relieved laugh to himself. "I swear to you, Laes, my loyalty will remain always with you, and should fate allow it, my fidelity will forever belong to Nessix."

Laes worked his tongue against the roof of his mouth as though trying to rid it of a sour taste. "Continue your duty as if we never had this discussion and act in no way on these... impulses until I have time to sort through this matter. You will know when I am ready to accept this arrangement."

He didn't wait for a response, not wanting to hear any elaborations on Veed's interest in his daughter. Instead, Laes pushed his hands against the table and stood to full height. Turning sharply, rigid strides drew him out of the war chamber. The door fell shut with a thud.

Inwan slapped Veed on the back and gave him a jovial grin.

"Well, my boy, sounds like it's up to you now. Don't screw this up."

Veed met Inwan's laughing eyes and before he could blink, the god disappeared. The commander looked around the vacant chamber, bewildered. He'd thought coming forward with this confession would grant him some sort of release from his suffering. All it did was leave him stranded in a confused whirlwind, wondering what he was getting himself into.

SEVEN

You look so sad.

Nes's voice had grown increasingly persistent the harder Brant tried to suppress it, pushing him to the point of accepting it as an appealing new facet of reality. "Yeah? Have any ideas how to fix that?"

We could go for a ride. Maybe spar if you're up for a match. I'm game.

Brant sighed to keep from choking on a fresh surge of sorrow. He scratched at the unusual growth of beard on his face.

You know, the ladies'll like you a whole lot more if you'd cheer up.

Two days had passed since Nes's funeral and Brant still hadn't managed to make it out of his chamber. Sulik brought him meals and spoke at him, but Brant's dismal mood clung to him like the grime of battle.

"I'm not looking for ladies right now."

Nes's memory laughed at him. *That's not the Brant I know!*

"No," he muttered. "I'm really not."

Had Nessix truly been there with him, she'd have pouted and stomped a foot over Brant's gloomy disposition. But no matter how tenaciously these whispers tried to prove otherwise, she was gone. Brant rubbed the meat of his palm with his thumb and stared at the edge of his rug. A knock alerted him to Sulik's arrival, but Brant didn't greet him. He hadn't answered any of the other times his comrade came by and, just as before, Sulik invited himself inside.

Sulik took inventory of the small table positioned beside Brant's chair, pleased to note that while the bulk of the food still sat on its plate, there was evidence it had been picked at. He switched the plates then unbuckled the flask Brant had requested from his belt. Brant accepted it without a word, holding it in his lap.

"How've you been holding out?" Sulik asked, longing to coax life from the young man. Brant's unkempt appearance and exhausted, bloodshot eyes plainly stated that he was no better now than he'd been two days ago.

Staying calm came much easier when Brant was alone with Nes's voice. Though he appreciated Sulik's concern on the deepest levels, his steady presence reinforced that Brant no longer lived in reality. Brant leaned forward to rest his elbows on his knees, subdued eyes searching his friend's for hope.

"Do you... Do you think Nes is still... here?" He cringed at the last word, realizing the absurdity of his question. Of course she wasn't there; they'd buried her. "I mean, at least *part* of her?" Brant held his breath behind trembling lips, the slow nod of his head begging Sulik to deliver the lie he'd kill to hear.

Sulik looked away from Brant's pleading eyes, unable to face their doleful hope. "If what Sir Sagewind says is true, no. They've imprisoned her soul and until it's free..." He shook his head. "I'm sorry, Brant, I—"

Brant bit down on his lip and threw his weight back against the chair, tears flowing freely from between closed eyelids in the annoying way they'd taken to of late. It wasn't so much the fact that Nessix was dead which tore at Brant from the confirmation; the last rational part of him understood that well. It was the fact that no feasible part of Nessix could be talking to him, that this was all in his head. Brant Maliroch *was* going mad.

Now, you've always been a bit crazy, Nessix said. *Go easy on yourself.*

He bit down harder on his lip to keep from responding. The trust he shared with Sulik only stretched so far.

Sulik, assuming Brant's reaction sprang from the void of loss, frowned. "You've done all you can, son. Take what time you need.

We all understand."

Brant peered his eyes open, cramming his paranoia behind the determination he thought Sulik expected of him to the best of his subpar abilities. "There's no time to waste over something as trivial as emotions. We'll lay here, crying and sniveling, and the demons will pick us off, just the same."

Sulik's eyes stung at how harshly Brant looked in on himself. "Don't give up on hope."

Brant laughed bitterly and turned his head away until the urge to snap overwhelmed him. "Then find it!" he demanded, flinging the flask to the floor. "Go, wind your way through these halls, visit the Spring, lead these men and tell me *where hope has gone*!"

The older commander lowered his gaze. No one expected a graceful recovery from Brant, but his anger teetered on a destructive level. Mathias was the only other person with the mettle to confront Brant on this matter, and Sulik's gut warned him how foolish it would be to try arranging as much. He'd known Brant as long as he'd known Nessix, and he'd stand beside him until he met his end, too.

"Then will you just let the demons win?" Sulik asked, his voice even as he erected walls for Brant to flail against. "Have they taken everything from you?"

"Yes. They have."

"Even your pride?"

Brant's eyes narrowed and he leaned forward slowly. The greater part of him knew what Sulik was trying to do, but the part of him inching toward insanity, the part that hoped for Nessix to keep talking to him, warned him that repairing this damage posed just as many dangers as leaving it to fester. Every sense of etiquette urged Brant to thank Sulik for his efforts, but he wasn't in the mood to indulge in such formalities.

The hurt on Sulik's face, the way his middle aged features sagged in weariness, tugged at Brant's compassion, and he lowered his head. "I am doing you no service," he murmured. "Perhaps you're better off leaving for now." Brant tried to thank Sulik for his continued concern, but the heaviness in his chest silenced the rest of his words.

Sulik had tolerated enough in his lifetime between the likes of Nes and Veed that snappy words and harsh tongues seldom affected him anymore. But thick skin and a staunch sense of humor couldn't combat the nagging fear that Brant wouldn't be able to pick himself up the way Nessix had when they lost Laes and Inwan. Sulik pressed his lips together to keep from voicing his sentiments, afraid of opening the door to the wrong side of this sanity Brant struggled to cling to. He retrieved the flask and put it beside the plate.

"You're not alone, Brant."

Brant didn't look up again, and Sulik sighed, leaving without another word.

* * * * *

In his life before Etha, Mathias had believed a man was responsible for his own destiny, and parts of that belief were true. After Etha integrated herself in his life, he learned to understand and accept the role of fate, to invest faith in a greater plan, and that Etha had a valid explanation for every aspect of life. That was all before the demons trumped that time-proven theory, and that same vile grudge which drove Mathias to crusade against them in the past spurred him toward a heartache he'd been content to leave behind.

Mathias wasn't stupid. He knew the dangers of war. He knew the likelihood of losing Nessix to combat from the very start. And while that gutted him hollow, experience understood it. Where tolerance escaped him was in how the demons mocked fate. They had gone far over the line this time.

These emotions are not conducive to rest, my love.

Mathias blinked, catching his breath at the sound of Etha's voice. He hadn't felt her eyes on him. "I've already slept."

Etha glowered at his accusatory tone. "That was days ago, and you still haven't recovered from everything you've been through, neither physically nor emotionally."

He bobbed with a dry laugh. "I'm not tired."

She fixed his back with a steady eye that burned through his battered frame. Lying to Etha was a waste of breath, and while she entertained the thought of pretending not to see his dishonesty, the prospect of leaving him to suffer through this pain alone tore gaping wounds in her godly insides. Mathias had never allowed himself to accept such a shameful defeat, and Etha longed for the champion she loved to return to her.

"You *are* tired." She wanted to go up to him, to touch each of his injuries and weave her resolve back into him, but the set of his jaw suggested she was unwelcome to such invasions. "Or do I need to show you again?"

Too weary to deal with Etha's games, a ragged breath melted Mathias back against the chair. "If you're going to use your will against me again, do it quick and be done with it."

Etha cocked her head in contemplation of his impudent statement, eyebrows raised at the challenge behind it. She'd grown accustomed to Mathias's blunt tongue over the generations, but this sort of stubbornness had disappeared before their relationship had left its infancy. In those days, she'd accepted his defiance, setting him up for pointed yet harmless failures, creating public disturbances only he could take the blame for. Her seasoned temper urged her to revisit similar disciplinary measures now, but the tender side of her recognized a child in pain. Etha swallowed her irritation and breathed herself back into serenity.

"I have and I would again," she admitted freely. "For the sake of your people."

Mathias pushed himself forward in the chair, turning to face Etha at last. "*My* people!" he demanded with an acrimonious snort. "I am their shield, Etha, their false savior. They are not mine."

Disappointment wasn't something Etha enjoyed attributing to her dear paladin, but it consumed her ability to hold back on him now. "How did I teach you, Mathias Sagewind? Did I give you the courage to fight or the frailty to grovel in self-pity?" She studied the rigid tendons in his neck and the firmness of his brows, neither offering conclusive suggestions to his thoughts. "I order you to continue leading your men. They need you to overcome this. You are their general."

"No. These people belong to the noble house. Go talk Brant into leading them. I couldn't."

Etha trilled out a brief laugh and shook her head. "You think he has what it takes to bring these men to victory after how he reacted at the funeral? He may be the closest thing to nobility Elidae has left, but he's not Nessix—"

"And neither am I!"

"He is a frightened little boy!"

"As I once was, and Nessix was once a frightened little girl!" The coil of memories noosed Mathias by the throat, smothering his defenses, but Mathias would prove to Etha that there was still some strength left in him. "We all had to learn to cope with our stations after they were appointed."

"Perhaps you are the frightened one, then?" Etha didn't spend the time to care whether or not her words harmed him. "These failures you keep rattling on about, have they not daunted you? Are they not the reason you refuse to pull yourself back together?"

Mathias couldn't provide a response to her demand. Etha was right and shame prevented him from admitting it. If Nessix was still alive and the war waging steadily on, he'd wear his title with that humble pride of his, shouldering the burdens nobody else could carry. The demons had stolen that option, though, forcing Mathias to stare down the mistakes he'd made and all those bound to follow. He'd failed to keep Nessix alive—what chance did he stand at protecting an entire nation? Even when burdened with the demons' curses, he hadn't felt so insufficient. Trying to fight what stampeded its way from his heart was no longer worth the effort. The weakness and defeat gained faster than his worn mind could run and his shoulders sagged.

"Sleep," Etha begged. Not only did Mathias need to find his strength again, but she couldn't bear to watch him crumble before her, not when she had no means to fix it. "We could discuss this for days, but right now you need to save yourself and rest."

"Etha, no!" Tears stung Mathias's eyes at his disrespect, but the sinister fantasies taunting him from the other side of consciousness prevented him from closing them. "Forgive my defiance, but not with these dreams."

She frowned, sympathetic eyes searching out the thoughts racing through his mind. "What did you see?"

Mathias sank back again and put his face in his hands. "A future I'll never have." One he hadn't known he wanted.

Etha reached forward and lifted his head in cupped hands, wiping away his silent tears with her thumbs. "I am so sorry, my love."

"You tried to warn me. This isn't your fault."

"No, but—" She stopped her words abruptly; they wouldn't do him any good. Her gaze drifted toward the floor and Mathias's hands grasped her tiny wrists.

"But what?" he asked.

She shook her head and his hands tightened around her.

"Etha, what do you know? I'm begging you."

"What I will tell you will hurt you," she warned, soft eyes petitioning him to back down. "And that's the last thing I want for you."

"I'm already dead to my emotions," he said. "Please, tell me now while I'm still broken and spare me uncovering it in the future."

Etha cried inside at his request and thought again about forcing sleep on him or erasing this conversation from his memory. Neither option would protect him from those dreams he feared. Fate doomed Mathias to dream of Nessix nightly and if he'd had the sense to look back in his past, he'd see that she'd been there for years. Etha melted under the desperation of Mathias's stare.

She lowered her eyes from him. "I'd always meant for you to find Nessix."

Mathias's hands released their hold on Etha, dropping to his sides as he eyed her with startled suspicion. "That's not possible," he said. He didn't want it to be. "You said yourself that you'd never intended for me to reach Elidae, that it took the demons' actions to get me here."

A melancholy smile worked its way across Etha's face. "But under different circumstances, she was meant to reach Zeal. This would have been a happier time for her and for her country. That was what I'd intended for her."

"A happier time?" His voice cracked.

Etha nodded. "It was a time of a more diligent god and a

mother who lived. A *general* who lived. Her life made sense, just like she'd wanted."

"In my last dream, she'd been…"

Etha's tired sigh expressed her unwillingness to confirm the question he'd been unable to finish.

Mathias's lengthy life had given him his fair share of significant others, but he'd asked Etha to forbid them offspring. The thought of burying his own children terrified him, and he knew how sharing that sort of bond with a mortal would affect him. It was exactly the pain he trudged through now, and this time, he had to bury them all at once. The thought of asking Nessix to be rendered infertile hadn't even crossed his mind until faced with this unobtainable future. He turned back to Etha and found her eyes troubled at the damage she'd caused, hands open to accept Mathias when he needed her support.

Being strong was simply becoming too much for Mathias to handle. He'd given his life countless times for the sake of others. He'd given his eternal peace for the same. And right now, that responsibility crushed him under his desire to be through with it all. Mathias fell to his knees from his chair, sobbing before the goddess he'd sacrificed everything for. He was too tired to deal with this, Nessix had been too dear. He longed to beg Etha to make him forget what she'd just told him, make him forget about Nes's influence over him, about Elidae and the demons altogether, but he couldn't. Abaeloth needed him, and he could not let his selfish emotions stand in the way.

Etha's hands caressed his shoulders and neck. She rested them on the back of his head. With each brush of her fingers came the familiar comfort of her will to soothe him, only this time, the aching returned as soon as she moved. Through the reeling of his doubt and torment, Mathias vaguely made out the sound of Etha's gentle voice.

"I am so sorry, but you know I couldn't have kept it from you forever."

The memory of strength urged Mathias's sobs to subside and permit his ringing ears to receive her words.

"What you need now, and you must listen to me, is rest. I will safeguard your dreams. I won't let them hurt you tonight."

Sleep. Yes, his weary body needed sleep. His worn soul needed sleep.

"When your men need you, you will wake. I will not allow harm to come to them while you are not with them."

Mathias raised his head on a wobbling neck to look up at the one woman he'd always chosen first. Walls of tears blurred Etha's serene face as her hand graced his forehead. Mathias closed his eyes.

* * * * *

Every year, Mathias found banquet season a stuffy, tedious affair. Spring was an agreeable season on the continent of Gelthin, and Zeal brimmed to the limit with buffoons willing to be swindled and able to offset other nobles' distress. Grand galas, pretty clothes, and seasonal delicacies masked even the more legitimate political arrangements, but Mathias preferred to avoid the commotion and attention garnered to his station. Besides, he'd seen everything Abaeloth had to offer.

A hurried knock sounded at his chamber door, one he opted to ignore. It repeated moments later, this time accompanied by his sister's fussy voice.

"Mattie, you *have* to come out! There's something new and exciting this year!"

He groaned and lowered his day's selected reading to his lap. "You say that every year, and all it ends up being is different colored flowers in the centerpieces. There are plenty of other men who would be thrilled to escort you to the parties. Ask one of them to go with you."

Julianna Sagewind produced an audible tantrum outside his door. "No." She drew out her debate with a frustrating, familiar obstinacy. "This is *big*. Nobles from *Elidae* are here this year!"

That prompted his genuine consideration. Mathias didn't care quite so much about the tenacity which had allowed the banished elves and their foolish human guides to survive the voyage to the distant island, so much as he was interested in the fact that Elidae was a far holier land than even Zeal. Reflecting on his sister's manipulative ways, Mathias narrowed his eyes. She always knew the right things to say to bend him to her will.

"How did they manage to get here?" he asked.

"That lazy god, Inwan, brought them."

Mathias twisted his mouth as he thought over the degree of honesty in Julianna's voice.

"There's three of them," she continued. "The general's twins and some lieutenant. Mattie, one of them's a *girl*!"

He rolled his eyes at her last sentiment and raised the book again.

"Come *on*," Julianna begged, drawing out the demand in the manner exclusive to younger sisters. "I've got to go do boring Council stuff with the two young men. You could pick the girl's brain about what Elidae's like. Mattie, I want to know!"

Mathias sighed and closed his eyes. Not even Etha had mastered the skill to sway him quite the way Julianna could. "I hate banquet season."

"I know," Julianna said, her words quickening. "But when do you think the next chance to talk to one of these people will be?"

Mathias suspected foreign noblemen wouldn't have brought an eligible young woman with them simply to see the sights. She'd likely spend the rest of her life as some lord's trophy, giving Julianna plenty of time to arrange a meeting in the future, but he kept these dismal musings to himself. "Fine," he caved. His book snapped shut as he dragged himself to the door. "I'll go interrogate that poor girl for you while you deal with her groveling brother." Mathias pushed the door open, met by Julianna's glittering green eyes and enthusiastic clapping.

"You're the best!" she chirped.

Mathias grumbled a vague consent and allowed his chattering sister to tow him away from the serenity of his chamber to the bustling main halls of the Citadel. Banquet season was the absolute worst.

Julianna trusted Mathias perhaps a bit too much. Leaving him behind, she entered the conference chamber to carry out the political duties bound to her title of High Priestess. Mathias crossed his arms and leaned against the wall, wishing he'd learn how to stand up to his little sister's goading. He grumbled to himself and glanced down the hall at the young fleman woman. She wore a simple dress cut high up her legs to allow an untraditional range of movement, and schooled her focus out an open window overlooking the courtyard. Mathias sighed and looked away.

With his eyes closed, the mirthful shouts of men sparring and the occasional clash of steel reached Mathias's ears. He put minimal thought into the young woman's interest in the scuffle—there was little else to occupy her mind as she waited—until he heard her hand slap against the windowsill and the flutter of a stifled laugh. Peering an eye open, Mathias gave her a second appraisal.

Normal women of nobility were soft and smooth, untouched by the ravages of outdoor activity, but it was evident that when the sun kissed this girl's olive complexion, she enjoyed every moment of it. Her arms were toned and capable, and the excitement which illuminated her expression as she watched the soldiers batter one another conveyed a comfortable familiarity with the more rough and tumble side of life. She wore her gown and elaborate coiffure with adequate grace, given her apparent elven heritage, but Mathias wouldn't dare venture to assume her a meek lady.

Pushing himself from the wall, Mathias wandered her direction, smiling at her enthusiasm as she silently cheered for one of the combatants below. She held herself with the poise of a self-assured girl, unafraid of her own authenticity—a trait Mathias valued in the fairer sex. He joined her at the next window over and studied the swordplay.

"Does fighting interest you?" he asked.

She jerked at his voice, batting flustered lashes as she turned from the action to look Mathias over. A sheepish smile accompanied murmured words Mathias only grasped the vague meaning of. He smiled back at her and nodded in understanding to their verbal barrier, touching a hand to his chest.

"Mathias Sagewind." A warm smile and polite gesture requested the same from her.

She opened her mouth and an empty puff of a response came out. Mathias gave her an encouraging nod and her lower lip curled between her teeth. She glanced away before replying, "Nessix Teradhel."

Mathias lowered his head in respectful acceptance, but stopped short of the customary gesture of kissing a lady's hand. No matter how seamlessly Nessix pulled off carrying herself in feminine attire, her casual posture and apparent interests suggested she was unaccustomed to the sort of fuss most women craved. Instead, Mathias waded through the speech pattern of her initial response and paired it with his knowledge of her purported heritage to wade into a dialect she might understand.

"From Elidae?" he asked brokenly, focusing on her lips as he listened for how she constructed her reply.

Nessix brightened at his effort at clear communication, pretty lips lifting into a smile as she nodded. "Yes. I am the general's daughter."

Mathias picked her words apart, wielding the full extent of the linguistic skills time and travel had given him. "Your visit to Zeal has made quite the pleasant fuss. It's not often anyone gets to see natives of your homeland."

"Your city's beautiful," she beamed, smile sweeping wider and lighting her eyes. "It's a new adventure for me, as well."

He appreciated her choice of words, perhaps a bit too much, and joined her at the window she'd selected. Julianna had requested information about Elidae, and Mathias would get to that in good time. For now, he was more interested in Nessix.

"Do you like sword fights?" he asked again, now that he knew how to request it.

Her face eased in contentment and she followed his gesture toward the scuffling knights. "I enjoy them, yes."

Mathias peered at her, intrigued by the slight twitches of her muscles and sharp, calculating eyes. He looked again at the slits in her gown's skirting, cut on four sides and reaching halfway up her thighs and guessed with reasonable certainty that she wore breeches beneath the delicate layers.

"So what are you carrying?" he asked.

She blinked and turned to face him. "Carrying?"

"You don't strike me as the type to settle for simply watching a sword fight. If I was a betting man, I'd say you're more than capable, yourself."

Her smile broadened, cheeks touched with a wash of blush. "Is this how you speak to every foreign lady you come across?"

His eyes glittered. "Only the interesting ones."

Nessix giggled and glanced away from Mathias as her hand deftly swept into the fabric of her dress's skirting to produce a dagger he assumed she'd carried strapped to her thigh. "It's not my most preferred selection, but it was all I could get away with."

"You feel the need to be armed in my fair city?" he asked.

"I'd rather have it and not need it," she replied in step.

Mathias loved this Nessix's practicality. Comfortable with her and enjoying her banter more than he'd intended, he decided to fish after the information Julianna wanted just as the conference chamber's doors swung open.

"Nes!" a man's voice barked from behind Mathias, followed by a disgusted scoff. "In great Inwan's name, put that away and get over here."

The happiness receded from Nes's eyes, dampening the peace Mathias's heart had enjoyed in her company. Whether or not that blunt voice belonged to Nessix's brother, Mathias hadn't felt such an instant distaste for another man in quite some time. Nessix sighed and gave Mathias an apologetic smile before obediently shoving the knife back into its sheath. She executed an awkward curtsey and bowed her head in a dutiful submission Mathias resented.

He caught her hand as she moved to dart past him, holding her with him a heartbeat longer. "It was my pleasure, Lady Teradhel."

She smiled once more, this time a bit sadder. "And it was mine, Mathias Sagewind."

He forced his hand to release its hold and she hastened over to the two men who exited the chamber. The sharper dressed of the pair scolded her in harsh tones that she met without debate. Everything about this encounter twisted Mathias's stomach, except for one fact. Nessix was so natural and honest with him, the first person outside of Julianna and Etha to speak to him as an equal.

There was no Sir Sagewind from her, and even if she'd known his proper title, he doubted she'd have used it.

A fresh pair of nobles approached the conference chamber, and before Mathias had the opportunity to try sneaking Julianna away to confirm his suspicions of Nessix's purpose in Zeal, the guards pulled the doors shut. Nes's brother placed his hand at the base of her neck and steered her away. Mathias tapped a finger against the windowsill, watching until the trio disappeared down the hall. Blessed with a foolish amount of pluck, Mathias accepted the unspoken challenge of making Nessix smile again, and headed back to his quarters.

EIGHT

Julianna's anxiety levels were often directly proportional to the rise of her brother's vivacious demeanor, and today was no exception. With a poorly concealed grimace, she followed Mathias toward the great hall. "Anything in particular make you start *liking* banquet season all of a sudden?"

He pursed his lips and shook his head, eyebrows raised in mock innocence. "Of course not." He nodded to the guards' respectful bows and ushered Julianna into the elaborate hall that bustled with nobility from all across Abaeloth. Squinting, he scanned the social hour's attendants, eyes lighting as he grabbed Julianna's wrist to drag her along. "I just didn't have the chance to ask the lady about Elidae for you yesterday and figured you'd be disappointed. You and your foolish Council didn't take nearly long enough occupying her brother."

Julianna trotted along to catch up with his driven pace and weaseled free from his hold. "There wasn't much to discuss."

"What did they want?"

She sighed, but the chatter around them enveloped her distress. "They're here to marry that poor girl off to someone influential to secure relations between Elidae and Zeal."

A tiny—but loud—part of Mathias's heart protested the anticipated confirmation. He noted how Nes's brother worked the

91

noble crowd with admirable charisma several paces from where his cousin stood bored guard over the dreary young woman. The practical gown Nessix had worn yesterday had been replaced with the more confining heaps of fabric preferred by Zeal's noble women, and she hunched her shoulders, face flushed as her fingers plucked and tugged at the garment's restrictions. Both of the men wore whisper pendants, allowing them to breach language barriers through divine means, while leaving Nessix woefully in the dark to the nature of the nearby bids for her hand. The Council retained a generous stock of whisper pendants for use, presenting pitifully few acceptable reasons to hold Nessix captive by ignorance. Typical political marriages didn't bother Mathias, but they did without the full disclosure and consent of all parties involved.

"See if you can occupy her keeper for a bit," Mathias said to Julianna. "I need to have a talk with the lady."

Julianna looked forward to the season's events because of the food and music and pretty fashions, not because she actually wanted to mingle with anyone. Regardless, she recognized the resolve set in Mathias's jaw and hoped to avoid causing the scene he'd make if she initiated a debate in front of so many foreigners. Julianna grumbled and stepped ahead of her brother, approaching Brant Maliroch with a warm smile. Mathias waited until she coaxed the young man to turn from Nessix and drew him several steps away before walking up to the forlorn fleman.

"Are you enjoying yourself?" Mathias asked.

Nessix sighed and cast her gaze toward the ceiling. "Considering you're the only person who's even bothered to speak to me…" She wrinkled her nose to stem off any offensive thoughts she had of his city. "The food's good."

Mathias bit back a chuckle at her honesty. "You don't care for the company?"

Nessix gauged his glittering eyes carefully before replying. "It's all just a bunch of old men and their stuffy wives fussing over me, talking to Nev, and pushing about to other priorities. It's boring."

Mathias nodded at her astute observation of this wretched period in Zeal's annual calendar. "I cannot say I disagree."

She let out a slow breath, shoulders loosening and brows

relaxing at his amiable acceptance of her criticism. "I didn't expect to run into you again."

"Oh?" He treasured the smile she offered and shifted a step closer to her. "The Citadel's my home. I like to keep my eyes on the commotion around here, that's all."

A touch of content ebbed from Nes's eyes and she crossed her arms. "I'm a commotion?"

Mathias frowned. He hadn't meant to upset her. "You aren't, but your brother seems to be."

Nessix rolled her eyes and let her arms fall back to her sides, directing her gaze away from her two escorts. "My father raised him a little too right. All he cares about is Elidae and how good she looks. Please forgive him for any obnoxious impressions he's made."

Mathias wanted to laugh at her apology, but the statement's assurance of her brother's cold outlook stifled his humor. "I've seen too much of this world to let the actions of one man determine my opinions."

Nessix smiled. "On Elidae's behalf, thank you for that kindness."

Mathias had seen and heard enough regarding Nes's plight. Every ounce of his wisdom knew where his thoughts belonged, but he'd never cared much for politics. He cleared his throat. "Lady Teradhel, I'd like to know more about you and your homeland, but it's best if we're not seen together in public."

She rubbed a knuckle against her lips to smother a laugh. "Are you a dangerous man, Mathias?" Her eyes shone with a disturbing fascination.

Mathias doubted she wanted—or would believe—the honest truth, and his most sincere hopes lay with her never needing to witness just how dangerous he was capable of becoming. "I don't think I am, but I do seem to have an intimidating effect on my peers." He hesitated. Even after all these years, he still struggled with reading women. Nessix appeared to enjoy his company, though, and he was nothing if not brave to a foolish fault. "Would you be willing to meet me tonight after things calm down a bit?"

Her expression fell and she tilted a shoulder away from him.

"If tonight's anything like last night, I won't be able to. As soon as this nonsense is through, they'll usher me back to my room. They've posted a guard and won't let me leave or anyone other than Brant, Nevius, and an attendant enter."

Mathias's opinion of Nevius Teradhel deteriorated even more upon mention of Nes's confinement. Chivalry rallied Mathias's motivation to rescue Nessix from her brother's selfish plans. "Don't worry about the guards. If I've got your blessing for a meeting, I'll see to it they won't cause us any problems."

She raised an eyebrow, a faint gasp revealing her hope. "You can do that?"

"I can do just about anything."

A short burst of laughter slipped from her this time, garnering an irritated glance from Brant. Nessix straightened herself with a quick jerk, clasping her hands at her waist. "I'll believe it when you show up."

Mathias grinned, accepting her challenge. "Then keep yourself decent, my lady. I'll be by to show you around Zeal this evening."

Enjoying the warmth of Nes's nature, regretful—though selfishly a bit pleased—that she had no one else in Zeal to talk to, Mathias forewent further formalities. Sweeping past Brant's suspicious gaze, Mathias nodded once to Nessix and turned to leave. Bored with her bothersome task, Julianna hastily dismissed herself from Brant and jogged to catch up to Mathias.

"So?" she urged. "What did you learn about Elidae?"

"Elidae?" Mathias asked. "Nothing. But I did snag myself a date tonight."

Julianna gasped and slapped her grinning brother on the shoulder.

Mathias woke with a start, uncertain as to when his guard had slipped to allow sleep to take him. Weakened from the aftershock of his dream, he sat up and pressed a hand over his eyes. These hints of a life never lived delighted him in the moment, always more welcome than the lies of a future he'd never see, but it was no easier to wake from them to grasp a cold, lonely world again.

"You've still got me. And you'd better hope you've got an army."

Mathias dropped his hand from his face and opened his eyes to see Etha perched on the edge of his desk. She pointed to the window and the siege bells tolled on her cue. Not one ounce of Mathias wanted to get up; the comfort of his blankets and wisps of memory begged him to stay in their warmth, but the battlefield's call refused to be ignored. Fighting off the places his mind tried to drag him, Mathias pulled himself from bed and stumbled his way to get dressed.

Etha frowned at his lack of coordination and disheveled composure. Pale cheeks and haunted eyes were traits of school children whispering ghost stories in the dark, not her immortal paladin. She dropped her weight to her heels and slid off the desk to sort through Mathias's armor and assist him with his preparations.

"You don't want to rush this one." She held her focus steady on the blessed steel in her hands, rubbing the pads of her thumbs across the metal to imbue it with her grace.

Mathias wiped the residual sleep from his eyes and frowned as he walked over to accept the pieces his goddess held out for him. "Are you doubting our ability to win?"

Etha's deft fingers went straight to work, snugly securing the buckles. She caressed his arms to impart in them bolstered strength, his chest to embolden his lungs. She pressed her hands against his heart and creased her lips. Mathias's expression fell at her silence.

"You are, aren't you?" he asked.

She bowed her head. "Mathias… Their numbers…"

He couldn't recall the last time Etha hadn't been willing to provide at least a rough estimate on his odds. With the army only just beginning to pull itself back together, Mathias felt even worse. "Then I pray I've recovered enough to make up for the difference."

Etha heaved a dainty sigh, her eyes hooded with trouble. She opened her mouth to speak, but a second set of tolls from the southern towers, signifying the approach of someone bearing Veed's colors, interrupted her efforts. Mathias hoped whatever part of the filthy man's force headed this way did so with peaceful intentions. The lay of this entire scenario already tested Mathias's nerves, and he hadn't even assessed the field yet.

"Mathias…" Etha murmured, frightened by the assertive glint in his eyes. "If you're slain—"

"If I die, I come back."

She shook her head. "Yes, you do, but you're the only person capable of holding this off."

"Then I'll just have to stay alive."

Shouts sprang from the hall, indicating the Teradhel army's mobilization to meet this threat. Etha gathered up Mathias's hands and kissed his fingertips.

"Stay alive, love."

He wanted to answer her with something playful, any form of jest to convey his confidence, but the words fluttered from his grasp. Batting down the dread sprouting in his core, Mathias secured his sword belt and grasped Nes's pendant on his way out the door.

* * * * *

The truth about the demons was that not much in the reaches of Abaeloth frightened them anymore. Those who survived the Divine Battle had faced the worst horrors imaginable. They'd learned how to thrive in a world which rejected them, fought armies of righteous knights and hordes of the undead, monsters and beasts unfathomable to all but the darkest of mortal imaginations. The only deity able to ignite their fear was Etha herself, and not even she manifested close enough to their realm to cause them any grief. Shand had secured them an excellent foothold, rendering her use to them fulfilled. With Nessix buried, the fleman armies still stirred about in confusion, and the demons commanded a staggering reserve of troops to do as they wished.

The Teradhel army had already begun to gather in force when Mathias exited the fortress and he found Brant cantering Armina up and down the lines of cavalry, delivering orders. The commander shot a twitchy glance back toward the fortress and surprised Mathias when he wheeled his mare around and rode up to him.

"The cavalry is accounted for and I've rallied the forces in position."

Mathias hesitated at Brant's proactive support, but he didn't question it. "Thank you."

Brant coughed and looked away. "Don't get used to it," he muttered. "It wasn't—" He caught himself before he blurted out that it had been Nes's idea. "Sulik's briefing your clerics. I'm not the commanding officer, but I can tell you that we don't have any more time to fool around." He left his words with a short snip and turned Armina to ride back toward the rest of the cavalry.

Mathias wasn't ready to attempt compromising with Brant, resigning to allow the commander to set about his own way so long as it didn't prove hazardous. Brant had a sharper tactical mind than Mathias gave him credit for, and the paladin would continue to value him as a critical player for as long as he held out. Bracing himself, Mathias reached out to Ceraphlaks in his mind and skipped the rest of the way down the stairs to take the field, striding toward the masses.

Is there anything you can give me, Etha?

Her silence persisted as before, and an angry grimace flawed Mathias's face. Scanning the skies, he turned a slow circle, unable to spot Ceraphlaks. Not holding out much hope for success, he reached out to summon his pegasus again. With the current disorder plaguing the divine realm, all of the unknown variables lurking in the political side of this war, the emotional condition of his army…

Mathias drew his sword. "Looks like it's you and me, old friend."

Dust curled up into the air from behind the enemy lines as they rushed ahead, and Mathias hastened his pace to the front of his force. At last, Ceraphlaks flashed in the sky, banking on the currents before landing nearby. Mathias swung onto his back, internalizing his frustration. There was nothing productive to be gained by faulting Ceraphlaks for his tardiness, and once Mathias secured his position, the pegasus leapt back into the air.

Mathias guided him toward the south first, catching his breath at the sight of Veed and his modest escort of four soldiers riding toward the Teradhel fortress. Discomfort wriggled within his gut at what Veed's arrival meant, but he grit his teeth and focused on more immediate concerns. The cordial response would be to warn Veed that he'd chosen a terrible time for whatever he wanted to fuss over, but Mathias grudgingly figured the other man's sharp mind had figured that out for himself. Either way, with any luck, Veed would jump at the promise of bloodshed and pad their kill count. Mathias directed Ceraphlaks back to the front lines.

Brant turned in his saddle to track Mathias's flight as he surveyed the threat raging toward them. Ceraphlaks swooped lower to dart ahead, and Brant threw an arm in the air, hollering for a charge. Trusting the movement of the army to Brant's capable hands and vindictive mind, Mathias allowed Ceraphlaks to press well ahead of the main body of the army.

Etha watched Mathias struggle to accept their mediocre level of contact, but more pressing matters demanded her attention. She swept fluidly through the tides of combat, interpreting the demons' goals to the best of her abilities, and hung close to Mathias as he guided his blade through dangers which prevented her from taking physical form. Fretful prayers surged her way from hundreds of hearts and several strained voices as the vicious swell of demons pressed into the ranks of frazzled flemans. The distress pulsing around Etha terrified her on a level she hadn't felt in centuries.

Trusting Mathias to find his way despite her silence, Etha snaked her conscience through the tangle of bodies to better assess the field and status of the other officers. She wound her way up one of Armina's powerful forelegs, skating along the mare's breast collar to stare Brant in the face. Less forgiving than Nessix had been, but of a more stable mind when at his best, Etha saw only one flaw in the earnest commander. His eyes raged without guidance or restraint, a broken heart driving him away from any thought of compassion as he tore his enemies down.

Brant hissed and rolled his eyes then shouted, "I know!"

Etha glanced her senses about to see who he'd spoken to, but found nobody willing to invest their attention anywhere but their own survival. She studied Brant carefully. A distinct shimmer illuminated his wild eyes as he spun Armina around.

"I've got this," he snapped. "Go find your own front!"

Curiosity won over Etha's sensibilities and she dipped into Brant's mind, regretting the action as soon as Nessix's voice popped up amid the mania.

You're going to have to think faster than that if you want to make it home.

A crushing swing sent another demon to the ground as Armina plowed through the fray, parting the enemy force with her body. "We'll make it home," Brant growled. His foot flung from the stirrup to catch a demon under the chin and topple it off balance. He drove his sword through another's skull.

Etha frowned at the depth of Brant's mental deterioration, but restrained herself from prying deeper where she had so little business. There was nothing she could do to help Brant cope with his torment right now. The concentration steeling his brows suggested he'd resigned to this unusual attention to a functional extent, and Etha trusted Nes's voice—no matter how contrived—would motivate him to see this through. If Brant managed to keep his focus, he'd survive, so Etha left him and Nessix to the games they excelled at.

Sulik had stationed himself toward the back lines, fulfilling the roles once tasked to Mathias. The commander fought the wounded free from combat, passing them along to the medics and clerics in training. His eyes ached with exhaustion. While he carried neither the familial nor soul bond to Nessix that drove Brant and Mathias toward madness, he'd yet to find the luxury of recovering from that first march. Etha nodded resolutely and rushed ahead to fortify his efforts.

My scholar! she cried above the roars around them. *Dear son— you must endure!*

Sulik jolted at her mental intrusion, still unaccustomed to Etha's tangible nature. Bracing himself, Sulik pushed on to the next of his comrades in need of assistance.

Not sparing the modesty to feel foolish, he answered. "I won't lie to you; I'm not sure I can."

You will through me. Etha reached forward and cupped a palm of air over his mouth. *Breathe in and be renewed. Mathias taught you well.*

Etha's intricacies evaded Sulik yet, but he'd witnessed enough evidence of her presence and wonders to not question what he accepted as a direct order. Sucking in a deep breath, an insurmountable will embraced him, intoxicating his drained body. Strength snapped across his senses, sharpness reclaiming his weary mind from where this war and loss had dulled it. Fueled by Nes's memory, the gentle commander's eyes darkened in determination and he pressed ahead aggressively.

Satisfied, Etha left Sulik's side, smiling as a fierce shout ordered his lines forward. Dusting the troops with any hope they could gather, Etha flit across the field to resume hunting out insight for Mathias, interrupted one last time by a ferocious yell and a shower of blood.

Veed had chosen the worst time to come harass Mathias, but between never turning down a chance to fight and quite literally having no other option in this critical situation, he engaged with the turbulent enthusiasm expected of him. He spun from Etha's conscience and pushed his might against his current opponent. Etha settled herself a bit longer to scope out the foul man's tempered madness as he slaughtered his targets with the same compassion they directed toward him.

Much earlier in the war, before the demons dared to sully Abaeloth's order, Veed's cruel conduct appalled Etha, and while she still had no taste for such violence, she no longer blamed him for it. These people, even those as disgusting as Veed, had waited for months to retaliate in a manner worthy of demons. She stared at Veed for a dozen of his heartbeats before the momentum of one of his swings landed him facing her direction once again.

A lengthy moment passed, prompting Etha to wonder whether or not Veed was alright. He stood staring at the ground, sword lowered at his side. Heavy breaths rattled his sturdy frame, but he'd taken no apparent injuries. Veed's characteristic ferocity refused to claim him in full, and he ignored the press around him. He made no motions toward either defense or offense, nor were any attacks thrown his way. A surge of restless misgivings writhed about in the core of Etha's being, and she glanced around in case the demons had left their vicinity. Her apprehension intensified when she found the demons still clashing against the flemans.

Her eyes flashed back to Veed. She was one thought away from inserting herself into the putrid dungeon of his mind when he looked up and stared into her eyes, expression cast with a deliberate calm. Etha stifled a gasp and immediately reassessed her appearance in case she'd somehow slipped into a physical form. Still thoroughly hidden to the untrained eye, she gazed back at Veed, a growing resolve settling over her. She couldn't explain how Veed saw her, but the intense perception of his eyes assured he had. The rush of combat pitched around them and Veed broke their stalemate with a purposeful blink before throwing himself back into the fight.

Free from the encounter but still riddled with a nagging suspicion, Etha pulled herself from Veed and swept deeper into the demon forces. Directly behind the last active line, demon reinforcements churned about, squabbling with one another in their impatience to join the fray. The mass of bodies condensed over the span of a mile. A dissatisfied rumble sprouted from these ranks, and Etha guided her attention toward the source of their ire.

A blot of darkness swelled from the northwest as a full army of alar flew in for the final insult. If Etha had needed breath to sustain her, she'd have lost it.

The goddess tore across the field, following the flow of divine energy and cracks of holy power to Mathias. *My dear, you need to do more! There are too many on the field and reinforcements in the sky. Wield my blessing in whatever way you see fit and those you cannot stomach to think of!*

She waited anxiously for his reply, rhythmically sweeping her conscience across the approaching threat. Battered but far from beaten, Mathias continued his mission of cutting down whatever was foolish enough to throw itself in his direction. He made efficient work of slaying his enemies, foregoing the torture Etha hated to see from him. A lucky few struggled to escape his wrath in search of easier prey. As his immediate location cleared, Mathias turned, sending his gaze right past Etha as he hefted himself toward the next pocket.

A tremor shook deep within Etha's essence. Even beneath the pressure of such horrific odds and perverted by this cold determination, Mathias wasn't the kind to ignore her advice, but he hadn't even acknowledged her presence. They hadn't last parted on terms poor enough to merit one of his silent tantrums, and dread welled inside Etha's all-knowing being. If her insight went unheard, the flemans would die with absolute certainty. Whatever fogged Mathias's mind now forced Etha into a most dire situation. More disturbing than Mathias's blocked status was Veed's lack of one, his intelligent, sighted eyes engraved in her mind. Why had he been able to see her but the dearest of her devout couldn't hear her screams?

Etha was not meant to intrude upon fate, but the flemans stood no chance at coming out of this. Their sole hope for survival relied on her direct intervention. Etha bore down on her resolve, turning her back on how filthy and wrong her pending actions made her feel. No war was won on its own, and if the fate of her blessed homeland counted on her taking a stand, she would ensure no more harm came her way.

Up until the demons had surfaced, inland Elidae flourished from a temperate environment, presenting an ideal climate for the invasion now wreaking havoc on her beauty. This nation, Etha's very first creation, would persevere through whatever the goddess threw at her. After all, Elidae was as strong as her mother.

Etha swept before Mathias again, grasping him by the shoulders to hunt for his attention. *Signal the troops in. Get them close and be prepared to give the most obvious order.*

No response came her way, and the uncertainty provided by Mathias's silence worked Etha's divine insides into a disorganized cluster. Whatever stood between her and Mathias wasn't something to test wits against with disaster pressing so near. Every second wasted on trying to push through this block cost too much time and with it, precious lives.

You cannot take this force on your own! she screamed to Mathias with one last frantic effort. *Call your troops in and prepare a hasty retreat!*

She held her ground through the span of Mathias's slow breath before he turned to scan the area to locate the nearest herald. He still hadn't confirmed receipt of Etha's warning, but his instincts served him just as well. "Bring the forces in!" he shouted. "No one goes more than three lines deep. Go on, sound the command!"

Etha had hoped to disengage the entire field before dropping her interference, but would compromise with what Mathias gave her. As the field shoved its way closer toward the fortress, Etha snapped beneath the demonic insult she'd pardoned for too long. Drawing her will up toward the heavens, she spared a whim of righteous pity for those below, surrendering to the divine power exclusive to her. Never again would her home be a battleground.

Twin streaks of blue lightning severed clear skies above the mortal chaos, striking down on adjacent sides of the field. It was the only warning Etha would deliver. Everyone—fleman and demon, Mathias and Veed—stood stunned as the ground popped in agony from the impact. Obsidian clouds spun about from every distant horizon, ravenously rolling toward the battlefield.

Mathias caught his breath, understanding the ache in his heart at last. Not one to dismiss his gratitude for Etha's assistance, he didn't particularly look forward to the promises which accompanied this ominous display. The weather was among the few forces not even he or demons could fight against, and if Etha's anger had driven her to step in, Mathias would put nothing past her. His heart quickened.

"Get the men moving faster! Run! Return to the fortress!"

The field quaked in fear of the great power thundering their direction, but Mathias's fierce orders shook both forces from their shock, restoring the most primitive instincts to stay alive. Fighting with twice the passion to free themselves, desperation pressed the flemans toward home.

Mathias removed himself from combat as the army mobilized, backing out of the scattering fray to watch the skies for what Etha had planned. He thought he'd caught warped whispers of her previous instructions, just enough to convey that she'd lost her calm, and he knew better than to attempt to stop her now that she'd taken action. This was no longer his time to fight, but to lead. Whatever shame came with fleeing would be nullified by the relief of avoiding death. Etha was a compassionate goddess, but without Mathias's immediate action, the odds of survival seemed limited at best.

A blustery chill swept across the land from the mountains in the east, hilts stinging to the touch mere moments after the gust. A second wind met the first from the west, rebounding the cold back against the warring armies. Unaccustomed to such low temperatures outside the mountaintops, the flemans steeled themselves as firmly as their shivering limbs and searing lungs allowed.

Finally, the demons began to falter. Ages spent dwelling in the moderate climate of the hells had sapped their tainted blood of its tolerance for the hardships of mortal environments. As the demons crumbled to the cold, the flemans pushed hard to free themselves from their enemies in this brief time provided to them.

The clouds amassed overhead, devouring any warmth the sun might have thrown them. A thick ceiling muffled the sounds of battle as voices hushed from the burning cold. The demons among the back lines struggled to comprehend the sudden change as the wings of the alar in flight chapped from gales of frigid wind. In the final throes before inevitable destruction struck, the demons tore through those scrambling flemans who their hands and weapons could reach. The first flakes of snow drifted to the ground, their destination intercepted by bodies both standing and dead.

With what Mathias feebly hoped was the conclusive development, he understood Etha's plan and the actions she meant for him to take. Woefully unsuited for arctic conditions, the demons would either be pushed back to their depths by this movement or perish where they stood. A natural barrier would rise to protect the innocents. Mathias knew as well as Etha did that it would take much more than a few inches of snow to thwart the demons' devious plans. The alar still aloft in the icy updrafts lowered their flight, unable to stabilize in the turbulence or temperature, but held course toward the front lines.

"Keep falling back!" Mathias shouted, shoving his allies ahead of his retreat.

The rate of snowfall increased, taking a firm hold on the heads and shoulders of the combatants. Wind roared across the field, threatening to drown out any further orders, and a curtain of sleet cut against them. In light of this abrupt upheaval, the men heeded

Mathias's command, forced to invest faith in him once more. There was no excuse for this tumultuous interception other than divine intervention, and to cope with that, they needed their paladin.

With Etha's law of not involving herself in the affairs of mortals already broken, Mathias knew she wouldn't back out now that she'd come this far. The conditions relentlessly grew worse, and with each step the demons faltered, so did the weary bones of the flemans. They clutched their wills to fight for their lives, but not much else could be salvaged beyond that.

"Ignore whatever gives chase!" Mathias coughed on the rasp that clenched his throat at the effort of shouting. "Fall back!"

The horns articulated Mathias's orders, answered by the snow's increasing intensity. Visibility faded fast, and Mathias didn't know how much longer they'd even be able to see their opponents if they tried to stand and fight. Songs of retreat flung through the thickening air, muffled by the natural insulation of snowfall, and Mathias banked his faith on his men following the command. He clenched his teeth and generated warmth with power lent to him from Affliction, holding his position on the field to cover those on foot. He'd lost sight of Brant and Sulik, but trusted their common sense to flee. When the snow impaired his ability to distinguish friend from foe, Mathias abandoned his combative efforts. Praying for any who might have fallen behind, he turned and followed the cries of fleman souls as they plowed toward the sanctuary of home.

"Hold your ground, cowards!"

Mathias dug his numb feet into the snow as Veed's harsh reprimand weaseled through the sheets of ice slicing down around him. Disgusted by the dark general's tenacity, the paladin struggled to balance the value of Veed's life with their rivalrous past. Mathias snarled. Let the son of a bitch find his end here. He'd rather looked forward to personally tearing into Veed's flesh, but leaving the beast to perish to Etha's will would spare him from feeling obligated to beg forgiveness for unusual cruelty. Mathias hunched his shoulders against the wind and blowing sleet and staggered his way through the knee-deep accumulation.

"You spineless fools!" Veed barked. "They're crippled! Take them now!"

"*Sir!*" an urgent cry demanded as a soldier stumbled into Veed's field of vision.

"What?" Veed spat.

The soldier raised an arm in case Veed felt compelled to turn his blade on him. "Sir, look!"

Veed followed his subordinate's pointed finger and the strength abandoned his sword arm.

The demons' howls succumbed to the roar of wind that spiraled down from the heavens, sucking bodies up into its heaving vortex. There was no hope for any of the alar in flight as the storm devoured them, and sense overpowered Veed's aggression at last. The snow fell in curtains around him, masking the fates of Solvig and the four soldiers who had accompanied him. The side of Veed that still acknowledged loyalty ached to know what became of his mount, but seeking the warhorse now guaranteed his own demise.

Instinct trumped any attempt at clutching to pride and Veed spun to plow a path away from the tornado. His legs inched in agony as the snow's depth climbed from knee to mid-thigh and his lungs seared with each breath he sucked down. Vague shouts from those fleeing ahead of him popped through the howling storm, and Veed concentrated the entirety of his focus on maintaining true to his heading. Blinded to his surroundings, he was unaware of panicking horses resorting to bold leaps through the banks.

The snow pressed past his hips and Veed was forced to use his entire body to move ahead, almost swimming as his lower extremities protested in numbness. He no longer feared falling victim to the demons—even if they somehow survived the conditions, poor visibility would prevent them from finding him, and the cold and ice vowed to claim Veed before his enemies had the chance to.

A glow emanated in front of him and will power alone drove Veed closer to it until strong hands hoisted him up by the arms through the windows of Nes's fortress. His eyes burned from their exposure and he squinted, rapid blinks trying to aid his adjustment to the comparatively dim lighting of the keep's interior. A pair of soldiers, Nes's men, stopped by to check on his status, but he brushed them off as he panted on the cold stone floor. Nothing more could be done at this point, and no amount of coddling would change that. They'd lost the battle, and the only blessing he counted on was that Renigan had stayed behind with his army. His fortress would be stable, but that said painfully little for the memories that raced and laughed through these old, familiar halls.

Veed flailed his arms to gain the momentum to sit upright and dragged himself to his feet. He stumbled down the corridors, the effects of battle and ache of cold in his bones hindering his motion more than he cared to admit. Unforgiving air assaulted his lungs and as soon as he escaped the rush of confusion around him, he sank against the wall. Physically and emotionally exhausted, Veed succumbed to his mind's tormenting.

NINE

Twelve years ago, the Teradhel fortress had served as a different sort of prison for Veed. Days passed without Laes approaching him with anything other than the typical orders and discussion of battlefield tactics. These casual interactions spun Veed closer to snapping under this self-imposed pressure. Laes moved on about his business, heedless to his friend's misery.

Veed executed his duties with unrelenting obedience and Nessix continued to flit about as innocently as ever. Each trill of her laughter and exuberant smile tore at Veed's patience, driving him to avoid all but the most mandatory social obligations. He requested his meals delivered to his chamber to spare himself from the usual familial dining arrangements. Even these meals often found their way out the window or fed to a wandering dog.

He carried out his orders with fiery enthusiasm, using the comfort of combat to focus his mind through more productive outlets. It seemed to Veed that Laes made an active effort to occupy Nessix's time, to the point that Veed only managed to snatch the briefest exchanges with her between assignments. He savored the glimpses he caught of her absorbed in the dance of sparring with Brant or conditioning Logan. When Laes finally approached Veed, the commander had grown ill with the strain to his mental health.

Veed answered this call to the war chamber with a desperate agitation unbecoming of a commander. No matter what answer Laes was destined to deliver, Veed needed this suffering to end. Laes sat alone in the chamber, or so Veed assumed. The general said nothing upon his friend's entry, not so much as glancing up as he sorted through papers and pouches set across the table. Veed cleared his throat. Several more tense breaths passed before Laes sighed and looked up. He studied Veed longer than necessary.

"You're gaunt, my friend."

Veed's eyes wandered away at the observation. "I've been working hard, General."

Laes frowned at Veed's dampened tone and lack of gusto. "That was not meant to be an attack."

"Then thank you for your concern." Exhaustion leached the sincerity from Veed's response.

Laes continued to roll up maps and check over the packs' supplies. "Have you been eating?"

Veed internalized his irritation at this pointless small talk behind taut tendons in his neck and scratched his ear. "Enough to sustain myself." This approach tried his patience on every level, just as he was certain Laes intended. He steadied himself with a deep breath and tight frown. "Surely, you didn't call me here to discuss my diet."

Preparations continued in silence for some time longer. The occasional hum of attempts to speak reverberated against Laes's throat, but his words remained tangled in his mind. Veed clenched his fists rhythmically and shifted his weight to rein in the flare of his agitation. He'd expended the bulk of his bravery during their previous discussion and doubted he'd retained the mettle to deal with whatever test Laes planned to put him through now. Confidence faltering, anxiety led Veed to tremble and just as he gathered the brass to speak up, a rowdy commotion skipped down the hall. Nes's feigned screams and winded giggles preceded her bursting through the war chamber door. She spun to try pushing it shut, but a stout shove from Brant knocked her to the ground, where she rolled, laughing.

"You're... interrupting... things!" Nessix gasped for air,

blocking her face with her arms and pressing a foot against her cousin. "Important things. *Order* things."

"You should have thought about that before you took notches out of my practice sword." Brant's eyes softened under irate brows at Nes's merriment.

Laes cleared his throat, the mischief of his daughter and nephew giving a temporary reprieve from the strictness in his eyes. "Is everything alright?" he asked.

Nessix held one hand out to fend against any potential assault from Brant and curled her legs beneath herself to stand. She still choked on her laughter. "Everything's fine here." She poked her cousin with an impish glance. "Well, it is with me. I was *trying* to be here on time—"

"Ha!" Brant tossed a hand in the air. "That's not what it sounded like when—"

"Oh, stop!" Nessix kept her arm outstretched to block Brant, and Veed could have sworn he caught her smile his direction. "I was trying to get here on time, I swear. He started it."

Brant crossed his arms and rolled his eyes.

Laes smiled his tolerance at the young officers and cast an admonishing glance toward Veed. Age ranked both Nessix and Brant as adults, but if this behavior didn't speak of Nes's propensity toward innocence, he didn't know what else would. Laes nodded to Brant. "Thank you for seeing her here on time, Brant," he said, "but I believe you've been tasked with duties at the stables this afternoon?"

Brant speared Nes with a stern look, jabbing a finger at her in promise of a rematch once he completed his responsibilities. She flashed him a cocky smirk and Brant left the chamber with no more fuss. The door fell shut, leaving the general, his daughter, and the agitated commander alone together. Veed shifted his weight between his feet and watched Laes for his next strike.

Nessix caught her breath and smiled with a warmth which life hadn't yet managed to dampen. "You said you had an assignment for me, Father?"

Laes sent a long glance to Veed, holding the commander's attention in a crushing grip, and heaved a sigh. "There have been reports of raids near Phyta," he said, his voice schooled with patience. "There haven't been any culprits sighted, so we don't know if it's minotaur or locals, but we've been asked to investigate it."

Nes's expression swirled between thrill and apprehension. "And you're sending *me* to look into it?" she breathed. "My first solo assignment?"

Laes's chuckle only snuffed a little bit of her light. "No, little love." He sucked in a preparatory breath and braced himself. "I'm sending Veed along with you on the off chance you run into trouble."

Veed gasped so sharply he nearly choked, trying to disguise his shock behind a cough. The sudden reaction gained a furrowed brow from Nessix. Catching himself before he'd need to come up with an explanation, Veed fabricated a smile to ease Nes's confusion. She returned the smile and nodded.

"Only as long as I get to take lead, right?" Her eyes danced with excitement and grand expectations.

Veed crossed his arms to keep from reaching out to her. "A lieutenant leading a commander? How do you suppose that would look?"

"I think it would look ideal." Laes's words wiped even the most decent of Veed's musings right from his mind.

Nessix, blissfully unaware of the duel waging between the two men she loved so much, grinned at her father's words. "It'll be good practice, though, don't you think, Veed?" She smacked him on the chest with the back of her hand. "I mean, one of these days you *will* have to answer to me, you know."

Her words, filled with jest and promise, sifted out a fresh vein of discomfort. Veed's smile never fully developed and he was afraid his expression reflected how ill he felt. Laes took careful consideration of this fact through narrowed eyes, and he nodded in approval of the commander's fleeing nerves. Picking up the packs, Laes walked around the table to hand one to Nessix. The second, he held out for Veed's wavering hands to accept.

"It shouldn't take much longer than five days; one day of travel on either side, and three to investigate." Laes retrieved his map and wrapped Nes's fingers around it. "If you're gone any longer than that—" He pointed those words at Veed. "I will send support troops to see what has happened. I trust with the two of you, there will be no problems. Don't you agree, Veed?"

The chance to savor any sort of elation escaped Veed under Laes's stony demeanor, one which anticipation of the forthcoming mission rendered Nessix oblivious to. Veed breathed deeply through his nose, wishing he could quit shaking. "There will be no problems, Laes," he answered shortly. "This sounds like a straight forward assignment with no reason for mishaps."

Laes nodded, more contemplative this time, and grasped Nessix by the shoulders. She beamed up at her father, unwittingly making the bite he'd brandished toward Veed more severe. "I want you to keep your senses sharp and your morals in check while you're out there, do you understand me?"

She cocked her head and wrinkled her nose at his strange request. "Of course, Father." A nervous laugh tinkled out of her. "Do you doubt I would?"

Laes smiled in forced contentment and glanced at Veed from the corner of his eye. "Absolutely not. That would be absurd."

Nessix grinned, blissfully unaware of the tension cramming the room past full capacity, and dismissed herself to prepare her personal belongings for the road.

"You can talk to her about whatever you'd like, but if you act... if you *touch* her outside of saving her life, Veed..." Laes growled, keeping his gaze directed toward where his daughter had flit from the room.

Veed didn't need Laes to finish the statement. His promise was clear enough.

TEN

The demons' war against Etha predated any other credible lore, and they knew her wretched ways better than most. In all that time, she'd only gone against her laws once before—when she stepped in to put an end to the Divine Battle. Since then, Etha had taken to hiding behind Mathias and Julianna and that ridiculous Order, and that timid reaction from one so ripe with power provided the demons with no end of entertainment. Etha's direct involvement in the affairs of the mortal world never came without massive repercussions, and the effortlessness with which she decimated their ranks to intercept the most recent battle proved a sobering reminder of the demons' bleak reality.

The inoga assigned to Elidae contended neck deep in debate over the fouled events when a classless underling skittered in to blubber about Shand expecting an audience. Tables were flipped at the announcement, chairs broken, threats and accusations thrown about. Grell spat and shoved past the rumble of his peers.

"I've got the bitch," he groused.

Nobody ever *wanted* to deal with Shand, and so Grell's offer received no complaints. He stormed his way through the tunnels, sending the less formidable of the population scurrying out of his path. Winding through the halls, he reached the room Shand preferred for her meetings. Small and near the surface, faint wisps of fresh air trickled into the chamber from the cavern's entrance. Grell drew a calming breath and crammed his way through the door.

"You filth!" Shand shrieked as Grell resituated his wings with a nonchalant shrug. "Didn't you listen to a damn thing I said?"

Grell appraised the level of insanity in Shand's scorching eyes and how she'd bloodied her palms courtesy of long nails embedded into her clenched fists. He smirked at her distress, cultivating the ugliest scowl imaginable from a woman so otherwise attractive.

"I listened to every word you said. A voice like yours is hard to miss."

She hissed at his rebellious disregard and rushed at him, her petite frame poised with what Grell assumed she thought conveyed danger. He bit into his smirk, reading the goddess's intentions with the clarity of a centuries-old warrior's instincts. Glancing away only to ensure his mass cleared the doorway, Grell backed away from her, arms open to his sides.

"This is *not* what we agreed on!" Brows rising in delight, Shand squared her shoulders and continued her steady pursuit.

"*I* never agreed to anything."

Shand sputtered at the demon's insolence and continued to press toward him. "I've been given the demons' word! You are *my* soldiers! You obey *me*!"

Grell maintained his retreat, holding her eyes calmly as she drove him deeper into his realm. "Let me make something clear. We've been at war since before your puny mortal self was even born. All you've done is provide us a shield."

Her eyes widened. Nobody spoke to her like that—nobody was stupid enough! "I am no one's shield," she growled.

If Grell had been of slighter stature or slower mind, her tone might have intimidated him. "But you are." His smirk broadened into a grin as Shand hunched forward and quickened her pace. "Because you know how easily we could uncover your identity to Mathias. As much as he hates us, he's still convinced there's good in us somewhere. I heard he gave up on *you* years ago."

Shand shoved Grell back, her shrill scream mocking her precious efforts of keeping a hold of her composure as it bounced off the cavern walls. Grell stumbled before catching himself, eyes losing their mischievous glint at Shand's attempt at using force against him, and he glowered back at her scathing fury. He remained still and let Shand stalk up to him.

Toe to toe with this brute, Shand stared searing needles up into his stony face. "How *dare* you defy me!" Her voice struck with little more than a whisper, one her egotistical eyes suggested had meant to daunt him.

Grell's nose curled at the goddess's fresh, outside scent, and a slow chuckle resonated in his throat. "You are a fool." He shook his head at Shand's pathetic misfortune.

"You have gone—"

Before the rest of Shand's blistering retort flew off her tongue, Grell crushed her wrists in his grasp and spun, slamming her back against the wall. After the alarm of physical assault had passed, Shand's eyes laughed at Grell's ignorance. Sneering at the abhorrent beast, she flexed her muscles to pull away from his hold. Divine strength failed to free her, and she pulled again. A startled gasp later, Shand twisted against him, shrieking her frustrations until they grew into panicked yelps. She kicked at Grell's sturdy frame through her elegant skirt, the skin of her wrists burning as she tried to tear away from him. When was the last time her heart rate had climbed from fear? Having lost the ability to adapt to such rudimentary reactions, the primal need to run overtook Shand's senses and she thrashed to escape Grell's control.

Grell devoured the terror in Shand's eyes and he leaned over her, his chin tapping her shoulder as he murmured into her ear. "Not even Etha's might can penetrate this deep in our realm. It's how we caught Mathias before and how we could just as easily catch you. Watch yourself, goddess."

Heart in her throat, Shand sucked rapid breaths through flaring nostrils as Grell slowly righted himself. His cold eyes were rich with an eerie intelligence that turned Shand's stomach. She whimpered, earning Grell's satisfied smirk. Had this been the demons' plan all along? What could they do to one of her power in these depths?

"Would you have still wanted to deal with us if you'd known

this before we began?"

Shand doubted her ability to control the timbre of her voice or even the words that needed to come out, and so she kept silent. In the days of her mortality, she'd been among the most brilliant of magic users, apprenticing beneath one of the pioneers of necromancy. After binding herself to her god shard, she developed a fierce reliance on divine might over superior intellect, allowing many parts of her mind to grow dull. And right now, she regretted nothing more.

Just as she braced herself to resign to the fact that she wouldn't escape Grell, the inoga opened his hands and stepped back. Shand didn't even risk a gasp, bolting terrified toward the tunnel's exit until she could once again spin fire in her palm. She wheeled around to face Grell, who followed in a casual swagger with relaxed shoulders.

"You are stupid!" she hissed, too shaken to notice the tears streaming down her cheeks. "All of you! Today's devastation—"

Grell stopped and clasped his hands behind his back. "Indeed, it was devastating."

She frowned at his calculated calm and sniffed back against this filthy fear. "If you would have listened to me, you'd have been spared those casualties."

Grell's chuckle shook against Shand's chest. "You have no idea of Mathias's true destructive force, do you?" He gave her the chance to sputter one of her arrogant opinions, but when she offered nothing but a gaping mouth, Grell continued. "We're going to take casualties, regardless. Might as well have some fun in the process."

"Do not try my patience, ingoa." Her tone pierced with timid threats but, like all demons, Grell enjoyed his share of pain.

"And if I do?"

"You only have this one portal left. I could stand out there and pick off each one of you that comes close with very little effort."

Grell hummed his consideration and nodded a dubious agreement. "You are aware that we have plenty of access points across Abaeloth, aren't you?"

"But they won't yield you Elidae. Isn't that what you're after?"

He shrugged. "They won't yield us Elidae while you're still here, but you can't watch the whole world at once, and you're not the type to trust another god to help you. You can keep stamping your feet here on Elidae, and we can access anywhere else we want, visit with all sorts of people. Lots of voices to go crying your frightful name and terrible sins to Zeal."

A sharp breath filled Shand's lungs. Her entire scheme of luring Mathias to Elidae was to separate him from the Order and especially his sister. Shand could pick them off one at a time, but not while they actively backed each other. Arrogance had drawn her into the same trap which had claimed most everyone else on Abaeloth, assuming the demons were stupid and incapable of controlling their destinies. It didn't dawn on her until hearing Grell's implied threat that the fallen had survived these centuries by wielding minds more devious than her own. Shand had invested too much in her plot to back out now, but as Grell smirked at her folly, she began to realize that if Etha's power couldn't harness the demons, she'd never been near controlling them.

"You would have never made it this far without me," she sneered, hoping to stoke some sense of loyalty from the inoga.

"If that helps you sleep better." Grell turned and strode back down the hall. "Come back when you have something useful to offer us. We've got Mathias under control."

Shand stood in stupefied silence as Grell faded from view, wondering what he'd meant by the last statement. The demons couldn't have Mathias; he belonged to *her*. As plans fell in tatters around her, Shand pinched her eyes shut and doubled over with a shriek of scathing fury.

Down the hall, Grell grinned.

* * * * *

Even the children had grown tired of the cold, calling snowball fights to disappointed draws as nimble fingers succumbed to the numbing frost. Soldiers struggled to maintain their posts, feet burning in the depths of snow that covered the battlements and drifted through the windows. Small fires lit areas of adequate ventilation, surrounded by thick huddles of dreary flemans. Together, the entire fortress suffered through this frigid fate and concentrated efforts were made to shake what salvageable joy could be found in it. Yet through all of this misery, only Veed considered himself a true captive to the fortress.

When Veed left the Teradhel army all those years ago, he'd been determined to start his own life. It wasn't until his intimate encounter with Nessix that he even entertained the idea of smoothing over past wrongs. It wasn't until her death that he realized how wrong he'd been. And it wasn't until this exact moment, pining for comfort within an icy cage, that he realized though he'd left this keep, it had never left him.

He hadn't expected any sort of welcome to greet him after being pulled into these halls, and once he shook off his shock of the battle which so nearly claimed them all, he invited himself to the only place in the fortress he considered secure. His old chamber occupied the fifth floor, well above Nes's and centrally located within the halls. Always a man of tremendous material needs and no shame in displaying as much, he'd managed it as the most lavish chamber in the fortress, besting even Laes's fine furnishings. He'd taken the bulk of his possessions along with him when parting Nes's company, but left enough behind that he wouldn't hurt for physical comfort in the days to follow.

If Veed took the time to scour the hallway, he'd still find officers' quarters, but for the most part, it now served as a general barracks for the soldiers. Shoulders hunched in frustration, Veed stalked to the rich wooden door of his former dwelling and frowned at the cobwebs clinging to the frame. Of course, it had only been in the loftiness of his imagination where Nessix had curled up on his couch, clutching one of the few items he'd abandoned as she mourned his departure. Instead, he was received by a door nobody had bothered to lock, revealing a musty room full of furniture left exactly as he remembered it. Dust coated his belongings, confirming years of neglect. If he'd had either the appropriate standing in this fortress or the gumption to care, he'd have sought someone to clean the filth away. Breathing in the stale stillness, Veed stepped back into a past he'd contently left behind.

This vacant chamber had remained frozen in time, and the goodness which lurked in the deepest rifts of Veed pondered what might have happened if he'd conducted himself in a manner better suited of a fleman commander. He'd insisted that destiny wanted him to carry his stolen title for so long that the concept of servitude had escaped him. This room that once overflowed with pride earned through loyalty refused to let him continue in such indifference, dredging up memories of a time when he'd cared about matters greater than himself.

Trophies of minotaur horns lined one wall, something he once beamed at as a display of courage. Just below them hung badges of merit awarded to him by both of the generals whom he'd served under, Inwan, and in a less than official exchange, Nessix. Eager to escape the honor that had earned such acclaim and the weight of happiness they possessed, Veed hadn't intended to see these awards again. This single wall summed up the entirety of a life that made much more sense than this catastrophe he floundered in now.

Veed crept closer to that wall, worn down from glaring at it. He didn't need fancy trinkets to gloat of his bravery or abilities, and those trophies earned through heroic deeds all ran together. Their value was little more than an ostentatious form of gratitude, anyway, and if Veed's eye for pretty things hadn't been common knowledge, he suspected most of these awards belonged to far more worthy recipients. Only one item held any meaning for Veed, and he frowned at the bite of tears that greeted it.

Draped atop the tip of a minotaur horn a hand above Nes's frustrated and humiliated reach, the one memento Veed never should have parted with was that dainty, blood-stained cloth. Pushing Nessix toward improvement had consumed Veed's life at one point, occupying much of his time between battle and politics as he schooled her in swordplay and the finer points of hand to hand combat. In those more innocent days, Nessix had trusted Veed too much and disbelieved he had it in him to try a true attack on her, a lesson she should have taken closer to heart. The assault had promptly ended that day's session, leaving Nessix with a clean slice perpendicular to her upper lip that resulted in a scar only the two of them ever spoke of. That was the first time Veed had witnessed Nessix back down from conflict, and she'd declared it the last with the informal trophy, claiming her blood would never again be drawn in combat. He'd believed those words as little then as he did now, but her rebellious declaration hadn't managed to quell the respect earned by her determination.

Veed snatched the handkerchief from the its resting place, holding it with a baffling tenderness as he stared at the blood flecked on its faded fabric. His breathing tapered to shallow heaves and the splotches blurred in his vision. Curling the cloth in his trembling hand, Veed brought it to his lips. When Laes died, Veed hadn't fathomed a more intense pain from loss, but Nessix had meant the world to him.

The fondness Mathias had used to speak of Nessix at her funeral infuriated Veed, as if that arrogant human had known her at all. He lowered his arm and sniffed back the surge of emotions, scanning his room through bleary eyes. Too many remnants of what used to be haunted these walls and aged fineries. Laes's watchful gaze followed him, knowing things Veed never would and now able to see far more completely. Even Inwan had a place tucked in this room. Constant reminders of the glory and splendor which existed when Elidae thrived beneath one just hand mocked Veed's attempts at dominance and control. He didn't regret the actions he'd taken or the consequences fit for them, but he could regret what his rash actions had stolen from him. Memories of the past, treacheries of the present, and remnants of dreams that would never be. He would have preferred Nessix to have torn his room apart, if only to justify being angry now.

ELEVEN

Twelve years ago, a far more daunting storm had cornered Veed. Thunder crashed and rattled the windows as he tramped his way down the hall. This entire predicament was beyond foolish, and he now believed Laes had sent him and Nessix out alone with the purpose of torturing him. Whether the general hoped to teach Veed a lesson or set him up for some grand failure remained to be seen, but it succeeded in sowing enough discomfort for Veed to abort both his assigned mission and his personal one. He stopped outside the door of Nes's rented room and listened to the storm welling up outside. Heart pounding and breath coming heavy, he knocked on the door.

"Come in," came her muffled reply.

Veed hesitated at the invitation, unsure if he'd heard correctly, then tried the doorknob. It turned without question and he pushed the door open to find Nessix in a nightgown, tucked under her sheets and reading over reports by candlelight. She gave him a warm smile that faded in confusion at his strict brows.

"Your door was unlocked?" As adamant as Veed had been about leaving, the danger Nes's inexperience proposed left him conflicted. "Have you always left your doors unlocked?"

She nodded, one eyebrow cocked as though Veed was a fool for not knowing. "Why wouldn't I?"

Veed blinked, too stunned to offer an immediate reply. At Nes's age, she should have been capable of living on her own, of understanding why women ought to keep themselves protected when in public. After all of the guidance provided to Nessix through her life, *how* had this lesson escaped her? Veed coughed. "Nessix, we're not at home. That isn't... safe."

She rolled her eyes. "You sound like Father. Nobody would want to hurt me, you know that."

He shook his head, eyes wide in disbelief.

"And even if they did..." Half a heartbeat later, Nessix produced a dagger from beneath her pillow. "I'm fine, Veed. A locked door is just one more barrier between me and the people. There's going to be a day where that could be the difference between success and catastrophe." She craned her neck and furrowed her brows. "Why are you packed?"

Fear for Nes's safety compounded Veed's previous concerns, but he forbid himself to chance the alternative. "Eh, you've done a fine job and we'd be going back tomorrow, anyway. Something's come up. I'm heading home."

"Right now?" Her voice shivered with a charming uncertainty.

"Yes."

"In this storm?"

Veed rubbed the back of his neck and voiced a modest chuckle, suppressing his impulsive side by looking away from her. "Yes."

Nessix shook her head and slid out from under the blankets, dangling her legs off the side of the bed. "Inwan came by for a visit just half an hour ago and told me to stay inside. He said this storm was going to be horrible."

Veed batted a dismissive hand at her. "I'll be fine."

"Wait. Why aren't you in your room?"

He sighed. "A traveler came by needing board. The inn keep asked if I'd be willing to let the man stay in my stead. Our way's always been to offer comfort to the people before ourselves."

Nessix shook her head, loose hair bouncing about her shoulders. She popped to her feet and rushed forward to grasp his arms. "You are not leaving in this storm."

"Nes, I'll be fine." Uncomfortable with her demand in light of his desire, Veed tested the young woman's hold and found her firm in her motives. Ideally, he'd have chosen a more controlled scenario to pique her concern for him, but nature had provided them other plans. "I have nowhere else to stay, and going home now beats sleeping on the streets."

"You could stay here."

Her innocent suggestion set free a whirlwind of flutters in Veed's heart. Though a far cry from a sultry invitation to her bed, Nessix had just asked him to share her quarters with her. Decency swept over Veed in a hurry and this time, he succeeded in yanking his arms away from her. "And risk the rumors that'd float around in the morning?" Her offer was delicious, but one Veed was certain Laes would refuse to swallow.

Nessix snorted and grabbed his arms again to drag him into the room. "It's either that or risk Father's disappointment." She shoved him with all of her slight might farther in and shut the door. This time, she locked it. "Besides, what if something happened to you on the road back? I'd never forgive myself."

Veed pressed his fingers to his forehead, knowing Nessix had no idea how her words tempted his lewd mind, but that raw side of Veed thrived off her spunk. He drew in a slow breath to ground himself back to propriety. "I appreciate the offer, but you need to trust me. It's better if I—"

"No." Nes's chin jutted with a provocative authority and she arched a challenging brow.

Veed shifted his weight and rolled his neck, forcing his breath out once more. "You're being childish. It sounds like the rain's letting up, anyway."

Her eyes darkened and she set her jaw somewhere in a cross between her habitual immature pout and the discipline she'd recently acquired. "It will start up again," she assured, a less than sensuous heat backing her claim, "and when it does, you'd be stuck in the middle of it. I will not allow that."

"I promise you, I'll be fine."

"Veed!" she hissed. "I *order* you to stay!"

The ferocity of the command immediately struck Veed both

123

with shock of her severity and an immense attraction to her power. At least he could be certain she welcomed the idea of him staying. Laes couldn't possibly fault him for that... could he?

"You may be the general's daughter, but I still outrank you," Veed said. "On what grounds do I have to obey your order?"

A temperamental dissatisfaction pulled Nes's brows to a glower Veed hoped to never receive again. "You outrank me on the field. You obey my blood at all times."

That reminder of his loyalty to Laes soured Veed's stomach and he swallowed in an attempt to buffer it. "You'll make a fine general someday, Nes."

The stern mask she'd worn fell away to reveal the slightest hint of blush at his compliment. "So that means you're staying, right?"

Great Inwan, keep me honest. "I will." Veed glanced through the modest chamber for the most appropriate place to stow his pack and, more importantly, himself. Now his only tasks were to avoid further offense and maintain a solid line between friendly and frightening. He'd never doubted himself in the past and this wasn't the time to start.

"Make yourself comfortable." Nessix padded her way over to the plush couch furnished in the rented room of nobility. She pushed piles of papers and spent clothing to the floor and gathered the fur draped across the back. With a few swats of her arms, she wrapped the cover around herself.

"What are you doing?" Veed asked.

"Getting ready to turn in." She perched on the cushions as she snuffed the trio of candles on the table beside her. "There's still a bit more scouting I want to take care of in the morning."

"I've already inconvenienced you by imposing my stay here and will not be the reason you leave your bed." Veed plopped his bundle of belongings on the table and grasped Nes's arms, thankful for the fur serving as a barrier between their flesh. He hauled Nessix back to her feet.

A tremor of delight danced through Veed at their nearness, enhanced by the privacy they shared. Reservations and integrity be damned, this felt *right*. He ached to tell her the thoughts that pestered his mind and vexed his heart, to pull her close, to kiss her. Decency wasted no time in scolding him for such fantasies, reminding Veed of both Laes's promise and capabilities, and so he settled for a brisk sigh as he pushed Nessix toward the bed.

"You are my guest," she fussed, pulling against his superior strength to no avail. "I will not discomfort you by forcing you out of a bed."

How Veed cursed the testosterone flowing through his veins! It took the greatest extent of his will power to keep from suggesting they share the bed and put this debate behind them. Through Nes's eyes, Laes fit Veed with a steady, trusting gaze. He sighed brokenly and shoved Nessix backwards. As she toppled onto the bed, Veed turned and retreated to the couch.

"Your father would prefer it this way." Veed forbid himself to look back at Nessix, unwilling to chance putting another crack in his resolve. "You may be his flesh and blood, but I've known him since I was younger than you are now. Give me that fur and tuck yourself in." He held an open hand behind himself, and only after several beats of his racing heart passed without Nes's compliance did he turn to face her.

Nessix was on her feet again, eyes strict and petite frame braced to manhandle Veed the way he'd just tossed her around. Instinct craved her touch, but with so many dangers tied to engaging in a physical altercation, Veed shook his open hand to reemphasize his demand. He received a belligerent glare in return.

"This is how it's going to be." Veed needed them both to hear that affirmation. "Unless you'd prefer I go out in the storm?"

The indulgent side of Veed wanted to hear her voice again before sleep overcame them. Instead, Nessix huffed a pout and pelted the fur in his direction. She slid beneath the thick quilts of the bed and turned her back to him. Veed watched her in silence as her breathing slowed toward slumber before turning to put out the final candle. He hesitated beside the bed, giving impulse an excuse to tug at his vows of loyalty. Clenching his teeth, Veed wrapped himself in the fur and laid down on the couch.

Sleep never found Veed and he didn't know why he bothered trying to find it. The darkness chilled him in his lonely fur and the steady beat of rain against the window tugged his mind toward thoughts of all the other ways to spend such intimate hours. Caving to his misery, Veed sat up and ran his hands through his hair. A flash of lightning outlined Nes's sleeping form and he couldn't look away from her. Mouth dry, he waited for his eyes to adjust to the dark, then got up to fetch his wineskin. A reluctant sip preceded a ravenous chain of gulps before he lowered it and turned back toward the couch.

He stared at Nessix on his way past, taken in by her innocence and the refined beauty nobility bestowed on her. Vanity had never concerned Nessix, and Veed wondered if she even realized how attractive she was. Clicking his teeth together a few times, he sighed and pulled a chair over beside the bed. He seated himself there, watching the steady rise and fall of her shoulder as she slept on her side.

Carnal desires urged Veed to reach out and touch her, to sweep a stray lock of hair from where it rested on her cheek, or to clasp her hand in his. He refrained from those desires, scolding this depraved side of himself with how she'd mentioned needing sleep. It'd be rude to wake her. Beyond that, how would he explain why he was watching her? The need for that question's answer came rushing toward him as the next flash of lightning revealed Nes's open eyes as she gazed back at him, caught in the haze between slumber and wakefulness.

"Veed?" she murmured. "What's wrong?"

What was wrong? Perhaps the fact that he couldn't think straight with her near, or that she never left his mind? Maybe how he was nearly three times her age and looking at her weakened him in ways no woman ever had? Possibly, the biggest problem was that Laes's warnings refused to dislodge from where they'd cornered his courage. Inwan help him, even in his most coveted dream, if he and Nessix had the chance to raise a child together, the intimacy which passed between them would be clear. Veed's heart rate quickened.

Nessix propped herself up on an elbow, preparing to leap to action at Veed's call. "Veed, what's the matter?"

The tremble of Nes's voice betrayed her earlier bout of boldness, but the words to reassure her evaded Veed. All he could do was watch her, take in her beauty, shameless thoughts persisting against the screams of moral obligation. The uncertainty behind Nes's eyes, matched with an unshakable belief that Veed would never lead her to harm, commanded the entirety of his focus. Those eyes snared his heart, pulling him closer to her. Before Veed's tired senses registered his movement, his hand cradled the back of Nes's head and guided her closer to him.

The confidence with which Veed controlled the situation swapped Nes's fear for confusion, but she stayed silent. Her faith in him complied readily with his actions.

With Nessix offering no blatant objections, Veed's wild urges—the ones which had led him to refrain from taking a wife to allow him the pleasure of more rowdy and spontaneous romantic encounters—ran rampant with his self-control. Nessix was so innocent and naïve, and she trusted him explicitly. All he had to do was assure her that she'd be fine, that if she banked on that trust, he'd show her delights she'd never dreamed of. He'd tell her how beautiful she was, how much he loved her, and he'd teach her how to love him back. Blood racing hot through his veins, Veed's fingers curled into Nes's loose hair and he hadn't been aware he'd kissed her until he drew his lips back from her forehead.

Nes's wide eyes muddled with indistinguishable reservations. She held her breath as she stared into Veed's dark, lusty gaze. His name stammered from her lips, not at all the sensuous whimper his renegade desires craved. Her apprehensions riddled holes throughout this perverse determination.

What am I doing!

The hand worked into Nes's hair clenched into a brief fist and Veed pulled his shoulders back. His breath came quick and shallow and as hormones assaulted him, he found it increasingly difficult to see straight. This wasn't right in the greatest stretch of the imagination. Shaking, Veed released his hold on Nes's hair and repelled from her side.

She called after him and Veed fought hard to block out her urgency as he snatched his bag from the table. "Lock the door behind me," he growled, refusing to turn back to face her.

A rustle of covers announced Nessix had initiated pursuit.

"Please tell me what's wrong!"

Veed squared his shoulders, clenching his grip on the bag. "If you've ever trusted me before, trust me now. I need to leave. Lock the door behind me and I'll see you back at the fortress."

Nessix gasped his name, hurt and confused by the chill in his tone, and Veed forbid himself to continue tempting chance. He strode to the door and left with a rigid purpose Nessix wouldn't dare question. Standing quietly in the hall, head bowed, Veed waited until timid footsteps approached the other side of the door. Silence hung between that negligent barrier for several heavy breaths before the lock clunked into place. A disappointed sigh relaxed the tension in Veed's chest, and he continued on his way out of the inn. With the door locked, Nessix was safe, even from him.

TWELVE

While the lingering cold succeeded in crippling Elidae's more mundane inhabitants, flying through the chilly updrafts offered no more discomfort than increasing altitude for Ceraphlaks. He enjoyed the freedom of his position, but took his responsibility of maintaining a strict watch over the mountains quite seriously. Etha's actions had driven the demons from the surface, but that didn't promise they'd stay gone. If anything, these beasts were masters of adaptation, and Ceraphlaks doubted they'd sit around and wait for the snow to melt before clawing their way out for their next assault.

Over the past few weeks, Mathias had quit reliably communicating with him once again, and so Ceraphlaks appointed the duty of scouting for danger to himself. No matter where his rider's silence originated, whether grief or preoccupation with comforting the civilians, under Etha's guidance, Ceraphlaks gave Mathias his space. The goddess assured Ceraphlaks that she still heard Mathias's prayers, and that alleviated his immediate concerns.

Very little of Elidae had escaped Etha's hammer of divine intervention, but at least she'd spared the island from the fires and terrors which had sheared Abaeloth apart during the Divine Battle. A compassionate and smart goddess, she'd learned from the oversights of her past and would not risk such devastation again.

After all, that recklessness was what gave rise to the demons in the first place.

Snow teetered in precarious deposits atop mountainous ledges, sealing thick frozen walls over the ominous caverns that could someday serve as portals between this world and the demons'. The forests huddled beneath a heavy white canopy, providing an insulated cave to protect the wildlife and whatever villains had the sense to hide before Etha's wrath claimed them. Veed's fortress was covered, but activity still buzzed through the walls, and Ceraphlaks kept his distance to avoid trouble. Roofs burdened with the weight of ice and snow began to collapse on the vacant houses and business throughout the evacuated townships of the north. This was not the beautiful Elidae Ceraphlaks had first discovered, but at least she was alive.

He surveyed extensively, scouring the places he most expected to disclose signs of trouble, but it wasn't until his return flight home that he noticed a vibrant patch of green against the otherwise barren landscape. Etha's mercy had spared Logan from the storm's consumption, protecting both him and Nes's tomb from the drifts and cold. The pegasus came so close to leaving the fecklan to his misery, but too much had changed since their first squabble by the Great Spring. Ceraphlaks banked back around and came to a gentle landing on the outermost edge of the open patch of land. He inched closer to Logan, neck outstretched.

Created by divine means, Ceraphlaks was more removed from the mortal world than even Mathias. He knew right from wrong, good from evil, but the concept of emotions never registered to him the way he often wondered about. He protected himself from the self-defeating handicap of bonding to mortals, as he knew them best for dying. Mathias was the first and only being he felt kindred to, and even in that relationship, he considered Mathias a trusted comrade more than someone to love. They took care of each other and had established a mutual fondness for one another, but Ceraphlaks was reluctant to label this kinship as any mortal emotion.

For these reasons, he hadn't understood Mathias's devotion to Nessix, able to escape the downward spiral that claimed the island.

In fact, his greatest regret amid all of this tragedy was that the demons had found a way to step ahead of Etha by intercepting a soul's final passage. A typical death was no more than the last chapter of life, and Ceraphlaks had seen the ends of countless men and women who he considered more deserving of such a devastated response, but Logan's despair lashed out gripping tendrils, seeking closure, pulling Ceraphlaks near.

As far as his understanding went, fecklans and their generals shared a bond much more intimate than the average mount and rider team, likely even closer than the bonds which linked two people. Just as he and Mathias had been custom tailored to serve each other, Logan would not have existed if not for Nessix. Ceraphlaks couldn't fathom a sense of camaraderie to rival what he shared with Mathias, but the glaze which tarnished Logan's eyes begged to prove him wrong.

Seeing Logan so thoroughly defeated chilled Ceraphlaks. Logan had trod up to his death willingly and alight with fire more times than Ceraphlaks thought prudent, but the great warhorse's heart had been torn out, buried with his rider. Ribs peeked through his raven coat, uninhibited by the lackluster mess malnutrition had forced upon him. Muscles had wasted, depriving him of the strength needed to thunder into battle. The vacancy of Logan's gaze confirmed his spirit rejected any attempts of reclaiming that passion, warping his youthful heart far into his twilight. Etha had protected Logan from the elements, but not even she could save him from his own destruction.

Wings tucked against his back, Ceraphlaks sorted his cautious grudges aside and approached Logan on timid hooves. Whether or not Logan intended to suffer alone, Ceraphlaks's compassion forbid him to do so. Nobody this selfless deserved that. Logan stood in a detached stupor, not even batting an eye at Ceraphlaks's advance.

Dismayed by the lack of response, Ceraphlaks nickered a kind greeting, the first civil exchange he'd given Logan since their relationship began but that, too, never received a reply. Troubled by this unsettling change in the fiery steed, Ceraphlaks nabbed a mouthful of hay from the generous buffet presented beside the head of Nes's grave and held it out, neck fully extended. If Logan didn't eat, he'd die, but Logan was intelligent enough to understand that. Ceraphlaks prayed that wasn't his goal.

As Logan continued to ignore the offering, Ceraphlaks gave in to eating the bite himself, wisps of hay falling from his mouth to sprinkle atop the mound of stones at their hooves. Mechanically, Logan lowered his head to brush the litter from the sacred spot with his lips. Ceraphlaks held his breath, waiting for Logan to snatch up the nourishment, but was left disappointed.

Lifting his wings at the ready in case Logan's old temper required it, Ceraphlaks crept one step closer to the grave. Ears pricked on Logan, he took another stride. Desperate to shake life out of the fecklan one way or another, Ceraphlaks lowered his head toward Nes's tomb and leaned his weight onto his forehand. At last, Logan's eyes swelled with a tumult of anger and warning, but his greatest effort to chase Ceraphlaks away culminated in the form of pinned ears, bared teeth, and a halfhearted snake of his neck.

Keeping his head low, Ceraphlaks honored Logan's attempt at guarding his rider and retreated a step. After failing to protect Nessix in life, Logan continued his heart wrenching duty even after her death and at once, Ceraphlaks understood. Logan would carry out his duty until the last of his days, and it wasn't Ceraphlaks's place to demand otherwise. Nessix had fallen with her pride intact, and Logan deserved the same opportunity. The flemans seemed eager to deny him this right, obvious from the food strewn before him and the blanket crumpled on the ground nearby. No, the flemans didn't seem to respect Logan's decision, but Ceraphlaks did, and he wouldn't impose any more.

The pegasus trembled from the emptiness welling inside himself. Instinct begged him to flee, but rationale assured him that he couldn't escape it that easily. This was why he no longer sought emotions and the burdens tied to them. Blowing out a resigned breath, Ceraphlaks unfurled his wings and carefully walked around the grave to nuzzle his condolences to the mortal horse he'd never seen eye to eye with.

Retracting the gesture challenged the whole of Ceraphlaks's will, and he wasted no more time before spiraling up into the cloudy skies. So little remained of Logan, and it plucked at all of the primitive flight responses that hid dormant in Ceraphlaks's blessed body, weighing him down with the urge to find Mathias to soak up his comfort. He was, after all, dreadfully fond of his rider. Ceraphlaks refused to look back, unable to witness the decay of such a proud spirit any longer. That wasn't how he ever wanted to remember Logan.

Ceraphlaks kept his senses on alert, begging Elidae to provide him a distraction from the worrisome sensations which cursed the mortal world. A flurry of movement and dash of red rewarded his effort and suddenly, he wished he hadn't been so selfish. Fighting the impulse to drift closer, unclear of this person's alignment or objective, Ceraphlaks rode an updraft to silence his presence. Despite his sharp eyes, the snow's glare dulled his vision and distorted his view of the traveler. Ceraphlaks snorted. This wasn't helping his anxiety at all.

In more peaceful times, he'd consider approaching the man on his own, but under the current circumstances and with demons as devious as ever, he wouldn't chance it. Whoever this was, he'd set his course straight for the Teradhel fortress. Ceraphlaks had seen enough. He flew hard.

* * * * *

If Brant hadn't been going crazy and Nessix was actually in the room with him, he suspected she'd be tapping an impatient foot against the side of her chair or flicking the toggle of his curtains until he snapped at her to stop. Instead, he only got to hear her voice yammer on about how bored she was and fussing at him over his foul mood. All efforts to tune her out had failed, and her constant chatter prevented him from catching decent sleep. Elbows rooted atop his knees, Brant leaned his head against his hands, propping his face up with his thumbs and index fingers.

Go see what Mathias is up to.

Brant's eyes darkened back into focus at the suggestion, but his gaze stayed low. "The fuck would I do that?"

You haven't seen him in a long time.

This time, Brant leaned back in his chair and scorned Nes's mischief with a caustic laugh. "I don't really consider that a bad thing, you know."

Aren't you the least bit curious about what he's doing with the army?

"What do you *think* he's doing?" Brant muttered, grateful for the privacy of his chamber. "There's nothing that can be done right now; we can't go anywhere through this snow."

I think he's doing something about that ruckus in the hall.

Brant turned his head to look at his closed door and quieted his mind. Of course, Nessix stayed still when she wanted to make a point. Just as she'd said, clipped shouts shot between the brisk flow of soldiers rushing in the hallway. The siege bells hadn't tolled to announce danger and even if their hinges had frozen, no horns raised to back them. Brant narrowed his eyes. This wasn't an attack, but neither did the voices outside his room echo with the exuberance typical of celebration.

See? Something's happening.

Brant didn't want to move for anything short of trying his luck at a glorious death in battle, but Nes's persistence stoked the faintest embers of his curiosity. Besides, if he hoped to keep his body in any sort of combative condition, he couldn't afford to sit around all day. Sighing away his inner desires, Brant stood and stumbled his way to the door. Sleep deprived and only half sober, Brant staggered from his chamber, slamming against the adjacent wall for support.

You're a mess, Nes teased.

"Shut it."

He leaned against the wall to let his head settle from the cyclone brought on by his sudden movement, and shook sense into himself. Light reflected in through the windows off the snow-covered landscape, forcing Brant to squint as his eyes adjusted to the unaccustomed brightness. Given the amount of noise which had filtered through the door, Brant had expected more people to occupy the hall, but in his current condition, he preferred the relative solitude. Blinking several times and breathing in the sharp coldness of the air, he coughed and addressed the next soldier to pass, beating Nes's chance to begin pestering him.

"Have you seen Sagewind?"

"He's at the gates, assessing our visitor," the soldier replied, an apprehensive twitch trying to pull him away from the respect demanded by Brant's station.

Brant shook his head and frowned. "Visitor—What?"

Told you Mathias was—

"Sagewind," Brant corrected.

The soldier's brows furrowed, but he stayed quiet.

Told you Sagewind—Nes drew out the correction obnoxiously—*was up to something.*

"A man appeared in the snow, marching this way." The soldier resumed his path toward the stairs now that he'd caught Brant's interest. "He's on his own, as far as we can tell. But where'd he come from?"

Brant followed, eyes narrowing. "Where, indeed…"

"As I said, Sir—General Sagewind is waiting to accept him and weigh his intentions."

Brant frowned over this new development. Nobody caught in any part of that blizzard could have survived its brutality, and the snow was still too deep for anyone from Veed's territory to make it this far on foot. Nes's incessant chatter over how they were overdue for some excitement grated on Brant, but he grit his teeth against her mischievous quips. The soldier he accompanied kept a wary eye on Brant's less than stable conduct, dually discomforted by this bizarre report. The pair walked on in silence until they reached the main level, and Brant shoved his way through the crowd.

I'll bet Mathias is on the steps.

Brant sighed his frustration out through his nose and refrained from correcting Nes's casual address yet again. Following his cousin's goading, Brant found Mathias standing at the top steps of the fortress's main entry, arms crossed and with no apparent effort taken to bundle himself against the biting air. The grave glower flawing the paladin's face suggested the temperature was the last thing on his mind. Rubbing his sleeves to generate warmth, Brant stopped beside the human.

Mathias flicked a look at Brant, making a swift appraisal of his haggard face and tattered expression. The commander wore his facial hair unusually rough and the bloodshot dullness of his eyes spoke of negligence to his personal welfare. Mathias would make sure to mention these concerns to Sulik.

True to the soldier's report, a lone man tottered through the snow with spent determination. No doubt, the trek would have proven difficult for a man even in peak physical condition, but this man slipped and flailed with exceptional difficulty, as though he'd long ago forgotten the concept of walking.

Brant...

Nes's voice was no more than a broken murmur, as empty as Brant's heart. He'd have given his soul to be able to turn to her now, to read the thoughts she broadcast in her eyes the way he'd been so skilled at doing. But then again, he'd have given his soul to have her back at all. Brant clutched his upper arms in a defensive shrug.

Whispers bubbled up from the crowd gathering behind the two officers as the traveler struggled closer, wondering why Mathias didn't venture out to help a man so in need. Brant took his turn to glance at Mathias, startled by the bitter scowl which tainted eyes that typically held so much warmth.

Brant, go help him.

Her voice was pathetic and small, a tone Brant hadn't heard since she was little more than a spoiled child. He lowed a gentle negative in his throat, hoping it passed unnoticed to Mathias.

The man in the snow pressed ahead, his course set with clear purpose. He was unarmed and uncoordinated, dressed for the weather even more poorly than Mathias. In light of the paladin's stern reception of this mysterious visitor and Brant's closed posture, the soldiers behind them shifted nervously, unsure what to anticipate.

Please, Nes pled brokenly. *Brant, it's—*

"No!" Brant snapped in fierce denial, no longer able to hold himself back. "It's not!"

The harshness left Mathias's eyes as he turned his attention to Brant, who flushed at his slip up. Sulik had mentioned these lapses of Brant's sanity to Mathias, but he'd been reluctant to believe it until now. Putting past animosity aside, Mathias turned to the crowd behind him. He would not allow the proud commander to fall any further.

"At ease." Mathias waved a dismissive hand as the soldiers clutched their weapons at the ready. No hint of his jovial nature had been present in the command. "This man is no threat to us."

Puzzled speculations accented the hushed murmurs from the crowd as Mathias turned his back to them, and Brant scoured his actions for signs of ridicule.

"Commander, I've got this under control if you need to take your leave."

Relieved by the formal dismissal, Brant managed to shift his weight to a heel before Nes's begging stopped him.

No. Stay. You have to.

He frowned and cast a glare at the ground away from Mathias. "I'm fine."

In happier times, Mathias would have gladly debated Brant's weak declaration, but for now, he let it slide. Brant, of all people, deserved to be part of this.

Speculations continued to pop up from the growing crowd, each one grating on Brant's resolve in light of Nes's consistent insight. Was this some demon? A survivor from one of Veed's townships? Maybe even one of their own? Could this all be some grand illusion? Brant wished it was, but as the man got close enough for the fog of his breath to clearly be seen, his existence became undeniably tangible.

The man stumbled to his knees at the foot of the stairs and neither Brant nor Mathias moved to offer even a word of assistance. Nes's pleading elevated to frantic screams and Brant bit into his cheek to keep from shouting back at her. Even as the visitor slipped and fell on the ice of the great stone steps, Mathias remained parked at his station, lip curled in disgust at the pathetic man below him.

Still scratching for an excuse to deny what rapidly appeared to be true, Brant sneered as the man looked up to reveal a strained expression and cheeks beaten red by the biting wind. Brant clamped his jaw shut as Mathias descended one step. The traveler pulled his feet back under himself and clutched at the stairs as he crawled upwards, damp hands sticking to the icy stones. Thrown by this cheerless reception, he looked up again, this time spearing Brant with a glare from intelligent golden eyes, before dragging his attention back to Mathias.

"Might I find food and rest here?" His voice rasped against a cough in his dry throat. "My mortal bones ache inside this frozen skin."

The request came with a smug sense of entitlement Mathias would have spit upon if he was an inch less of a man. Beside him, Brant trembled with suppressed motives Mathias was happy to let him keep to himself, and the paladin shouldered the duty he was best equipped to handle. He sneered at the ragged traveler.

"You are pathetic."

Everyone but Brant flinched at the cruelty in Mathias's tone, and it seemed to alleviate a significant portion of the commander's concern. "Just let it go," Brant said beneath his breath. "You said Sagewind had this, anyway."

Brant had spoken his words softly, unheard by the mortals present, but discerning suspicion narrowed those golden eyes. Mathias clasped Brant on the forearm, gave him a supportive nod, and stepped forward to intercept the newcomer's scrutiny.

The man found his balance, arms outstretched to his sides, and straightened as much as the subpar footing allowed. "I meant to offense, stranger," he said, matching the chill of Mathias's judgement.

"Perhaps that was something you should have thought about before all of your wayward adventures." Unafraid to turn his back to this man, Mathias faced the fidgeting crowd. While he had no plan to hide the truth from the army, he wasn't prepared to open the stage for ridicule quite yet. "Go arrange the necessities for this beggar. I believe he has answers for many of our questions."

Confusion toyed with the soldiers and few civilians in the crowd, and it took Brant half turning to deliver a single, stiff nod for the group to disperse to carry out the request.

Mathias seldom succumbed to personal grudges, finding them petty and shameful, and refrained from turning back to face the visitor until he found purchase on civility. It didn't surprise him in the slightest that Brant still stood firm, fists clenched and jaw set against glistening eyes. The longer Brant and Mathias dawdled in silence, the more impatience swirled about their guest, and the humble composure he'd donned to wheedle his way into good graces ran fluidly from his grasp. The flemans wouldn't *dare* deny him entry. He squared his shoulders and resumed climbing the stairs.

Perhaps the flemans wouldn't forbid his passage into the fortress, but a human owed nothing to this delinquent. Mathias turned at last and halted the man with a hand pressed against his chest, batting aside the anger that glared back at him.

That simply wouldn't do! Armed with untold means of obtaining what he wanted, the traveler chose to start with devotion. "I've been a simple wanderer for so long," he said, sizing up this man he'd heard so many warnings about. "Tell me, how is my dear Nessix?"

The few rebellious soldiers who lingered above gasped between their shock and disgust. Brant couldn't distinguish their heated remarks over the volume of Nes's demands, but those, he ignored outright. Roaring with the rage once reserved for the most vile opponents, Brant sprang forward and dug his shoulder into the man's chest. The force of the impact paired with the perilous footing pushed his target off balance and they both fell backwards down the stairs. A flash of red announced at least one of them sustained injury from the fall, and the crowd's gasps sharpened with concern.

"Someone, go find Commander Vakharan," Mathias called as he hustled down the stairs to pull Brant off the other man.

Blood flowed a steady path from a gash across Brant's forehead, and his eyes swept vague passes across the scene around him. Mathias felt briefly for his pulse, deciphering snippets of a garbled argument with Nessix, and he eased Brant upright to prop him against the stairs. Their unwelcome guest bled more profusely from the back of his head, but he sat up calmly and on his own accord, eyes alert and burning pretentious fire for the disrespect used against him. He opened his mouth to protest, but met a timely silence courtesy of Mathias's fist.

As the man rolled to his hands and knees to pull himself back to his feet, Mathias returned his focus on tending to Brant.

"I demand to see—"

"You can't!" Mathias said, turning his head sharply. He wouldn't protect this man any longer. "Great and mighty Inwan, your chosen is dead."

* * * * *

Anxious gossip filtered beyond the small gathering and into the deeper reaches of the fortress like an invasive disease, infecting even the most resilient minds. Mathias's credibility was still shaky at best, but the stern conviction behind Brant's actions and the scathing accusations he spouted once Sulik resolved the damages from his self-destructive assault urged the fortress's inhabitants to believe that this was, indeed, the god who had turned his back on them so many years ago.

News trickled its way from the main arteries to where Veed had stationed himself to contemplate the frozen landscape through one of the communal picture windows. Reports of Inwan's return, spoken of in muted tones by passing soldiers, unearthed the better part of Veed's interest and drew him from seclusion. He'd adjusted more comfortably than most to life without Inwan, and the wealth of information the god carried of him left Veed in no great hurry for a reunion. Regardless of his personal desires and stubborn denial, the reports continued to accumulate, building assertively until Veed's mind itched to intervene.

Finding where Mathias had harbored this abomination wasn't difficult; a throng of prying soldiers huddled around the war chamber's closed door, hushed and straining to hear what transpired inside. Not surprising Veed in the slightest, the crowd denied him the respect due to his station, and he shoved his way through the cluster of citizens and soldiers, pulling nosy men away from the door to reach it himself. Of course, it was locked, but that didn't deter him. Whatever favors Inwan had granted him all those years ago no longer mattered to Veed. Little about the past mattered anymore, only this wretched present. Veed pounded on the door.

"I demand entry to this interrogation."

He ignored the scowls and skeptical gibes flung his way. In a time where he still possessed the motivation to preserve his reputation, he'd have spit insults right back, but his mind was weary from travelling so many bittersweet roads of late for him to care what anyone thought of him. The scoffs died out in a sea of stunned expressions as Sulik cracked the door open to pull Veed inside.

Veed made a quick appraisal of the room's inhabitants, not at all surprised to find both commanders and Mathias present. The same exhausted tension which had plagued Sulik over the past few weeks still etched premature age across the older commander's brow, and Mathias stood at the head of the table, arms crossed and expression stony. Brant sat off by himself, shielding his face with a hand and muttering heated snips on muffled whispers. His chest shook with aggravated breaths.

If this fourth man truly was Inwan, Veed had been given a prime opportunity to thrust the blame of Elidae's downfall on someone far more deserving of the burden than himself. He studied the stranger sitting at the far end of the table with the intensity of a shrewd gambler. Inwan had been fond of taking multiple forms, but those eyes never lied. In a sea of clear blues and murky browns, his yellow eyes stood as out of place as Mathias's green ones, and the entitled glint within them shamelessly bragged of fabricated greatness. Veed had no doubt this man was, indeed, Inwan. His breath snagged in his throat.

As Sulik secured the door, Inwan abandoned his unsuccessful attempt at staring down Mathias as his attention shifted to Veed. Where Veed might have once shrank from the pressure laid upon him, he held his ground now. A flicker of hope passed from Inwan's gaze as he realized Veed had no intention of providing him political sanctuary.

"Commander—"

"General." Veed's correction carried a bitter snip not even he had expected.

The god-man's face sagged, drained of the illusion of power as he surrendered to the thought that his precious Nessix was gone. "You took her station?"

"No. I abandoned her not long after you did and brought up an army of my own." Veed salvaged the tiniest mote of pleasure from Inwan's discomfort. He jutted his chin in the direction of Mathias and the insane commander in the corner. "She left her army between those two."

Inwan leaned forward, hiding his shame behind an antagonistic sneer. "So you have even less of a reason to judge me."

Mathias glanced for half a heartbeat in Brant's direction as his muttering spiked in volume and he threw his hands down to his side. The paladin looked to Veed next, burying his hatred of the vile man beneath the leverage Inwan's defensiveness suggested he had.

"Let the miscreant judge you," Mathias said. "You owe that much to these people."

"Veed owes me his head!" Dilated pupils flashed Veed's direction.

"Just shut *up*!" At last, Brant sprang to his feet and launched himself to the edge of the table beside Mathias. He braced his arms against its solid security to keep from acting further on the desires Nessix begged him not to take. "You *left* us and dare to return like nothing was wrong to people who fucking *hate* you! None of us would have dared admit it to Nes when she was still... still... here, but after... Damn it, we were finally able to forget about you!"

Inwan's former talent of skimming the conscience of mortals settled amid mere speculation on what drove Brant's vehemence. "I never planned to return—"

Brant dropped his head as bitter, bordering maniacal, laughter rattled free from him. He bit down into his lip to keep from engaging Nessix in debate, a shrill growl all that escaped him.

Acutely aware of Brant's struggle, Mathias stepped forward to spare the commander further embarrassment. "So you weren't ever going to show your cowardly face to these people again?" he asked.

"Didn't you hear the whelp? They don't want me." The level of respect Mathias's status demanded hadn't yet occurred to Inwan, but that didn't stop annoying beads of sweat from marring his skin.

Brant glared at Inwan through narrowed eyes burning with condemnations. "But Nes does." He pinched his eyes shut and hissed at his slip. Nes's crying had worn him down to his bare limit. "*Did.* Your timing, great master, is as impeccable as always."

As far as Inwan was concerned, he owed nothing to Brant, or this human, and least of all to Veed. Their questions and judgements slid off his back, mind too ravaged by the implications behind his untimely return. Banished from Abaeloth by the Divine Council for inappropriate interactions with those outside his reign, Inwan had grown quite comfortable in the purgatory carved out for him. There, at least, he'd still commanded the comfort of his godly gifts to generate entertainment. It came at the hefty cost of the people who loved and worshipped him and the affection of his chosen daughter, but he'd trusted the flemans' ability to forge ahead in his absence. Faithful in his people, Inwan opted to enjoy his banishment as a pleasant leave from responsibility.

Now, for reasons unknown, he'd been snatched from that paradise; cast out into the cold, trapped in a body that completely defied his divine abilities, and to find that he no longer even had Nessix.

Despite how easily the insight which Inwan harbored could annihilate Veed, the dark general's disgust flooded past a containable level. Brant wasn't the only one breathing fire over the god's terrible timing. "You never should have left Nes. She needed you."

Unwilling to face whatever repercussions might arise from staying present any longer, Veed's eyes danced away from the others and he turned to dismiss himself. Sulik silently saw him out and stood facing the door for some time after it fell shut. He secured the lock with a heavy thud. Veed's timid resentment hadn't escaped Mathias, drawing an unsettling concern from his gut. Mathias couldn't recall a time when Veed didn't at least pretend to wield authority and ease. Inwan's lips pressed in a smug smirk as Brant kept his eyes pinched shut and jerked his head in pathetic attempts to silence Nes's broken appeals.

Mathias frowned as he realized how little he knew about the

relationships entwined within fleman nobility. With a grimace, he worked his tongue against the filthy taste in his mouth. "Veed was right. Nessix never quit loving you. The rest of Elidae had given up on you, but she always knew you'd come back. I'd sworn to her you would."

Brant growled and slapped his hands on the edge of the table. "Where is she?" He delved into Inwan's eerie eyes, his previous turmoil swallowed by a menacing delirium. Inwan's noncommittal shrug spurred the commander to shove the bulk of his might against the table, eliciting a yelp from Inwan as it slammed into his ribs. "Sagewind can't find her, his goddess can't find her, but you... *you* are connected to her! Where. Is. She?"

Inwan gasped for breath, arms wrapped around his midsection and eyes wide at the foreign sensation of pain. "Have you buried her yet?" He accepted the silence of Brant's glower as an affirmative. "Then she's in the ground. That's all I can tell you."

Sulik grasped Brant by the forearm before the young commander could invest momentum behind his lunge forward, providing Mathias the chance to contemplate Inwan's reply. No more satisfied with the god's answer than he'd been with those he'd concocted for himself, his concern wrapped around Inwan's physical reaction to Brant's tantrum. An action as mortal as the one Brant had taken against him shouldn't have come close to affecting a god. Meeting Sulik's eyes, Mathias nodded his appreciation of keeping Brant in check, and strolled around the table. Inwan tracked him with a glare accentuating his tight frown.

"Love me or hate me," the god continued, "but the flemans are still my people. You owe me respect!"

A dry laugh shook Brant as he pulled against Sulik's steady hold. "Then take a look around you. Walk on our battlements and gaze at our fields. See what's become of your beautiful Elidae. Wait for this snow to melt and look at the carnage your lack of guidance threw on us. Pass through the halls below, where we've had to harbor an entire kingdom, ask the widows if their devotion to you rivals that to the husbands and children they've lost to this war. Tell me then what the fuck we owe you."

"Blasphemous child!" Inwan bellowed, shoving the table back.

144

Even restrained and thrashing for purchase against his distress, Brant had the strength to catch it. "Do not threaten me with what has become of your home."

"Then who do I blame?" Brant asked. "Did I ask for this? Did Veed?" His eyes narrowed. "Did Nes?"

Inwan gulped his uncertainty down a restricted throat. In truth, he grasped but a vague awareness of the carnage and ugliness Brant referred to and proving his ignorance and incompetence by asking for clarifications now would only serve against his bid for authority. He flung a bitter look at Mathias. Nobody in the heavenly realm had escaped the stories of the White Paladin, and meeting him in the flesh rendered Inwan unusually subdued. He searched Mathias's righteous calm and cursed the power Etha's favor granted this human over the lesser gods.

"If Nessix would have prepared herself more soundly, perhaps she'd have been more capable of preventing what happened."

Brant, let up on him… Nes's voice trembled.

"No!" Brant insisted. If she was so bent on staying the course of defending her negligent god, Brant would buckle down on the last duty he cared about. He would protect Nessix from harm. "Nessix could have never prepared herself, not for this, and you know it. Laes couldn't have faced it, En couldn't have faced it. Fuck, even Sagewind's struggling! You were her sanity, Inwan!"

It's not his fault!

"Then that was her weakness," Inwan said.

He's right, you know.

A temperamental jerk freed Brant's arm from Sulik and he spun from Inwan, eyes glistening with a ravenous vulnerability. "No, he's—"

Mathias had allowed Brant's torment to run ahead long enough. Striding over to the commander, he grasped Brant by the shoulders and ducked his head to catch distraught eyes. "You don't have to listen to me, but Nessix does. This isn't something either of you need to worry about right now," he said, compelling the young man's mind to cease its charge down this destructive path. He backed Brant over to his chair and eased him to sit. "Tomorrow, you can go back to hating me, but today, you both need to trust

145

me."

Sulik hustled over as Brant leaned his head against the back of the chair. His chest heaved and tears rolled unchecked from his eyes as sense seeped back within his grasp, mind clear for the first time in weeks. As Brant's eyes drifted closed, a grim frown pressed across Mathias's face. What he'd done was nothing more than a patch, one waiting to crumble the instant Brant's madness found a reason to reawaken. Leaving Brant in Sulik's compassionate hands, Mathias turned back to Inwan.

He wouldn't help a traitor, but neither could he disgrace the station Etha had burdened him with by lowering himself to such a petty argument with a god. Whatever reason Inwan had for choosing now to return, Mathias would uncover it on his own through time and prayer. Keeping this toxic assembly together any longer, though, promised to deteriorate the fragile pretense of stability holding the fortress together, and Mathias didn't want to have to raise his voice. He stalked forward with a confident air which Inwan cowered away from, slapped a palm against the god's chest, and removed them both from the room.

Teleportation was not a foreign concept to Inwan, but he hadn't been prepared to move in this fashion from a mortal shell. Neither had Mathias anticipated the familiar action to strike him with a nauseating dizziness. Had he really expended that much energy to heal Brant's injury and calm him? It seemed unlikely, and Mathias shook coherence back into his mind.

"You'd be wise to stay in this room." Mathias steadied himself from staggering by backing up against the wall. He crossed his arms, hoping the startled hunch of Inwan's shoulders suggested the god had missed this unexpected debility. "I suspect as soon as either Veed or Brant begin talking about you, there will be quite the mob demanding answers you don't seem to have."

Inwan ceased his hasty appraisal of the simple interior barracks to sneer at Mathias. "You think you have authority over me?"

"I am the avatar of Etha's will," Mathias said. "I *know* I have authority over you. Now, behave, and I'll come sort things out with you after I've calmed the masses."

He didn't need to hear more of Inwan's belligerent replies to know they were there, nor did he wait for them. Masking his exhaustion behind an irritated sigh, Mathias turned with no fear of this shackled god and departed the windowless room. With his last ounce of magical reserves, he placed a divine lock on the door. If his suspicions were correct—and he was almost certain they were—Inwan's current limitations would prevent him from tampering with such a simple blessing.

THIRTEEN

Twelve years ago, finding peace from his racing thoughts came no easier to Veed. Phyta was one of several cities without an active curfew, a fact Veed took grateful advantage of that night. Repulsed with himself, guilt drove him to the town's brothel, where he used the honesty of his coins to satiate the sensations Nessix had unknowingly shaken out of him. Physical desires addressed in the second best way he knew how to find, Veed sat down at the establishment's quaint bar as he unsuccessfully tried to decompress from the whirlwind of events thrust on him over the course of the evening.

Outside, the rain continued a steady downpour and Veed glanced at his cloak where he'd left it to dry by the fire. He was such a fool! His promiscuous past gained on him rapidly, mocking him for all the time he'd wasted not learning how to court a woman through proper means. The tryst he'd just bought proved that nights cozied up with a random woman no longer satisfied him quite the way they used to. From the back of his mind, a dark voice cursed him for leaving the inn so hastily, for not at least investigating Nes's willingness. An angry growl interrupted the trail his lustful side tried to drag him down. He'd made the right decision, he was convinced of it, and such vile notions were not welcome.

The barmaid hustled to the front once she saw Veed sitting there, blush glowing brighter as she fell over herself upon recognizing the station he wore. "C-commander Astaldt, what can I do for you?"

Veed lifted his jaded gaze from his study of the callouses on his hands to meet hers. "Water." The chill of his tone chased away any invitation for small talk, confirmed by the young woman's blanch.

"Two of the tallest of your most potent brew," a voice from behind Veed corrected, "on my tab."

The maid, eyes wide and red lips gaping, looked from Veed to this other man and took two reluctant steps backwards, face riddled with confusion.

"Go on, young lady," the man said kindly. "Bring the commander his water, but know he'll be long into his ale before we're through talking."

Veed clenched his jaw to contain his irritation as the maid flounced off. He turned slowly. "I'm not in the mood for—" A dreadful chill struck his heart, putting a quick stop to his stony correction.

Yellow eyes gazed at him with the patience of an old schoolmarm. Voices and physical appearances often varied, but those eyes… Veed swallowed hard and looked away.

"Forgive my defiance," Veed murmured. His stool squeaked beneath his uncomfortable fidgeting as Inwan pulled back a neighboring seat to settle on.

"I will," the god answered, "but I figured you needed to do some talking."

Veed scratched the back of his head, still unable to look at Inwan. "What's there to talk about?"

"For starters, were you aware you called that whore you were with 'lieutenant'?"

Veed flushed and ducked his head between hunched shoulders. No, he hadn't been aware, and had absolutely no desire to discuss it right now.

Inwan shrugged at Veed's sheepish silence and continued. "More than once. Ah, thank you, my dear." He accepted the barmaid's delivery of their drinks with a grin of gluttonous anticipation, ogling the young woman's backside as she walked away. With a snap of his fingers, time froze around them, stilling even the dance of the candles' flames. Inwan rested an elbow on the bar and turned to face Veed. "I answered your prayers as accurately as I could within my godly guidelines, and *this* is what you decided to do with them?"

It was wrong—potentially dangerous—to question a god, but that didn't stop Veed's scathing glare from dragging away from the amber poison in front of him to meet the challenge in Inwan's eyes. "Aren't you supposed to be a little more invested in Nes's integrity than to encourage what I could have done?"

"You're assuming she'd have put up a fight."

Veed choked on the water he'd just about thrown to the back of his throat. He knew Inwan and Nessix shared a unique relationship, but would she have disclosed that sort of information to him? Did Inwan have any way of knowing this as fact? Veed's timid gaze darted away from the god. "She's a child."

Inwan shook his head, brows raised in that cocky amusement Veed had always resented. "And she needs a teacher."

Veed eyed the ale once more, frown etching deeper. "I promised Laes I would go about this properly, and I aim to keep my word."

Inwan slapped the bar top and laughed. "If what you did to that whore was what you'd been planning for Nes, there's nothing proper about your intentions. This is the man you are. Why are you trying to hide from it?"

This was not a conversation Veed wanted to indulge, especially with the god who hand-picked Nessix as his golden child. "I'm not hiding from anything."

"You are a terrible liar."

Unable to stop the heaviness of his breathing, Veed struggled to swallow a heated retort. It was in his best interest to stay on Inwan's good side. "I will not hurt Nessix. I will not frighten her. She is too important to me. I thought you of all people would understand that."

Inwan swigged his drink and shrugged. "This was meant to be

your chance to find a place—a warm one—in her heart. You really think you'll be comfortable trying to court her with Laes breathing down your back?"

Apparently, Veed wasn't comfortable trying to court her three cities away from Laes! "I am a good man," Veed insisted, hand clenching around the mug of ale in front of him. "And I will conduct myself in that manner."

Inwan picked at a flaw on the counter. "I never said you weren't. If you're doubting as much, that's on you." A lazy smile crossed his face. "Nessix isn't a warrior without good reason. She's capable and curious, and she trusts you."

"That's the problem!" Veed cried, turning to face Inwan at last. "She *trusts* me!"

Inwan's brows furrowed and he soaked in that desperation so foreign to see in Veed. "You're complaining about that?"

The dizzying rate which Veed's breath came forced him to lean forward and brace his elbows against the bar. Of course he wanted Nessix to trust him. He wanted her to do a whole lot more than that, but it was her trust in him that would open her up for him to take advantage of, and he forbid himself to do so. A sudden thought speared Veed's mind and he sat up slowly. Inwan had doted over the Teradhel family for generations, and while the god himself had backed Veed's initial request, there was no way to ensure this conversation wouldn't leak back to Laes.

Veed eyed the barmaid again, how her skirt hung suspended in the air from her gait, her eyelids closed halfway through a blink, and he prayed to the devious god beside him that all of her senses were frozen in the same manner.

"She can't hear a word," Inwan promised.

Veed swallowed the lump in his throat. "I love Nessix," he said, "and I want to do nothing to hurt her. Taking advantage of her trust in me is not how I want to win her over. What happened tonight, what I thought, I didn't mean for any of it to happen that way."

"Of course you didn't." Inwan laughed and drank some more. "But the fact of the matter is you did."

"That doesn't ease my mind."

Veed's eyes flicked uncomfortably through the room, and his hands couldn't settle on whether or not to pick up his ale for a drink. His left foot shook from where he'd rooted it on the bottom rung of his stool. Inwan laughed again at the discomfort he'd caused, slapping Veed on the shoulder.

"My boy, I planted these storms here, told Nessix to stay inside, for a reason."

Coughing on the confession, Veed blinked to try to clear his head. He drew his shoulders back slowly as this new information soaked in. "You set me up." He wondered briefly what Laes would think of this, considering how close it had come to rushing out of control.

"Laes doesn't get to have an opinion on it," Inwan said. "And I didn't set you up. I set up the potential. All of those thoughts were your own."

Veed's hands clasped around the ale and he pulled it centered in front of him. He lowered his gaze. This conversation succeeded only in piling more uncertainties on top of his overwhelmed mind, and Veed couldn't help but feel some hidden agenda lurked behind it. Not even Laes loved Nessix as much as Inwan did; Veed was lucky the god chose against raining fury down on his pathetic soul for the scandalous impulses beating inside him. This assistance Inwan seemed willing to provide didn't add up and honestly, it frightened him. The deeper these thoughts set in, the more the entire scenario seemed like a carefully baited trap, and Veed looked back on his past to try to identify where he'd gone wrong to land himself in this position. Inwan began to hum, not answering the thoughts tumbling about the commander's laden mind. Veed picked up the ale and drank at last.

"Well, my boy," Inwan sighed, plopping a small coin purse on the counter. "I've given you heaps to think about. The rules say I'm not supposed to tamper with mortals like this, so I can't tell you what you should do, but my little Nes won't be a child forever. Laes doesn't intend to remarry, and that bloodline must live on somehow." He stood, exaggerating a stretch before sneaking one last glance at the barmaid and finishing the rest of his ale in one long pull. "She's going to end up screwing someone. Unless you think there's a man out there who loves her more than you do..."

Inwan pressed his lips together and raised his eyebrows. He snapped his fingers and the maid stumbled forward, glaring behind where her foot had left the ground. The candles danced wildly, caught in the wind of time rushing back to them. By the time Veed blinked, Inwan was gone, leaving him in wide eyed silence.

FOURTEEN

Mathias had spent far too long walking in the living world to not hear what went unspoken. With his grief finally leveled out so he could dedicate his concentration on matters beyond self-pity and the weather providing an artificial safety net for the citizens and army, his thoughts tore between how to manage Brant's mental instability and what to make of Inwan's untimely return.

Whether or not Brant wanted to hide behind the excuse of indirect ties, he was all that remained of the noble house and would have to accept the station required of him when Mathias's time on Elidae was through. No matter what differences the two of them shared in the past, Mathias had faith in Brant's ability to serve in the required capacity, provided he kept his head together. The frequency which Nessix seemed to visit her dear cousin, though, made the prospect of Brant's long term sanity less certain than Mathias was comfortable with. Hypnotism only offered a temporary fix and a competent leader could not function under constant sedation.

Perhaps more pressing were the concerns wrapped around Inwan. Everyone connected to the divine realm knew the nature of the god's banishment, often using it as the butt end of jokes and providing a constant reminder that though the gods swelled with power, a delicate web of laws governed their actions. Mathias hadn't known where they'd tucked Inwan for his sentence, and even after meeting Nessix, he hadn't cared enough to find out. Improper conduct deserved appropriate punishment, and Mathias had refused to tempt Nes's hope by disclosing the few answers he did possess.

How little Inwan proved to know about the flemans' plight, though, vexed Mathias. Gods held an intricate connection to the people and lands they oversaw, and under normal circumstances, Mathias had assumed Inwan would have felt the ache of tragedy rending this island the instant his feet hit Elidae's soil. Even Laes—limited to the confines of a devoted and desperate soul—had experienced the nation's pending terror.

Mathias plunked down on his bed and stared at the ceiling. Days had passed, longer than he'd intended, since he last spoke with Etha, and he needed to pull his way out of this oppressive brooding. Opening his mind, he laid back and set down a lazy path in search of his goddess.

"I know you're behind this," he murmured, closing his eyes as he sifted through the expanse of eternity few knew how to access.

Silence. Mathias tried to breathe away his frustrations, but it proved a massive undertaking in light of current events. He knew better than to think Inwan willingly brought himself here—the god's contentious conduct assured as much. It tore at Mathias how Nessix's faith had insisted Inwan would return for her people. He bled for the fact that she'd needed her god every bit as much as he needed Etha. His goddess glowed with justice and compassion, and it made no sense to Mathias why she waited until weeks after the demons had claimed Nessix to drag Inwan back to Elidae. There had to be a greater purpose, he just couldn't fathom what it was.

"Why did you send him here? Why now?"

More emptiness pounded throughout the chamber, mocking Mathias's loneliness, and his eyes flashed open. Etha wasn't just withholding information from him. She wasn't even in his mind. No silent embrace wrapped him in inner peace, no flitting laughter or soothing voice bounded through his room. There wasn't even a frantic cry as she tried to reach out to him. Mathias slammed a fist against the mattress and sat up, racking his brain over when another curse could have landed on him. Some sort of power still beat inside of him, evident by his ability to heal Brant's head injury and soothe his maniacal mind, but Mathias was sure that Etha was unable to reach him right now.

He longed to blame the coincidence on Veed's presence in the fortress, but as he scanned the recent past, he found plenty of times when his connection with Etha was shaky even before the last battle forced them into communal confines. At least this explained why Etha's drastic measures to purge the demons had blindsided him. Limiting his options to events that happened prior to that fight, Mathias grudgingly cleared Inwan from having any involvement. He shook his head. The demons hadn't even been that active before Nes's funeral. Commanding control over his thoughts before they worked themselves into an indecipherable frenzy he couldn't sort out on his own, Mathias fell backwards again and shut his eyes.

Unless Etha came to him on her own accord, past experience told him his best bet at gaining her attention relied on him somehow reaching the temple. He needed full access to his divine connections to summon Ceraphlaks, and though travel conditions hadn't deteriorated further, Mathias didn't favor the prospect of fighting through the accumulation of frozen snow on foot.

One terrible method of escaping the malaises of reality existed for Mathias, a feat which he treasured in the precious hours he claimed it and loathed all over again once it passed. All that was left for him to keep from fretting over matters beyond his control were the blissful lies of sleep.

* * * * *

Mathias knocked on the door and took a step back, clasping his hands behind his back. By a count of ten, no answer greeted him, and so he knocked again. Just before he made a third attempt, the door creaked open a mere hand's width to reveal a cautious blue eye. Mathias smiled broadly.

"How did you—" Nes's shock silenced the rest of her whispered question.

"I thought I told you not to worry about it." Mathias made no attempt to keep his voice down. He cocked his head to sneak a better view of the young woman and smiled. "But as late as it is and with you still dressed so pretty, it would seem you had some amount of faith in me."

Color kissed Nes's cheeks and she took a step back. "I was getting ready to change."

"I'm sure you were." He waited politely on the other side of the door, unwilling to encroach on her sudden burst of modesty. "Either way, I have the guard situation taken care of and adequate distractions set for both your keepers. I've got someplace to show you, if you'd do me the honor of accompanying me?"

Nessix narrowed her eyes in legible suspicion, but pulled the door the rest of the way open. What was Mathias's goal here? How did he know how to speak with her? Why did he care more about talking to her than Nevius? Common sense beat Nes in the head with these demands, but her gut asked something much more appealing. What in Inwan's name did he want to show her?

Mathias stood before her with warm, clear eyes. He'd swapped the formal rigidness of his pressed and polished attire for the more relaxed appeal of simple pants and a tunic. The slightest murmur of caution reminded Nessix how little she knew about this intriguing man, yet a far louder voice complained of how bored she was and that her lungs provided her a strong capacity to scream for help, should the need arise. Nessix grounded herself with a quick breath and firm nod then stepped into the hall. As the door fell shut behind her, she glanced to her right to find her guard sprawled on the floor, eyes closed and weapon fallen free from his grasp.

She reached back to grope for the door's handle. "What did you do to him?"

Mathias turned and looked back at her with a sheepish smile. "He's fine," he assured. "Just got a little tired is all."

Nessix eyed Mathias, suspicion holding her fast in place. "I will ask you again, Mathias Sagewind, what did you do to him?"

Her bid for authority pleased Mathias more than it probably should have. He'd found such a delightfully willful young lady. "I told you I'm capable of just about anything. My skill sets are a bit different from the average knights and nobles."

A touch of reluctance left Nes's expression, replaced by a healthy dose of fascination. "So you use magic?" She didn't have the knack or patience to grasp the divine arts for herself, but delighted in their wonders just the same.

"Something similar to it, yes." Mathias grinned at how the cogs in her mind churned through her curious gaze. "But I'd be lying to you if I said that was my limit."

Nessix crossed her arms and inclined her chin, the first hints of a challenge sparking in her eyes. "I could take you in a one on one fight at arms," she declared, confidence brimming past Mathias's chuckle, "but how do I know you won't use your magic against me?"

His charming smile made her heart flit about stupidly.

"Well, I suppose you don't," he said. "But I haven't used it against you yet. Besides, if you're aware you're a target, it's much harder for spells to have negative effects. You're safe with me, my lady." He extended his hand to her. "Now, may I please show you my city?"

Once again, common sense locked horns with impulse and the side of Nessix which her father ignored and her brother found humiliating won. She placed her hand against Mathias's palm and his fingers curled around hers to lead the way down the vacant hall. Not entirely sure of what sort of fate she flirted with, Nessix stayed quiet. Mathias didn't press for conversation as he hummed a cheery tune, and it didn't take long for suspicion to get the best of Nessix.

"Is the Citadel always this quiet after dark?" she asked. It was difficult to navigate these halls without constant curtseys during the daytime, but she'd yet to see anyone passing by tonight.

"Nope."

Mathias didn't venture to elaborate, sealing her curiosity. "Did you put the entire building to sleep, then?"

He grinned at the depth of her imagination. "That would have been quite a tedious task. No, I didn't put them to sleep, rather, I found another way to occupy their time."

She laughed at his answer. "It seems you're quite the influential noble."

"Knight," he corrected politely.

Nessix cocked her head at the thought of Mathias deliberately veiling such a lucrative station. "And you didn't introduce yourself as such?"

He shrugged. "Would it have made any difference?"

Nessix chewed on the inside of her cheek as she thought this over. Whatever strange things Sir Sagewind still hid from her aside, he was the only person in all of Zeal who had put forth any effort to show her kindness independent of seeking Nevius's favor. Mathias was funny and gentle, and what it came down to was that Nessix didn't care if he was a full-fledged prince or an escaped convict—she enjoyed his company. She frowned.

"It would make a difference to my brother."

Mathias swallowed his distressed sigh and shoved his mind deeper into the present. "You put an awful lot of concern into what he thinks."

She huffed. "I have to. He's in line to become General once my father retires. Dumbest thing ever, since I'm the oldest."

Mathias felt his expression try to harden and fought to push his misgivings aside. "What is it you're here for, anyway?" He'd waited to find a chance to ask her since they first met.

"Some political bullshi—" Nessix cut off her crude statement, despite Mathias's encouraging smirk. "Political *business*. I thought it would be more interesting, but Nev and Brant seem to have everything under control. I have no idea what purpose I'm even serving."

Mathias's stomach hit his feet. She honestly had no idea.

If you don't check your gloomy mood, it'll catch her attention.

Etha's words siphoned a sigh from Mathias and he pulled his smile out again. "The purpose you're serving, Lady Teradhel, is to enjoy your stay in Zeal. Let's not worry about your brother right now."

It took until they'd reached the grand entry of the Citadel, but Mathias's suggestion lightened Nes's mood at last. "Alright, then. You said you could show me around?"

He nodded. "I can if you can ride."

That gained her laughter. "If I can ride! Our horses are part of our culture. I could outride any man in this entire city."

Had Mathias intended to startle or discourage Nessix, he'd have summoned Ceraphlaks to have a little fun at her claim. As his goal was to keep his enchanting charge content, he chose to rein in his mischievous impulses in favor of leading Nessix from the Citadel. He entertained her steady flow of questions with polite half-truths that served their purpose far better than their full counterparts until they reached the quiet side street where he'd ordered two horses picketed. His amusement peaked when Nes's face twisted in repulsion.

"What is *this*?" She plucked at the single stirrup hanging from her horse's saddle as though she'd found a hair in her food.

Mathias nodded to the skirt of her dress. "It's a side saddle to accommodate a lady's fashion."

"Ha! This fashion is absurd!" Nessix wasted no time lifting the saddle's flap to loosen the girth. She pulled it from the horse's back, hiked her skirt to a proper lady's indecency, and dug out the dagger she still kept strapped to her thigh. Without an ounce of modesty, she cut jagged tears on either side of her hips and one down the front of her skirt. Mathias hid his smirk behind his hand. Nevius would most certainly disapprove.

"Are you needing a leg up?" Mathias asked, stifling his chuckle.

Nessix arched a brow and grasped a fistful of mane to vault astride the horse's bare back. "Are you?"

Before this tragic noble lady arrived, Mathias had enjoyed the occasional fling with women he could easily cut ties with. The nature of his existence had kept him on Abaeloth too long for him to not find the urge to seek intimate and romantic contact, but an ingrained response actively sought to protect him from the heartache which immortality complicated such relationships with. Bantering with Nessix and soaking in her spirited manner encouraged Mathias to forget that reluctance. He swung aboard his horse and indulged the young woman's silent goading. Cueing his mount to a brisk canter, Mathias led Nessix on a chase right out the gates of Zeal, foregoing the tour he'd promised her. Instead, he guided her up the hill of Northfork Road to his favorite spot in the realm.

An ancient tree welcomed them to the rise and Mathias dismounted to secure their horses to a low hanging limb.

"I thought you were going to show me your city," Nessix teased, sliding from her horse's back.

Emboldened by their interaction, Mathias grasped Nessix by her forearms to turn her around. He leaned over her shoulder and pointed back to where they came from. "I am."

Looking on from the outside, Zeal was even more impressive than Nessix had imagined. It was a massive city, easily three or four times the size of Elidae's largest township, neatly wrapped around the Citadel. Towering over every other building by several stories, the Citadel's alabaster elegance wasn't what snatched Nes's breath away. The fast pace which they'd climbed the hill had prevented her from noticing the generous expanse of snowy lilies that carpeted the outskirts of Zeal. Filling hundreds of acres, they spanned clear up the walls, forming a circle of white around the holy city. They glowed warm in the moonlight, bobbing gently in the breeze.

"It's beautiful," she murmured.

At least she likes it.

Mathias frowned. *You're not making me feel any better, Etha.*

"You promised me a good time," Nessix said, tugging Mathias's mind away from Etha's dismal reminder.

It took him a moment, but Mathias salvaged a smile from the bliss and wonder in Nes's eyes. "I did," he agreed. Walking to the side of the tree, he picked up two dulled swords and tested their weights. Nodding his approval, he tossed the lighter of the two to Nessix.

She caught it and grinned. "You *really* know how to charm the ladies, don't you?"

"I can't be sure. Am I charming you?"

Her cheeks lit with color, lower lip pinched between her teeth. She glanced away from him, refusing to answer his question. "So you think you can take me at swordplay?"

"I'm pretty sure I can." He suspected Nessix was the kind to prefer a challenge over simple flattery.

Nessix arched one brow at his declaration, and stepped back into a preparatory stance. "Alright, then. Let's see what you can do."

He grinned at her eagerness and engaged her readily.

Mathias appreciated Nes's willingness to embrace their unconventional dance, and he thrived off the beauty of her enthusiasm. He didn't have the heart to tell her he wasn't giving it his all and the more feisty she ventured with her attacks, the harder he pushed back. They continued pressing each other, Mathias always half a step ahead, until Nes's expression shifted away from entertained and closer to frustrated. Mathias almost pulled back, but Nessix twisted unexpectedly to the left and the flat of his blade slapped against her bare elbow.

Nessix yelped and recoiled from Mathias, hunching over to nurse the point of impact. Mathias hadn't thought he'd pushed too hard for her and immediately dropped his sword to tend to whatever damage he'd caused.

"I'm sorry, I hadn't meant—"

As soon as Mathias entered striking distance, Nessix squared her shoulders and hunched down to drive into his abdomen, toppling him to the ground. Her sword sang with brisk laughter as she swept it to point at his throat and she placed a victorious foot on his chest. Mathias blinked a few times as his mind processed what just happened. He met her glittering eyes and confident smirk, and couldn't help but laugh.

"Who taught you swordplay?" he asked as Nessix lifted both pressures from him and extended her hand. Mathias sat up, but declined her gesture, patting the ground beside him instead.

"My Uncle Veed." She took a seat in the grass and lilies they'd trampled in their scuffle.

Shaking his head, Mathias brushed the grass from his sleeves. "Your Uncle Veed fights dirty."

"All's fair in combat," she said.

"I suppose so."

They sat in the quiet for some time, gazing down at the flickering lights of Zeal's night owls. "So, now what?" Nes asked. "What else do you have to show me?"

Mathias turned to face Nessix, the glow about her thrilled face, the light in her eyes, the way she didn't even notice how her hair strayed from its bindings. What else did he have to show her? A subtle warmth coursed through him, but he was far too much a gentleman to advertise as much. He looked from her eyes to her lips and back again. Her vivid smile and willingness to follow his ridiculous leads confirmed that Nessix enjoyed his company, but Mathias hadn't yet convinced himself she'd gone along with him for any reason other than his offer to alleviate her boredom. He wanted to show her how gently he'd learned to kiss a woman, he wanted to show her there was one man in this city who knew how to treat her right, he wanted to show her that when she was ready, he knew how to share much more thrilling experiences than sparring offered.

Mother, what am I doing…?

Etha chose one of the best times to keep her opinions to herself, leaving Mathias to gaze into Nes's eyes until her expression settled into a naïve confusion that melted his heart. "Lady Teradhel…" He wanted to tell her how beautiful she was and that he'd kiss her if she'd allow him, but all he could murmur was her name.

"Sir Sagewind?" she asked, deliciously ignorant to the trouble warring inside of him.

Mortal desires nagging at him, Mathias licked his lips and reclined back on the grass. He pointed to the starry sky. Right now, he'd accept any available distraction.

"What do you know of astronomy?" he asked.

Nessix wrinkled her nose and sounded another trill of laughter, lying down beside him. She scooted her shoulders over to rest her head against his bicep. "I know there's stars up there, but that's about it."

He glanced at her and smiled, heart singing to him jubilantly. "Well then. Let me tell you the story of the heavens…"

* * * * *

Well over a week had elapsed since Shand last attempted to

contact her pawn, a neglect which he relished. He'd occupied his time tailoring borrowed goods to cater to his fancies, but as each day came and went with the fortress locked in its icy shell, the more the concept of home escaped him. The sole source of comfort he pilfered came from knowing that Shand didn't dare come to him with so many potential witnesses confined within these walls.

With each additional day between the pawn's last encounter with Shand and the inevitable next, the more doubt of his security in this entire escapade scratched at his resolve. The demons had already assured him of their capability to halt Shand's rampage and had invited him along for the ride. All it would cost him was his exclusive control over Elidae once the war found its end. He'd made great strides in establishing his influence among the flemans and was confident in his ability to command the respect and fear of at least half of the nation. Maybe that was good enough.

Good enough wouldn't solve his problem of how to escape Shand, though. It was laughable to imagine a mortal slaying a god, a bold assumption to trust the demons to honestly assist with such a notion, and saying he was on poor terms with the only immortal he knew was generous. Divine powers aside, how would a man even begin to fight a god?

The pawn knew Shand's physical form was tangible, and as such, able to be attacked, but the only blood he recalled flawing the perfection of her skin belonged to her unfortunate victims. Even if he scrounged up the fortitude to challenge Shand, her intellect and abilities would sniff out his intentions in seconds. Cold sweat prickled the back of his neck. What if she already knew of his deceit? The demons' casual approach to the situation promised him none of these concerns deserved merit, but they'd yet to provide him with a practical solution to the problem named Shand.

Irony burst into a fit of giggles as a searing gust scattered papers from the pawn's desk and Shand blustered into his chamber.

He leapt to his feet, flushing with poorly concealed guilt and sputtering an incoherent greeting. Shand paid mind to neither infraction.

"*Fix this!*"

He silenced his failed words as Shand's frenzied eyes darted between the elaborate adornments of his new chamber, her knuckles blanched white against clenched fists. Over the past several years this goddess had kept the pawn in her pocket, he'd seen her lose her composure often, but never trembling with this sort of instability. Among all of the impossible and unfair demands she'd made of him, this was the first time Shand had implied needing help from his mortal hands. If not for his imbedded terror of Shand, the pawn might have plucked some amount of amusement from her plea. How was he supposed to fix something a goddess couldn't touch?

The pawn coughed to clear the tick from his throat. "My lady," he croaked. "I'm an average mortal. I can't do anything about the weather—"

"It's not the weather!" she screamed, swatting an arm at her side.

Twisting his hands around each other, the pawn cast a nervous glance at his closed door. If he couldn't soothe her into stillness soon, her shouting would gain attention.

"Stop the demons!" she insisted.

His jaw sagged. "Stop… the—?" Had they begun some sort of movement without his knowledge? Far be it from him to challenge any of the demons' desires, but that didn't answer how or why Shand thought him remotely capable of influencing them. "I thought we were supposed to be paving a path for them?"

Shand's shoulders rose and fell from sweltering breaths on the verge of exploding. "They're trying to forge their *own* path now, and we cannot allow it. Your army has to do something. Make. Them. Do. *Something!*"

This wasn't quite how the pawn had expected this coup to play out, and facing Shand without immediate backup from his unlikely allies made him wish he had a stronger knack for foresight. "Once the weather clears, I'm sure I can begin working on something, but what about Mathias—"

"I'll deal with Mathias," she snipped. "I've got more than enough to use against him now. All you need to worry about is how to get the demons back in line."

The sweat on the back of the pawn's neck condensed and

rolled thick trails down into his collar. Even if he hadn't bound himself to the demons, he couldn't fathom how Shand expected him to quell them. He swallowed, relieved Shand's rage blinded her to his insecurity. "The only way I can think of to stop them is through Mathias." Oh, how he resented that the paladin seemed to be his key to freedom from both the demons and Shand. "And that would mean I'd need him functional and unbroken."

Still too shaken by Grell's seamless manhandling, Shand didn't even react to how close she just came to letting her servant secure control. "I don't care what has to be done. Those beasts must remember their place."

He glanced about, searching his room for the nonexistent answer to his goddess's demands. "I'm not sure what *I* can do about that."

Shand struck a fierce step in his direction, gaining an instant cower from the twitchy man defying her. That flare of power, of influence, of *control*, placated the most feverish parts of her mind, allowing her an even breath. Blinking back the dampness of fury in her eyes, Shand uncoiled her fingers to smooth out her skirt. "You will do whatever you can, *use* whoever you can, to force the demons back into submission."

Bitterly, the pawn twisted his mouth to keep back how Nessix and the influence she'd commanded could have spun such a convenience without even trying. His hatred for Shand grew an inch. "You have my word, my lady. I will do everything I can to set order back into place."

A handful of steady breaths later, Shand concocted a confident smile to hide away her fears and delivered a curt nod. "See to it you do." Relieved by having delegated her problem to someone else, someone she could hold responsible for any failures to avoid placing blame on herself, Shand departed.

The pawn sat back down and glowered at the gaudy tapestry on the wall, wondering how to report this to the demons.

FIFTEEN

Inwan's unexpected return had given Veed a feeble hope of redirecting some amount of animosity away from himself, but a chillier result of the god's presence met him instead. Bundles of ire and regret roiled within Veed in light of the dark memories lurking through the walls of the Teradhel fortress, unbecoming sensations overlooked by all but the very few people who thought they knew how he worked. In the unsociable bustle of the masses, he continued playing the part of a pompous ass, but once removed from those he felt compelled to impress, when he gave himself permission to accept weakness, the past devoured Veed. Subdued under the crush, time continued to pass until all that remained for him to cling to was the defiance he'd rallied behind so long ago.

Only Brant managed to take gouges from Veed's forced resolve. The commander had grown up considering Veed family, and if memory served right, a bountiful wealth of suspicion riddled the young man's mind in regards to Veed's integrity. These doubts drove Veed through the frigid days. He escaped the hassle of public ridicule in favor of torturing himself with reminiscing on the mistakes of his past and the bleak future he saw ahead. These walls closed in on him by the day, twisting him into a pathetic rendition of the man he'd once been.

As long as Elidae kept him imprisoned here and Inwan's

boldness continued to thrive in that mortal frame, Veed forced himself into a crude mold of sufferance. What he needed, more than any sort of recognition or deliverance, was to go home to his army. Backed by men who had vowed obedience to him, free of this torment, he'd teach Mathias and Inwan and Brant all about hospitality and respect. Once he had his troops, his pride, no need to grovel to people who spat in his path, Veed would find himself again. This was not the life Veed had ever intended to live.

Such bitterness—as he refused to call this heap of anxiety anything else—confined Veed to his chamber. Memories mocked him and battered against the hardened and arrogant walls he'd constructed over the past several years, but he no longer sought to deny them. As much as he regretted the way losing Nessix had destroyed him, he accepted that she was gone, quite possibly the first man to do so. Clinging to that closure as if it would save him, Veed dragged himself through this dismal chill.

Veed wasn't the only one wearied by the dreary conditions. The guard towers had stood unmanned for some time, the soldiers appointed to those posts frustrated with such an idle position in light of the unforgiving environment. No significant threats could march on them through the ice and snow, allowing the soldiers to justify relaxing their patrols and diligent watches. Ground conditions didn't affect those capable of flight, though, and the demons had narrowly clung to their patience for this exact opportunity.

Too few men watched over the battlements to prepare for a full assault, and most of the archers dozed at their posts or huddled around small fires to keep the blood in their fingers. Of the handful of lax guards, only one managed to reach the tower upon sight of the first line of alar. The great bell fell silent after a single toll as one of the winged brutes landed on top of the soldier and released a pair of aranau onto the borders of the flemans' prison. Too stunned to take timely action, the remaining guards dropped helplessly as swarms of aranau arrived by air delivery and weaseled their way across the maze of the rooftops.

The archers scrambled to attention after the brief warning and subsequent cries of their falling comrades, flexing feeling back into their fingers to take aim. Reports of the attack raced down through the interior levels of the fortress and it took but brisk moments for the army to jump at the chance to reinforce the sparse numbers on the walls. Too much time had passed since their last call to arms, and every soldier had chewed on their stewing resentment long enough to compensate for their stiffened limbs.

Brant strode through the halls with an authority he hoped rivaled his cousin's. "Archers, to the walls! Shoot down what you can!"

The order reached Mathias as he completed his preparations, stirring concern in his otherwise calm mind. That couldn't be right. He knew the demons and their limitations well; there shouldn't have been anything to shoot down. The alar's fragile wings would tatter at the smallest trauma in this sort of cold. They'd still maintain their combative strength as long as their bodies held out, but they wouldn't stand a chance at mobility or escape. Mathias frowned. The alar were smart enough to know this.

Etha, tell me what's coming. He didn't hold his breath for a reply, but it never hurt to ask.

"Archers, hold your ground!" Mathias countered the previous order firmly as he moved briskly through the assembling mass in the halls to reach Brant. "Get the refugees well below ground. Commander Vakharan will lead the guard over them. Captains, gather your troops in the stairwells and man the doors."

Brant clenched his fists and spun on Mathias, the bags beneath his eyes tattling how unfit he was to lead this attack. "We'll miss our targets."

All attention swept to the nearest doorway leading to the battlements as a steady force pounded against it. Mathias growled and rushed ahead, Brant close at his heels. The door gave way and a wave of twisted men and women flooded down the stairs, falling over one another in their lust for combat.

"Our targets have found us," Mathias muttered. He called over his shoulder, "Men, do not let them enter! Take your posts!"

Mathias left Brant behind him, pressing forward in defense of those crowded near the stairwell. He wielded the confining space and his superior experience to his advantage. Whatever crammed too near to dismember with his blade was slammed against the wall, crushed between enchanted steel and unforgiving stone. Fingers clawed at Mathias's face, grabbing for his eyes and neck, but it wasn't until one of those foul hands clasped around Nes's pendant that all semblance of restraint snapped from him. Grasping that demon's wrist, he hacked its arm off at the elbow and sent it screaming into the fray of its brethren with a kick to the gut.

"You've faced this before!" Mathias shouted to the allies around him. "Push to the roof and remind them who we are!"

An earnest rush answered his rallying cry as men who no longer accepted pain as a hindrance zeroed in on their enemies. Beyond losing Nessix, every mind revisited Sarlot's devastation as the snarling faces of aranau attempted to storm the keep. They remembered the blood and terror. They remembered the civilians torn to pieces, the children strewn through the streets. The army had matured into a fierce and formidable force since that battle, and while Nes's vivacious shouts no longer led them, vengeance lit a raging blaze behind their desire. A solid mob of flemans backed Mathias as they wedged their way up the stairs, no longer caring whether or not they held him responsible for the tragedy they'd only begun to overcome.

Brant stood frozen, gawking at the troops' enthusiasm. He had no idea how many demons waited on the battlements, and though he yearned to deny his concerns about whether Mathias lived or died, a lance of doubt struck his gut, taunting him over how much he'd come to rely on the paladin.

What are you talking about? Nessix breathed, her excitement catching in her voice. *This is why we live!*

The corners of Brant's mouth twitched toward something a hair brighter than bitterness. "Use every passage!" he called. "If the door opens, expect them to use it."

That's it!

Brant leapt up the stairwell Mathias had cleared and exposed himself to the enemy force flown onto the rooftops. No amount of danger would stop him. He'd already lost his family and was now confined with the three men he hated most. The demons meant less than a damn to Brant. No hearts beat in their chests. They had no sentient eyes, no souls. Never again would they set foot on his home as long as breath filled him. Nes's excited encouragement backed his determination, and he fought as a warrior ought to.

The aranau berserked around the fleman army, concentrating their gleeful assault in clusters instead of utilizing any concept of advanced tactics. Brant hadn't anticipated such simplicity to their attack, thankful the bloodthirsty foes neglected to spread out across the remaining expanse of the battlements. Whatever worked to keep them compacted for slaughter, the better. Brant didn't waste his effort to locate Mathias; a circle of dying gargles streamed from behind him, and Brant comfortably assumed those death songs came courtesy of the paladin.

Mathias found his rhythm in combat, efficiently holding the enemy at bay. It took talent and fortitude to frighten aranau, but even through their bloodlust, they knew to pick the easiest fights available. As a handful of troops resorted to flinging the wingless demons from the wall, Mathias's heart sank.

"Don't!" He cut his way closer as the toppling demons whipped around to grab a hold of the nearest flemans as they plummeted off the wall.

With the most lucrative target distracted by his concern for others, the demons swarmed over Mathias, weighing his limbs down with their mass. They latched to his back as he flung his might against them until a final demon jumped onto the pile and sent him forward. Mathias threw his right arm in front of him, crushing one of his enemies as he fell. Claws raked at his face and pulled at his hair. Adrenaline fogged Mathias's response to the pain and with Etha so far from him, he braced his limbs against the stone floor, forced to rely on his own strength.

A hoarse cry burst from Mathias as he thrust his shoulders back, only to be pressed down again. He curled a leg beneath himself, but no matter how hard he attempted to push back, the ice prevented him from gaining adequate traction to rise against the combined weight of his armor and assailants. The jolt of a sword ricocheted off the plate on his back and urged Mathias to duck his head, but the following stream of profanity gave him heart. As fast as an arm could capably swing a blade, Mathias's burden grew increasingly lighter until he could stand at last, and he looked into Brant's stern eyes. Breathless and bleeding, Mathias nodded his gratitude.

"Keep yourself alive long enough to get rid of these beasts," Brant said.

He'll remember that, I promise.

Brant smirked, through with his concern over Mathias. "Alright, what next?"

Press ahead!

Mathias didn't attempt to interrupt the intimate conversation this time, too busy regaining his composure and relieved to see some sort of twisted bliss in the young man. If Brant's hallucinations had excavated civility from his temperamental demeanor, Mathias accepted it gladly. For now, he let the action speak for itself, content allowing Brant exclusive insight to his motives. The thick of combat was not the proper time to try coaxing sanity into the commander.

As Brant dashed off, a volley of arrows swept out from the lower levels as warning calls raced up to the active combatants to announce the alar's return. They flew lower this time, their feet skittering across the battlements' icy surface as they deposited a fresh round of aranau. Those not grappled by fleman warriors banked back into the sky, but several of those went down, paper wings pierced by arrows. Disorder persisted on the rooftops as wearied troops struggled to determine where to concentrate their efforts. Despite the generous dent taken from the original wave, the flemans didn't risk turning their backs to the replenished threat. If the demons reached the inner levels, the fortress would be breached, and all of their efforts, all of Nes's dreams for Elidae's future, would be lost.

Between the archers picking off the alar and the soldiers holding their ground, reliable progress chipped away at the demon numbers, but the threat was far from under control. Mathias and Brant both had their hands full trying to manage the troops in their vicinity, staggering in resolve and stamina, when a radiant flash of steel and thunderous roar intercepted their focus.

Veed, only partially clad in his armor, rushed from the fortress and headlong into the fray. A solid force of Nes's troops backed his charge, but Veed alone danced into the opposition. Each demon he touched crumbled like brittle parchment and Veed's aggression soared with every life he claimed. He thrived on tempting fate and toying with sin. Nes's memory still tortured him, Inwan's presence still unnerved him, and his current location still frustrated him to the brink of madness, but right now, he seized this fight, savoring the surge of power that came from each defeated foe.

Pummeling his way through the demons with a natural efficiency, it took a shot of friendly fire sinking into his unarmored right shoulder blade to hinder Veed's tempestuous progress, sword arm rendered incapable. Snarling at the ineptitude of the Teradhel army, he continued his destructive assault off-handed. The switch slowed his pace, but his drive for destruction burned strong.

Chaos continued to churn across the battlements, but for a moment, Mathias stood gaping at Veed's conduct. Even wounded, the vile man radiated brutality and a sharp air of entitlement, flinging all of Mathias's reasons for hating him to the forefront of his mind. Tolerating Veed after he'd been repressed by isolation was a feat in itself, but beholding this beast in his element, alight with dominance, ignited memories Mathias preferred to leave buried. Hatred was a foul emotion and one Mathias tried his best to dismiss. He'd justified the demons' wrongs, but try as he might, there was no justification for a man as filthy as Veed.

Mathias raised his sword and braced to lunge toward the disgraceful general, stopped not by any code of morals, but the army's response to Veed's violent spree. The surrounding troops rallied around Veed's progress, drawing enthusiasm from his energy. Even partially crippled, Veed set an admirable pace and kept his fierce sights trained on his opponents. Raw emotion screamed at Mathias to take this chance to cut Veed down here in the tumult of battle, to pretend the execution was a tragic accident, but the wizened tactician in him whispered just within his perception that the army needed Veed's skill and gusto. Gritting his teeth, Mathias flung his attention away from Veed, trusting he'd stay alive for Mathias to tend to later.

As Mathias used experience to shift his focus back into action,

Brant stared, transfixed as Veed rapidly worked his way farther from the safety of the army and into the unknown guarantees of battle.

Where in Inwan's name did that *come from?*

"I don't know," Brant murmured, matching Nes's disturbed wonder. He'd never before witnessed Veed use his divine abilities on the field.

Blade radiating a menacing red, Veed's magical threat succeeded at keeping a reasonable amount of demons at bay, but something more powerful than awe of such fantastic talent captured the cousins' attention. This was the same Veed who had charged into battle in defense of the fortress he loved through his love of Laes. In this moment, Veed fought on the side of light, crusading for a cause much greater than his own glory. The ice around him failed to impede his efficiency and he left a red trail in the compacted snow to track his progress. Veed wouldn't be slowed until the demons fled, were killed, or took him. This was the man who Brant once called his uncle.

He'd been our teacher before, Nes whispered. *Follow him.*

With a resolute nod, Brant threw himself back into combat. He'd fight for himself. He'd fight for Nessix and the innocents who relied on his strength for their safety. Both Mathias and Veed were much more capable than him, and so Brant invested his efforts where he felt they were most needed. Working as the mindless force insanity had tailored him into, Brant tasked himself with cleaning up the stragglers who slipped past Veed's brutality.

The aranau maintained a vicious flow, and it didn't take long for Veed to cross Mathias's line of vision once again. As the paladin's rage flared at the clarity in Veed's eyes, he watched in morbid pleasure as a trio of aranau shifted their attention to the dark general. Mathias held his breath, inwardly yearning for the damned beasts tear Veed apart, but then a stark reality hit him.

There was something important invested in the depths of Veed, something Mathias both needed and hated. No matter what his most sincere hopes screamed for, he couldn't risk losing whatever value Veed carried inside of him to a grudge, no matter how well deserved it was. Mathias threw himself forward, his shoulder bashing a demon aside as his sword swept down to scatter the opposition.

Brant had set the day up to be one of rough gratitude, and Mathias picked his way through the caving ranks of demons. He stepped as lightly as possible on his advance toward Veed before degrading himself to using the bodies of the fallen warriors to gain better traction on the ice.

The version of Veed before him was different, but not in the way Brant had observed. Mathias didn't see Brant's level of familiarity, no fond memories he longed to forget. Mathias barely recognized a soul in Veed at all. What struck Mathias about the way Veed conducted himself was the man's hasty brashness. Veed had grown accustomed to power and indisputable control, demanding the loyalty of his underlings and citizens. Now, trapped away from the comfort of his reign, amidst a population that, at best, resented him, Veed struggled to hold on to that pride Mathias resented. Weeks had passed since the last time Veed set out to purposefully cause grief. After Inwan's arrival, he'd even gone as far as to remove himself completely from the public eye. There was no reason at all for Veed to rush to the army's defense, and as the fleman soldiers whittled away the opposition's threat, Mathias allowed that inconsistency of Veed's disposition to drive him to seek answers.

"I didn't expect to see you in arms," the paladin said at last.

Veed took his time mustering the will to straighten as far as the broken shaft in his shoulder allowed. "It was this or lay down and let the demons take me when you failed."

Mathias's eyes followed the injured shoulder. Veed wouldn't let him touch it, which worked for Mathias just fine. A bitter whisper reminded Mathias of Veed's own capabilities to seek divine assistance, and the paladin snarled against the motives warring between his practical and emotional sides.

"Why are you here?" Mathias asked.

Veed didn't look at Mathias. "Where else would I go?"

"No, why did you come here the day of the storm? You came without force. What had you been after?"

Veed sneered and spit out a mouthful of blood and battle

residue. "I'd been coming to tell you I was pulling my support. Guess that bit me in the ass."

The confession didn't raise Mathias's miniscule opinion of Veed, and so he settled for a short nod of acceptance. "Regardless of your objective then or now, my tactical side demands I thank you for your assistance today."

"Of course it does," Veed snorted, trying in vain to reclaim the authoritative presence he once managed to harass Mathias with. Bravado and tenacity didn't veil the doubt in his eyes. "All these people you say you'll protect are too busy huddling beneath each other, trying to escape reality. They're all waiting for their deaths. You must know that."

Mathias's eyes narrowed. Despite any recent changes born of stress, showing concern for others was well out of character for Veed. Maybe Nessix had changed him, after all. Mathias's sword wobbled in his grasp.

"We're all waiting for our deaths," he replied evenly.

Veed scowled at his rival's disdain, but kept his mouth shut. He'd already expended too much effort to hold his own in a debate and wouldn't risk compounding the shame of his mental state with humiliation. His shoulder throbbed as the surge of adrenaline settled, and Veed awkwardly navigated his bloodied sword back into its sheath.

"I know none of this is easy for you," Mathias said through Veed's stony glare. At least he was starting to look like the man who had earned so much hatred. "It must be hard being a prisoner."

Veed barked a short laugh, still keeping his gaze from Mathias. "Don't think you're holding me captive." He longed to blame all of this on the weather, but neither Nes's memory nor Inwan's brooding eyes allowed Veed to leave until they deemed him adequately punished.

Mathias recognized that fact well. "I never did."

Veed nodded. "The only thing that's changed here is who's alive. I owe you nothing." Robbing Mathias of the chance to respond, Veed turned and abandoned the confrontation, grasping his wounded shoulder as he descended the stairs.

Mathias clenched his jaw as Veed disappeared into the fortress. Even when lost in his blatant misery and forgetting himself in defense of the Teradhel keep, Veed ducked behind that loathsome demeanor that caused so much pain. Mathias would never forgive Veed for his attempt at claiming possession of Nessix, just as she'd never seemed to let go of how Veed had abandoned her after Laes's passing. For as long as Mathias had known him, Veed kept his motives rooted in selfish and disgusting desire. It wasn't Mathias's place to judge a soul's worth, but he wouldn't waste any sleep praying for Veed's salvation. Too many wrongs beat in that heart and Veed had set himself up for these troubles long ago. All Mathias had to do now was uncover how badly those past flaws had affected the present.

Packing his bitterness away in a tattered box, Mathias looked across those strewn across the battlements, fleman and demon alike, suffering and living and dead. He detested fighting, and not one battle passed that he didn't resent his proficiency at dealing death. Etha had crafted him to act as her iron fist, and he accepted her will without question, so he carried on with few complaints. If none of this existed, if there was no such thing as evil intent, Nessix would still be alive, and Mathias would be happy.

His brooding would not mend the battered or bolster the weary. It certainly wasn't helping his own mental clarity. A sigh shook Mathias and he turned to follow Veed back into the fortress, reinforcing the orders already called to clean up the combat zone.

As weary troops dragged the wounded back to safety, Inwan crept across the battlements, wide eyes soaking in the sight of spent soldiers hastily ending the lives of the writhing demons at their feet and helping those who obtained grievous wounds back inside. The flemans weren't strangers to war, but this scene was foreign to the once-god. Fighting the common, simple beasts of Elidae never carried this weight of dread. There was no gentle way to go about warfare, but Inwan never realized the raw brutality and torture which demons excelled in and coaxed from the flemans. Always one to advocate the use of any necessary means in combat, not even Inwan had condoned this sort of violence. Here they were, though, comfortable fighting with filthy conduct, not because they wanted to, but because their survival hinged on it.

Nes's memory wailed hearty victory hymns, too satisfied with the fight to weigh in on the matter, but Brant remained rooted in his duty, dealing final rights to the creatures who sought to destroy his home and hauling his battered comrades to their feet.

"This isn't what you expected to come back to." Brant stood with his back to Inwan, but was acutely aware of the god's nearness.

Telling Brant that he hadn't planned to come back in the first place wasn't an option. Not after seeing the young man's savagery. "It's always hard to see your people suffer," Inwan said.

Brant waited for Nessix to voice her opinion, but she kept on rambling through her songs. He turned to face Inwan, eyes rejecting the god's hope of finding an ally. "And I suppose you would know all about that."

"Look at what happened while I was gone, boy!" He swept an arm about beside him.

"What other option did you leave us? You're lucky we even made it this far." Brant grit his teeth at Nes's jubilations. She *hadn't* survived this long.

Unaware of Brant's inner struggle, Inwan crossed his arms and squared his stance. How did returning to this horror and devastation make him lucky? He'd yet to determine how he ended up back on Elidae to begin with, let alone where his divine powers had gone. Every attempt he made at utilizing his divinity had failed by mere inches, the power still bubbling deep inside him but always a breath out of reach. His dear flemans were suffering through a war, through the loss of their beloved general, and he was left to slog through the greatest fear a god could fathom. He was a failure.

The finality of Nes's death struck him suddenly, a powerful blow that sucked the breath from his fragile form as his mind flooded with questions he was too afraid to ask. Had she suffered? Who was with her in those final moments? What was the nature of her demise? Had she gone out as a hero or as pathetically as her father? Inwan had spent most of his time since Mathias's last warning trying in vain to reach the spiritual realm in search of her, but his efforts repeatedly came up bare.

Brant sneered at this man he once held in such high regard. What a coward he'd become! In the past, Inwan seldom engaged in battle personally, preferring to hide behind officers he swore to love and protect, tossing about fierce encouragement and brassy claims. But he'd stayed with them. He'd faced their tragedies and guided them to brighter futures. Nessix had loved Inwan with stalwart ferocity. Brant had accepted it at one time, but looking back at how little this god was willing to sacrifice for them, he began to wonder why.

"Nessix died wanting nothing more than to see your face," Brant said at last. "I'm glad you never got to see hers."

Indifferent to whatever offended response Inwan would sputter at him, Brant resumed his duty of hefting the wounded to safety and left Inwan to contemplate the carnage around him.

SIXTEEN

Twelve years ago, returning to the Teradhel fortress offered Veed a welcome breath of comfort. Inwan's words still rang loudly in his mind, but he was confident he'd chosen the correct path and went home without reservation. He arrived before Nessix, pleased by the fact that she hadn't had a chance to mention his shifty behavior from the previous night to her father. Veed spent the ride home rallying his courage, patiently schooling his conscience over how, per Inwan's reassurance, he had nothing to worry about. He'd maintained his honor and Nes's innocence. Far more relaxed than he'd been mere hours prior, Veed made his way to the war chamber to check on any pending reports or orders. Brant and Laes both waited in the room, the younger man's arms crossed and a deep concern etched between the older's brows.

Veed sucked in a sharp breath. "Is something wr—"

Laes's fist dug into Veed's jaw, forcing that last word to an abrupt end. Raising an arm to block a potential second blow, Veed attempted a hastened retreat. Laes's shoulder drove against Veed's breastplate and slammed him back against the wall.

"You son of a bitch!" Laes growled. "I gave you one order!"

"Laes, I didn't—"

A primal yell burst from the general as he grabbed Veed's arm and flung him to the ground. Veed scrambled to face this threat, bewildered eyes locked on Laes's as a stomp to the chest emptied his lungs and forced him flat on his back. "Give me one reason not to carve such insubordination from your flesh!" Laes's foot slid forward to press deadly promises against Veed's throat.

Veed hardly registered Brant's presence any longer as he grasped his best friend's ankle with both hands. "Sir, I did nothing."

"Nothing!" Laes spat. "Carry out your orders, Lieutenant Maliroch."

Veed held his breath. If luck smiled on him even in the slightest, Brant would pitch one of his typical arguments to pull Laes's concentration off Veed and allow him to form a composed response to these accusations. Veed reluctantly raised his eyes as the concept of hope spat in his face. Brant stalked past him, a delicate disgust shining through the pity in his glare. The door thudded shut with firm purpose.

Rapid heartbeats passed in silence thick enough to gag Veed, though the strength of Laes's foot on his neck contributed to the effect. The general's respiration rate teetered on the cusp of hyperventilation, and though guilt was wrongfully thrown on Veed, not even all of that bolstered confidence allowed him to meet his friend's eyes. Veed didn't know what trials he'd have to pass to regain his lost favor, but braced himself to pay whatever was required to settle this debt that wasn't his.

"Laes, I—"

"She is a *child*, Veed." Laes's words hissed low and hauntingly calm. He kicked his foot free of Veed's grasp and placed it on the floor once again.

While Nes's age ranked her just on maturity's side of adulthood, Veed refrained from revisiting that debate. "I swear to you, I did nothing."

"You followed her with corrupt intentions."

"Sir, I did nothing besides—"

"The man you gave your room to, Veed, he was one of ours."

A chilly fist pummeled Veed in the gut, sucking the breath from him as sensibility restrained the wisps of temper that wriggled free. If Laes intended to discuss matters of trust, he'd just handed

Veed a frightful blade of his own. Pride urged the commander to retaliate, but the steadfast loyalty which still stood for his general and friend refused to permit such hasty measures. Veed held his tongue behind a tight frown. Laes wouldn't allow him to finish a thought until he was ready to listen, anyway.

"You went to her room."

Veed propped himself up on his elbows, training a cautious eye on Laes. "I did."

"Were you seeking entry?"

This time, Veed hesitated. He was still torn about whether or not he'd meant to leave last night, but figured he stood a better chance at talking his way out of the answer Laes expected to hear than trying to justify the truth. "Yes."

"Did you sleep with her?"

The thought skipped across Veed's mind to tell Laes of Nes's adamant demands for Veed to take her bed, but he wanted the general to think of his daughter as a brazen whore even less than he wanted his own redemption. "No." Laes's eyes sought to keep Veed pinned down, but he sat up despite their pressure. "I did not."

Apparently, the truth didn't satisfy Laes. "Did you do anything at all that I would deem inappropriate?"

Veed's mouth opened to respond, but reluctance held his words at bay. While he was free to plead his innocence with a clear conscience, the fact that he'd so very nearly succumbed to his lust slammed him in the chest. Desperate to fight the claws of undue shame as they tore at his resolve, Veed drove off the indecent thoughts that vied to creep back into his mind. He only had to answer the question.

"I slept on the couch and left as soon as the storm passed enough to allow me safe travel." He knew Laes wouldn't accept anything he hadn't previously decided to believe, but even Nessix could confirm this answer during her inevitable interrogation on the matter.

Laes nodded slowly, his steady gaze locked on Veed. "Put yourself in my shoes, Commander."

"I can't." A flare of belligerence escaped Veed's grasp before he managed to contain the rogue impulse. "But if I'm ever given the honest chance to raise a family of my own, I'll get back to you on it."

A roar tore free from Laes's throat and he swung his foot back to kick Veed down once again. Veed flinched and raised an arm to protect his face, but Laes stopped the action before he struck forward. Great strain contorted his face as he took a step back and turned away, shaking his head. Veed lowered his arm reluctantly, afraid to guess what sort of thoughts rained down upon his friend's mind.

"Get out of my sight," Laes growled.

Struggling between fealty and defiance, Veed dragged himself from the floor, still watching Laes with the expectation of another attack. Once his feet solidly supported him, Veed scurried from his friend at a shameful rate, unable to vacate the room fast enough. Orders had been delivered, and while the disturbing urge to strike back against this injustice plagued the bolder corners of Veed's mind, he figured it would serve him far better to listen.

SEVENTEEN

Not even in the escape of his dreams could Mathias find peace, and a rough shove in the shoulder from a delicately slippered foot roused this carefree version of him. He blinked his eyes open against the offensive rays of dawn. Reclined on his back, he looked up at his sister's stern glare and breathed in the coolness of the morning. His right arm ached from how it curled upwards and back to serve as a makeshift pillow. It was what nestled in the crook of his left arm that had earned Julianna's disapproval.

Nessix lay soundly asleep with her head on Mathias's chest, his arm draped across her shoulders. He looked away from his sister to cast a fond glance at the young woman and a smirk played at his lips. Far be it from Mathias to object to it, but this hadn't been in the previous night's plans.

"What are you thinking?" Julianna demanded, her voice stretched thin across a firm whisper.

Mathias worked down a chuckle with the flex of his jaw and mouthed a "Shh" at her.

"I will not 'shh'!" she snipped back. "What in the Great Mother's name do you think you're doing?" Julianna gestured to the length of Nessix's slumbering form, and Mathias gave the sweet young woman a second tender look.

Her hair had come undone during their sparring and little bits of foliage and withered grass had woven themselves in her dark tresses from their period of star gazing. Her sword still rested nearby and her skirt draped about their legs in filthy tatters. Warm memories flooded Mathias's mind with each of these tiny flaws, but he would grant to Julianna that it must look rather inappropriate to an outsider.

"Don't worry, Jules," he murmured, watching Nessix carefully for signs of her stirring. "Everything's fine."

"No, everything is not fine," she scolded. "What do you think will happen when her brother finds out?"

Mathias rolled his eyes, conveying exactly what he thought of Nevius's opinions.

"This is a serious offense, and you know it."

"It's a serious offense to look at the stars?"

Julianna's lips puckered in a firm reprimand, her dainty fists shaking at her sides. "Get her back to her room before they find out she's missing."

His brows faltered in discontent, the light dimming in his mischievous eyes.

"Mathias…"

He sighed his frustration. "Fine." With the sun at such an invasive point on the horizon, it wasn't as though there was much time left to enjoy this peace undisturbed, anyway. "Now, run along."

Julianna arched a brow at him. "And trust you'll obey me?"

"Who's the older of us again?"

"I've got three hundred years on you these days."

Mathias rolled his eyes again. His issue wasn't with returning Nessix to her room, considering she belonged there, but he suffered over the idea of letting her go. She roused such a youthful joy in his jaded soul, allowing him a carefree escape from this world that demanded so much of him, and he liked to think he made her feel at least something akin to pleasure. Her fate here promised a fair amount of sadness, and she glowed so full of life. Mathias wanted to stay lying with Nessix in the field of lilies forever, if only to save her from the future her brother was selling her into. Selfishly, Mathias wanted her free to banter and spar with him, to count the stars and find pictures in the clouds. He blinked and drew a slow breath as his truth reached clarity. This was no longer a quest to save Nessix from her role as a political bargaining piece.

As Mathias's face fell with his realization, Julianna shook her head. "Meddling with—"

"I'm a grown man, Jules," Mathias said. "I can handle whatever problems I get myself into."

She frowned. "Where your mind's going, it won't be your problem, it will be hers." A nagging tumble in Julianna's stomach reproached her for being the cause of the regret creeping into her brother's eyes. After all the sacrifices he'd made for Abaeloth, he deserved to find his happiness. Julianna hated that he'd chosen to seek it in Nessix. "Sometimes the right thing isn't what we want. I trust you'll keep that in mind."

Julianna turned and walked down the hill, leaving Mathias to sort through matters for himself.

* * * * *

Mathias blinked himself awake, the disappointment of his dream slipping away enhanced by an abrupt recollection of the recent attack on the battlements. Groaning, he rubbed his eyes in an attempt to shoo away both his taunting fantasy and the flashes of Veed rampaging on his aggressive quest for dominance. Torn between conflicting desires, Mathias didn't know if it was worth his frustration to keep Veed around to capitalize on his valor, or if he should toss him out in the cold or slay him in his sleep. No matter how many disgusting memories assaulted the sacred parts of Mathias's mind, he kept snagging on an unsettling anomaly in Veed's performance the previous day.

The fierce demeanor wielded by the vile man was a valiant and outwardly convincing act that hid a fragile component Veed couldn't possibly want uncovered. Behind the bravado and established personality flaws, Veed had no more confidence in his position than Inwan did in his. As it stood, Veed was a fraction of the villain he'd been in warmer times, but that didn't mean he harbored any fewer secrets. Mathias was certain Nessix had known her fair share of them, but even with all of her hatred of Veed, she'd taken them silently to the grave.

Even now, Nes's unique code of ethics baffled Mathias, as he couldn't figure out what had motivated her to protect Veed after the volume of wrongs he'd made against her. Mathias accepted that Veed had served as an uncle to her in the past, but could her honor and loyalty persist after the cruel ways he'd torn her down? Nessix had claimed Laes's death drove Veed away. She'd been young and afraid, and despite her grandfather's mentoring, she'd doubted her ability to govern the entire nation on her own. Veed's grab for power amidst Nes's grief of losing her father had been the first time Mathias had witnessed Veed willfully take advantage of her, and it absolutely hadn't been the last.

Mathias raked his fingers through his hair, craving these answers he feared he'd never get. "No," he growled to that whisper of doubt. "When I free her, I will find out then." Affirming as much left a hollow void in the pit of his stomach. He'd quest for the rest of eternity to find Nes's soul, but he didn't even know where to begin looking.

He'd wasted too much time and energy making assumptions about what had and could have been. Mathias shoved himself to his feet. He needed these answers, whether or not he wanted them. Sulik, as honest as he'd proven himself to be, had never been fully immersed in the noble line's political loop. If Mathias had any desire to play games—and if he thought Inwan would give him even half an ounce of respect—he knew the god would be an erupting fountain of knowledge. Only one living soul remained who could possibly have even a remote inkling to share Nes's secrets with Mathias.

The decision to leave his quarters hadn't been a fully conscious act, and Mathias stood in front of Brant's door as doubt wagged a cautionary finger at him. Mathias had never considered himself a timid man, but mustering the courage to commit to his chosen task kindled the faintest glimmer of reluctance. After all, he wasn't even convinced exhuming the ghosts of Nes's past was what he wanted. Mathias knocked on the door. The scuff of chair legs and rumble of Brant's undertone answered, and it wasn't long before Mathias was met by the commander's stony face.

Oh, it's Mathias! Invite him in. We haven't talked to him in a long time.

Brant's frown pinched closer to a glower. Mathias must have known how unwelcome he was.

That's nonsense. I've missed hearing what he has to say.

The deeper down this hole Brant fell, the harder it was to tune out Nes's enthusiasm. He swore he caught the slightest hint of pity in Mathias's eyes and turned his face from his unwelcome guest.

What are you so ashamed of? He knows you can hear me.

The flare of Brant's nostrils kept him from a verbal response and he had to remind himself that no matter what Nessix said, Mathias couldn't hear any of her nonsensical swooning. Mathias's face had settled with the rigid lines of tortured purpose, plainly declaring his intention to stay until he achieved his objectives, whatever they were. Brant frowned and glanced at the floor, pulling in a slow breath before facing this challenge.

"Can I help you?"

Mathias pinched his lips together and took a turn to avert his gaze. Brant never made an effort to hide his distaste of him, and Mathias's pending questions promised to drag the commander down roads he'd contently left behind. This past had been hidden for a reason and Mathias prayed it was a history he wouldn't regret visiting.

Words found Mathias slowly, creeping out from behind his regret. "I know this won't be easy for you, but it's killing me not knowing. What was the relationship between Nes and Veed?"

A chill skittered up the back of Brant's neck at the inclusion of his beloved cousin and the man she'd hated most in the same statement. He sucked on his tongue and crossed his arms, prepared to retreat back into the seclusion of his quarters.

You can tell him. Nes's voice was small and timid, unusually subdued. *He'd have gotten it out of me eventually.*

Nessix's preferred method of protecting herself from the past had always been to refuse speaking of it, and Brant had never questioned that approach. He leaned against the door frame. "Friendly foes," he said. "Neither wanted the other dead as far as I could tell, but they never seemed to mind making the attempts." That answer sufficed better than the truth Brant knew, and it was all he felt Mathias deserved.

He already knew that, Nes insisted, *and he deserves to know it all.*

Brant cleared his throat to hold back his objections and lowered a hand to pull his door closed, but Mathias slammed his palm against it to stop the action. He knew the honesty of Brant's reply, but everyone's reluctance to speak of these buried memories proved the past was much more complicated than the commander let on. Mathias had come too far to back out now. Brant could hate him all he wanted, but Mathias refused to leave until he received the answers he needed.

His sorrow was no less evident between his brows or in the grim tuck of his lips, but Mathias set his eyes with resolve. "Veed had a vested interest in keeping Nes safe—"

"Not too unlike you, then?"

As Mathias winced and coughed on his reply, Nes murmured, *Brant… that was low…*

Brant scoffed and returned his hand to the opposite elbow, assessing Mathias with leery eyes. Whatever intimacy Nes had shared with Mathias, he didn't know her. There was no way he'd loved her, not enough to insist Brant revisit the events which had ripped the kingdom apart.

Mathias's cheeks paled and he refrained from looking at Brant. "He had more than just her welfare in mind, Commander. We both know that."

"Just like how I know about the lust that's run through your virtuous veins?"

Please stop, Brant. I really loved—

"Do. Not. Say it." That time, Brant's self-consciousness couldn't catch his seething correction from escaping through clenched teeth. He didn't know why he tried so hard to hide his insanity from Mathias; the paladin had confirmed his awareness of the condition some time ago. Even if Brant wanted to deny it, the decreasingly rational side of him suspected Mathias was his only chance at coming out of it in the end. Brant looked up through hooded eyes, and Mathias stayed silent.

He's trying to understand, Nessix said. *He wants to. He's the only person who can get us out of this war and he needs more insight than I can give him.*

Brant shook his head and grumbled at the sense she made. Mathias had limited his response to a lowered head and firmly clenched jaw, forgoing that obnoxious jest and arrogant authority he usually used when he didn't get his way. Had Brant not stood right there, facing the subdued paladin, he'd never believe Mathias capable of accepting these untimely accusations without dispute. It was eerie seeing Mathias so fragile, and after so much effort spent aiming to discredit and defeat the paladin, Brant suddenly wondered why he'd tried so hard to do just that.

Veed has information. Mathias knows it. You know it. I can't answer his questions anymore. I'm counting on you. Please.

Nes's pleading picked away at Brant's hostility. As much as he wanted to run from it, Mathias had loved Nessix, and if her memory spoke with any sort of accuracy, she'd shared at least part of that notion. Mathias had a right to the things Brant knew, and if the truth scarred him, then so be it. The commander hefted a sigh and stepped aside.

"If you plan to pry further, you'd better come in and sit down."

Mathias's shoulders sagged, tightened expression relaxing on a relieved breath, and he stepped forward. Sulik had mentioned in passing the state of disarray in which Brant currently lived, but Mathias hadn't put much thought into it until now. Scrolls lay curled haphazardly on the floor where they'd been dropped and kicked aside. His bed was unmade and the rumpled sheets and strewn pillows provided evidence of disturbed sleeping patterns. The remains of two wine glasses lay shattered on the floor beside his desk, a third partly drained sitting on top beside a fourth that was full and waiting for company that wasn't coming.

Frowning that he hadn't taken the reports of Brant's degradation to heart, Mathias reached out to pull the closest chair around.

"Not that—" Brant sprang forward at Mathias's action before sheepishly retracting both his hand and his objection. He winced and rubbed his forehead, shifting half a step away from Mathias as his cheeks burned with a shameful flush.

Mathias paused and cleared his throat. In the case of any other patient, Mathias would have jumped on this opportunity to work toward closure, but Brant had found a functional peace within his turmoil. "I'm sorry," Mathias said instead. "It was rude of me to assume."

Lips pressed to keep them from trembling, Brant gave a single nod and gestured toward the chair he frequented. Breaking the uncomfortable impasse, he snatched up the bottle of wine as Mathias took his seat. He found a fresh glass to pour a drink for Mathias, topping off his in turn, and leaned back against the sturdiness of his desk. Closing his eyes for the span of a slow breath, Brant sniffed back his grief. "You're aware Veed was our uncle of sorts, right?"

Mathias politely accepted the drink, but refrained from tasting it. "I was told."

Brant nodded and sipped his wine, frowning. He'd quit tasting it weeks ago. "What you probably hadn't been told—we'd shoved it under every rug we could find—was that he developed an... unhealthy fondness for her when she was still more girl than woman and shook apart the entire structure of our nobility."

Mathias nodded, his upper lip curling the longer he thought it over. Even with these revelations falling into place, his mind eased no more than he'd expected.

Brant's blank gaze stared across the disheveled room, failing to register Mathias's reaction. "We were never able to *confirm* if he'd acted on those impulses—"

I confirmed it, the youthful memory of Nessix insisted.

"No," Brant growled, brows pressed in scolding, "you didn't." He blinked, eyes leaping to sharp focus as he sent a hasty glance at Mathias. No sense of ridicule laughed from the paladin's tense gaze, no hint of pending judgement at Brant's feeble state, and the commander heaved a sigh. Not even as recently as two weeks ago did he ever think he'd drop his guard around Mathias to display such vulnerability but here in this room, he felt at last that Mathias understood. Brant shook his head to scatter Nes's words from his mind and continued to chase the paladin's objective. "When she was still a child, we never confirmed foul acts against her, but Uncle Laes had hefty suspicions that remained clear up to his death. After that, Veed snapped, left the fortress, and continued lusting after Nes from a distance."

Mathias read the worry wrinkling Brant's forehead, the listlessness in his bloodshot eyes, but nowhere on Brant's face raged the anger of knowing that Veed had ultimately succeeded in reaching those goals. It surprised him to think Nessix never told Brant the devastating truth of how Veed had used her, as Mathias had believed the cousins had kept no secrets from each other. Maybe it all boiled down to Nes's desire to protect her kingdom before all else. Alienating Veed through the actions Brant would have inevitably taken against him would have disrupted the war in ways Nessix didn't know how to cope with. Her death managed a much more efficient job at that. Right now, Mathias was in a greater need to find strong allies and renewed vigor, even if it had to come from mutual hatred and the risk of civil unrest. He'd never find a way to bury these thoughts or the regret that would come from divulging them to the grief-stricken commander. Mathias swallowed hard.

"Did she ever tell you what happened?"

The question jolted Brant's wandering mind to the present and his tired eyes met Mathias's. "What do you mean? She didn't have to tell me. I was there when he left."

Mathias shook his head. "No. Did she tell you?" It took him a pair of rapid heartbeats to gather the nerve to complete his statement. "About what happened between her and..." The idea of speaking Veed's name twisted Mathias's stomach. "Him. About Logan?"

Brant had heard rumors but had paid them no mind, as there was no shortage of them flitting about for the past several years, thanks to Veed's lewd tongue and unscrupulous army. This time, with Mathias's unusual lack of words and obvious struggle to find grace, Brant was forced to recognize some vein of truth in them at last. His lips parted and he shook his head as he waited for Nes's commentary to chase away such frightful notions. Her refusal to deliver on Brant's expectations solidified Mathias's broken claim and Brant's eyes tried to spring with tears that had dried up days ago. Mathias swiped the glass from Brant's hand before that one fell, too.

Mathias wouldn't press the issue of how Nessix had withheld her repulsive act from Brant, saving the commander from that side of his shame. "The suspicions from her youth had been worthy of your concern. Had—" There was that unusual hang up again. "*Why* had he been after her?"

Brant held his breath, praying for Nes to weigh in on the subject, but she disappointed him yet again. Why wouldn't she? She wasn't real. She couldn't be. Brant's eyes bore blindly through the floor, shoulders drooping as shock exhausted that last pinch of pride left in the commander. "I don't know," he murmured, voice cracking with a strain of defeat Mathias wanted to run from.

I'm so sorry, Brant… Ah. There she was. *You didn't need to know. Nobody did.*

Mathias pounded a fist against his thigh as he threw his weight against the back of the chair, interrupting any reply Brant might have wanted to blubber back to Nessix. "We're missing something," he said. "What is it?"

Brant dragged his eyes up to Mathias's and he squinted to sift through his mania. "Why are you asking me?"

Mathias blinked and refocused on Brant, but he didn't have that answer. "Had he always been after her power?"

"Yes."

"In the same way as he is now?"

Brant wanted to confirm that, too, but honesty caught the accusation in his throat. He attempted to clear that reluctance free but failed, and settled for shaking his head. "There was a time when a man with the same name fought for something other than himself. But I'm not sure what happened to him."

This was a confession Mathias fought to accept. It would have fit his agenda much better if Veed had always conducted himself as a monster. "Do you remember when he began to fall?"

Brant shook his head again, this time with a throaty sound of resistance.

Think, Brant! Nessix urged. *You remember when Father pushed him away. You remember all of it. You were there. Please. This is important.*

"No," Brant murmured, tears welling in his eyes. Those were the last days of Nes's innocence, when dreams still meant something. When nightmares could be woken from.

Mathias nodded in what he thought was understanding and resumed his questions, but Brant didn't hear them past Nes's voice.

Tell him! Tell him how scared I was without Father, about how I was scared of Veed. Tell him, Brant, please!

A fierce growl erupted from Brant as he pushed himself from his desk's support, wheeling around to try confronting the voice of his torment. The glass he'd left filled for Nessix fell and shattered on the floor with the others. "You're not real! You're not Nessix!"

His chest heaved, eyes too deprived of any sort of rest to allow him to register the empathetic look sent his direction. Brant couldn't take any more of this, and for the thousandth time, he contemplated how tall the fortress was, how many sharp objects were available to him. He looked to his sword belt where it lay in a heap on the floor and wondered why Sulik still let him keep it. Brant wanted out of this infernal damnation; he needed out of it. He was loyal to his army, had vowed to protect the citizens, but he was so lost without Nessix.

But you have Mathias.

Brant wept openly, covering the shame of his anguished face as he sank back against the top of his desk. Mathias lowered his eyes to his hands as he waited for the surge to pass. If he hadn't been in such a similar place as the commander, witnessing this breakdown would have discomforted him. Instead, Mathias directed his prayers to plead for Brant's peace. Regardless of what history said of their past, Mathias and Brant had one very significant thing in common.

Etha saw to Mathias's petition and she eased calm back into Brant. His breathing slowed and all those inner demons flailing against his sanity fell back to their dark holes. When strength returned and Brant looked up, he was surprised to find no pity on Mathias's face, only a steeled resolve. The commander sucked back his tears, seared the phlegm from his throat with a quick chug from the bottle, then wiped his nose with his wrist. Brant prepared a hasty explanation for his sudden breakdown, but Mathias beat him to speaking.

"I don't know what hell you're going through, and I won't pretend I do, but I swear to you I *will* find her again."

Brant blinked at the statement. It seemed impossible, but Mathias did have an annoying knack for delivering on such feats.

"Her soul never made it to the heavens. That means it's still somewhere on the mortal plane."

Hope—innocent and genuine—sparked to life in Brant's reddened eyes. His mouth gaped open to facilitate the rise of his respiration rate. Old habits and a stubborn streak wanted to insist Mathias was just spouting his usual overblown drivel, but cruelty wasn't in the paladin's nature. "Can you still fix her?"

The truth would disappoint Brant, and that same lack of cruelty forbid Mathias's honesty to taint the faint light Brant clung to. Even once Mathias located Nessix, he doubted his ability to restore her life, but he prayed she'd receive peace when that day came. "When we get through this war, I will devote myself solely to saving her and you will be the first to know when she's back in my reach." Mathias stood and placed a hand on Brant's shoulder. "In the meantime, I ask that you do what you can to sort out anything that might help me. Honor Nessix by not giving up. She needs you, Brant. Always has."

Brant's bowed head and the way he pointedly looked away from Mathias confirmed his inability to continue speaking of this subject, and Mathias wasn't convinced he wanted to press the matter. "Get some rest, Commander," he said, "and trust that I will see this through."

With nothing else left to say, Mathias left Brant to Nes's attempts at rallying cheer out of him.

* * * * *

Inwan groaned, the ache in his bones protesting his effort to rise. As he swept the fuzz from his mind, freeing his thoughts to contemplate what circumstances had landed him here, the god hauled himself to a seated position on the crude cot he'd woken on. He hadn't remembered his physical form hurting so much, but comfortably blamed that on how out of practice he was coming out of his imprisonment. What did scratch at his calm, though, was how he seemed locked in this single useless body. This limitation made it that much more confusing that he'd woken in a setting he didn't recall falling asleep in.

Wary, Inwan coaxed his creaky joints into compliance and hefted himself to his feet.

He stood in a simple room, bare other than the cot and himself. Smooth stone walls surrounded him on all sides, including overhead, and he turned a slow circle in search of a doorway instinct told him didn't exist. He completed a full pass to come face to face with Etha's stern eyes. Sucking in a sharp breath, Inwan narrowly limited his reaction to a flinch of embarrassing proportions. Ego catching up to the annoyance of his racing heart, Inwan crossed his arms with a short and haughty roll of his eyes. He was as bad an actor as ever, but that was the last thing on Etha's mind.

"Have you figured out why you're here?"

As powerful of a man as Inwan hoped to emulate, his knees trembled in the petite woman's presence. He rocked a single step backwards. Etha's glower followed Inwan's casual retreat and assured him that she had a very specific agenda behind dragging him back to Elidae. There was no escaping the Mother Goddess, but the flop of Inwan's gut suggested it wouldn't hurt to try. Mouth clamped shut, Inwan turned from Etha and resumed scanning the room for an escape from this encounter.

Not even the greatest of Inwan's feeble efforts bested the weakest parts of Etha's power. She rattled the ceiling with the stomp of a tiny foot, sprinkling flecks of dust and bits of crumbling stone down on them both. "I asked you, you mockery of my child, if you know why you are here."

Inwan allowed himself to cringe without attempting to hide it this time, coming to terms with the fact that Etha would get her answer one way or another. The smartest thing for him to do was give it to her as readily as possible. Even if he wanted to continue defying her, the righteous glory of her fixed brows refused to let him turn away from her again. For one of Inwan's capable physique, being so afraid of this overbearing waif should have been ridiculous, but he stumbled over even the most basic of replies.

"I've served my time?" A hint of accusation snuck past the sound practicality of his reservations. Some habits, not even fear could completely negate. "I don't know."

A scowl tarnished Etha's gentle face. "You mean to tell me you have *no* idea?"

In days past, Inwan had enjoyed the luxury of a clever mind, one fond of trickery and games. He'd prided himself on his ability to hear what went unspoken, and the subject of this confrontation was no exception. Inwan shook his head with so much force he almost believed his gut's conviction to stand against Etha.

"No," he growled defensively. There was no other reason for Etha to drag him back to Elidae other than to deal with the loss of his dearest child. He'd have given anything in his power—and stolen from whoever necessary to give even more—to have stopped what had become of Nessix. "You will *not* pin Nes's death on me. It wasn't *me* who failed her."

"Then who was?"

Inwan glanced away with a bitter hiss. "I couldn't have failed her. I wasn't the one watching over her."

Irritation boiled inside Etha, threatening to bubble over the refined calm she hoped to employ against this unruly child. No matter how badly Inwan wanted to escape her interrogation, that was one indulgence Etha refused to grant him. "No, you weren't. But you should have been."

That succeeded in provoking Inwan to wheel back around to face her, an arrogant curl of his lip speaking his resentment more clearly than any heated words could have. "How, *great* Mother, would I have managed that? I was banished. Do not think for a second that I ever wanted to leave her."

Etha's eyes narrowed and she jerked her head to the side. "You were banished, but not without fair warning. If you weren't willing to deal with the consequences of your actions, you shouldn't have strolled with chance."

Inwan snorted and crossed his arms, and Etha frowned at his utter refusal to accept responsibility. How had a cretin like him ever been found worthy of a god shard, much less Nes's fierce devotion? It was an answer Etha suspected not even Inwan had figured out yet.

"Nessix died trying to justify her faith in you, and you still have the nerve to stand up for yourself?"

Inwan was tired of Nes being used as leverage against him. "What's done is done," he said. "Not even you can change the past. What do you want me to do about it now?"

This disgraceful man's attempt to display authority tempted Etha to laugh, but disgust choked the expression away. She shook her head, lip curled. "I want you to prove to me it's worth my effort to keep you around."

Inwan rolled his eyes. "If you didn't want me here, you should have left me in my cell. Nobody *forced* you to drag me out."

"That's just it." Etha's words were clipped and laced with a terrifying keenness that snagged that long forgotten fear of the unknown buried deep inside Inwan. "Your banishment didn't faze you in the slightest. The entire time you were supposed to be reflecting on your actions, you didn't once worry about what was becoming of your nation or your people, not even your chosen child. You trusted everything would be fine while life itself failed Nessix. And you have the audacity to consider yourself among the spectrum of light!"

"You think I wouldn't have stayed with her if I'd been given the opportunity?"

"You had plenty of opportunities to control yourself," Etha sneered. "You chose punishment over virtue, and that cost Nessix her life."

Inwan had never run from his pride, but he had enough intelligence to keep from reacting to Etha's accusation with the anger he'd throw at anyone else. This same intelligence also understood that Etha continued to bring up Nessix for a very valid reason, one which Inwan resented to the depth of his being. He had loved Nessix with the same devotion which she'd loved him, and her death devastated him on both divine and mortal levels, but no amount of devastation could bring someone back to life once their soul was gone. He squinted in contemplation as he toiled over Etha's true agenda.

"Why are you so interested in her?" he asked.

"Why shouldn't I be?"

The steadiness of Etha's tempered glare pulled at the hairs on the back of Inwan's neck—a sensation forgotten by him through ages of divinity—and he fought off the urge to shiver. "You're making this great fuss about how *I* should have been here when I'd been held against my will and how *I* should have been watching over Elidae. But you were the one who was here, and this is—what do you call it?—your sacred homeland?"

Inwan's efforts did not amuse Etha. "Blessed," she snipped.

He barked out a caustic laugh. "Blessed homeland, then. You dragged me back here, blamed me for crimes well above those I'll admit to committing, and shackled me in this useless form, but somehow you expect some sort of greatness out of me?"

Etha returned the laugh, her bitter tone betraying the serenity much better suited to her. "Don't flatter yourself. I've never expected greatness out of you."

Inwan scoffed at the disdainful ease which Etha delivered the insult but didn't pursue it. He traipsed down a dangerous path in trying to combat Etha, her tone and the increasing hostility in her eyes made that clear. Even if he'd had the full extent of his powers at his disposal, Inwan doubted he'd stand a chance against challenging Etha. His muscles yearned to tremble from the strain of containing himself, but stifled the sensation beneath his greater desire to survive.

Etha raised her brows at Inwan's silence, the first flicker of approval she'd given. "I trapped you in that mortal shell for a reason, and your current lack of power reflects your diligence. Do not think for a second that I am deaf to your thoughts. I have no reason to go gently on you. Abandoning your people is one thing, but leaving them helpless to demons is another."

He coughed and looked away. "Forgive my lack of respect."

Face twisting at Inwan's sheer insolence, Etha stepped forward and slapped him. "I don't have to forgive you for anything.

As fragile as you've become, you ought to keep your pride in check. Mathias and I are the only two beings who know your current limitations. Do not give me a reason to shine light on them to your peers."

Pin pricks of pain tapped across Inwan's cheek and he pressed timid fingers against his flesh. What was this conversation supposed to yield? He'd known Etha's low opinion of him for years and was no more surprised or moved by it now than he'd been all along. Inwan frowned, remembering where the day's discussion began.

"Why *am* I here?"

Etha drew in a slow breath. Progress at last. "To face your guilt."

Inwan threw his head back and groaned. Hadn't they *just* gone through this? "My guilt in that you let Nessix fall? No, I—"

"In how you left your people to suffer!" Etha's delicate voice rebounded from the stones around them, assaulting Inwan from every direction. The impish side of Etha laughed and clapped its hands at how he cringed from her reprimand, but her disgust in the flaws he still allowed to flourish held her humor captive. "In how hopeful they were to see you return to them, just to be more useless than ever. It's time for you to take responsibility for your charge."

"And how do you expect me to overcome any of that while trapped in this pathetic body?"

"Eh." Etha shrugged and turned to walk toward the wall. "Your actions are the only thing limiting what power I'll restore to you. Prove to me you deserve to be a god. Make it up to your people, even if it kills you."

This time, the timbre of Inwan's puff of laughter tattled his growing self-doubt, a fault he hoped to hide from the general population. "I don't even know *how* to use a mortal body. My powers use to be limitless—"

"Your powers were always limited." Etha stopped and faced him, lips pursed and arms crossed. "And don't make yourself more of a fool by thinking otherwise. You can either find a way to redeem yourself or die to the demons. Either option is fine with me."

Etha snapped her fingers and in a flash, they were back in the room where Mathias had first secured Inwan. Etha appraised him a final time, lip curled in dissatisfaction at how much wasted potential laid dormant in Inwan.

"You can't disappoint me any more than you already have," she said. "Do whatever you must to keep from disappointing yourself."

Inwan stood in mute silence, even after Etha vanished from his sight. He couldn't remember the last time he took responsibility seriously, but Etha's ultimatum rang a firm warning in his head. If he wanted to survive, to reclaim any sense of the power he craved, he needed to find a way to look after his people. Missing Nessix and her enthusiasm even more, Inwan sank onto the bare cot to fret over his options.

EIGHTEEN

Twelve years ago, it took nothing more than a simple invitation to dinner to destroy Veed's appetite. The family and officers' dining hall was unlikely to provide him a remotely welcoming environment, but turning down such a direct request would raise more suspicions that he'd rather avoid. Already nauseous from his emotional burden, Veed delayed his arrival for as long as he could find excuses then trudged down to the main level to see what sort of disgusted glares waited for him.

He responded to the greetings of passing soldiers and junior officers with tight smiles and brief nods. Each step taken toward the dining hall twisted the knife in his gut another quarter turn until he almost preferred the thought of execution. A deep breath loaned Veed a halfhearted attempt to steady his mind when he reached the door, and his clammy palm pulled it open.

Seconds after entering the room, before the door fell completely shut, the cessation of dishes clanking and Nes's startled gasp greeted Veed. The legs of Nes's chair honked against the polished floor as she pushed herself from her seat and ran around the table to him. Her petite hands reached up to cup his face as she turned his head to better appraise the bruises Laes had branded him with earlier in the day.

"What in Inwan's name ha—"

Acutely aware of Laes's curled lip and Brant's patronizing glare, Veed grasped Nes's wrists to pull her hands away from him. He shoved her two steps back, released his hold, and strode past her to his seat. "I'm fine." He hadn't intended such coldness to come from his tone, but he'd known before he even showed up that Laes wasn't through judging him.

"You were *fine* last night," she argued, trotting up behind him. "What in the world could have happened between then and now to—"

Veed wheeled on Nessix, halting her stubborn debate and belligerent advance. "Don't worry about it, Nessix. There was an accident. I'm fine."

Part of Veed's heart died at the way Nessix's lips pinched together and her brows hanging unevenly over her eyes. Sighing, he put a hand on her shoulder to direct her back to her seat, Laes's preconceptions burrowing deeper into him. Nessix had no idea how her innocent actions complicated Veed's situation, and he couldn't fault her—even treasured her more—for her concern. When she obediently followed his guidance, the tiniest glimmer of relaxation offered his racing heart a reprieve. Veed took his seat beside Sulik, the chair to his left still vacant. Nessix sat across from Veed, flanked on either side by her father and cousin. As Laes calmly went about his meal, Brant's suspicious eyes scoured Veed between bites. Veed made a few uncertain shoves on his plate and managed to stab a bite of something he neither saw nor tasted. Sulik sat rigidly beside the commander, unsure who it was safe to talk to.

"Your report, little love?" Laes asked after swallowing a bite. He smiled at his daughter. Veed knew Laes far too well to miss the scheming in his eyes.

Nes's expression brightened from the uncertainty dumped on her by Veed's arrival and subsequent actions. "We didn't find anything the first day out, but after we'd scouted around a bit and went to talk to the guards, they said most of the activity had been at dawn, so—"

Her eyes fleeted up from where she'd been diligently cutting the meat on her plate, and her expression fell as she soaked in the friction jolting through the room. "What's wrong?"

Nobody answered, and her chair creaked beneath the shift of her weight. Veed would have given his sword arm to ease her confusion, but suspected he'd land in heaps of trouble if he leapt to her defense. Head still lowered, Veed looked up through his lashes, brushing past Brant's glare and catching Laes's for much too long. He swallowed the ashy bite in his mouth, grimacing as the bolus raked its way down his throat. A gentle tap brushed his foot and he raised his head to meet Nes's confused eyes. Questions streamed from her silently, innocently.

Why is everyone so upset? Why won't Father just tell me I failed his expectations? Veed, she demanded, *what did I do wrong?*

"Tell them what happened," she murmured, voice quivering with an internal panic that she'd disappointed her father.

"Yes, Veed," Brant echoed smartly. "Why don't you tell us?"

"I'm not asking Veed," Laes snapped. "Nessix, what happened out there?"

A frustrated frown flawed her expression, but at least it eased the trouble from her eyes. "I was telling you, but no one was listening."

Laes's focus never shifted from his food. "You weren't delivering the right information."

"I—" She stared hard at Veed a moment longer, cultivating a distinct fear inside of him. "I've never given a formal report before. I thought—"

"Backtrack, Nes," Laes cut in, an unusual harshness for him to use against the daughter he loved so dearly. "Start from what happened just before your return."

Nessix flinched at his interruption, lost at how to navigate such strictness when she had no honest idea how to fix it. Veed lowered a hand to his lap to hide the clench of his fist. Laes was more than welcome to stomp on him, but Nessix was still his daughter and, as Laes himself was so adamant to emphasize, still a child.

"There's no need to speak to her—"

"I've heard enough from you."

Brant's hand found its way to Nes's arm when she gasped at

the venom in her father's correction, as if a simple touch could make her eyes less wide or bring color back to her cheeks. She placed her knife and fork down with deliberate care and looked across the table as calmly as her racing heart allowed. Only Sulik could relate to the poor girl's confusion, both of them drowning in the static passing across the table. As the tension spilled over, Sulik followed Nes's lead and quit eating.

"Am I needed here, sir?" the young man asked, flinching at the sound of his own voice.

"Leave."

Nes's mouth sagged, her breath coming in quick, shallow puffs as Brant squeezed her arm reflexively to her pain. Veed hung his head away from them, clamped fingers tingling. Sulik had been the only sign of safety in the room, and hearing him move his chair back to stand and leave grated on the last of Veed's nerves. Veed expected a hit to his station before Laes would allow peace restored between them, and he faced legitimate apprehension over the physical damages that might be paid to him, but this was the first time concern for Nes's welfare came to mind. Veed doubted Laes would deliver actual harm to her, but neither had he imagined such harshness directed her way. Veed would accept whatever punishment Laes felt he deserved, but if any threat flew toward Nessix, not even Brant would have a chance to react in her defense, and Laes would get to see firsthand the depth of Veed's devotion to her.

"I'm waiting for your report," Laes said.

Brant's hand eased from Nes's arm as she darted her frightened gaze across the table. Veed remained pinned beneath Laes's glare but peeled his attention away to meet Nes's eyes. His heart ached for having catalyzed her pain and as helplessness etched across her face, the seldom seen glimmer of tears lurking close at hand, Veed ground his teeth and looked away.

Nessix drew a few more sharp breaths until she found her tongue. "Father, help me." She reached out to touch Laes's arm but stopped short. "Please. I don't know what you want from me."

Laes climbed to his feet, palms pressed against the table. He stared down at his plate as he organized his thoughts before turning his head toward Nessix, face softening to convey that he was still her loving father. "Nes, my little love, I need you to tell me everything you remember about last night."

A nervous breath led Nes's struggle to compose herself enough to speak. "We took out a small troop of minotaur." She cleared her throat but still didn't manage to chase off her uncertainty. "Most of them fled, and I went back to the inn feeling pretty insufficient. Inwan came by, treated me to dinner, and told me I did well for my first mission. He said you'd be proud."

Veed held his breath. After his own discussion with Inwan, he'd have preferred to go without the god getting dragged into this.

"So Inwan was with you?"

Nessix pulled out a nervous smile. "He always is."

"When did he leave?"

"What does—" Nessix cut off her question before anyone tried to do it for her. "The storm started up, he told me to stay inside, and then said he had to leave."

Laes drew a deep, patient breath, leaving his place to move behind Nessix. His eyes held a predatory focus on his friend as his hands latched around the back of Nes's chair. "You stayed in your room, then?"

Veed scowled and shook his head, despite the confusion it drew from Nessix. Laes had good reason to accuse Veed of foul acts, given his past, but the implications he made of his own daughter? Subjecting Nessix to this torture put the final twist in Veed's stomach. Swallowing his reservations and concepts of self-preservation, Veed snapped his eyes to meet the general's.

"She does not need an interrogation, sir."

"Nessix, you will keep telling me," Laes commanded, ignoring Veed's attempt to leap to Nes's rescue. "Everything that happened before you went to sleep." He sent a pointed look at Veed. "And I want it in your own words."

Nessix straightened slowly at her father's tone and glanced between the stony faces that usually held so much warmth toward her. Her brows stitched closer to each other as an air of contempt swirled about her.

"Inwan left." She dictated her words with care, in case her

previous statement had somehow been misunderstood. "And I started to log my report. The storm rolled in and Veed came by to tell me he had to leave. After the warning Inwan gave me, I wasn't about to let him head out."

"So Commander Astaldt stayed with you?" Laes pressed.

"Yes."

"By whose suggestion?"

Nessix shook her head. "By my *order*. He wanted to leave and I told him he couldn't. I don't understand why this is such a big deal; you wouldn't have let him leave, either." She paused to see if her father would confirm her assumption. When he stayed silent, she sighed in irritation. "He put up a bit of a fight on the matter, but in the end, I convinced him he wouldn't be allowed to go out in the storm."

Laes glared across the table as Veed stared at his plate as if it would offer him sanctuary. Was that guilt he displayed? Shame? Nes's report had flowed off innocent lips, and she had no history of lying to her father.

"You don't have to protect him," Laes murmured at last.

"Protect him?" A delicate confusion swept across Nes's face and she shook her head before the reality of her father's accusations dawned on her. Her cheeks drained of color and she half rose in her seat to turn to Laes, a disgusted scowl twisting her face. "What is it you're saying?"

Laes balked at the heat backing her words. Always obedient, always adoring, Nessix had never used such a tone against him before, but Laes refused to allow any disappointment in himself to exceed his concern. "I'm saying that Veed has gone a long time without the company of a woman—"

"And you think—" She shot a quick glance over her shoulder, lost eyes questioning Veed as to whether or not he knew they were being judged in this manner. "You would think so low of us?" While Laes struggled with coordinating his tongue to stammer a reply, Nessix growled a murmur of distaste and forced her small frame against the chair until she had room to rise in full. "I love you, Father, but it's repulsive that you'd imagine such shame of me."

It was the first time in Veed's recollection that Nessix stood up to her father, and Laes stared at her, muted and stunned both by her bold declaration and his faulty assumptions that had launched her over the edge. Nessix's apparent opinion of Laes's insinuations was conveyed with too much honesty to permit questioning any hidden motives to keep Veed safe. She didn't return a look to Veed, nor did she spare another glance at her father as she pushed her way out of the room. Brant sprang to his feet to dart after her.

A small swell of victory rallied in Veed's core as Laes's devastated eyes tracked Nes's exit. "Calling your daughter a whore," he sneered. "I hope you're proud of yourself." With nothing else left to say, Veed also vacated the dining hall, chased by angry demands for his return.

Veed disregarded Laes's furious orders and strode back to the safety of his quarters. He knew better than to follow Nessix and Brant to wherever the girl had run off to. His concern, regardless of its degree and purity, would only broaden the violent path which Laes's irrationally decisive mind crashed down. Veed wasn't a coward by any stretch of the imagination, but neither was he stupid. Given time, Laes would find his calm, but until that happened, Veed resigned to keep his head down to avoid receiving any more cheap shots.

Reaching his quarters without incident, Veed passed the rest of the evening lying on his bed, scouring the ceiling for answers that couldn't possibly exist. After the previous night's discussion, he saved himself the effort of asking Inwan what went wrong, and Veed wasn't even convinced he wanted to find out at all. His head pounded with the barrage of accusations strapped to him, with the conclusions Brant and Laes had made, the reports delivered by that planted soldier. What role had Inwan played in all of this?

Veed groaned and rubbed his forehead. Out of all the trouble he'd squeaked his way out of in the past, why couldn't he see a way free now? At least he found solace in Nes's defense of them both. If Veed knew Laes at all—and despite the allegations pending against him, he was sure he did—the general would fold on the issue soon. Nessix's appalled reaction spoke for itself and Laes was too smart to not realize the intimate role he'd played in drawing it out.

Preferring to contemplate the evening with a clear and sober mind, Veed opted against consulting his wine rack for guidance. The silence in his room begged to challenge his choice of sobriety when the floor gently protested the weight of a moving body. Veed blinked and held his breath to listen more carefully. The arsenal of thoughts which battered his mind assured he hadn't nodded off, and the locked door hadn't opened since he secured it upon his arrival. Veed sneered. At this point, he almost expected Laes to try planting spies to monitor his actions, even if it involved invading his private quarters. Part of Veed almost hoped for the situation to develop as far as an assassination attempt so he could release his steam and fight back. Maybe that would send a clear message to his old friend.

Either way, Veed ran out of patience to tolerate any further discussions somewhere between the first time Laes struck him and the general's callous treatment of Nes's emotions. If whoever lurked in the room with him had orders to watch him, they were in for a dull evening. If they had any greater plans, well, he'd just see how much repressed anger the past few hours had generated and act accordingly.

The floor creaked again, plucking at Veed's curiosity. Any spy or assassin worth receiving payment wouldn't have made that mistake twice, which meant the intruder didn't care if he knew of their presence. The creaks gave way to distinct steps, cat-like strides accented by the click of a woman wearing heels. Veed frowned, gaze darkening as he continued staring at the ceiling. So *this* was supposed to solve his problem?

Veed didn't bother to look around the room, keeping his focus directed at the rafters. "I don't appreciate whatever effort's being made here," he warned. "Whoever sent you for whatever reason, you'll just have to accept that I'm not interested."

"I came here myself."

The voice crept through the room, cool and calm and delicately feminine, and it belonged to a woman Veed didn't know. Brows furrowing, his eyes spun into sharp focus at last. Women of Elidae approached him often, each dazzled by his station and reputation, unable to hide their hopes of making it as far as his private quarters. But this woman invaded Veed's privacy without a hint of that familiar desire. He still had no idea how or why she was in his room, but the authority in her voice assured her motives didn't involve the more exhilarating activities that happened in his chamber. Setting his jaw, Veed rolled to his side and sat up to face this intruder.

There was no woman in his room. He straightened slowly and cleared his throat.

"Perhaps I didn't make myself clear," he said, voice maintaining its calm, despite his mind's ominous warning that this marked the beginning of madness. "I'm in no mood for games." He refrained from expressing the aggressive insults and accusations he'd have thrown at a less mysterious guest. Even unable to see her, he heard this woman clearly, and her presence stifled the air around him. A chill blew across the back of his damp neck as gentle laughter floated through the chamber.

"You think I'm just an average woman? I'm not here for what you think."

In a flash, a brief whisper of time which slipped free of Veed's grasp, the woman appeared beside his bed. Elegant fingers traced their way along his shoulder and down his arm before he grabbed her wrist to force her a step back. His glower aimed to hold her at bay, but faltered at the glitter behind exotic purple eyes and chin length silver hair. Her lips closed in a dissatisfied scowl.

"It is not wise to take your disappointments out on others," she warned, snatching her hand free from his grasp. "Especially those you do not know."

Veed sneered. "Do not lecture me in disappointment."

She twisted her head to the side and studied Veed with a deep, intelligent gaze he flinched from. "You are hurting."

A bitter chuckle attempted to hide Veed's discomfort. Shoving her back another step, he sprang to his feet. "What is your purpose here? I will not tolerate mockery."

"Mockery!" Melodic laughter echoed Veed's sour humor. "No, my dear, I'm not here to mock you." She appraised him with those critical lavender eyes. "I feel for you."

"Pretty words won't take my mind from where it's settled," Veed said. "I know why you're here, and I know where such reports will end up. I've no use for any of that."

She crossed her arms, lighting her smirk with a challenge. "Why am I here?"

"To prove my weakness as a man and give Laes more fire against me. He thinks he can prove my indecency."

She gasped—a gesture even this suppressed version of Veed found insincere—at his statement, pressing a hand to her chest. "I am *here* to sympathize for your loss!"

Veed pinched his lips together and closed his eyes, trying to dig up the patience to deal with whatever was happening here. "To sympathize with me?" he spat. "What do you know of what I'm going through?"

"Good people are always the ones trod upon and taken advantage of. They're the ones who never get what they deserve." The intensity of her gaze shifted at last, swelling with a depth Veed couldn't quite consider warmth. "I lost all that I love in my life, and it seems you've been treated the same. How can I *not* feel for you?"

Veed stared into those foreign eyes, eyes devoid of relatable emotion and deep enough to lose even the most valiant of men in a storm of doubtfulness. He'd trusted his instincts his entire life and credited them for the man he'd become, and right now, those instincts told Veed this woman posed a danger greater than he'd first assessed. The calm smile she slid him coincided perfectly with that realization, solidifying his eerie notion.

"I am done talking to you," he said abruptly. Unable to gauge this woman's integrity or the limit of her power, Veed refused to engage in her game. "Leave me alone."

She shook her head, a crooked smile settling on her face. "You cannot deny a heart in love, and I will not deny yours."

She hadn't attempted another advance on Veed, content standing just out of his reach, and perhaps that was what hooked his interest through the tumult of anger and regret. The sincerity etched between her brows, even if absent from the glint of her eyes, tugged at Veed, vowing it was safe to trust her. He crossed his arms.

"What do you know of me?" He stepped back to lean against the edge of his bed.

"More than you ought to be comfortable with." She gave a dainty shrug and watched him sit, still not moving from her position. "Be neither surprised nor startled that I know of your affection for young Nessix."

That chill returned, this time brushing over Veed's arms as his mind sharpened back to clarity. No matter how angry Laes was with him and how indecent Veed thought Inwan was, that sort of insight should not have made it to any remotely public avenue. Veed himself would see this woman dead before he let Nessix be involved in whatever she was after.

"How did you get in here?" he growled.

"If you want my assistance, you will leave the questions to me." Her gaze hardened and lodged a splinter of insecurity in Veed's heart, but he gave no implication of reacting quite yet. She smiled. "Do be aware that I'm capable of both ensuring your safety for eternity or ending it in the blink of an eye. Doubt me, if you will, but know that I won't serve those who won't serve me."

Laes had lost interest in pursuing any form of the magical arts or those who specialized in their use before he'd even met Veed, and Inwan routinely promised the flemans that they had no need to worry about employing such measures. Veed longed to demand for this woman to identify herself, but the same instincts which had gained him his station insisted he heed her demand for no further questions. Instead, he met her eyes, searching as deeply as she allowed him, and a firm ring of calm wound its way around him, embracing him in a reminder of the courage which made him the frightful opponent he'd always been. Words failing him, Veed lowered his head at last. He might have preserved Nes's integrity and favor, but with both Brant and Laes now against him, Sulik soon to follow, Veed knew his chances to find peace were limited. Emotionally battered, he opted to listen to this strange woman's proposal.

"How much does that young woman mean to you?" she asked at last.

"I would die for her."

Her brows raised in approval of the conviction which drove Veed's immediate reply and a delicious smile crossed her lips. "Ah, yes. But would you kill for her?"

Veed grasped his elbows and raised his chin. "I have before and I would again, without a second thought." He couldn't tell if this was a threat or an invitation, but a twisted glow of hope pulsed its way to life inside of him.

"Then we might be able to make ourselves a little deal..."

She still made no advance on Veed, casually keeping a respectful distance. Veed's heart beat at an unusual rate for something as simple as a conversation, as though preparing for combat. His fingers clenched around his sleeves as he debated who his opponent was meant to be.

"Go on," he said.

The woman moved now, hands clasped behind her back as she wandered over to look out the window. She turned back to face Veed after a brief observation of Elidae's dusky fields. "How would you like to get your way for a change?" she asked, meandering his way. "To have your hard work and dedication to this land finally pay off? To finally get the appreciation and recognition you're due?"

As Veed looked into her fathomless eyes, he felt his mind slip toward a frightening void. "I *am* appreciated." Laes had valid reason to safeguard Nessix, and as much as it gutted Veed to admit it, he understood that much.

"You deserve Nessix," this woman scolded, shaking her head at him. "You've been good to her father. You've been good to *her*. If you work with me, you will win her. She'll come to you willingly and lovingly, without fear of repercussions. The two of you would have a future together, any one you want to make."

Veed didn't know why he bothered entertaining this woman and her tempting tongue in the first place. He was a smart man with a sound mind. She had unknowingly gained access to his chamber, knew things about him she had no way of knowing, yet somehow, that same brilliant, rational mind screamed at Veed to accept her implied promises, no matter how firmly his heart stood against them. The closer she inched toward him, the more he craved the indulgence of her beautiful words, and the more obtainable they sounded. What it came down to was that she was right. Veed deserved Nessix, and he'd do anything to have her.

"I'm listening."

A breathy sigh enhanced Shand's smile and her eyes darkened into liquid pools of deceit. "Only one man stands in your way," she murmured, slipping a narrow vial into Veed's hand. "One I have my own reasons to get rid of..."

NINETEEN

History had forgotten the time when Kol boasted one of the strongest political minds on all of Abaeloth, but he hadn't. It was what allowed him to remain among the most influential of the alar and to maintain authority over such intricate projects as the one he'd harvested Nessix to complete. It also gave him sound intelligence to know when to keep his opinions to himself. The rank he'd carved out through his years of ass kissing and hard work had secured his position beneath Grell, and where the inoga went, Kol was typically expected to follow. He learned early on to hoard away his thoughts during the dysfunctional meetings between these greater demons, and contented himself to sit quietly in his seat, hands encircled around the bottom of Nessix's prison as she spun about in a brilliant fire of irritation.

Could she hear what they talked about? Of the future the demons had planned for her dear Elidae? Kol had interrogated plenty of his first trials once they regained the ability to speak, but none confirmed any sense of coherence at this stage. As Nessix churned into brighter shades of red as talk of demon occupation continued, Kol gave the jar a brief rattle to redirect her fury. It had to have been a coincidence. Nessix settled herself into a grumpy indigo and Kol sighed.

"And how much longer do we have to wait?" Inek, an inoga

so obese it baffled Kol how he managed to take up arms at all, demanded. "That blasted snow's melting and the puny flemans have been growing tender in their homes. We should move *now*."

Ehsmil chuckled and shook his head. Intelligence was a rare commodity among inoga these days, as they preferred to rely on brutish strength and size to control those they deemed inferior. Fortunately for the sake of tactics, Ehsmil had been a scholar in his mortal life. On good days, he still was. "We need to wait to see what Shand plays next."

Inek spat and sneered across the table. "Grell was stupid to let her go when he had her."

"*I* was stupid?" Grell growled. The legs of his stool griped at the abrupt shift of his weight.

Kol sighed and gathered up Nessix as he stood. In that same moment, Grell flipped the table at Inek and rushed ahead. Shaking his head at the incompetent hierarchy he was forced to serve under, Kol backed up to the wall to remove himself and Nessix from the impromptu brawl.

The drive for power had gone to the heads of all inoga and leached the concepts of honor and reason from them. Kol watched fists fly between his lord and Inek, well past the point of cringing at the sound of crushed noses and the snaps of breaking limbs. He glanced at his charge, tracing a vein of brilliant green crackling through her confines. He narrowed his eyes and adjusted his hold on the jar, allowing Nessix a better view of the rumble. Coincidence or not, the degree of cognizance she appeared to command intrigued Kol. If Nessix truly was capable of observation in her current state, allowing her to gather insight now may prove beneficial in the future. Once this meeting and its subsequent hazards had concluded, Kol would sit down and talk at her about her options and his expectations.

After the exchange of a few good blows from both parties, Ehsmil and Turit, the largest of the inoga stationed for Elidae's occupation, had their fill of the scuffle and dragged their comrades off each other. Inek flailed for Grell's neck, and Grell spit a mouthful of blood at the other demon. Turit barked a harsh reprimand and drove Kol's lord up against the wall until Grell regained control over his desire for combat and relaxed.

Kol sighed again.

Ehsmil released Inek and backed away from the frazzled demon, hands open and arms positioned to grapple him again if necessary. "What matters right now is seeing what she will do next. In all things, we must remember that she is a goddess and betraying her will not come without consequence."

Inek grumbled and scorched Grell with a haughty glare as the only winged inoga in the room clomped his way to the toppled table. He righted it again, grunting as it tipped on a broken leg. Too impatient to attempt manipulating balance from it, Grell gave it a shove and let it crash back to the floor. With one ear trained on Inek, Grell walked up to Kol, who lowered his head in respect born of his desire to keep all of his limbs attached to his body.

"Alright then." Grell leaned a shoulder against the wall and crossed his arms. "We have to wait on Shand. So what can we do? You figured out what to do with *her* yet?" Grell turned his glare to the swirling mist contained in Kol's jar.

Kol looked over the other three inoga, demons he shared little history with. Out of all of them, he only trusted Ehsmil's logic, and Kol banked on the fact that his research was important enough for Grell to protect him from the others, at least for now. Claiming the right to brag about the army Kol and his cohorts were building looked too impressive for Grell to risk messing up.

"Yes, sir," Kol replied evenly. "But forward progress with her hinges on a few key factors."

Grell grunted at the prospect of complications. In his simple mind, this operation should have been successful and done with months ago. "What do you need?"

"Nessix is not just another trial and her revival must be conducted with care. I cannot proceed with her until the snow melts, to start with. We'll have to launch some sort of disorder within the flemans—something to keep them distracted. And I'll need to determine the most aggressive of the priestesses."

Grell nodded with each of the first two conditions, but stopped at the last. "You mean the ones in the cells?" When Kol nodded, Grell bellowed with laughter. "They're all such timid things. You expect to find aggression in *them*?"

"I don't have any other choice. If reports from our troops on Gelthin are accurate, Zeal has recalled most of the clergy and are on high alert. I doubt we'll get another chance to harvest fresh options anytime soon."

Inek snorted. "You want aggressive? Someone should go snatch up that pretty Julianna. Get us some more Sagewinds in this realm."

Kol closed his eyes, temper beating against the foolishness of crossing an inoga. "If you think the High Priestess is an ideal prospect, I'd be delighted for you, Inek, to bring her to me."

Grell belted out another laugh. "And wouldn't that cause all sorts of problems for our good friend Mathias! His sister and his lover in one body. Ha!"

The rest of the inoga romped right off the only topic Kol cared about, spurting lewd thoughts he had no interest thinking about. He flicked another glance at Nessix. She swam with a muted yellow of uncertainty, spinning at a slower, insecure rate. No. This couldn't be a coincidence. Kol had theorized from the moment he first saw Nessix in life that she harbored something unique inside her, a trait she proved more by the day. Now, Kol had to hope he could forge that zest into an obedient, useful servant. One he wouldn't regret bringing back to life. Kol frowned, tucked Nes's jar into its pouch, and left the room.

* * * * *

Just as in the days when Veed still held influence over circumstances which concerned him, guilt overran his remaining emotions. This cold had worn on him. His position trapped in a fortress and surrounded by an army which resented his very existence had stripped away the confidence which allowed him to feel he was in control of the world around him. Having these memories reawaken… Now that devastated him. As long as external conditions rendered him immobile, pinned between Inwan's knowing glare and the suspicions from Mathias and Brant, Veed had no access to peace. He'd made mistakes in his life, horrible ones he never bothered to dwell on until now, but loving Nessix hadn't been one of them. The only way to escape the crushing past was to face it.

Against his better judgement, Veed requested a meeting with Mathias and his officers, vowing to put an end to the ignorance that had prolonged this war. He approached the war chamber, disregarding the nagging voice that warned him how much he'd regret this. A gentle baritone of voices rumbled from behind the door, and the twist in his gut told Veed it wasn't too late to stand them up. Even if he chose to flee this discussion, where would he go? He couldn't simply hide in this fortress, not with them expecting to hear what he wanted to say. Veed sneered at how his mind had shriveled during these weeks of neglect and silent torture. Unfamiliar with the feeling of self-doubt, Veed yanked the door open before he could attempt to talk himself out of it.

The conversation halted abruptly, Sulik's voice clipping to a stop as four sets of eyes set across stony faces leapt up at Veed's entry. Brant and Inwan each flanked the seat Nessix once occupied. Sulik sat between Brant and Mathias, leaving only one chair vacant. Centered across from the panel before him, Veed placed his hand on the back of the seat, still silent. His heart sang a valiant petition for his eyes to stray to the empty chair to Brant's right, but Veed staunchly forbid opening that door. An invitation wouldn't come to him, so Veed pulled the chair back to take his seat. He cleared his throat, folded his hands on the tabletop, and bowed his head.

Silence persisted, gnawing at the artificial calm Veed had concocted for the occasion. The other men waited for him to speak, as they'd gathered on behalf of his request. Now, all Veed had to do was find some way to force his words out. The travesties locked up in his head had burned inside him for too long. Veed kept his face directed at the table, but shot a brief glance at the paladin.

Mathias scorned Veed with righteous eyes which vaunted of justice and wisdom. The same justice that had failed Nessix. The same wisdom that had allowed her to die. Detestation was a mild word to describe Veed's opinion of this man, and his reliance on Mathias only dug that intense hatred deeper. After all, this righteous clod was Veed's best chance at finding answers about Nes's fate.

Veed scowled at himself over his prickling nerves, curling his booted toes to keep from squirming from the knowledge he alone carried. Why should *he*—the mighty and intrepid Veed Astaldt—be afraid of this room of broken men? He couldn't flex away his tension, confirming the suspicion that picked at him over the past several days. Even hiding behind an accumulation of pride and valor, Veed was no less broken than anyone else in this room. He studied his hands as they sat clasped atop the table and breathed in a ragged sigh. Choking on his instinctual desire to rehash past disputes with Mathias, Veed approached his objective as civilly as his grudges allowed.

"I'm not behind this, but I know who is."

There were several replies Veed had prepared himself to deal with—physical attacks, furious demands, pointed accusations, even the faint possibility of an outburst of relief—but he hadn't anticipated silence. He gulped past the ringing in his ears and pulled his eyes up from the table to meet gaping mouths and wide eyes. Of the four other men, only Brant showed any sort of reaction, his eyes pinched shut and lips twitching as if fighting an outburst.

It still stood to be seen whether or not Veed knew about the fragility of Brant's mental state, but Mathias was not so callous as to expose it intentionally. He knew Brant was preoccupied battling Nessix's badgering for more information, and Mathias would beat Brant to demands for Veed to elaborate. After all, he loved Nessix, too.

"Then tell us."

Brant blew out a rapid sigh at Mathias's words and blinked his eyes open.

The chance to back out of this conversation now past, Veed struggled to grasp a firm heading. His eyes darted through the room, not necessarily from fear of the men present, but of those forces unseen to mortal eyes. "Is your goddess protecting this chamber?"

Mathias crossed his arms, watching Veed through narrowed eyes. That hadn't sounded like a threat, but reminded Mathias of

Etha's current absence. "She's with me," he said, believing it as truth, regardless of her current silence. "And so far, you're the only evil I've been able to—"

Veed snarled and leaned over the table. "*I* am evil?"

"How else can you justify your indecency to Nes?"

That propelled Veed to his feet and he slammed his fists against the tabletop. "Indecency? I *loved* her!"

Mathias rose to meet Veed's aggression, fist crumpling the corner of the map in front of him. Beside him, Brant jerked his head to the side, lips working rapidly through his side of a hushed debate. "Don't you start with what Nessix meant to you."

Too focused on Mathias's opposition, Veed paid no mind to the insane commander. "She meant more to me than she could have ever—"

"You were the bane of her existence! She loathed you!"

"She loathed my power." These past weeks holed up amid more pure memories of when honor and honesty meant something to Veed backed his declaration. "You can never take loyalty from a fleman."

Mathias braced himself against the table and hissed, struggling to keep his patience under control. "*Loyalty*?" he seethed. "Is that what you call it?"

"You couldn't begin to understand."

Aching fingers uncoiled from the crumpled map and Mathias's darkened glare bore deep into Veed. "Nessix meant more to me than you'll ever know," he growled. "I cared for her. *I* never raped her."

Those words lanced a tortured cry from Brant as he dropped his head in his hands. Going into this meeting, nobody had expected a particularly peaceful exchange, but with the situation unravelling at an alarming rate, Sulik sprang to his feet and pounded a fist on the table, glaring between the two generals.

"Neither of you are solving anything!"

The words filtered through Mathias's conscience, heedless of his desire to assert himself over Veed and coaxing his internal reactions closer to normal. For the sake of whatever information Veed intended to share and the benefits uncovering it would give the war, Mathias clenched down on his final remarks and cast his gaze aside.

Ever willing to spurn decorum, Veed snatched the opportunity to claim the last word. "Better her body than her mind."

Mathias's head snapped up, fury alight in his eyes at Veed's disregard toward the weight of his crime. Sulik held a hand up in front of the paladin to prevent him from jumping back into the scuffle. Forcing a firm breath, Mathias grit his teeth and turned his head to meet Sulik's eyes. The commander's lips pressed disapprovingly, eyes schooled with harshness he hadn't pulled out in years, and he shook his head. Mathias prayed for composure, disappointed by the rate which it trickled into him. Damn it all, Mathias needed to keep Veed willing to talk. He slammed back down in his chair, allowing Sulik a tentative breath of relief.

"Fine," Mathias seethed. "This chamber is the second most secure location on the island." He didn't know that with certainty—Etha hadn't yet chimed in with such assurance—but Mathias had few qualms with the idea of lying to Veed. "If you have any information that will help us, you owe it to Nes."

Adrenaline settled in Veed's system, and his eyes tracked Sulik as he left his post by Mathias to console Brant. Veed closed his eyes and sighed. This simple meeting had already launched astray from his plan, hindering his ability to rely on the course he'd calculated and its expected reactions. Ultimately, none of these complications made a difference to Veed; he planned on leaving the Teradhel fortress at the earliest opportunity. He'd return to his army and continue this asinine war to defeat the demons. As much as he hated to admit it, Mathias was right. Victory relied on the information locked inside of him, and Veed should have disclosed it to Nessix that first time she'd gone to him with reports of demons.

"There's another goddess," he said slowly. "A filthy, manipulative bitch named—"

"Shand."

A fearsome chill possessed Mathias's voice, one nobody in the chamber had heard from him before. It rivaled the vehemence he'd thrown at Veed the night after he'd manipulated Nessix into submission, but his hatred found its roots someplace far deeper than a conflict of morality. Veed blinked, unsure how to handle Mathias's fury directed toward someone other than himself.

"You... know her?" Veed asked.

Mathias stared at the table, the slow shake of his head scolding his own ignorance. More power hungry than any of her peers and one of the few gods who had a direct history with him, Shand's involvement in this war made too much sense. How hadn't he seen this sooner? A new thought struck Mathias, one that took immediate concern off this oversight. Veed still had secrets, more interesting ones than Mathias had originally anticipated.

"Do you?" he asked.

All eyes fell on Veed, expecting enlightenment from the answer to Mathias's question. Even Brant pulled his gaze up to scour him, brandishing Nes's judgement alongside his own. Veed swallowed the tickle of remorse from his throat, holding their gazes with the strongest front he could manage. Not even his strongest efforts could keep his eyes from stinging with reflections of the truth he never wanted to face again. "Yes."

Mathias sighed out his initial response to do away with Veed here and now, committing himself to extract every last detail Veed had hidden from the flemans he'd sworn to protect. "Would you care explaining how?"

Veed did mind explaining himself, increasingly so. He didn't need these patronizing glares or to hear Brant's crazed mumbling to know that much. "I..." Veed looked away, mind clawing for excuses that fluttered just beyond reach. Resigned to the fool's path now that he'd set down it, Veed kept his eyes from those around him. "I had a run in with her several years ago."

"And what did she want?"

Mathias's question hit without a flicker of hesitation, as though he knew a deal had been made. Veed had been a fool back then, and he was one now. Of *course* Mathias had put things together. The bastard lived in the divine realm. He communed with gods, apparently frightened a fair share of them, too. Veed forbid Mathias's unique position to stop him from trying to protect himself; he'd delivered the important part of his message, the one that made a difference. The only part he'd have been able to tell Nessix.

"I never said she wanted anything."

"Shand wouldn't have wasted her time on a man like you unless she could work it into her own agenda." Mathias's tone, the familiarity with which he spat his opinion of Shand's character, uncovered a hateful dimension of the paladin he'd kept well hidden from others. He stood poised over the table, tearing bricks down from Veed's walls. A moment later, his brows rose as the truth—at least part of it—registered. "Blessed Mother…" he muttered with a shake of his head. "Shand's where your divine gifts come from. Am I right?"

Brant's rambling clipped to a sudden stop at Mathias's question, and his head snapped up to gauge Veed's tangible level of guilt.

Veed found a certain degree of comfort in peril and had thrown himself into some of the most dangerous situations a man could ever expect to face. He needed only one hand to count the number of times he'd experienced genuine fear, and under the eyes of these experienced officers, his racing heart spurred a shameful desire to flee from this discussion. Given the number of opponents he faced, Veed discarded escape as a viable option, and it would take little more than a shout for backup for guards to complicate matters. Veed bowed his head and buckled down for the inevitable. He'd run from this for too long.

Looking up after the silence threatened to pick holes in his trembling resolve, Veed met Mathias's eyes with steeled deliberation. "Yes."

Mathias shook his head again, accompanied this time by a caustic laugh. *How* had he not seen this? "So what did you give her in return?"

Veed clamped a firm fist around the rapid drumming of his heart. "What makes you think she wanted anything from *a man like me?*"

"Because Shand does *nothing* without gain to herself," Mathias said. He allowed Veed the span of two heated breaths to continue his case. As usual, he met disappointment. "Did she get you to scout out the safest locations for the demons' portals?"

Veed's eyes darted away as his heart pounded free from his attempt to confine it. He shook his head.

"Offer them cover as they gained their foothold?"

"No." Veed flinched at the crack in his voice.

Mathias's eyes flashed, searing the scraps of confidence Veed clung to. "Did you have anything at all to do with the ambush that killed Nessix?"

Shaken or not, that was one accusation Veed refused to tolerate, and before sense grabbed a hold of his pride to restrain him, Veed slammed his fist into the table. "I killed Laes!"

The briefest silence embraced the room as the confession penetrated its occupants, interrupted only by Sulik's gasp and the sound of Veed's ragged breathing. He kept his head bowed as the shock of his outburst siphoned through his system. Blood pounded in his ears, blaring a firm order for him to find his calm or lose his consciousness. Veed blew out a sharp breath, struck by a cascade of conflicting emotions, and threw his weight back in his seat. He raised his gaze to meet blank eyes. All but Brant's.

"I'm not proud of it." Veed's voice cracked again and he raised weakened hands in a feeble bid for placation. Not that he expected it to do him any good. "It's why I left. I killed Laes to be with…" He couldn't finish his rush to defend his foul action. Not this time. Lips numb, he forgot why he ever thought this confession was a good idea.

While the others reeled over what this meant, Brant already knew. It was what he'd known all along. Tearing his gaze from the center of the table, Brant dragged his absent eyes to Veed, who looked as though he'd just been run through.

"Give me the order," Brant whispered.

The past weeks of anger and hurt, of sleeplessness, caught up to Brant all at once, shoving him to the edge of the realms of his sanity. And then, Nes's order hit him, cold and fierce.

You put him in the ground.

Brant stepped over that ledge.

Alive in an instant, Brant launched himself over the table. He crashed his way through wine glasses and tactical pawns, tearing maps in his mad scramble. Veed had been too stunned by his own foolishness to foresee this reaction, and Brant's hands wrapped around his neck before anyone so much as stood to intervene. The commander drove his weight into Veed, tipping the chair over to throw them to the ground. Brant crushed his grip tighter around the throat of the man he once idolized and slammed his head against the floor.

Rallying instinct to seek defense at last, Veed reached up to grab Brant's arms, desperate to free his windpipe. Possessed by bloodlust thanks to Nes's savage encouragement, Brant's desire to kill Veed belittled the man's drive to survive. The commander drew his right fist back, allowing Veed to suck in a quick breath, before connecting a punch square in his face. That precious breath fled Veed as he cried out against the strike, the nip of blood passing over his tongue as it ran down his nasal passages. Aborting his attempt to gain control, Veed raised his arms to try protecting his face as Brant pulled back for another strike.

By now, only Inwan remained seated, indifferent to the commotion around him. Sulik started to rush around the table to intercept Brant's violence, but Mathias grasped his arm, pulling him to a stop before he managed to travel a full stride. The commander looked to the just and gentle human, color draining from his face.

A perverse pleasure illuminated Mathias's eyes, the slightest hint of a justified smile pulling at his lips. Each strike Brant landed sapped part of what Sulik recognized in Mathias, and the paladin indulged himself on this brutal punishment until Veed's pleas for mercy no longer came in complete and coherent statements.

Mathias channeled his rage and loathing into the force of a fist clenched at his side as he let go of Sulik and strode around the table. The commander followed behind with the foolish notion of intercepting any offensive actions his mentor might try. Once Mathias reached the tangle of men, he cocked his head, savoring the sight of Veed's bloodied face. Speckles of blood accompanied each of Veed's gasps and the light of terror flooding his eyes delighted Mathias on a disgusting level he'd never experienced before.

Etha should have been there to remind Mathias that Veed still had information. She should have soothed him, telling him that while Veed deserved to be punished, it should not culminate in this sort of brutality. But Etha remained silent. That realization plucked the morbid joy from Mathias, and he caught Brant's arm as it drew back for another swing.

It took the commander a single breath—and they fell rapidly—to redirect his attention to Mathias, but the paladin caught his other arm as Brant sprang to his feet.

"Let me go, you son of a bitch!" Brant sputtered, throwing himself against Mathias's hold like a deadly child caught in a tantrum. "He will die by my hand!"

"No, he won't." Mathias conveniently left out the fact that he wouldn't allow Veed to die until he had the chance to settle the score himself.

"She told me to!" Brant sobbed, his struggles ebbing as exhaustion hailed him. "She wants him dead!"

Mathias squared his hold on Brant and tried unsuccessfully to meet his eyes. "He might still have information for us."

"Fuck his information!"

"Brant!"

"He will *die*! She ordered it!"

Mathias's lips tucked in a grimace. Brant's hysterics prevented him from listening to reason, leaving Mathias few options. "Then Nessix will just have to trust me. Veed will have his time, but right now, he needs to live."

Brant roared and flailed against Mathias once again before ugly weeping drained the strength from him. Sulik inched closer to grasp Brant's shoulders and Mathias briefly nodded his gratitude as he released his hold on Brant. The young man slumped over, staggering backward as Sulik eased him to perch on the edge of the table.

Even the most remote sense of cordial conduct demanded Mathias at least offer to help Veed up after the thorough beating he'd suffered. Instead, Mathias crossed his arms and concentrated against his urge to spit on the wretch at his feet.

Veed's chest heaved violently and it took him several

moments of cowering on the floor to realize he was no longer in danger. Groaning, he eased himself to his side and spat out a mouthful of blood. Ever aware of the nearness between his face and Mathias's foot and how steeply the odds currently stacked against him, Veed kept his head bowed and his thoughts to himself.

"Do you have anything else to share?" Mathias asked once it became evident that Veed was not about to offer anything on his own accord. Such a pity. The first time Veed attempted decency, things had to end this way.

Veed ran his tongue along the backs of his teeth, hunting out damage. He sent a spiteful glare up at Mathias, one that almost aimed to threaten him.

Mathias frowned. "And to think, all it took was a beating to silence you. We could have arranged this months ago if I'd have known."

Intermittent mumbling and Sulik's good nature preoccupied Brant, temporarily alleviating Veed's concern of a second round. He centered his attention on Mathias. "You pathetic ingrate," he growled, gasping against a cracked rib. "You will not threaten me, not after what I just told you."

Mathias turned away to fend off his impulse to kick Veed to the floor again. "What you just told me was that you are the reason Nessix lost her hope."

Veed shoved himself to a seated position, hissing against the aches of his trauma. "It hadn't been my idea, not something I'd asked or even wanted to do."

Inwan leapt to his feet at last, his scowl harboring hints of divine fury he hadn't grasped since his return. "That doesn't make it any less your fault it happened!"

Veed clenched his fists, not daring to turn away from the threat posed by Mathias. He narrowed his darkened eyes, tipping his chin toward his shoulder to address the god who loomed behind him. "*You* cannot judge me. Not after—"

Mathias pelted a laugh laced with bitter arrogance. "Of course he can. In fact, I welcome it."

Veed clenched his teeth, brown eyes ablaze. If he'd trusted his body's ability to obey him, he'd have jumped up to punch Mathias in that smug face. "You have no right—"

"I have *every* right!" Mathias shouted, silencing even Brant's murmuring. "I am Etha's avatar, and I will do whatever I deem fit. This is my commander's home by right, my army you're mingling with, and my mother's blessed land you've fouled with your lust. I will ask you once more. Do you have anything else worthwhile to share?"

The time spent wasting away in the Teradhel fortress had destroyed much more than Veed's mental fortitude; it had eroded his sharp mind that should have seen all of this coming. Veed owed nothing to these miserable worms. Mind spoken more than he should have allowed, Veed was through with his audience. The only thing left for him to claim was the pride he'd cultivated from the years spent building his kingdom, and it was that pride he used to push himself to his feet. He cradled his side with his left arm and leaned his right against the table for support. Despite the rapid swelling of his left eye and the whirlpool in his head, Veed met Mathias with familiar hatred.

"I've got one last thing for you," he growled.

Mathias crossed his arms, narrowed eyes piercing at Veed's air of conceit. "And what's that?"

"You can torment me. You can beat me. You might even see me dead. But you will always have to carry with you the knowledge that Nessix came to me willingly. And I had her first."

Sulik leapt to reach Mathias just in time to intercept his lunge toward Veed. From the start, Mathias had staunchly claimed that the war needed Veed on the field, whether or not anybody wanted him there, and with emotions raging so high, Sulik appointed himself to ensure Veed would make it to the next battle. Mathias permitted Sulik's restraint, allowing the commander to relax.

Those words had been Veed's final blow, the extent of what little strength remained in him. And somehow, it still didn't make him feel better. Hiding behind a swollen smirk and a pompous chuckle, Veed turned to exit the chamber, keeping an ear on the positions of the men he left stunned in the room.

The door fell shut

TWENTY

Strictly on the most practical level, Mathias understood Veed's reasons for coming clean the way he had. The same stress Mathias's resolve creaked under—trapped with these memories, unable to make progress on the warfront—had crushed the foul man beneath its burdens, delivering a slew of additional concerns to try sorting into place. If not for Mathias's age and experience, he suspected he'd have also cracked by now, but his determination and commitment to Elidae forbid such an emotional response.

"How do you want to proceed?"

Mathias whipped around at the sound of Etha's voice, gripping the edge of his desk to keep from reaching for his sword. He hadn't noticed her presence in the room until she spoke, and Mathias heaved a sigh at how distracted he'd been.

"I don't know." He shook his head and gave a halfhearted shrug. "We should have seen this from the start."

Etha watched Mathias's thoughts zip through his mind and pinched her lips together. His hatred of Veed wrapped around him so tightly that his long-standing rivalry with Shand seemed to be forgotten. This was not the time for Mathias to lose focus on the root of this war. Etha frowned and walked over to him.

"Do you think we can trust him?" She rested a hand on his shoulder.

"In this?" The bite behind his laugh melted at Etha's touch. "Inwan hadn't let any other gods near Elidae. He'd even kept *you* hidden from his people. Veed would've had no way to know who Shand is if she wouldn't have come to him herself, and the entire situation reeks of her schemes." He slammed a fist against his desktop, jarring Etha's hand from his shoulder. "Damn it! How hadn't I seen this?"

Etha gnawed on the inside of her cheek. No matter how many times she saw Mathias try, it never got any easier to watch him burden himself with blame for matters outside his control. "The ways of evil are manipulative. I hadn't seen it clearer than her normal treachery, myself." When her words failed to release the clench of Mathias's jaw, Etha sighed and turned to sit atop his desk. "You do know that none of this is your fault, don't you?"

Mathias blinked and shook his head, turning from Etha until he got the scowl out of his system. "I don't know anymore." He propped an elbow on his desk and pressed his forehead into his hand. "Fighting demons, that's straight forward. Fighting *gods*…?"

Etha tried a smile that she felt conveyed only a small fraction of her compassion. "You fought one before. And you won."

He shook his head and cast his gaze toward the ceiling, hand falling to the table. "The god of the undead? No, Etha. Nobody *won* that. All we did was bottle him up to taint the corner of Abaeloth we condemned to him. And I wasn't even the one responsible for that. That was Jules."

Silence crept between mother and son, picking holes at their threadbare resolve. Etha's smile faltered even further. "Do you think Julianna would stand a better chance against Shand than you do?"

Mathias sighed. Pushing his chair back, he rose and tried to release his agitation by pacing. "I don't know," he muttered. "We can't risk her leaving Zeal, not with Shand watching the field. I'd give anything but my heart and my sword arm to have her backing me right now, but she's needed at home."

Etha nodded slowly. "Shand must have separated the two of you intentionally." She pinched her lower lip and narrowed her eyes, contemplating the possibilities of the evil shrew's plans.

"So what do you want me to do?" Mathias asked, interrupting Etha's thoughts. "How do I stop her?"

Etha hopped down from her seat and walked up to Mathias, grasping his forearms to cease his pacing. She laid a hand on his chest. "You've had quite some time to bond with Affliction since your last clash with a god."

Mathias blinked, eyes widening at Etha's vague implication. "Are you suggesting I might be able to *kill* her?"

Her eyes flickered with hope for the briefest instant before a frown cast a gloomy cloud over her. "I don't know. But if it's possible, you'd be the only man alive who could."

That lacked the reassurance Mathias hoped to hear for a topic as substantial as this. He cleared his throat. "I suppose we can save that as an option, but I'd prefer something we both felt a bit more confident about."

"Me too."

"The demons told me their goal with this war was to make me suffer and given my past with Shand, it's not a stretch to assume she shares that motive."

"But Mathias…" Etha directed her gaze away from him before clasping his hands and raising them beneath her chin. "They've already done that, yet the war is still raging."

He drew a shuddering breath, soaking in the comfort of his goddess's touch. "The demons will never be through coming after me," he said. "And I doubt Shand will be, either. I can't be killed. Maybe I should try speaking with her to see what specifics she's after. Try to strike a bargain?"

Etha squeezed his hands and let them drop. "You'd have to find her first. She's been absent from the divine realm for days now and put up a fair share of blocks to secure her location. She could be anywhere."

Of course she had… "I doubt she'd be too far from this war. You're finally letting us thaw out. The demons will resurface soon and I'm sure Shand will come out of hiding in time."

Etha turned and shuffled away from Mathias, tiny shoulders sagging. She reached out and touched the blanket on his bed, grasping the folds of fabric in a shaking hand. Mathias watched in silence, unable to predict the course of his goddess's mind.

"This wasn't supposed to happen…" Etha's dismal whimper flooded the room with despair. "Never, ever again."

Mathias frowned and rubbed the back of his neck, resuming his pacing to redirect his trepidation somewhere other than the urge to argue matters which stumped even Etha. The last time Etha truly lost control over any of the deities beneath her, she'd launched the Divine Battle to put a stop to their tantrums. That war had cost Abaeloth her physical integrity. That war had created the demons. That war had forced Etha to slay her children. It devastated Mathias to see his goddess so fragile, so helpless, and he snarled. Nessix had suffered. Elidae had suffered. Now, that suffering had found Etha. And all of this, Mathias tied directly to Shand Heltsa.

"Mother, it will not happen again," he vowed. "If you cannot find another way, then I will. The world has learned from the past, even if some individuals haven't. I am here to be your shield and I strictly forbid any harm to befall Abaeloth as long as you allow my heart to keep beating."

Etha turned to face Mathias and he gasped at the tears rolling down her cheeks. "I will never be able to repay your devotion, Mathias."

His eyes softened. "All I ask is that you allow me to find Nessix when this is through. That is the only reward I seek."

Etha knew continuing to debate the soundness of that pursuit was a lost cause. He'd made up his mind on the matter, and so she accepted it. Wiping the tears from her eyes, she pulled out a trembling smile. "Thank you, Mathias."

Unable to return the gesture in light of the room's heavy air, Mathias took a knee. "I live to serve you."

Etha sniffled, took a quick breath, and nodded. "If you come up with any ideas…"

He looked up at her, a smile finding his lips at last as Etha rebuilt her composure. "I will tell you immediately," he said. "And the second you catch Shand's scent?"

"I'll point you in her direction." Etha blinked several times, each passage of her eyelids rekindling some of her spark. "Now that we've sorted through these matters, I'd better go pass the information along to the divine realm. Keep your wits about you. I hardly suspect Shand will be pleased to learn she's been outed."

Mathias rose at Etha's gesture and nodded. "I will stay diligent."

Etha's smile tightened and she flitted forward to catch Mathias around the torso. He accepted her embrace, closing his eyes at the peace that wrapped around him, and several soothing heartbeats later, Etha was gone.

Emotionally battered and burdened with reservations over the prospect of battling a goddess, Mathias sank to his bed. Duty would never escape him, no matter how badly he or Etha wanted it to. The White Paladin, the hero, the avatar of the Mother Goddess, would defend Abaeloth from all that sought to wrong her. He fell backwards with a groan and rubbed his forehead. No, this duty would never escape him, but he still had one last method of freedom. Taking advantage of the moment, possibly one of the last quiet times he'd get to enjoy in the foreseeable future, Mathias closed his eyes, arms wide to the bittersweet dreams awaiting him.

* * * * *

Julianna fit into social events seamlessly, accepting the fawning praise and polite gestures granted to her station with a refined grace trained into her from years of practice. Even as she ate, she composed herself with an elegance that Mathias never hoped to match. He sat beside his sister, receiving just as many gilded words and attempts to flaunt some obscure connection to him, and all he felt was awkward and a little bored. He'd lived both phases of his life to serve and protect others, but he preferred his place out on the front lines. Even if he was the type to revel in attention, his own was rather distracted tonight.

Pairs of men approached the head table that seated Elidae's nobles, the less well dressed introducing his charge to Nevius. He and Brant listened attentively to animated attempts to impress them as they dined, understanding the exaggerated accounts courtesy of their enchanted pendants. Nessix, still lacking such a simple luxury, sat to her brother's right, picking at her plate and only cracking a forced smile when attention was noticeably brought to her. Mathias sighed, every bit as disappointed in the evening as she appeared.

Julianna leaned closer to her brother, as not to be overheard by the crowd. "You're awful gloomy tonight."

"You think?" His absent question prompted Julianna to follow his gaze for what must have been the hundredth time that evening.

"Her situation isn't ideal, but this is how politics go," Julianna said. She pouted when her brother refused to bite and laid a hand on his forearm. "At least she's here in Zeal, where people are decent, right?"

Mathias sneered and pulled his arm away. "I'm not sure where your lines of decency are, Jules, but even the Council wouldn't entertain this sort of arrangement if they weren't looking out for their own motives before anything else."

"*I* am part of that Council, you know. It's just… there's nothing we can do about this, Mattie." Julianna knew Mathias better than anyone else alive, well enough that she should have chosen her words with more care. That reminder rushed up to her in a flourish as Mathias narrowed his eyes and squeezed his teeth together. "Mattie, no—"

He popped to his feet with such force that his chair nearly fell to the floor. Julianna's hand snatched at his arm, but too late. She rose halfway, debating the consequences of chasing after him. If she tried to interfere with his mission, they were guaranteed to make a scene that would reflect poorly on the entire Order. Groaning, Julianna plopped down in her chair and clutched at her handkerchief.

Mathias lengthened his stride to cut off the next pair of noblemen who approached the head table, thanking their perturbed glowers with an easy smile. He strolled ahead in that casual way of his, focused so solely on Nevius that he missed Nessix look up and gasp. Mathias marched his way up to the table, slapped his left hand on the surface, and extended his right.

"I am Mathias Sagewind."

Nevius blinked at Mathias's blunt introduction and Brant briefly choked on a mouthful of food. Out of all the proper, courtly addresses delivered to them over the past four days, this coarseness was rather unexpected. Nevius wiped his mouth, drew a steady breath, and laid his hands flat atop the table. People of different cultures from all across Abaeloth considered Zeal their home, and he wouldn't risk offending a potential ally due to a careless discrepancy.

"Alright." A cordial reluctance drew the word out longer than necessary. "And who are you introducing?"

Mathias had expected a much sharper mind from Elidae's future general, given Nes's wit. "I'm… introducing Mathias Sagewind?"

"Have you no decorum?" Nevius gasped, glancing at the guards who hadn't so much as twitched to detain this barbarian. "Are you aware of how serious this is?"

Mathias continued his address in Nes's native tongue, allowing her insight to his side of the following discussion. Nevius, sporting his borrowed whisper pendant, would be none the wiser of Mathias's intention. "Oh, I'm quite aware. I'd been under the impression that all noblemen were invited to have an audience with you." Since it still hadn't been accepted, Mathias shrugged and retracted his hand.

Nevius cleared his throat and sat back in his chair. "You are a noble, then?"

"I am a knight," Mathias confirmed, just as he had for Nessix.

Nevius sighed. "Very well, Sir Sagewind. How many generations has your family served Zeal?"

This wasn't going to go as smoothly as Mathias had hoped, but he'd expected the evening to culminate in an explosion, either way. Might as well press ahead to the inevitable. Confident in his abilities and status, Mathias set down the honest path. "I would be the first."

Both Nevius and Brant's mouths gaped open, but Nessix watched Mathias with wide, hopeful eyes, showing interest for the first time that night.

Nevius rolled his lips between his teeth and glanced down, obsessively pressing nonexistent wrinkles from the tablecloth. "Then I'm hoping you have something extraordinary to offer your fair city and my nation of Elidae?" He looked up at Mathias, a politically contained pity laughing in his eyes.

Mathias smiled at the challenge and nodded. "I don't mean to brag, but I am Zeal's—you know, I'd venture to say all of Abaeloth's—most proficient demon hunter."

Nevius chuckled, drawing the same from his cousin. "A demon hunter!" he said. "Demons haven't been a problem on Abaeloth for ages. You think *that's* supposed to impress me?"

Mathias shrugged. "It seems to impress everyone else here."

Nevius pulled his eyes from Mathias and looked across the expansive chamber. Just as Mathias suggested, clusters of nobles whispered along the perimeter of the dining area, pointing nervous fingers in their direction. A few of those still seated grimaced and pushed their plates away. Nevius looked back at Mathias, seeing an average man with average credentials, save his lack of propriety. Still committed to maintain his appearance, Nevius salvaged his patience and cocked his head. Too invested in conning Mathias into discrediting himself, Nevius missed the way Nessix leaned forward, lower lip pinched between her teeth, to hear more of Mathias's goading.

"What is your purpose here, Sir Sagewind?" Nevius asked at last.

There was the question Mathias had hoped to hear. Donning a sly smirk, Mathias reached forward to lift Nes's hand from the tabletop. He bowed low enough to kiss her fingers, winking at her modest blush as he stood upright. Audible groans filtered through the buoyant music and a few patrons went as far as to dismiss themselves from the hall. Nessix curled her fingertips against Mathias's, unwilling to let him go. That was bound to sit poorly with her brother.

"My purpose here is to dote on your lovely sister," Mathias said, "just like everyone else."

Nevius's fist clenched around the tablecloth, ruining his previous effort of making it so pretty, as he fought to cling to a proper public bearing. "And *what* do you possibly have to offer Elidae?" he snipped.

"What can I offer Elidae?" Mathias repeated the words for

Nes's benefit, assuming she'd yet to hear them spoken. "Well, my dashing good looks and superior bloodlines to start—"

Nessix snatched her hand away with a gasp and spun to face her brother. "Superior bloodlines?" she asked, startled eyes flashing back to Mathias. "What—"

Nevius rose and leaned over the table. "Nessix, do not listen to—"

"What in the world do you—" she tried.

"He means nothing—"

"You mean your dear brother didn't tell you?" Mathias's voice boomed past Nevius's hushed attempts to take control over his sister's indignation. "By the end of the week, he plans to have you wed to whoever bribes him with the fanciest promises and leave you here to play house and make babies for a complete stranger."

Had Nessix not been sitting, her gasp would have floored her. One look at her brother's closed eyes and clenched teeth confirmed Mathias's claim, and suddenly, a greater swell of loneliness caved in around her. Nevius pulled in a deep breath and turned to her.

"Nes—"

His mouth snapped shut as Nessix emptied her chalice in his face. "You asshole!" Her voice burned with an ugly rage unbecoming of a noble lady. Not even able to look at Mathias, Nessix turned and fled from the hall.

Nevius trembled and sucked the wine from his lips, sighing the fragile crumbs of patience back into himself as he studied the tabletop. "Brant, go tend to her."

The cousin obediently darted off between hushed socialites as Julianna's displeasure seared straight through the back of Mathias's jacket. Mathias bit the inside of his cheek to fend off his smile. After all, this wasn't funny.

Silence snuffed the banquet hall, the last notes of the brass honking pathetic ends to their chords. Nevius's chest heaved and he slowly wiped his flushed face with one hand, flicking droplets of wine onto the floor. His other hand clenched in a white-knuckled fist on top of the table, and he stared away from Mathias with a rigid jaw. The paladin watched his opponent with calm, keen eyes. If Nevius wanted to make a scene, Mathias wouldn't rob him of the opportunity to display his nature to the grand public.

Nevius swallowed hard and still couldn't bring himself to look up. "Mathias—"

"Sir Sagewind."

The correction gained Nevius's ire and he tipped his scathing glare to meet Mathias's cunning challenge. "You think throwing around a title makes you better than me?"

Despite his flourishing obstinacy, Mathias opted to keep his smile at bay. "I think throwing around *my* title does."

The chamber grew quieter still as prying ears sought to catch the conversation to come. Nevius blew out puffs of breath, baring his teeth in the most unconvincing smile Mathias had ever received. "Do you have any idea what you have done?"

"I've informed your sister of something she should have agreed upon before you even left—"

"That is not for you to decide!"

Mathias slammed the flat of his hand on the table and leaned closer to Nevius. He had reached his limit. "Zeal is *my* home, and in my home, we do not take advantage of people. Don't you even care about your sister?"

"Of course I do," Nevius seethed. "But as my country's future leader, I care about that more. Nessix understands."

Mathias scowled. "Her conduct just now suggests otherwise."

"Are you intending to stand in my way of negotiations with Zeal?"

Considering Nevius's blissful ignorance of who Mathias was or the dangers which came with accosting him, Mathias let that slide. "If you would look around you, child, you would see that I am not the one impairing your negotiations with my fair city." He jerked his shoulders back to stand upright and tugged at the hem of his tunic. "You would be wise to take that into consideration next time you're in public."

Mathias turned on a heel, disinterested in the remainder of Nevius's righteous sputtering, and strode back to his seat. Julianna's eyes poured with humiliated reprimands and she slowly shook her head, lips turned downward in strict disappointment of his behavior. The closer Mathias neared her, the more determined light swirled within his eyes. He walked around the table to take his seat, and Julianna fixed her gaze at her plate, ashamed to be beside her impulsive brother.

"Now, go on," Mathias called out to the crowd. "Get back to your dining. Maestro—" He gestured toward the band. "No need to stop on account of a temper tantrum." He glanced up at Nevius who still shook in rage, shrugged, and resumed eating.

TWENTY-ONE

Veed had known the likelihood of his confession turning south from the moment he committed to deliver it, he just hadn't anticipated how steeply. He accepted the incrimination which came from the connection he once shared with Shand, but the nature of their relationship, of the actions she'd conned him into carrying out, had never been part of Veed's plan. The crushing weight of this detestable fortress continued to smother him, and Veed's compulsion to escape from its confines peaked to overwhelming.

After retreating back to the relative safety of his chamber, Veed did what he could to mend the injuries Brant had delivered to him, hating the divine power that allowed him such a convenience more than ever. Necessity beat out his repulsion; if the weather continued its current pattern, in two days' time, Veed suspected he'd be able to leave this fortress behind once and for all.

The door swung open and Veed leapt to his feet to grab his sword, ready to fend off whoever thought it wise to come after him. Inwan, armed with nothing but a tray of food, hesitated in the entry, blinking in confusion at Veed's unusual level of reactivity. Veed, as aloof to the god as ever, flushed and lowered his sword. With a shrug, Inwan stepped the rest of the way inside and closed the door behind him. He walked over to deposit the tray on an end table and Veed sank back down on his couch, keeping his blade free and ready.

Inwan watched Veed, lips pursed and locked in an internal struggle between resentment and regret. Veed planted his focus on that wall of minotaur horns, and Inwan invited himself to take a seat.

"As bold as ever, Veed." The god's voice lacked remorse and sympathy, but Veed hadn't expected either. "And I would like to thank you for that."

Veed swallowed his irritation and dragged his eyes to Inwan's, facing a meek and almost laughable expression. "Why is that? I thought you adored Laes."

"Oh, I had. And I'd love to see you burn for what you did to him. But that wasn't what I was referring to. Thanks to your outburst, you've pulled their attention away from me."

Veed allowed himself a dry laugh and slouched deeper into his seat. "Glad someone's found a benefit from it."

Shifting his gaze about the room, Inwan was as reluctant to pursue his current objective as Veed had been in the war chamber. Inwan didn't fear a reaction from Veed; rather the thought of an honest answer—one he didn't want to hear—drove the god to meekness. Lacking the resolution to put up a strong front now that he was trapped in this mortal body, Inwan stalled over the purpose of this visit.

"You can eat that, you know." Inwan nodded toward the food. "It's safe, you have my word. I never told them where I was taking it."

"When have you ever given me reason to trust your word?"

Inwan shrank at Veed's scrutiny. Maybe he should have invested a bit more effort to accommodate Veed in the past. Over a decade after his sentence, Inwan still struggled with this business of serving others before himself. He scratched the back of his head and frowned "Here." Inwan stood and retrieved the tray to sample a pinch of bread. The warmth had left it, but not its softness, and Inwan swallowed the bite, nodding with satisfaction. "See? It's safe enough for me and as sharp as you are, I'm sure you've caught on to my disability by now."

The slip of humility drew an abrupt laugh from Veed, a bitter sound which troubled the once-god. "You call it a disability?"

Inwan dropped what remained of the morsel and rubbed the crumbs from his fingers. He slid the tray back onto its table and took a step closer to Veed. The man radiated with hostility, repelling Inwan's desire to sit beside him. This wasn't going well. "Is it true?" Inwan asked gruffly. He missed the days of diving into the conscience of mortals, the freedom to extract what he wanted on a whim.

"How would I know?" Veed grunted. "You're the one in that body."

Inwan closed his eyes and crossed his arms with a huff. "Did you have your way with her?"

A less subdued version of Veed would have found no end of amusement from the grief lacing Inwan's question. Now, it simply dug the chasm of his grief one foot deeper. "Not when anyone willing to stop me stood in the way."

"Brant?"

"Was never a concern of mine."

Inwan frowned at how easily Veed disregarded the young man. "Until tonight, I presume."

Veed hissed his opinion of Inwan's observations and cast his gaze aside.

"And that Mathias?" Inwan pressed. "He clearly had feelings for her."

Veed's embarrassment drowned in the welling bitterness pooling inside of him. He growled at the irony of facing this rival for Nes's affection only after she was no longer here to fight over. "He wasn't man enough to try to stop me." Veed opted to save Nes's memory the confession that she'd consented to his coercion. "I was not violent with her, as all of you seem eager to think."

Mortal emotions subjected Inwan to mortal responses, and if he hadn't understood the limitations of his fragile frame, he'd have tried to claw the stabbing twist out of his gut. Through the extent of his banishment, only Nessix had found her way into Inwan's mind. He'd gone along contently, confident in her abilities and the flemans' adoration of the Teradhel line. Not once had he imagined he'd return to find Nessix slain in his absence and betrayed by the man who once professed such a deep love for her. Was this the sort of realization Etha had hoped he'd find?

Inwan's eyes fell to the floor. It must have been. If he'd taken his position seriously when he still had the chance, none of this would have happened. His people wouldn't be crammed in a dungeon. The nation wouldn't be divided in chaos. Nessix would still be alive. *Laes* might still be alive. Inwan no longer wanted to defend himself from his guilt. He'd earned it several times over. Elidae had fallen apart without him, left vulnerable to whoever wanted to strike her. Inwan believed with every thread of his being that Nessix had led the best she knew how to, but even through her bold façade, Inwan had known her heart intimately. She'd needed him.

That nauseating storm brewed up in Inwan's stomach once again, raking its way up his throat. He stood in silence. As terrible as Veed was, how could he claim to be any better? Contemplating that answer built on the knot in his core until only one viable option came to mind. Inwan fled from the room.

Inwan's hasty departure gained a glance from Veed, but he couldn't quite scavenge enough arrogance to laugh at the god's discomfort. The door closed, blocking out the sound of Inwan's retreat, and Veed sighed out his tension. He'd never shared a particularly good relationship with Inwan and though he knew the god's bond to Nessix, he didn't know the lengths he'd go to in defense of her integrity. The beating Brant had delivered more than satisfied any hidden masochistic whims of Veed's and given the opportunity, he'd pass on taking another one. Both the confession of his involvement in Laes's death—no, his murder—and confirming to Inwan how he'd defiled Nessix topped off Veed's list of unpleasant tasks. With both obstacles behind him, all Veed needed to worry about were assassination attempts and means to get back home.

A knock sounded, too polite to be an aggressor, or so Veed hoped. His attempt to feign confidence didn't quite fool his proliferating dread and he held his breath as he grabbed his sword, stood, and walked to the door. A hand's span from grasping the knob, Veed paused to rally his courage. Fatigue and paranoia cautioned him against opening the door, but pride sneered at this pathetic response. Why did it matter who waited on the other side? Veed growled in shame, flinging the door open before he caved to all those timid warnings.

Even if everyone else in the fortress wanted Veed dead, Sulik would always be the voice of reason. Often the last to know of Veed's schemes, the last to anger, Veed was certain Sulik was also the last to offer the most remote sense of security.

Sulik rocked back on a heel to glance down the hall, then back at Veed. "General Astaldt." He cleared his throat, holding Veed's twitchy gaze. "I've been asked to order you to vacate the Teradhel grounds."

Veed drew in a slow breath. "I plan to do so, Commander, once the snow melts to allow safe passage."

Sulik creased his lips. He loathed defying authority, even that which he hated. "The order was made for your immediate departure. Your haste will benefit us all. Yourself included."

The thought of setting out through the still treacherous landscape was only slightly more appealing than the prospect of Brant or Mathias showing up to reinforce Sulik's message. Maybe it was for the best. "Any chance Brant will lend me a horse?"

For the first time in Veed's recollection, Sulik wielded an inflexible glare. "You're lucky he lent you your life."

Veed bowed his head, the tumult of witty retorts he'd have thrown back at that statement a month ago rolling through his mind. Now, he quaked at the prospect of pressing his luck.

"Since all you arrived with is your sword and armor, I suspect it's safe for me to report your compliance within the hour?"

The finality delivered to him brought a squirm to Veed's insides which he hadn't felt since his rebellious youth. He'd held a senior rank his entire adult life and had long ago forgotten how it felt to receive the ultimatums. Just one more memory to run from. "I'll be gone as soon as I'm able," he muttered. "Forgive me for being unable to thank your superiors for their hospitality." He moved to shut the door.

Sulik caught it, the sternness of his expression embedding concern deeper into Veed's troubled mind. "I'll be sure to pass that along." He shoved a modest parcel in Veed's direction and unclipped the water skin from his belt. "I only prepared the drink." Whether or not Sulik cared for Veed, he considered himself among the few people the dark general could trust. "But my conscience couldn't send you out without provisions."

Veed's brows furrowed as he reached out a reluctant hand to accept the offer. "And are your fellow officers aware of your kindness?"

Sulik's eyes darted away and he crossed his arms, shoulders shrugged. "It was Sir Sagewind's idea. Brant knows nothing about it. I'll let you decide what that means for yourself." He looked up once more, frowning as the briefest memory of the man Veed once was flickered through his mind. He wanted to pray for Etha's mercy to reach Veed, but after all the pain and disorder brought on by this man's selfishness, just thinking such a request felt blasphemous. With silence and a brief nod, Sulik stepped back and disappeared down the hall.

* * * * *

Veed discarded the strips of dried meat and the half loaf of bread Sulik had given him, very nearly the water, too, but he trusted Sulik more than any of the others. He replaced the rations with the least perishable items Inwan had brought. Of course, Veed didn't particularly trust the god either, but at least he saw that food be tasted. Careful to tuck that bloodied handkerchief in his pocket before donning his armor, Veed departed from the Teradhel fortress without fanfare for what he swore to make the last time. Even if he managed to restore what passed as a welcome, he disliked the honest man he became when inside those walls.

Despite the warming temperatures and rapid melting, the voyage proved more taxing than Veed anticipated or appreciated. The time spent trapped indoors added to the difficulty, as Veed's legs protested finding reliable traction and his stamina had taken a hit. Ice packed thick on the road and growing deposits of slush enhanced the hazards of his passage. By the time Veed reached Nes's grave, his feet burned from the cold.

He stayed with her in silence, wanting to speak words he couldn't decipher, but Logan's wasted condition chilled him almost as deeply as his guilt did. The massive horse stood with his legs splayed to maintain balance, not even registering Veed's presence. If not for the fact that Logan still had his feet beneath him, Veed would have thought him already dead. It couldn't be more than a few more days. Disheartened, Veed bowed his head, vowing to come back to visit Nessix at a later time. Logan deserved what peace he could find in his final days.

Veed pressed on across the ice, guided by the landmarks peeking through their snowy shells as he scoured the horizon. He squinted against the brightness, nearly blinded as he trudged south. It took until the sun had passed its peak for Veed to recognize the form of a person standing several paces ahead of him. He stopped, blinking rapidly in a vain attempt to clear his vision, and raised a hand to shield the sun from his eyes. The figure was gone. Sighing at his clear lapse of sensibility, Veed took a step forward and froze as the scent of lavender wafted on the breeze from behind him.

"Of course you're not hallucinating."

Eyes wide, Veed stayed rooted in place, not even bothering to reach for his sword as Shand's laughter trilled at his back.

"Come now. Are you afraid of me?"

She stepped around Veed to stand before him, her traction flawless atop the ice. Her smile held the same calm deception that had seduced Veed when they first met. He closed his mouth to contain his startled gasp and swallowed hard.

A second bout of laughter rolled about in Shand's throat as she watched Veed's nerve scramble for purchase amidst his shock. "Oh, my dear Commander Astaldt," she said. "You are right to be afraid of me, no shame in that. Do you have any idea what you've done?"

Weighing his options and his odds, Veed reached an unsettling conclusion. Trying to escape Shand was no less ridiculous than trying to escape his past. He'd managed to survive his confession, despite Brant's enthusiastic efforts to assure otherwise. Maybe luck still rode in Veed's favor. Besides, would it be such a terrible thing if Shand killed him here in the snow? That thought—the sheer and generous disregard for his own life—sobered Veed. He met Shand's eyes. This was the manipulative bitch who started it all.

"I suppose you want to punish me."

"For outing me to Mathias?" She shook her head, a devious smile warming the deceit in her eyes. "He'd have figured this all out eventually. No, what that troublesome confession of yours did was remove their suspicion of you. What purpose do you serve me now?"

Veed's glare hardened as he constructed the same barriers he brought with him to combat. "I quit being of use to you years ago. This isn't news to me."

Shand appraised Veed's clenched fists and the manner which he hunched his shoulders forward. Veed's treachery still called to her in the worst ways, and her lips quirked with the hint of a pout that he'd escaped her grasp all those years ago. She shrugged. "If that's how you see it."

Veed's fingers twitched, ready to reach for his sword. "So do you plan to kill me?"

She rolled her eyes and planted her hands on her hips. "Of course not. As you are right now, you *want* to die. Just like you did when you killed Laes. Foolish little mortal, you'd think you'd learn. Your pride won't allow you suicide, so I'd be doing you a favor." She smirked as Veed clenched his jaw. "No. I've always had a use for you, and I'll find one again. Don't you worry."

Veed had run out of tolerance for Shand two months after their first meeting. He should have known he'd never escape her. Regardless, she just confirmed that she planned to keep him alive, and so Veed shoved his way past her to resume picking his way toward his fortress.

Shand's face lit with a wicked grin and she turned to follow, gliding behind Veed's carefully placed steps. "You're so anxious to get home."

Veed knew she'd never allow him to ignore her, so he answered before she made a hassle out of it. "I'm anxious to leave behind my hell."

He refrained from even glancing back at Shand, and she cocked her head to study how rigidly he carried his shoulders and how he held his arms so slightly out at his sides to assist his balance. Mortals were such funny creatures. She wished yet again that she'd found a way to effectively control this one. "Are you sure you're not marching into another one?"

Her question beckoned Veed to pause and think over those implications, but the sharpness which came back to him with each step suspected that was the sort of reaction she'd hoped to catch. Through giving anything at all to this fiendish woman, Veed trudged along. "Falk's a competent man. My fortress will still be standing when I get there."

Shand's lips turned up in a smile, eyes narrowing in delight. "But are you sure Falk *wants* you back?"

This time, Veed did stop. He'd trusted Renigan with his army's management, confident in the commander's obedience and experience. Renigan complimented Veed's objectives well enough, but never expressed signs of noteworthy ambition. That had been Veed's greatest motivation for granting him the rank of commander. Veed turned back to ask Shand if this was what she'd meant by toying with him, but by the time he'd spun around, she was gone.

Spitting at Shand's memory, Veed muttered a curse about the bewitching wench and continued toward home.

* * * * *

Commander Renigan Falk detested being called from his quarters—now much more elaborately furnished than they'd been a month ago—and into the chilly air that accompanied duty. With his sights set on claiming the title of general upon the inevitable discovery of Veed's demise, he needed to take initiative if he wanted to avoid challenges for the position. Grumbling to himself over the ineptitude of the troops, Renigan tugged the heavy, fur-lined cloak about his shoulders and went to investigate this inconvenient fuss.

He burrowed his chin into the cloak's lining, crossing his arms against the lingering cold as he followed a messenger to the battlements. The soldier stayed close to Renigan's side, no doubt aiming to use the current political instability to snag a promotion for himself, but Renigan ignored the fawning glances and animated conversation his escort prattled about. Instead, Renigan strained his eyes against the blanket of twilight to study the figure creeping their way in the snow. This man was the first living being greater than wildlife to dare approaching the fortress since the storm struck, but that misgiving wasn't what set Renigan's heart to racing.

"Shoot him down," Renigan commanded the nearest archer.

Not as smitten with Renigan as his guide was, the archer cast his commander a speculative glance. Veed prided himself on how efficiently his army functioned, but common sense and an innate loyalty to his rightful general gave the bowman pause. It was no great secret that the bulk of the army resented Renigan taking command in Veed's absence, but he was the highest ranking officer. For now.

"Sir," the archer said flatly. "Do you truly consider this man a—"

"What are you being paid for?" Renigan growled. "I gave you an order."

Clenching his jaw, the archer nocked an arrow and took aim ahead. Renigan held his breath as it loosed, striking a comfortable ten yards from the intended target. In the snow, the traveler's attention jerked to where the arrow struck before his shoulders squared in distinct agitation. Clenched fists accompanied his prowl forward.

Sweat beaded against the thick fur of Renigan's collar. "What *are* you being paid for? That was your best shot?"

"It was a warning shot," the archer replied, taking a brief appraisal of the number of allies present on the wall. Renigan wouldn't risk remedial action over such a reasonable call with so many watching.

"And you were ordered to take him down," Renigan said.

The archer eyed his commander suspiciously, unclear how Renigan identified the man who staggered toward them as anyone other than their missing general, but given the commander's recent ego boost, he wasn't quite foolish enough to confront him about it. Untethered from Veed, Renigan was a cowardly pig, one unworthy of the army's respect and obedience. Veed ruled harshly and with high expectations, but he'd always been fair. The archer bit down on the insides of his cheeks.

One wrong move was all it would take. He had to follow Renigan's order to maintain his immediate safety and potential job security, but he refused to become the man who struck down Veed Astaldt. He couldn't risk missing a second shot with the same margin as he'd missed the first. It would have served him much better if Veed hadn't resumed walking, as the slick footing rendered his movement unpredictable. The heat of Commander Falk breathing down his neck disrupted the archer's concentration even more. Drawing on discipline alone, he focused on his aim and let the next shot fly. As the arrow soared past Veed's ear, the archer sighed out that weight of distress, allowing his eyes to ease closed.

At the receiving end of a second missed shot, Veed stopped again, throwing back his cloak to reveal his crest and colors. Expression distorted by the distance between them, Veed's focus on their location stole the archer's relief and forced him to shrink back in frightful guilt. Renigan stood beside the chastened bowman, arms crossed as he stared back at Veed and contemplated his options.

Did he dare order a third attempt? He knew the men distrusted him and doubted this archer would accept an offer of promotion for landing a successful shot. Renigan also had fair reason to expect this archer—or any of the other silent witnesses present—to run off to tell the army of the attempts he'd ordered on their general's life. Trapped, Renigan kept his mouth shut as he drafted out a list of excuses.

Before a viable reason for his outwardly impulsive conduct solidified in Renigan's mind, a group of soldiers darted from the main level of the fortress to assist their rightful general. With a modest audience gathered around him, Renigan pursed his lips to avoid incriminating himself further. Arms crossed, he scanned the disgusted expressions of a unit of men unwilling to continue participating in his disgraceful power trip. Gritting his teeth, Renigan spun on a heel to descend the stairs and meet his general.

The four soldiers who had rushed to Veed kept their footing

far better than his exhaustion had allowed, and he dragged himself closer to them, surrendering to the aches in his weary bones. Though the cold sapped his strength, Veed found renewed vigor as he neared his fortress. Each step pulled him closer to freedom from the misery which had so nearly defeated him, distancing him from the past he needed to leave behind, and he longed to return to the life he'd carved for himself. Years of guilt alleviated from his chest, Veed was eager to reclaim his position. His pride would heal with time.

Even with the arrival of his escorts, Veed kept his focus trained at the gates ahead, driving himself closer to sanctuary. Inside his fortress, he'd be safe. From Mathias and Brant, from Shand. From Nessix. As his soldiers reached him, Veed brushed off their offers of physical support, but graciously accepted the eager display of fellowship.

Renigan emerged from the fortress, arms open in an air of false humility. Veed had known Renigan for years and picked up the abhorrence behind the exaggerated relief in his commander's eyes within an instant. At once, Veed identified the nature of the shots fired at him and the closer Renigan got to his general, the stronger Veed's suspicions grew. The commander stopped two paces from Veed, held at bay by a curled lip and astute gaze. Veed might have been worn to the verge of collapse, but not so much that he wouldn't ream his wayward commander.

"I see you've done well for yourself while I was away," Veed said flatly. "Thank you for taking care of my men."

The calmness of Veed's words kindled the embers of Renigan's fear. He licked his lips. "It is my duty, sir." His contempt blazed through the shield of fabricated respect and Veed's eyes narrowed.

"I trust those shots were taken in defense of the fortress? In case a lone man intended to storm it?"

Renigan tried to interpret some degree of insight from the glint in Veed's eyes, but his general's superior will blocked the intrusion. Those shots *had* been taken against the only man who posed a threat to the fortress, at least the fortress Renigan wanted. "Of course, sir," he said. "We didn't know who you were."

Veed almost pitied Renigan for the pathetic effort he rallied behind. The commander wore clothes too fine for him. The soldiers Veed had encountered so far bowed in grateful relief rather than cheering in jubilation to see him alive. Veed's impulses urged him to wring the obvious betrayals from Renigan's neck, but his tactical side begged for a bit more patience. Renigan's refusal to meet Veed's eyes and the volume which he used to defend himself assured that the commander knew Veed wasn't fooled, and that served as adequate punishment for now. Besides, there were more memorable ways to discipline an insubordinate officer.

"If it was due to defense, I correct none of your actions," Veed said, donning a smile so friendly it quaked Renigan's resolve. Veed turned to address the troops who came to assist him. "Gentlemen, the snow is melting and attacks will resume sooner than we'd like to see. I am home now, ready to warm myself by a fire, then we will resume preparations for war."

Veed hadn't realized quite how much he'd missed obedience until the soldiers bowed and turned to file away. A smile crept to his face as power flowed back into his words. He had no need to watch for Renigan's response; the commander's glower struck against Veed's indifference hard enough to speak his mind. No longer governed by reluctance and self-doubt, Veed breathed in the cool air and moved after his men, entering the fortress with a broad grin.

How it felt to be home! Let Mathias and Brant and Inwan bury themselves in their safe house, fussing over his conduct. Their decision to evict him had landed him right back in power, free to control his actions and brimming with spite. Once the demons were more properly managed, maybe he'd even act on those malevolent whims.

Renigan followed his general with rigid strides, grasping the hems of his sleeves to keep from biting his cuticles. Words would pass between the two of them, they both knew it, but Renigan didn't know how much time he'd have to formulate a solid defense. If fate smiled on him, perhaps Veed would still consider him too valuable to risk losing his loyalty—or life—right now.

"Forgive the attack made on you," Renigan said at last,

desperate to direct his thoughts off their negative path. Veed's pleasant smile and calm eyes bothered Renigan more the longer they walked. "We'd assumed you were dead to the storm."

"Of course you did." Veed's smile persisted as he acknowledged awed greetings with cordial nods. "I probably *should* be dead, but you know I do my best to avoid disappointing."

"So it seems…" Renigan disguised his scowl with a forced yawn. "Might I ask how you survived?"

Darkness stormed Veed's expression at last, assuring Renigan that there were people Veed hated more than him. "I'd been lodging at the Teradhel fortress until I could make safe passage." He was too pleased to be home to step foot on the slope of what happened during his stay, and he redirected the conversation accordingly. "Did Solvig make it home?"

Renigan scratched his ear, thrown by Veed's vague answer. "No."

"A pity."

"Sir, what news do you have from our neighbors?"

Veed scowled and glanced over his shoulder, irritated by the manner which Renigan demanded answers of him. "Nothing worth merit. Mathias is still a fraud, Sulik is still his tool, and Brant's gone insane." He opted to withhold the insight which resulted in his hasty exile. Renigan deserved that knowledge even less than Mathias had, and Veed didn't want to revisit it again. He coughed and turned his focus ahead. "Our little Nessix would have been greatly pleased, though."

Renigan's brows furrowed at the ominous statement. "Oh?"

"Inwan's back on Elidae."

This news stopped Renigan cold. He'd neither expected nor wanted to hear of the god's return, not now. Not ever. "You can't be serious." Now more concerned for his safety than bitter over losing the coveted status he'd so nearly claimed, Renigan rushed to catch up as Veed pressed on.

"I only lie to my enemies," Veed said, unmoved by his commander's disbelief.

Renigan chewed over the complications this development implied, silently fraught with the same questions everyone else had struggled with. "This changes matters quite a bit," he murmured.

"Seems it does." Veed stopped to face his commander, catching him with calculating eyes. "And in light of these changes, I need your compliance now more than ever."

The firm tone of Veed's voice set Renigan's heart thumping even faster. How deep could one man sink into a war before stress eviscerated him? He scoured his general's expression, seeking even the faintest sign of weakness or doubt. Veed looked terrible, malnourished and of colder demeanor than before, but arrogance held his shoulders high and his stride shouted of his confidence. Renigan had no way of knowing what happened to Veed while he'd been gone, but he came back bearing more problems than Renigan knew how to cope with. Veed was supposed to be dead! Renigan needed this position! Inwan had been *banished* from this plane! Clenching his teeth, not at all pleased with the unravelling of his dream, Renigan gave Veed a stiff nod.

"Of course, General."

Veed's smile broadened, his cunning eyes lighting in a way Renigan never trusted. The general slapped him on the shoulder. "I've got to get out of these frozen clothes. Go help spread the good news that I'm home."

Veed turned and sauntered down the hall, whistling a jaunty battle hymn. Internally, Renigan seethed at his fouled luck, heart racing and with no clear heading to run toward.

* * * * *

Renigan hadn't claimed a solid night's sleep since Veed's return to the fortress. He knew well that his general saw through the schemes he'd implemented in his absence, though the two of them had yet to discuss it. Grumbling as anxiety pressed grisly notions through his overwhelmed mind, Renigan threw his weight to roll over, coming face to face with a demon parked on a stool at his bedside.

"Blessed—bitch's... name!" he sputtered as he scrambled upright, fingers wrapped snug around the hilt of the dagger he slept with. "How—No. *What* do you think you're doing here?"

Neither Renigan's excitability nor the weapon he clutched fazed this demon as he contemplated how such a useless man had ever earned worth in their ranks. "You were told you'd be notified when we were going to begin our movement."

Renigan's mind flailed about a sea of weariness, clutching to a line of hope at last. Veed wouldn't be able to touch him, provided Renigan could trust his unlikely allies to honor their bargain. That was something he still hadn't convinced himself of. Stifling a yawn, Renigan rubbed his eyes and released his dagger to climb from bed and fetch his water skin.

The demonic messenger said nothing, judgmental eyes appraising the fleman's attempts to wake up enough to hold a coherent conversation. Renigan assigned the bulk of his attention to his unexpected guest. Tied to so many powers that could—and would—obliterate him without a second thought, Renigan had to play each threat as it came. Heart drumming a sinister march, he drank of his water until its coolness sharpened his senses, and wiped his lips with the back of his hand.

"I take it you being here means this movement is in the works?" He kept his voice low, more paranoid of eavesdroppers than ever before.

The demon stood and stretched out his arms. "We're coordinating them, yes, and you will tell us which two towns your lord manages that would yield the greatest impact if they were to fall."

It was an indisputable demand, one which Renigan hadn't anticipated, and he bit his tongue against correcting the demon for addressing Veed as his lord. His tired mind waded through the consequences of losing townships. The terms he'd agreed to involved him obtaining control over Elidae, and control meant nothing without a kingdom. Failing to comply with this request, however, stood the chance of robbing him of something much more significant than a few thousand citizens. Renigan closed his eyes and rubbed his forehead. "Norrik and Retonim would have the greatest economic impact. Adessa has the largest population and greatest political pull."

The demon pressed a finger to his lips and nodded slowly,

tucking the information away to share with those of more superior wit. "Very good. In two days' time, we'll strike the two most significant targets. Your lord is not to have any insight of these attacks."

Renigan dropped his hand from his head and caught himself just short of sending his guest a retaliatory glower. "The greatest target on the island is still the Teradhel fortress with the volume of lives harbored there," he said. "Why not attack—"

The demon raised a hand, stifling Renigan's debate before it gained momentum. "This isn't a grab for power. This is a distraction to give us time to work on Mathias."

The words jerked Renigan upright and he furrowed his brows. "A distraction for whom?"

"Your General Astaldt, of course." The demon walked over to Renigan's desk, scanning the documents on top of it. "Having him get in the way of Mathias does not serve us at all."

Renigan snorted, but kept his distance from the demon. "If you want Mathias, keep Veed as free as you can. He'll go after him—"

"Veed cannot have Mathias." The demon wheeled to face Renigan so fast it elicited a yelp from the fleman. "And if we must take drastic measures to ensure it, we will."

Renigan's limited finesse for outfoxing his opponents crawled to action as adrenaline replaced enough of his fatigue to loan him the brazenness to speak his mind. "You know what, just jump ahead and take care of Veed now. Or is that what these attacks are for?"

The demon shook his head, irritated by Renigan's simplicity and wondering what his superiors had thought when incorporating him into their plans. At least Renigan proved consistent in his idiocy. "Neither you nor Veed are allowed to be touched for now."

Renigan jabbed a finger at his guest. "You told me we would get him out of the way." He retracted the gesture at the demon's curled lip and crossed his arms, shoulders hunched. "You told me I'd have Elidae."

"We agreed to allow you to govern Elidae. You made the assumption it would be yours in your own pathetic mind."

The ease in which the demon spoke that truth chilled Renigan worse than this blasted cold. He should have known better than to trust the demons in the first place. Between these beasts' power and Veed's suspicion, he'd dug himself a fine grave, leaving him only one place to turn to. Shand. And if she gleaned even the whisper of a suggestion of his devious arrangements... Renigan cleared his throat, eyes darting away from his company.

"I have betrayed my general for you. I have betrayed my people for you. I betrayed a fucking *goddess* for you, and you're telling me I did this for nothing? All I have is the word you gave me. How am I—"

"Supposed to trust us?" This time, a smug smile sharpened the demon's features as he paced through Renigan's spacious chamber. "Maybe you're not. But that's something you get to sort through on your own. We did keep our end of the bargain by warning you what's on the horizon. I'd like to think that's evidence enough."

In a less perilous war, maybe such a warning would suffice, but Renigan didn't even know whether or not he could trust his own general any longer. What other choice was left for him other than trusting the demons?

"Alright." Renigan shrugged in defeated compliance, hands flopping at his sides. He took a long drink, wishing it was anything more potent than water. "You've told me the movement, what else do you need from me?"

"All you have to do is make sure Veed takes the field. Encourage him to stay preoccupied with the campaign. We'll aim to keep him alive, but his numbers will be devastated."

Internal panic romped about Renigan's insides. Not only did the demons intend to take two cities, but a blow to the army as well? Renigan needed Veed's troops when it came time to seize power, especially if he planned to strike back against the demons. The plan which they'd pitched to him themselves relied on him leading a loyal fleman force in the end. Renigan looked up into the cunning eyes of his company, realizing he'd never had the upper hand in this dangerous arrangement.

"So Veed's supposed to take the field. What about me?"

"You stay right where you are," the demon said. "What sort of general would leave his fortress completely unguarded?"

Renigan's mouth hung open, but he couldn't sort through his confusion to form a reply. Was he meant to trust the demons after all, or was this simply another mode for them to use him? He gulped down his uncertainty, the guile painting his guest's expression assuring him that the demons not only knew he felt trapped, but intended to keep him there. Renigan wondered, not for the first time, how much better off he'd be if he'd just stayed loyal to Shand. He wiped the beads of sweat from his forehead.

The demon brandished a broad grin. "Will you confirm receipt of our message?"

Voice failing, Renigan held his breath and nodded.

Through with this tedious hassle, the demon flicked an impatient gesture in the direction of Renigan's bookshelf. An oraku stepped free of the shadows to join his companion, and Renigan choked on a gasp, heart thumping faster. Eerie whispers burrowed into his mind, emphasizing the imbalance of power between him and the demons, and his pair of guests whisked away.

Renigan collapsed into his desk chair, arms shaking and head spinning as he cursed his foolishness. So much for getting sleep.

TWENTY-TWO

The song of the watch tower bells invigorated Veed. He'd pined for their foreboding clang from the moment his fortress reached view, longing to take the field and remember who he was. Flooding from the snow melt threatened to impede a traditional march, and pockets of mud complicated navigation, but to go to arms! Veed prepared for this attack whistling a cheerful battle hymn, carefree and eager to resume the war's progress unhindered by leery eyes and the guilt they exhumed. With Nes's welfare no longer a complication to worry over, he was free to fight as recklessly as he wanted.

Securing the last straps of his armor, Veed grabbed the blood-flecked keepsake from Nessix and tucked it against his chest as he strode from his chamber. The guard he'd posted after his return obediently locked the door, securing Veed's wealth from the less trustworthy members within his ranks. Veed grinned, tugging at the final adjustments to his bracers.

Striding into the main arteries of his fortress, the busy hum of confusion passing among his men curbed Veed's vivacious mood. His army was more disciplined than this.

He snagged the nearest captain by the arm. "Is something wrong?"

The officer snapped to attention as thoroughly as Veed's hold allowed. "It seems the demons have infiltrated Norrik and Adessa, sir. Both towns are under siege."

Veed's eyes narrowed and he shook his head, no less confused than the rest of his ranks. Besides Nes's loss of Sarlot, the demons had shown no prior interest in striking at civilians. Both Norrik and Adessa bordered the far eastern fringes of his territory but weren't close enough to each other to be hit with one force. Veed could lead one front, but he barely trusted Renigan to keep his rank. Rubbing his chin, Veed pondered his options, deciding he'd prefer Renigan delegated to the field rather than stationed alone in the fortress. If nothing else, the commander would fight to save his own life.

"Have the town guards been able to hold at either location?" Veed set into motion again, cursing the disgraceful way his mind lagged over the report.

"They're holding the cities proper for the time, but we're still awaiting confirmation on the numbers they're facing. Sir, I've never seen the demons coordinate like this."

Veed frowned. He hadn't, either. An irritating voice from the practical side of Veed's mind, one he swatted flat the instant he caught it, nagged about how Mathias likely had. Let the pesky paladin have an answer to this; Veed would find his own. "Arrange a decoy to lure the force attacking Adessa toward the Teradhel fortress."

The captain swallowed the order and darted his eyes through the busy passageway in search of moral support. "Do you think the demons will keep interest that long?"

No, he really didn't, and that gave Veed no other choice but to treat his first battle back home as a campaign. Renigan jogged toward him, calling out with a voice draped in a laughable shroud of concern. Veed glowered at the annoyance, grit his teeth, then turned to meet his commander.

"Commander Falk." The sharpness of his address smeared the nature of Renigan's concern and Veed cocked his head. "Had there been any signs of this sort of unrest brewing while I was away?"

"No." Renigan answered too quickly for Veed to accept as completely honest.

Veed crossed his arms. "Is that because there were no movements or because you were too daft to notice them?" He glanced at the other officer in their company. "Captain? Can you confirm Falk's report?"

Renigan flinched at Veed's blatant insult and spoke before the lesser ranked officer had a chance to reply. "There was no movement, Veed. We'd been under the same snow and ice that held you up. You were the first sign of life we'd seen in weeks."

Veed's steady gaze dissected Renigan's behavior, slicing cleanly through his overconfident posture and unwavering eyes to expose the faintest glimmer of sweat resting on his brow. Veed continued to prod around, digging for the dishonesty carried by his commander until the pressure of his gaze drove Renigan to scratch the back of his neck and expel a nervous laugh.

"Are you doubting me?" he asked, discomfort now tittering on his voice.

"No." The answer came abrupt and smooth, no less suspicious than Renigan's own actions. "I'm not." Veed's eyes softened with an artfully contrived smile. "I do believe that nothing could have marched in force anywhere through that weather."

Renigan blew out a relieved sigh, waiting for his heart to quit racing.

"Alright then." Veed turned to the captain to shut Renigan out of the remainder of the conversation. "Begin distributing orders. The fifth and sixth battalions will stay behind at the fortress with me; the remaining force will be split evenly to head each front. We're treating this as a campaign. Don't prepare to get cozy."

"Veed, I—"

Veed held a finger to the captain to request his patience and shot Renigan with an admonishing glare. "In a moment, Commander." He turned his attention back to the captain, brushing off the interruption as though it held no relevance. "Find…" he hummed in consideration, "Captain Telvach to take command of the force attacking Norrik. After his recent practice, Renigan's got the northern front, I'm sure."

When the captain flung Renigan an uncomfortable glance, it gave the commander a nip of courage to press the matter. Veed was already on to him and he was sure it wouldn't be long before he'd be stripped of his station. He had one other option. He had to keep the demons happy. "General," Renigan snipped, afraid of his own boldness. "Why aren't you heading out?"

"Your orders, Captain," Veed said, sending the officer off with a firm nod before rewarding Renigan's foolishness with his attention. "Why do you think I'm staying behind?"

Renigan's mind reeled over the demons' instructions for him. Out of all the half truths and vague tasks they'd thrown at him, the only one they'd assigned him as a clear objective was to make sure Veed took the field and kept his mind too engaged with survival to worry about anything else. Renigan cursed his faulty luck. When this war began, he'd had everything planned out and his position secured. Shand had promised him she'd lost interest in Veed and assured she'd keep Renigan safe for his loyalty. Time had proven the goddess understood only a rough interpretation of what safety entailed. And then, he let the demons play him the same way. Now, Renigan faced his general, the man he'd served beside for the bulk of his military career, and his heart pounded every bit as hard as when he faced those other evils he tried to align himself with.

Veed's calculating eyes and the smirk that anticipated a defensive response sapped the confidence from Renigan. "I can't be sure, sir." It took all of his effort to keep from holding his breath.

Veed's lips broadened to a sly grin, one Renigan's years of service had taught him meant danger for its target. For him. "You managed the troops *so well* without me, I assume the soldiers respect you enough to serve you. I've been away from home, trapped in hostile confines, for too long. At least allow me to enjoy my homecoming."

Slapping Renigan on the shoulder, Veed strode down the hall, the cheerful battle hymn back on his lips as he loosened those straps he'd taken such care to secure. Renigan wished, not for the first time, that he had the brain power to keep up with anyone these days.

* * * * *

Allowing Brant to make the initial demand for Veed's eviction from the fortress had saved Mathias from the drudgery of shouldering the task himself. He'd struggled violently between his personal desires and the compassionate man bent on protecting life. Veed's presence in the fortress had turned Mathias into a disgusting caricature of himself, one who fantasized about torturing others. It was for the best that Veed had been sent away.

With clarity returning to Mathias by the day, he refocused his energy on Elidae's current dangers. Most of the snow had melted, allowing life to creep out across the island once again. Mathias suspected the demons anticipated a glorious return to arms, and he busied himself with preparations to ensure that return didn't come packaged with unnecessary losses to his army. The footing hadn't quite reached full traction, suggesting the demons might be reluctant to march, but that didn't secure the sky from alar.

Mathias frowned, tapping the end of his pen against his desk, sending tiny flecks of ink across the corner of his map. They had one option. One option that should have been secured and through with weeks ago. The option he'd *tried* to take weeks ago. They needed to reach the second tunnel, and they had to do it before the demons resurfaced in force.

He ran his free hand through his hair and sank back against his chair. Dread consumed him from a source he couldn't quite grasp. Nessix wasn't there to get angry with him anymore, and destroying that portal would seal off the demons' access to Elidae. So why did putting the army back in this same position seem like a terrible idea?

Mathias puffed out a laugh. "It had been such an easy decision the first time…" he muttered. "Why is it so hard now?"

He waited for Etha's answer, just in case she wanted to offer one, but she kept still. Silent, once again. Mathias sighed and placed his pen down to rub his eyes. He looked over the map. The sooner they got to that second tunnel, the sooner they'd end this. The flemans were capable of cleaning up whatever demons lurked about afterwards, allowing Mathias to move ahead and find Nessix.

Blowing out a slow breath, Mathias pressed his arms back to

stretch out his chest. Just as his fingers returned to his pen, the distant clang of Veed's siege bells disrupted the stillness of his room. Mathias frowned and straightened. Nessix would have translated their message the second they began ringing, but Mathias had relied too heavily on her insight to take the time to interpret the patterns for himself. The wicked side of Mathias that still fought for control urged him to ignore the warning, but his conscience kicked those whims to the dirt.

Mathias stood, his knees aching from how long he'd kept them stationary, and he powered his way down the hall in search of Sulik. Several soldiers he passed cast him curious glances, no doubt wondering whether or not he had an official response to deliver, but Mathias kept his mouth shut. It would reflect poorly on him if he expressed his thoughts on Veed's welfare, and he was still working to repair his good name.

The preliminary hunt for Sulik proved his friend missing from his usual haunts, so Mathias approached the first captain he found. Perhaps it was a good sign Sulik was scarce. That might mean those tolls were nothing to merit concern.

"Can you tell me what he's facing?" Mathias asked the captain, praying to any deity watching over him in Etha's absence that he could justify withholding assistance.

"Two fronts, striking in the east," came the instant reply.

Mathias grimaced at what that likely meant. "Two forces wouldn't target one fortress."

"No, sir. They're announcing townships in imminent danger."

Mathias shook his head and tugged at his lower lip. "I gather he wouldn't have those bells ringing for raiding parties." This didn't add up to the tactics Mathias expected of his familiar foes. The Teradhel fortress still served as the most attractive target.

"No. It's siege level."

Think! Mathias ordered himself. *This means something!* Deciphering this madness would have been much easier with Etha to consult.

The captain averted his eyes from Mathias's agitation. Brant had been vocal to the masses about what transpired in the war chamber upon Veed's confession and rumors had quickly grown more elaborate as they spread through the troops. The number of men willing to aid Veed's distress had diminished. Mathias couldn't possibly ask the army to move to that traitor's defense.

"Sir Sagewind!" Sulik's voice eased relief into both men, allowing them an adequate excuse to forget their desire to see Veed fall victim to tragedy.

Mathias turned to greet his friend. "Have you received a report on field conditions yet?"

Sulik shook his head. "By the look on your face, I suspect you're disinclined to assist?"

Blanching at how obvious his loathing had become, the filthy part of Mathias which he tried to overcome glowed with his affirmation. "I am, but I want to send scouting parties to relay intelligence back to us. Two at each front, and one in each direction surrounding our fortress. They're to keep out of Veed's sight at all costs. I cannot afford drawing his attention."

The commander eyed Mathias, put off by the coldness his warm comrade wielded in reference to Veed's prospective fate. Sulik had discussed this change with Etha, but she supplied him with answers just as unsatisfactory as those he came up with by himself. This battle Mathias fought was one he needed to face on his own, and she promised Sulik that no matter how frightening her paladin became, he'd make it out safely on the other end. Faith was still a relatively new concept for Sulik, but he aimed to apply it now.

"Do you anticipate an attack here?"

Mathias squinted in deliberation. "I don't know," he admitted. "I'd assumed they'd target us at the first possible opportunity." He tapped his lips, squeezing direction from past experience, but still yielding nothing productive. "Is there any reason they'd target Veed? Anything extraordinary about those townships?"

Sulik, much less seasoned in the ways demons fought, shrugged. "They've got economic impact, same as Sarlot did, but do the demons really have anything to gain from harming Veed's economy?"

Mathias flattened his palm over his mouth and shook his head. "Unless Veed's been lying about his wealth, no. It wouldn't affect someone like him during war time."

"I'm sorry, sir," Sulik said. "I don't have any more ideas than you do."

Mathias sighed then dropped his hand to his side, drawing out a weak smile. "You can't be blamed for it."

The commander attempted to return the gesture, but his tangle of apprehension dampened his efforts. "So you're letting Veed handle his own fronts. What are your orders?"

Moving past the uncertainty of Sulik's disappointment relaxed Mathias's expression. "The second tunnel."

Sulik grimaced and lowered his gaze, struck by a nagging sickness at the thought. "And you think... It'll work this time, right?"

Mathias breathed deeply, suppressing the regret unearthed by Sulik's timid response. "It will. The demons are focused on Veed. Veed's focused on them. If nothing else, we can occupy the passage and block them at their source."

"And you're leaving Brant behind, I presume."

"Brant and Inwan. I trust they'll keep our civilians safe."

The first time Mathias announced his intentions to collapse that second tunnel, Sulik had more than a few misgivings related to Nes's reaction. That dread ended up an alarming premonition, and Sulik was afraid to know why his heart felt so heavy now. "Do you expect either of them to comply?" he asked, just above a whisper.

Mathias patted Sulik's shoulder. "They will. I've got it figured out."

"Sir, that's what you said when—"

"It's different now." The clip of Mathias's interruption cast a hasty flush across Sulik's cheeks. "*I* am different now. It'll all be okay."

Sulik tried to smile to show his support of Mathias, but this was the second time he'd made such a promise. Unwilling to keep digging, too afraid of the answers, Sulik swallowed the lump rising in his throat. "Then your orders?"

"The peasant troops stay behind," Mathias said, relieved by Sulik's compliance. "Begin to rally the army proper. I'll speak with Brant and Inwan."

Sulik lowered his gaze. "Yes, sir." He turned to carry out his duty.

"Oh, and Sulik?"

The commander stopped, shoulders squared and back to Mathias.

"Thank you."

Bowing his head, Sulik moved forward. He didn't have the heart to go through this again.

* * * * *

Plans unfolded smoothly for the Teradhel army's push toward the remaining portal. Mathias hadn't yet spoken to Brant or Inwan about their roles in the attack, as incoming reports delivered by his scouts preoccupied his immediate concerns. Allegedly, Veed had yet to personally ride out, entrusting combat to his senior officers. It sounded out of character for the battle fiend, amplifying Mathias's reservations about the current conditions. Veed had no way of knowing Mathias's plans, but moving such a large force would be too obvious for Veed to miss. Mathias prayed there was one thread of goodness left in Veed and that he'd avoid complicating matters that did not concern him.

Mathias cracked his knuckles and looked over his map one more time. The plan was deceptively simple, provided they pulled it off this time. He'd wipe out the demons' access point, cripple Shand's indirect method of acting against the flemans, and force her to come out to confront him. At that point, Mathias would take care of her. He still wasn't clear how he'd manage that, only that he had to find a way if he wanted to see peace come back to Elidae. But first, he had to stop the demons.

The army was set to move out in the evening and anticipation rippled through the ranks. They'd spent so long immobile, stewing in their dismal thoughts, and were eager to engage again. Eager to end this war.

As Mathias shoved the map into his pack, a rapid knock sounded at his door. Before he could turn to convey a welcome to enter, a pressing voice called from the other side. "Sir! Come quickly!"

Mathias's heart stopped at the urgency in the messenger's voice. The siege bells hadn't tolled, so there couldn't be an attack coming. No swift rush of commotion signified that the fortress had somehow been compromised. Mathias's thoughts snapped to Brant and he dropped his pack to rush to the door.

"What is it?" Frantic prayers soared toward Etha that he still had time to prevent a tragedy.

"Sir." The messenger's mouth snapped shut. He swallowed hard and met Mathias's eyes, tears glistening across his own. "Logan's been killed and—"

Mathias's mind snagged on that word. Given the great horse's deteriorated condition, he'd expected him to pass soon, but that wasn't the report. Logan had been *killed*.

The messenger shook his head, posture slumped in a bleak cross between helplessness and terror. "And the general... Sir. Her grave has been robbed."

Mathias clenched his teeth, a sweltering breath drawing his shoulders back. "Robbed?"

The messenger lowered his head, timid gaze pointed at the floor. "Sir."

"What was taken?"

He snuck a glance at his interim general, balking from the storm brewing in his eyes. "E-everything. Including..." How could he say it?

"They've taken Nessix."

The messenger blinked back his tears, curling his lower lip between his teeth. He nodded.

Mathias's heart quivered around Affliction, his desire to brutalize the culprits striking so hard his head spun. Hadn't the demons done enough? Hadn't Shand? Rational thoughts and tactical aptitude sank in his fury, surpassing all concerns about strategy and tunnels and mortal rivalries. He was ready to demand justice through any means he'd have to take. Etha had told Mathias he needed to find Shand before he could tend to her, but now, finding her was his sole concern.

"Report this to Commander Vakharan," Mathias said sharply. "Tell him I trust his judgment on whether or not to inform

Commander Maliroch. He will carry out the movements as planned if I don't make it back." When the messenger's gasp of uncertainty dropped his mouth open, Mathias added, "In time."

A brief nod later, the messenger gulped and dashed off.

Mathias counted whatever kept Etha from his mind a small blessing. He couldn't afford the risk of her trying to talk sense into him, as the intentions burning inside of him would appall the gentle goddess. Intimately familiar with Nes's grave site by now, reaching it by teleportation should have expended minimal effort. Mathias steadied his stance, closed his eyes, and began to direct himself to the sacred ground, yet he never moved from where he stood. Was he too impassioned right now? No, that made no sense. The more emotional charge he carried and the stronger his urgency, the more effectively this technique worked. It all began to fall into place. Etha wasn't simply distracted by locating Shand or watching the demons' activity. The only divinity left in Mathias came from the power Affliction poured into his heart.

The paladin stormed out his door, not even bothering to try summoning Ceraphlaks. If his past taints were any indication, he wouldn't be able to reach his companion, either. He stalked down the hall, ignoring the murmurs and concerned glances chasing after him. The longer he wound his way through the fortress, the more abrupt questions went unanswered, until word of his instability made its rounds as thoroughly as Brant's had. At least the army still had Sulik to guide them. The troops and civilians huddled away from Mathias, watching him through troubled eyes.

Nobody attempted to intercept or follow Mathias, giving him a wide clearance as he left the fortress to trudge through the mud. It was for the best. Any mortal who followed him could only look forward to Shand striking them down, but that wasn't Mathias's greatest fear. Rather, Mathias was afraid to let the army see the way he planned to treat a lady.

He pushed ahead on foot, stalking purposefully to the sacred place where Nessix should have watched over her troubled nation in the afterlife. He spat at the thought. Who was he trying to fool? Nessix couldn't watch over anything; her soul was gone.

And now they have her body…

Mathias's blood seared, bringing a glow of fury to his cheeks. He wanted to scream. He wanted to tell the demons that he surrendered, that they'd won. Through desecrating Nessix, they'd tortured Mathias in a way he never thought possible. They'd cut into him in the hells. Forced him to watch barbaric measures taken against others. He'd witnessed them delight in destroying lives, but this level of sadism surpassed all expectations.

Even if Mathias hadn't loved Nessix, the demons had stolen her soul from Etha's grasp. How long had they practiced this atrocity? To how many others? They'd dug up Nes's body, the same body Mathias had so carefully preserved for the day he pried her soul from their foul hands. Yes, even if he hadn't loved her, this was unforgivable, and unfortunately for the demons, Mathias *had* loved her. He still did.

His feet dug into the ground as he belted out an anguished roar. "You wanted a fight, Shand?" he shouted to the openness around him, tearing his sword free from its sheath. "I'll face you now, coward!"

Tears stung his eyes and he turned to survey his surroundings, sword at the ready. He didn't know if he expected Shand to show up, but the part of him that remembered mortality breathed a sigh of relief when she didn't. Fist clenched around his blade's hilt, Mathias stormed ahead until Nes's grave came into view. At that point, he broke to a run.

As reported, Logan lay on his side, five arrows puncturing his barrel and his throat slit. His eyes remained open and as empty as they'd been since Nes's funeral. The last ounce of leniency left in Mathias whispered a prayer on the noble horse's behalf, but his more immediate concern revolved around the open hole in the ground and the pile of earth beside it. Mathias's jaw clenched rigid, nostrils flaring as he stalked up to the edge of Nes's open grave and looked down into it.

Nessix was gone and in her place lay the scattered remains of a white lily, crumpled petals torn from their stem and strewn through the tomb. Mathias drew a sweltering breath, neck aching from the clench of his jaw. This was a new low, even for beasts as warped as demons, and he had no doubt this boldness had

271

originated with Shand.

Mathias spun and paced around the grave, eyes darting across the sparse landscape. There weren't many places for someone to hide, but Shand wouldn't need one. "Alright!" he roared. "You've made your point! Come face me and let's end this!"

The rational side of Mathias still screamed that he had no idea how to take on a goddess, not by himself and especially not without Etha. He trusted Affliction's might even in Etha's absence, as he credited the god spear for keeping him alive in his previous visit to the hells. But surviving torture and surviving a bout with a goddess were two different challenges. Mathias growled his hatred, determination speaking bold vows that he wouldn't need something like the god spear to see Shand dead.

"Where are you, whore?"

A stiff breeze pressed against Mathias, strong enough to push his prowl to a stop. He straightened, the whispers of divinity riding along with the gust picking at his senses.

"No need to shout, Mathias, I'm right here."

Mathias's heart hesitated its rhythm at the sound of Shand's smooth voice. He knew the gods shared a certain degree of begrudging respect for him—after all, next to Julianna, he was Etha's favorite creation, besting the regard she held for any of the new gods with ease. The squabbling, lower ranked deities seldom hid their subsequent resentment from Mathias, but none of them had attempted to use force against him until now. With the past they shared, Mathias suspected Shand was after vengeance, he just didn't know at what line she'd stop. No matter. Even if she found a way to permanently remove Mathias from Abaeloth, Julianna would see her punished. Determination wrapping its fierce arms around him, Mathias tuned to face Shand.

She stood a solid six paces from him, hands held loosely in front of her and serenity painting her flawless face. Her lips lifted into a broader smile as she soaked in the tension of his stance.

"Mathias, dear, you look terrible."

"What do you want from me?" he asked heatedly. The sooner he got that sorted out, the sooner he could put things right again.

Shand gasped through an open mouth, brows arching with an

exaggerated confusion Mathias shook off. "You were the one calling for me." She pressed a hand to her chest. "Well, I'm assuming as much. It's been a long time since I've been expected to answer to such a crude address."

Mathias scoffed and would have shaken his head if he'd been willing to take his eyes off her. "You haven't changed at all..."

"Huh," she mused with a slight shake of her shoulders. "And here I thought I'd grown so much bolder. Certainly clever enough to fool you. Though I suppose that had never been terribly difficult."

His eyes narrowed. She'd play this game with him all day if he allowed her to. "I'll be generous and give you one chance to make this right."

"Or else what?"

"Shand, you are in serious trouble with those who outrank you, trouble I may be the only one who can help you get out of."

She closed her eyes, confident against the prospect of Mathias attempting an attack on her, and smiled. "Oh, I'm not wanting out of this trouble. Believe me."

Mathias's lips tugged at a snarl, knuckles begging for leniency as his fingers crushed around his sword. "Where's Nessix?"

Shand opened her eyes, revealing the same dark daggers Mathias had grown familiar with. Scrambling to catch his composure, he adjusted his grip on his sword and awaited an explanation that culminated as nothing more than a slight shake of Shand's head.

"Tell me where she is and I'll leave Elidae," he said. Sulik had Etha backing him now, and the flemans had the skill to hold out while Mathias arranged for proper reinforcements.

Shand laughed and clapped her hands. "Oh, that girl means an awful lot to you, doesn't she?"

Every trill of laughter, every glint in those toxic violet eyes, pulled a thread of Mathias's sensibility away, threatening to unravel the cordial demeanor he preferred to maintain. Shand was a fool. She only thought she knew what Mathias would do when he reached the end of his patience.

"This isn't a game, Shand."

"Of *course* it's a game."

"Where. Is she?"

Shand sighed with a shake of her head and disdainful flick of her hand. "I don't know."

"Where is she!"

The goddess rolled her eyes. She could harp on about Mathias's stupidity right now, but it wouldn't take either of them very far and that road seemed too dull to hold her interest. "All I can tell you is that the demons have her. They've been such…" She hesitated here, wrinkling her nose in light of her recent complications. Mathias didn't need to know about any of that. "*Loyal* darlings, I thought they deserved a little insight on my mortal studies as payment."

"You whore!"

The first time Mathias encountered Shand, she'd been a fragile mortal woman, apprenticing under one of the pioneers of necromancy. The Order had expended intensive measures to keep that school of sacrilege from the demons and, as far as Mathias knew, they'd succeeded in doing so. At least until now.

Shand belted a hearty laugh at the darkness that spun in Mathias's eyes. "What's wrong, Mathias dear? Where's all those bold words of how you'll strike me down for my dastardly ways?"

The desire to retaliate urged Mathias to rush her while he had the chance, but experience held up a hand of warning. Shand had obviously discarded any sense of her grudging respect for both him and Etha, and Mathias still didn't know what he could do against her. "Oh, Affliction is burning for you, you can be sure of that."

Shand meandered closer to Mathias, not sparing a glance at his sword. "Then why not let him out to play? Show me this great god-slaying power that beats inside of you."

Mathias clenched his jaw as she neared, trembling to hold himself back from making a stupid decision.

Gleeful eyes held his scathing gaze and narrowed as Shand cocked her head. "Or does Nessix really mean that little to you?"

Mathias's free hand wrapped in a fist so tight his knuckles ached. Forget his reservations. Forget the indisputable difference in their might. If Shand wasn't his best lead on how to find Nessix, he'd rip her to shreds where she stood. "I will not kill you." He forced those words out, needing to hear them for himself, each seeping with his true desire to rid Abaeloth from every last memory of Shand Heltsa.

Shand stopped a sword's length from Mathias and laughed again. "That's because you *can't*, isn't it?"

Mathias held his uncertainty in his heaving chest. If sheer desire would have been able to slay Shand, he'd have destroyed her the moment Veed so much as murmured her involvement with the demons. Instead, Mathias banked on a bluff he prayed Shand would buy.

"You can make this right, Shand. At least by me. Free Nessix from the demons, deliver her back to me, and I might be willing to work with you."

She grinned and shook her head, raising her hands to her lips. "You still don't understand, do you?" she asked. "Giving you Nessix back will do nothing for my agenda."

"Then what is your agenda?"

Shand strode closer, giddy at the snappy way Mathias righted his stance and threw his shoulders back. He did not, however, retreat. Pride and his silly sense of bravery forbid that.

"To punish the Order, of course," she murmured, cocking her head as a sneer traced ugly lines across Mathias's face. "You, specifically. With all of your clout, you could have kept me safe and comfortable in those ranks."

Mathias snarled. "I couldn't have done a thing to protect you after you attempted to steal that god shard. That's something you need to take up with Jules."

"Jules"—his sister's name snapped tartly from Shand's lips—"is not here."

His heart raced against Affliction's anticipation. He could have used his sister's strength right about now. Mathias swallowed those regrets; wishes would do nothing for him. "In the end, you got your way, didn't you? You *did* become a goddess."

"Not the way I should have," Shand corrected. "I should have ascended first—"

"You would have still been second."

Shand's eyes flashed at his cocky interruption and she curled her lip. "That shard would have been mine if it weren't for Etha's interference."

Mathias's brows furrowed. Etha had nothing to do with the assignment of the god shards, nor the events which had led to Shand's banishment from Zeal. "It was a decision made by the Order. *Mortals* of the Order. Etha does not tamper with fate."

Shand scowled at Mathias's faith, that petty trait which had earned him so much favor in Etha's graces. Frustration roiled against her calm until it nearly slipped from her grasp. She curled her fingers against her palms to curb her irritation. There was still too much she wanted to drag Mathias through for her to let her temper get the best of her now. "Of course she doesn't," Shand murmured. "That would explain how you ended up here on Elidae, why those storms were sent to cripple my army, how these pathetic, godless fools found her blessing. No, Etha cares not for tampering with fate."

Mathias's glare hardened. "She answers the prayers of the faithful," he said. "She does what must be done."

"The faithful?" Shand's lips lifted into a lazy smile and she reached forward. Before Mathias thought to flinch away, Shand cupped his cheek in her palm. A startled gasp stole the air from his lungs and his body jerked, growing rigid as Shand's heinous divinity flooded through his limbs and twisted its way into his mind. Instinct screamed at him to pull away, but Mathias couldn't move.

"Etha may be keen on doing what she has to, but I do whatever I want." Shand slid a step closer to Mathias and murmured in his ear. "Remember that."

Her lips traced his cheek, and Mathias fell into darkness.

TWENTY-THREE

When Kol first set his sights on obtaining Nessix, he'd had no way of gauging the extent of her worth. He realized the political sway she commanded, and that she possessed the challenge of a tactical mind, but not even in his loftiest dreams had he anticipated her to mean so much to the world around her, let alone to Mathias. She'd intrigued Kol from the first day he began investigating her. Nessix swelled with alluring potential and the longer Kol worked with her soul, the more he was convinced that potential was all he'd ever need.

He'd been nervous over the logistics of reclaiming her body, having assumed the flemans would have kept her under close guard. At the very least, Kol expected such invasive actions to draw attention from those still mourning the loss of their general. Fate seldom smiled on the demons, but it seemed to favor their retrieving Nessix. With her faithful warhorse easily trounced in his decrepit state, Kol's task force of two dozen demons and their alar escorts unearthed Nessix without complication and delivered her home to him.

Kol dipped a cloth in the shallow bowl of water sitting beside where Nessix lay and systematically wiped the dirt from her face. Tenderness was an unbecoming attribute for demons, but that suppressed side of Kol basked in delight as he worked. This petite

woman held all of the traits Kol coveted in his creations—
leadership skills, combat experience, a deceptive size and frame.
Most important, Nessix had a temperament that complemented an
authoritative position in the hells beautifully. Kol savored this quiet
time with her, certain it would be the first and only chance to enjoy
it.

After he finished washing the dirt from Nes's face, Kol shifted
his attention to her neck. He worked carefully, mindful of the
laceration he'd used to take her life, and as he uncovered the broad
wound, he cocked his head and smiled. As he'd hoped, her flesh
still gaped open, Mathias's feeble attempts at blessing her failing to
mend this cursed flaw. Mathias had otherwise done an immaculate
job preserving her corpse, undoubtedly with some twisted hope
that he'd someday be able to perform a miracle very similar to what
Kol intended. This worked immensely in the demons' favor, as
Nessix would need no further modifications, no attempts at
patching up decayed flesh, to resume function.

Thinking of Mathias brought a frown to Kol's face, robbing
him of his bout of pleasure. The paladin had proven some time ago
to be a nuisance to even the most carefully conceived plans, and
Kol couldn't help but think he'd try to intercept this one. That was
Nessix's one imperfection. She'd meant too much to Mathias. Kol
had a narrow window to make this work; a narrow window Mathias
could not interfere with. If any part of her recreation went foul,
she'd be lost to Kol forever. The past dozen years of experiments
and failures and eventual success gave Kol a general sense of
confidence, and it all culminated in this. His creations, the akhuerai,
needed their leader, one capable of launching no end of mayhem
before she was through. The akhuerai needed Nessix Teradhel.

Kol shook his head to chase off his concerns. It wasn't like a
demon to dwell on such unsavory sentiments. He concentrated his
efforts on cleaning the dirt from Nes's hands, revealing the
calloused skin of one who had spent life on the battlefield. This
roughness contradicted her delicate profile, and Kol had a hard
time accepting how much grief this tiny woman had caused him.
Nes's nobility had gifted her an attractive face and elegant build,
features the once-mortal side of Kol knew could prove every bit as

deadly as any skill at arms. Yes, Nessix was perfect for his cause.

"Grell is approaching."

The guard's crisp warning yanked Kol from his reflections, drawing out a frown as he flicked a glance to where Annin sorted through jars of medicinal components. He'd hoped for Grell to give him more time to prepare his course of action, but time was never something Grell was generous enough to give. The door flung open well before Kol had braced for it and Grell crammed his way into the room.

The inoga stood just inside the entry, scowling at Nessix. Kol gave up trying to decipher what Grell's scowls meant some time ago, as he used them to express both pleasure and disgust. Kol moved his hand to the pouch at his side, the pouch which protected Nes's soul. Soon, he could quit fretting over whether or not Grell would accidentally screw this up, and damaging Nes's physical body was far less detrimental than damaging her soul.

"So you *did* find her." Grell crossed his arms, looking anything but impressed. "You think it'll make a difference?"

Kol sighed and fetched a clean cloth to wipe the dirt from his hand, lips creased as he assessed Nes's immobile form. His survival counted on this working. Kol's eyes lingered on Nessix as he delivered his answer.

"I think it will make every difference," he said. "Returning her to the body she knows how to use, the body Mathias recognizes… I don't see how anything could serve us better."

Grell grunted—another expression Kol didn't bother interpreting—and narrowed his eyes as he appraised Nessix. She was so scrawny, it was hard to believe her body capable of anything greater than the typical responsibilities expected of a woman. Even some of those, Grell doubted she'd hold up to meet his standards. His scowl developed into a sneer. That one gained Kol's attention. That one meant dissatisfaction. As tiny and unassuming as Nessix was, it infuriated Grell that she had been so much trouble for his army. He hated this woman nearly as much as he hated Mathias, possibly more so since the pair of them meant so much destruction. Based on Kol's research and theory, though, he'd get to take these frustrations and then some out of her flesh with few consequences in the days to come.

Redirecting rage was not among inoga's strong suits, but Grell managed solely from his desire to put this project and the headache affiliated with it behind him. "So have you run your games yet? You know who we're sacrificing for her?"

Kol cleared his throat and tucked the cloth beside Nessix. He crossed his arms to keep from touching her pouch again. "About that, sir," he murmured. "I've, um, cancelled Nessix's games."

Grell straightened, wings flicking in offense. That was the only part of this entire operation he enjoyed. "You *what*?"

A swift flare of uncertainty threatened to shake Kol, but he shook it off, confident in the amount of thought he'd put into this final phase. He had to believe Grell understood the importance of Nessix functioning at full capacity, whether he liked her or not. Her revival relied on Kol and his research, and if his suspicions were correct, his new approach may be the best way to secure the safety of them both. Kol drew a slow breath and braced himself.

"I have cancelled her games," he repeated. "I believe she'll serve us best with blood sourced from a stronger donor than some random aranau."

"That is why we have *games*," Grell seethed. "It's not some random aranau. It's the most fierce we've got."

"The most fierce of the aranau have been used in previous projects," Kol countered, unclear where this bout of bravery spouted from. "And they are too chaotic, besides."

"So what's your alternative?"

Kol swallowed the regrets flailing inside of him. "I've yet to talk over the logistics of it, but I intend to source my own blood for her."

Grell stared at Kol as if he'd just sworn loyalty to Etha herself, too busy letting the words sink in to be annoyed at the boldness with which Kol held his eyes. A noxious laugh boomed from Grell at last, and Kol pointed his attention toward the ground.

"Would you listen to him, Annin?" Grell said, waving his hand at the Spirit Binder. "You're the magical consultant in this escapade. What are your thoughts?"

Kol held his breath, hoping he could work his colleague's

insights to his advantage.

"Master Kol's plan is reckless," Annin said without hesitation. He never hesitated when he spoke, even to inoga. *Especially* when he spoke to inoga. "But it wouldn't be one of his plans if it wasn't."

Grell frowned, having never cared much for Annin's casual addresses. "We bleed our aranau dry to bring back one mortal."

"Indeed, we do." Annin stepped away from his table of components at last. He stood just behind Kol, submitting to the alar's authority, but aiming to stake his status for Grell to notice. "Which is why I said it was reckless. With care, I believe it can be done. Just more slowly than what you're used to."

Grell growled. He didn't have a nearly sharp enough mind to understand the procedures necessary to reanimate a body, and though he felt Kol and his lackey were talking down to him, he had no grounds to debate. "How long is longer?"

Annin shrugged. "It'd have to be a slow bleed. Three days at least."

Kol grit his teeth to fend off his wince. If the aranau's thrashing and screams were any indication, this would make for an agonizing three days. Though he hadn't yet discussed the details with Annin, he hoped he'd be able to hold out that long.

"And in that time, I'd have no access to him on the field?"

"Have we even taken the field recently?"

"Annin, that's enough." Kol's reservations about this plan had robbed too much of his patience. The last thing he needed was Grell to flip tables or kill his oraku. "My lord," he said, looking up to Grell. "I have thought over our options and this is truly the best one we have."

"I think you've just grown smitten with the little wench," Grell snorted. "I told you not to keep carrying her around with you."

Annin's residual respect for Kol prevented him from voicing his agreement.

Kol bit back his retort, due in part to his confusion over the accusation, and laid his hand on the pouch where Nessix's soul burned against his leg. "I understand how the akhuerai function better than anyone, even our elite oraku. I studied how Nessix works on the field more extensively than anyone else. I created her final memories. I know her. I am the best fit for the job."

Grell grunted, disparaging Kol's impulse down his nose. "And if it kills you?"

"Then I die."

Grell looked Kol over a while longer before puffing out his arrogance with a shake of his head. "Then you die..." He turned and left the room. The guard pulled the door shut behind him.

Kol remained still, eyes focused on the ground as thoughts tumbled through his mind. He'd been around for a very long time. Long enough to remember the faces of the first children gods. And through all of those ages to make errors, this decision threatened to be the worst idea he'd ever concocted.

Annin interrupted Kol's reflection with a brusque sigh. "You hadn't discussed this with me," he said. "Is this about your rivalry with Grell or do you really intend to carry it out?"

Now would be the most convenient time to back out of this ludicrous fantasy, but Kol was just fool enough to stay his course. "Pissing off Grell is an added bonus, but this is my intent."

"You do know I wasn't bluffing. It could kill you."

"Yes."

Annin sighed and walked past Kol to lean over the table and look over Nessix with his critical eyes. "Do you have a priestess in mind for blessing her soul vessels?"

"The brunette's always been feisty," Kol said, distracted by much more sinister thoughts involving his death.

Annin nodded, glancing at Kol to take in the storm of regret and confusion tumbling through his mind. "And when would you like to proceed?"

It had been quite some time since Kol last grasped a firm semblance of fear, but it crept up on him now, urging him to flee from this threat he'd thrown himself before. Death in combat didn't bother demons. Death due to internal conflicts among their peers didn't bother them. But the thought of Nessix killing him from beyond the grave? Kol wouldn't speak the words out loud, but that awoke a tremor inside him that fought to bring tears to his eyes.

Buying time in vain hopes of banishing such juvenile weakness from his voice, Kol cast his gaze back to Nessix as she lay there so serenely. Though Kol suspected she'd prefer death over the purpose intended for her, Nessix had no idea the risk he prepared to take on her behalf. And if it failed him, he wouldn't want to survive to bear the consequences, anyway. These reflections did not ease the smoldering fear inside of him. Kol coughed on his sigh and glanced at Annin.

"Is there anything I should do to prepare?"

Annin shrugged and disregarded the tick in Kol's voice. "If you were still mortal, I'd suggest you pray. Since you are not, no. There is nothing I can advise you to do."

Kol rubbed his jaw and nodded, glancing through the room to try to find a distraction to calm himself. Weeks had passed since he last took the field in combat, so he had no injuries to weaken him. He hadn't been called to any greater action than walking the halls of the hells, so there was no worry about preexisting exhaustion. Maybe part of this fell back on arrogance, but nobody else was as fit for the task at hand.

"Then we start immediately," Kol said through numb lips forced into compliance. "Send for our priestess, bless those soul vessels, and let's get started."

Friendship was a questionable concept to demons, but Annin liked Kol more than he hated him, and the alar's palpable reservations breathed life to a wriggling discomfort in his own stomach. "Of course, sir." Not wanting to dwell on Kol's ridiculous notions any longer than necessary, Annin left, stopping for a brief consultation with the guard.

The door shut and Kol turned his attention back to Nessix. He picked up the cloth again, twisting it in his hands before he resumed the task of cleaning her flesh. His free hand gripped the pouch at his side.

"Do not make me regret this, little one..."

* * * * *

The following day, Mathias was the one dragging Julianna to the banquet hall, as his previous behavior had humiliated her enough to account for the next thirty years. In her heart, Julianna wanted to be happy for her brother, but in typical fashion, his happiness came at the express displeasure of someone it was imperative to not displease. She fidgeted in her seat, delivering smiles born of deeply ingrained politeness at the respectful gestures made to her as Mathias lounged in his chair and made a production of enjoying his meal.

He leaned over toward his sister. "Hey, why do you suppose Nes hasn't shown up yet?"

Julianna took a deep breath to calm herself. It didn't work. "Rumor has it," she said sharply, focusing her irate gaze at the table to avoid looking at her brother, "she tried to show up wearing pants."

Mathias laughed despite his sister's strict and obvious agitation. It wasn't as though he needed more reasons to like Nessix.

"This isn't funny!" Julianna scolded. She flung a hand toward the tension hanging in the air throughout the hall and when Brant entered before the general's twins did, she met his eyes quickly and looked away. "All of this is your fault for that stunt you pulled yesterday."

"I'd argue it's all *your* fault for dragging me to banquet in the first place."

A contented smile crossed Mathias's face as he swept his gaze past Brant's scowl and prompt address to one of the posted guards to watch Nessix be escorted to her seat. A petite, tawny haired maiden scampered along behind her, tossing a mischievous smile in Mathias's direction. Julianna dropped her fork, mouth gaping in horror. Nevius's frown far overshadowed Brant's discontent and moments later, a well-armed guard approached Mathias's table.

"Sir Sagewind." His voice strained between duty and terror, fingers twitching a healthy distance from his hilt. He wouldn't meet Mathias's eyes. "It has been requested that you are escorted from the evening's activities."

Julianna immediately wiped her mouth with a handkerchief and prepared to stand. Mathias grasped her forearm to hold her in her seat. "Has it?" He raised a brow at the guard's avoidance.

"Yes, sir," the guard stammered. "Please, sir, do not make this a conflict."

A conflict? This already was a conflict, one much greater than the guard could ever hope to bargain for, and Mathias was not the cause of it. Even if Nevius proved himself a decent man or Nessix contently accepted her role as a broodmare, Zeal was Mathias's home. The *Citadel* was his home! And this man, this pathetic excuse of a noble, dared to request Mathias to leave? He looked up at Etha, who gently tried to cheer Nessix, looked at the beautiful young woman's subdued expression, and his eyes darkened. His grip tightened around Julianna's arm.

"Mattie…" she warned on hushed tones. "Don't…"

If this was something which merited obedience, Mathias might have taken note of his sister's reservations, but he couldn't tolerate this disrespect any longer. Tearing his hand free from his hold on Julianna, Mathias sprang to his feet and slammed his fist on the table. Place settings skittered across the top and clattered to the floor. Julianna groaned and sank her face into her hands.

"I want everyone's attention," he called, clapping his hands to gain the eyes and ears of the entire hall. After the startled gasps died down, Mathias continued. "I, your White Paladin, Sir Mathias Sagewind, hereby declare my intention to take the hand of Lady Nessix Teradhel of Elidae in marriage!"

Nessix, still ignorant to Mathias's native language, looked up with confused eyes. Beside her, Etha covered her mouth with two tiny hands and scrunched up her shoulders before leaning over to hurriedly whisper a translation in Nes's ear. The noble lady's face paled and her jaw dropped. Mathias set his determination in his eyes.

"Any who wish to challenge my proposal are welcome to duel me for this honor."

The crowd of stunned locals all knew better than to raise objections. As disappointed as they might have been, nothing was worth challenging Mathias in combat. Nevius, however, was not a local, and he'd solidified his opinion of Mathias the previous night.

"You son of a bitch!" the fleman noble roared, too blinded by this blatant insult to his standing to care whether or not he

285

maintained a credible front. The crowd gasped at Nevius's foolishness. No sane man confronted Mathias Sagewind with aggression. "You have no right!"

Mathias held his arms wide and shook his head. "I have every right." He took a step farther from Julianna's attempt to snatch him. "I am a noble and a legal resident of Zeal. Wasn't that the only requirements you made for who could buy her?"

Nevius's nostrils flared. "You are unwelcome to our courtesy."

"What you are extending is not a courtesy. It is slavery."

"Guards!" Nevius sputtered, outwardly flailing to regain his self-control. "Won't *someone* do something about this beast?"

The guards shifted and fidgeted, unwilling to draw their weapons. If they'd been ordered to detain any other man, they'd have jumped to action. Mathias's devilish smile grew at the command he held over the room.

"Does this mean that *you*, Sir Teradhel, are challenging me?" Mathias asked. He strode ahead, an imposing air sweeping about his erect shoulders. "You know what? Bring that cousin of yours, too. I'll take you both on, for the honor of your beloved sister."

Fire raged in Nevius's eyes and across his flushed cheeks, and Brant threw down his fork to move to his cousin's side. Both men bit down on Mathias's challenge and shoved their ways to the open expanse intended to serve as a dance floor. Etha, wearing a broad grin, plopped herself down in Nevius's chair and propped her chin in her hands, elbows on the table. Nessix rose halfway out of her seat and held her breath.

This game had gone on for too long. "Mathias, stop this!" Julianna's authoritative voice rang through the hushed chamber.

Mathias hesitated, brows furrowed, but he didn't look away from his approaching targets to confirm the disgruntled ire in his sister's glare. "Are you seriously worried about me?"

"No!" she cried, exasperated. "I'm worried about them!"

Several patrons murmured their agreement, an action which only bristled Nevius further. He and Brant had both drawn their swords, formidable weapons in their own rights, but Mathias trusted his blade more than he trusted any mortal ally. He smiled and loosened his sword in its sheath. A dull splat connected with his back and Mathias turned to meet Julianna's glower. She must have been more upset with him than he'd thought for her to resort to a public display of such childish behavior. He glanced at the sad little lump of ruined cake on the floor then back at the icing covering his sister's hand and chuckled. Oh, yes. She was *quite* angry with him. With an amused shake of his head, Mathias turned and pressed on toward his opponents.

"This does not have to happen," Nevius growled, receiving concerned glances from the audience.

"I agree," Mathias said. "But I know I'm unwilling to yield, so unless you are…"

Gaping holes riddled Nevius's defenses, flaws torn wider by the goading he so poorly endured, and though Mathias didn't much care for him, he hoped against needing to injure or humiliate the nobleman in the manner Nevius seemed destined to seek. Agitation clouded the young fleman lord's focus and the enraged snarl across his face suggested he'd spent every last fleck of will power on not flinging himself at the paladin. Mathias twisted his lips and met Etha's glittering eyes. She nodded enthusiastically and Mathias buckled his sword back in its sheath.

"I'll tell you what," Mathias said. "It's obvious you care about your own honor more than your sister's, and you're willing to fight hard for it. It's also clear that you don't think I'm worthy of her hand or to have any connection with your nation—I'm still unsure which is more important to you. You couldn't hope to beat me in a proper duel, so I'll take you bare handed." He went as far as to loosen his sword belt and toss it in Julianna's general direction. He glanced back at her and found her clean hand pressed against her forehead. As much fun as he wanted to make of the current arrangement, it was time to take matters seriously.

Nevius glanced at Brant and nodded. The pair spread out, flanking Mathias the way a pair of novice hunters cautiously targeted a wolf. The paladin glanced at the band and then back at Nevius. "Mind if I request some music? Or would that be too distracting for—"

An intense roar announced Nevius's charge and half a heartbeat later, Mathias heard Brant's feet pounding toward him as well. Mathias sighed and held his position until they entered lunging distance then dashed a pace forward to avoid them both. He turned back to face the young men and shook his head.

"Come now, Nev. Didn't your Uncle Veed teach you better than that? Or were you just not a diligent student?"

Nevius snared Nessix with a filthy glare. She limited her flinch to the tendons in her neck, but that was more than enough to awaken Mathias's animosity. He stared Nevius down for longer than he'd expected his opponent's patience to hold out. Mathias couldn't be sure if nerves had finally gotten the best of Nevius or if his hesitation came from tactically holding his action to see what Mathias tried next. Either way, their audience sat captivated by the foolishness of the fleman nobles.

"Go draw your sword, coward!" Nevius hissed.

Mathias looked over the feral youth carefully, a slow smile drawing his lips. Nevius displayed his strategy so plainly on his face that even unarmed, Mathias felt this was an unfair duel. "How much fighting have you actually done?" Mathias asked. "And I'm not talking fancy fencing lessons and sparring with wooden swords. I was right, wasn't I? Your Uncle Veed didn't teach you a thing about actual survival or tactics, or if he did, you were too daft to listen."

Nevius scowled, cheeks blotched with redness. "My Uncle Veed has nothing to do with this."

Mathias shrugged. "Nessix would have taken me to the ground three times by now and you've yet to touch me once. You think you've got the experience to lead your people with skills like *that*?"

"I said go retrieve your sword!"

Nevius sputtered his rage like a boiling pot, but laughter no longer found any part of Mathias. It was a shame this reactive, entitled brat was the one destined to dictate the future of his country. Mathias sighed, rolled his eyes, and stepped forward, placing himself between the two cousins once again. Their deficit of experience did nothing to disguise their plan, and as soon as Mathias moved past them, they sprang toward him as he'd expected.

Nevius was stockier than Brant and had considerably more to prove, and so Mathias targeted him first. Ducking to the left to avoid the fall of Brant's blade, Mathias grabbed Nevius's sword arm beneath his and twisted to throw them both to the ground.

The crowd gasped at the first sign of actual combat and wailed their dismay as Brant dove toward the fallen men. Mathias allowed the young man to get awful close before digging his heel up and into Brant's gut. Unarmored, Brant clutched his stomach, keeled over from the impact. Mathias stood and resumed walking toward his sword.

"And to think, they called *me* a coward?" he asked Julianna, raising his voice for the audience to hear.

"Mathias, that's enough," she scolded.

He bent down and retrieved his sword belt. "Nevius, may I marry your sister?"

"To the hells with you."

Mathias swung his free hand back toward Nevius and shook his head at his sister. "I don't think it has been." He took his time unbuckling his blade to think over the best possible scenario. There would be no gentle with this young man, no easy. He tucked those reservations aside and looked up to Nessix. Trouble flooded from her eyes and Mathias ached for her in light of his pending actions.

"Lady Teradhel," he asked, "do you love your brother?"

Her breath came so shallow she barely had the sense of mind to process the events spinning about before her. Etha touched her arm and Nessix blinked.

"Of course I do." Her words were hushed and small.

"And your cousin?"

"Yes."

An air of fondness missing from her first answer backed the second and Mathias grimaced. He'd been afraid of that. Glancing at the local nobles, all pompous dolts who expected titles to earn a certain degree of respect, Mathias stretched out his shoulders. "I beg your forgiveness for what I must do."

Nessix didn't answer him and Mathias whipped his sword free, discarding his belt on the ground with the same motion. He stalked back toward his opponents, testing the weight of his familiar blade as he kept his eyes lowered.

"You see, gentlemen, there's a reason everyone in this room is nervous right now, and I assure you it has little to do with the fear of you being offended. Quite the contrary, really." He looked back at the crowd. "Am I right?"

A handful of murmurs responded, but wide eyes prevented any heads from nodding.

"Big talk isn't good for much on the battlefield," Nevius said.

Mathias chuckled and nodded, pressing his lips together. "Oh, I'm well aware of that. I'll ask you again. How many battlefields have you seen?"

"My people were born of warriors—"

"That isn't what I asked."

Nevius's teeth clamped down around his words and he sucked in a sharp breath. "I have led units against minotaur raids and was a commanding officer in a movement against the ogre hordes."

Mathias rocked back on his heels and raised his eyebrows. "And I suppose you feel quite experienced from those missions?"

"I *am* experienced."

Mathias opened his mouth to explain the battles he'd been through, but realized it'd take the rest of the evening, and he still had a duel to win. "You are experienced." He pinched his lips in a grim frown. *Etha, please do not allow me bloodshed I cannot undo.*

That's no fun at all.

He looked up at her through serious eyes to find a fiendish grin on her face. When his expression remained stony, she pouted and rolled her eyes. Mathias looked from Nevius to Brant and sighed.

"I'm sorry."

Before either of them drew breath to demand his elaboration, Mathias dashed forward, his sword twisting into a spear. He slammed the butt of it against Brant's throat, sending him staggering back and gagging for breath, then spun to sink the spearhead into Nevius's abdomen. The fleman noble's eyes flew open and his sword fell from his limp hand. Now, the crowd found their gasps.

Mathias wasn't smiling any longer as his weapon warped back

into a sword and Nevius's body slid free from the blade. Julianna shrieked her fury at him and Nessix's cry of disbelief tugged at his compassion. He paid neither of them any mind, as he hadn't yet accomplished his objective. Brant wheezed behind him, still unable to get to his feet, so Mathias had no reservations keeping his back to him. Instead, he caught Nevius by the arm and eased him to the ballroom floor as the sound of siege bells clanged in the distance.

"Treat these like the last words you'll ever hear," Mathias said. "I have known your sister for a week's time, and I love her enough to do what is necessary to end her distress. Remember this, next time you think it's wise to challenge me."

Nevius sputtered up a mouthful of blood as he tried to speak and his right arm shook as he raised it. Mathias watched the young man's eyes intently, waiting for the residual anger to surrender to fear of the unknown. Nessix continued to wail in the restraint of Etha's arms.

Can you hold her back and help me at the same time? Mathias asked.
What would you do if I couldn't?
Okay, now it's not funny.

Mathias turned his head to catch a glimpse of Brant, who had pulled himself upright to stare in mute horror at the growing puddle of blood Mathias knelt in. The bells tolled louder.

"You will not die today," Mathias said, bringing his attention back to Nevius. He placed his hands over the pouring wound, coaxing Etha's grace through Affliction's channel in his heart. "But I pray you have learned something."

Mathias hated that it took mortally wounding Nevius to make his point. Such aggression wasn't his style, but Nevius's agenda hadn't given him the time to sort matters out in a more appropriate manner. Those bells... they continued to pound, dreadfully familiar and distracting Mathias from his dire obligation. If his concentration faltered, Nevius would bleed out.

Closing his eyes against the steady sound of danger, Etha's grace pooled beneath his palms to flood Nevius's body cavity. Mathias frowned as Nessix continued wailing over her fallen brother and prayed his actions hadn't frightened her away from him. She was a resilient girl, he knew, and she was clearly more fond of several other people in her life than she was of her brother, but even Julianna and the other nobles of Zeal had disapproved of the manner which Mathias chose to assert himself. Perhaps he *had* gone too far this time. He sighed and closed his eyes.

Several moments passed before Nevius's hands worked into weak fists, a bit longer still before he hauled himself to a seated position to look around the startled banquet hall. His bewildered gaze met Mathias's calm eyes and his hands clawed at the torn fabric of his jacket, pressing through to skin that didn't even bear a scar. As Mathias anticipated, Brant hadn't made a move.

"I will ask you again. May I—"

"Mathias!" Etha's voice rang through the chamber, seizing his attention from the present. "*The bells!*"

Mathias blinked and turned to face her. Nobody else in the room so much as moved, as though suspended in time, but fear hollowed his goddess's eyes. With a firm jerk, Mathias woke. His entire body ached as though he'd been thrown from a horse, and it took him undue effort to motivate his limbs to obey his demands. The bells, very real, pounded from Nes's fortress.

TWENTY-FOUR

The bells continued to toll, but it took the connection of blunt force to Mathias's side, snatching the breath from him, to initiate his movement. Replenishing his supply of oxygen with a rasping cough, adrenaline fought against his stiffness and Mathias pushed himself upright to see Ceraphlaks standing alert at his side. The stalwart pegasus wore a veil of worry over the typical mischief in his eyes and blew a sharp breath of concern when he met his rider's muddled gaze.

Mathias groaned, pressing lethargic arms against the ground to rise to a seated position. His disoriented mind whirled about as though he'd been struck from behind and his limbs dragged as if pushing against a current, begging him to lay back down. Magic thrown about by the gods was much more powerful than Mathias and his little piece of Affliction, and this was the first time in ages that he felt like he'd spent the night drinking.

Ceraphlaks bumped him again, this time on the shoulder, and Mathias clutched at his hair in a poor bid to stop his head's spinning. Wincing, he stabilized himself with his other hand, the coolness of the dirt against his palm and earthiness of the air around him luring him back to the present, back to reality. Shand was gone, and Nes's empty grave sat beside him, begging him to answer those bells. Mathias curled his legs beneath himself,

293

grunting at the effort and wishing Ceraphlaks had hands to help him stand. The bells rang their alarm, urging Mathias to fight harder against the internal forces that tried to hold him down. He staggered to his feet.

Banking his trust in Sulik's ability to dictate orders and his faith in Brant's effective streak of violence, Mathias repeated to himself that his tardiness to the field wouldn't affect the battle's outcome. Ceraphlaks positioned himself to facilitate mounting and Mathias swung a leg over the pegasus's back, gripping a fistful of mane to stay centered.

"Thank you, old friend," he mumbled, wondering if he'd be able to maintain his balance to stay astride in flight.

Ceraphlaks reached his head around to bump the bottom of his rider's foot.

Mathias attempted a smile, but it was well worn in the wake of Shand's assault. "I'll be fine. Just give me some time to shake this off. I'll hold on tight."

His reassurance was vague and soaked through with dull skepticism, but Ceraphlaks had been instructed long ago to follow Mathias's instructions and wouldn't start doubting him now. Careful not to unseat Mathias with a rough departure as he might have done on any other day, Ceraphlaks sprang into the air. Even when escorting him from the hells themselves, Ceraphlaks had never seen Mathias so uncoordinated. Suspecting divine mischief, the pegasus wiped the whimsy from his mind and took care with bearing Mathias to the field.

Mathias floated through disorientation for the bulk of the flight, coherence leaking back to him as the combatants came into view. By the time they'd reached the active field, the battle thrashed in its final stages. Weeks pent up in the fortress had worn on the flemans' strength and stamina, but the heart with which they chased after their opponents' retreat assured Mathias that their spirits were still well intact. Ridden by guilt over leaving the army without their interim general, Mathias urged Ceraphlaks lower to gauge how big of a hit they'd taken in his unplanned absence.

As a solid force, the army pressed the demons westward, clearing the grounds around the fortress. Those active soldiers who hung back busied themselves with salvaging their injured comrades and dealing final rights to their dying foes. Their movements trudged slow and deliberate. All but one. Mathias flexed his fingers as he watched Brant throw himself onto a fallen demon, not bothering to reach out to Etha. If he hadn't been blocked from her before, Shand's little trick would have seen to it for now.

"Take me down there," Mathias told Ceraphlaks. "I have to make sure he's alright."

Still troubled by his rider's recent plight, Ceraphlaks landed at the clearing nearest to where Brant straddled his victim's torso, gouging at its face with a knife. Mathias dismounted and borrowed some heart from a firm pat on Ceraphlaks's neck as he viewed Brant from a safe distance. The commander's shoulders rose and fell rapidly with heated breath, and he staggered when he pushed himself to his feet to scan the area for his next target. His movement seemed to disobey his purpose, carrying him forward with erratic jerks and the grace of a baneful prowl. Mathias marveled that Brant hadn't yet passed out.

Focus solidified in Brant as he located fresh prey, and he flung himself onto another dying demon. "Where is she?" he roared.

The demon, eviscerated and pale, was so far gone that it couldn't have answered him even if it wanted to.

"Where did she go?" Brant repeated, voice trembling.

Mathias's heart ached for Brant's anguish and for the torture his need for retribution inflicted on these demons' last moments. As his head improved from swimming to merely fuzzy, Mathias turned away from Brant to assess the rest of the field.

Not far off, Inwan stood amid the fleeing carnage, eyes wide and jaw slack. He clutched a simple sword of mortal creation in his left hand. The tip of the pristine blade rested on the ground, and a golden aura wrapped him in an impenetrable shield. Inwan's presence served as one more pointless distraction for the worthwhile combatants to work around, his shock rendering him useless. Mathias's lip curled.

Divine energy and the shields created by it were effective at holding demons at bay and prevented unsolicited advances from prying mortals, but Mathias wielded a stronger power than Inwan had at his disposal. Ducking his head against the force of Inwan's barrier, the effort compounding his residual weakness into a fresh tremor of debilitation, Mathias strode up to the god.

Inwan jumped and gasped as his shield rippled at Mathias's intrusion. His right hand flew to reinforce the hold on his sword as he spun and brandished it clumsily in front of him. When his thoughts quit reeling and allowed him the clarity to identify Mathias, Inwan's disbelief still clutched him too closely to tend to his flush of shame. If Mathias would have been receptive to games, he'd have laughed at the god's startled reaction.

"This isn't what you expected."

Inwan blinked, unresponsive to the callous tone of Mathias's words. Overcome by horror and the urge to deny reality, he swept his helpless gaze across the field, trying to make sense of this devastation. "I cannot watch my people suffer through this. Not when it's this bad."

This time, Mathias allowed that dry laugh to escape him, an expression he regretted as a fresh wave of dizziness scolded him for the effort. "You have no other choice unless you want us to give up." He scrutinized the flawless armor Inwan wore. No dents or mars, not even a spray of blood. His sword bore no signs of engaging in combat. The coward, in all of the greatness he bragged about, hadn't even been brave enough to try defending his people. This critical observation told Mathias more than he wanted to hear. "We will continue to fight," he said, "whether or not you have the courage to join us. We got along just fine before and don't need you now if it's too much for you to bear. Laes sent me here to stop the demons, and one more body—*your* body—will not increase our odds of victory."

At last, Mathias's criticism wore through Inwan's dumbfounded stupor, demanding his retaliation. "You cannot tell me not to take the field."

"Of course I can't," Mathias said, "but I can tell you that your presence here won't make much of a difference. You are even less qualified to fight demons than any of your people are."

Inwan scowled at Mathias's casual disregard. If this human truly was a man of divine nature, he had to fear and respect the gods! Inwan stepped forward, but the sword faltered in his grasp. He opted to spare himself the embarrassment and kept it lowered at his side. "I will not tolerate your flippant tongue any longer!"

Unimpressed, Mathias held his ground. Even with whatever power Etha deemed Inwan worthy of recovering and with Mathias impaired by the residue of Shand's manipulation, this peacock's show didn't daunt him. "I am not criticizing you, I'm keeping you safe. Your status alone won't protect you on the field. The demons are far older than either of us and know more about your capabilities than you ever will." Mathias could have thrown more at Inwan, words he was sure would come out of him before he left Elidae, but he finally saw Brant drop his sword and sag to the ground halfway between one brutalizing display and the next. Someone much more vulnerable than Inwan needed Mathias's help now. He slapped the god on the shoulder. "But if you want to fight, welcome to the army. I'm sure you can find a cot in the barracks."

Mathias felt Inwan's glare pelt his back as he walked away, but that scorn slid off his blessed armor and reined temper. Instead, he focused on Brant as the young man sat bloodied and panting amidst the filth of battle. Mathias walked a wide circle around the commander to avoid startling him, a wary eye trained on Brant's sword. Inwan hadn't frightened Mathias, even with the god having recovered some amount of divine strength, but with the manner which Brant's mind had deteriorated, Mathias absolutely feared an attack from him.

Mathias crossed in front of Brant and crouched down to meet him on eye level. Head hung from slumped shoulders, Brant gasped so hard Mathias marveled that he still held on to consciousness. The paladin frowned, grasping his own hands to keep from reaching out to Brant.

"Commander, are you coherent?"

Mathias's voice picked at the one part of Brant's brain still receptive to the present and his head wobbled upright. Frantic eyes screamed like a lost child, softening with the pathetic glow of hope when he registered Mathias's worn gaze.

"Where is she…?"

Brant's murmur nearly escaped Mathias, and his heart sank at the desperation which seared him for answers. Both Mathias and Sulik had carefully monitored Brant's mental status after Nes's death, well aware of how close these delusions of his cousin crept toward destroying him. His interactions with what his mind recognized as Nessix had grown worse of late, so bad that drunken soldiers had begun referring to Brant as the Mad General. Brant's savagery upon Mathias's arrival to the field suggested Sulik had decided to inform him of the fate of Nes's body, and his broken, terrified question confirmed it. This hadn't been the way Mathias hoped for Brant to find closure, but he'd take what he could get.

"I don't know," Mathias answered gently.

"But you—" Brant raised a hand as if to beseech Mathias for something he didn't have, but the effort to hold it exceeded the commander's current capabilities. His hand flopped back into his lap. "She always said you knew everything."

Mathias bit down on his lips to keep them from trembling. The version of Nessix Brant had become acquainted with these past few weeks wasn't the same one Mathias had known. "No she didn't."

"But you should…"

Mathias bowed his head, faltering under the tenacious commander's forlorn daze. "I will find her, Brant. I will find her for you, for your people. I'll find her for—" His words choked to silence before sobs had the chance to betray him.

"For yourself?"

Mathias's head snapped up, expecting this fragile version of Brant to be after a fight, but instead caught the same broken gaze, tainted with uncertainty and devoid of hope. Mathias's eyes stung. "I will not rest until I solve this, and I will keep you informed of my progress to the greatest extent you'll tolerate."

The reassurance seeped through Brant's senses, easing a breath of the helplessness lurking in his eyes, but it didn't stoke the haughty fire that drove him when Nessix was still alive. Brant nodded at last, a slow acceptance, but progress nonetheless, and he tried to wobble to his feet. When his first attempt failed, Mathias reached out a hand to instruct him to stay down.

"Did Sulik stay with the fortress?"

Brant settled himself per Mathias's unspoken suggestion and nodded.

Mathias stood, using the action as an excuse to scan the horizon. "He'll have clerics out here shortly. As far as I can tell, you haven't taken enough physical damage for you to require healing, but they'll bring wagons to aid your return."

The broken commander looked up at Mathias, seeing at last the benevolent man who had won Nessix over. As terrible as Brant had treated Mathias in the past, the paladin hadn't abandoned his compassion and spared Brant the shame of helping him to his feet. Mathias truly was a man to admire, a man Brant should have trusted from the start. All it had taken for him to realize it was losing Nessix twice. Brant coughed and sniffed back the deluge of emotions rising to betray him.

"Would you go see to that?" Brant's voice shook out the request, jaw trembling. "I mean, to make sure our wounded make it home?"

Desperate to preserve that last, fragile thread of Brant's pride, Mathias forbid his shoulders from drooping at Brant's impending surrender with a deep breath and forced smile. This bridge should have been crossed in less trying times. "Of course, Commander."

Without another word, Mathias stood and turned to give Brant his privacy, pinching his eyes shut and pressing forward as the other man's sobs drove him toward home.

TWENTY-FIVE

In his lifetime, Veed had logged a generous ledger of poor decisions, but he hadn't gotten to this point by being a fool. Though he hadn't expected it, he recognized Renigan's attempt to grab power and might have been impressed by his commander's opportunistic tenacity if not for his irritated preoccupation with the fresh developments on the war front. Considering the number of times Veed had taken what wasn't his, a history well known among anyone who paid attention, he couldn't figure out why Renigan thought he wouldn't see through this scheme.

Veed had selected Renigan as his commander due to his lack of ambition and his willingness to obey. Renigan had never once shown a propensity for insubordination, and Veed had valued those traits in the early days when his political standing was still fragile. Of course, that was all years ago and until very recently, the whole country had grown comfortable in their positions, or so Veed had thought. After all, if a man was meant to lead by example, Veed himself had proven betrayal an effective measure to gain power.

But Renigan? He took orders. He delegated tasks. He was selfish but unmotivated, not at all the type to seek power. What did he think he'd do with it, anyway?

Veed yearned to take the field, to indulge in a productive and satisfying release of the surplus steam which had built inside him from his confinement within Nes's fortress. He wanted to bathe in the glory of battle, to strike down his opponents without fear of political backlash. As badly as he itched for action, though, he first had to tend to the most predominant threat, and so he stayed behind to assess the status of his fortress.

Observations of the troops who had been left with him revealed a deep exhalation of pent up worry, wearied eyes relaxed and laughter popping up in casual conversations as if they'd been given that form of expression for the first time. Nobody spoke of the manner which Renigan had managed them in Veed's absence, but this silence carried more weight than even the most polite criticism. For now, Veed held off asking for clarification on the matter, trusting Renigan's carelessness and sloppy form to expose himself eventually.

Neither the army nor the fortress seemed worse for wear, a fact credited more to Renigan's desire to own what would never be his than any respect for Veed. That the commander had ordered an attack on Veed upon his arrival was evidence enough of the festering contempt in their chain of command. Veed knew he unsettled his commander, and while he acknowledged the chance of those nerves interfering with Renigan's focus on the field, he trusted the army's ability to compensate for any mistakes the commander made.

Reflecting on Renigan's brush with defiance bored Veed the same way as watching a play no one had bothered to rehearse, and so he troubled over the greater, much more significant concern.

Why were the demons attacking his territory?

It was the first question to strike him when the bells began to toll and the one still hanging in his mind. Uncovering that answer firsthand had been the strongest argument for Veed to lead a front himself, but he chose the path which best led to his station's longevity.

At this point in the war, the demons had established a reliable pattern, always targeting a fortress or a mobilized military force. On very few occasions, they'd struck one of the few homesteads outside the proper city boundaries, but to Veed's recollection,

Sarlot had been the only city they'd pointedly gone after. Over a year deep into this war, it made no sense for them to veer from their path now.

Nes's territory in the north was vulnerable; keeping an entire kingdom stuffed between the walls of one fortress, growing soft and weak due to weather and lack of practice, should have made them the more appealing quarry. So what was the demons' objective? Why didn't they go after the easier—and far more substantial—prey?

The most obvious answer rested on the one man Veed actively tried to avoid thinking about. Rumor stated that the demons had targeted Elidae to coax Mathias away from the Order and open him to their torment. No matter how much truth rested in such gossip, Veed saw the significant threat the pompous human posed to the demons, and he suspected they knew as well. Veed sneered and tapped an irritable finger on his desktop.

He didn't care about the demons. He didn't entirely care about Norrik and Adessa, so long as enough of his kingdom survived after the war ended. What he did care about was Mathias and what the spread of his influence meant for Elidae. What he cared about was what dangers Mathias posed to *him*. Veed wasn't clear why that rotten paladin bothered him so much, considering Nessix was no longer in the equation, but all of his instincts told Veed that Mathias was a very real threat to him.

Six months ago, the thought of Mathias proving dangerous to Veed was laughable. The paladin had always been tolerant and calm, even when goaded to the point when other men would snap. He hadn't even reacted past a few heated words and furious threats the night Veed had slept with Nessix. But the past few weeks of living in such close proximity, facing the mental degradation which came with the pressure of unrelenting confinement, convinced Veed that it was best to challenge Mathias with care. Or not at all. Weighed down by so many unsavory thoughts, Veed grabbed his sword to go work his worn muscles. Battles far exceeding the war loomed in his future, and if he hoped to stand a chance at victory, he had to stay on top of himself.

* * * * *

"It's been so long since the old fool's even attempted to show humility, the least you could have done was *try* to be nice."

Mathias yawned and rubbed the back of his neck. Drained, thanks to Brant's breakdown and with a lingering headache from whatever Shand had done to him, Mathias was less than receptive to Etha's antics. At least she seemed in a good mood amidst this unrelenting torrent of misery. Mathias tried a smile, weak, but serving its purpose.

"I'm not convinced his show was entirely honest," he said. "It's evident you restored *something* in him, yet all he did was stand behind his shield and act like it all bothered him."

Etha frowned, tucking her face into the pout of a fussy child. "That was his first time seeing what has become of Elidae. It very well may be his second time seeing demons at all. You know as well as I do that his eyes only ventured to one aspect outside of Elidae through his entire existence."

Mathias grumbled and paced over to his window, glimpsing out at the land that should have flourished with so much beauty. He still didn't see inexperience as an adequate excuse.

"And you don't have to," Etha said to his thoughts.

He turned to meet Etha's raised brow, sheepishly pressing his lips together to hold back the disrespectful rant he so badly wanted to let loose. "Fine," he said. "I'll do my best to incorporate him into the plans from here on out if that's what you want. But it's up to you to decide if he's worthy of staying safe. I will not protect someone who has no desire to protect himself or his allies."

Etha's expression softened and she sat on the corner of Mathias's bed. "He has the desire to protect the flemans. He just doesn't know how to."

Mathias scoffed and rolled his eyes. "He's a *god*. How can he not know how to protect his people?"

In a perfect world, this conversation would travel in a more positive direction, one which suggested Mathias's compliance or at least acceptance of additional divine assistance beyond Etha's own. The demons, however, had skewed the concept of this ideal and

Etha twisted her lips. Mathias was worn, not just from the past day's events, but from this war as a whole, and she trusted his shortness found roots in that exhaustion. Right now, Mathias didn't need her reprimands, he needed her support.

"I've forgiven Inwan for his past transgressions," she said. "All I ask is that you try to do the same. He knows what he did wrong and he truly does wish he could fix it."

"Yeah?" Mathias asked, loosening the cuffs of his sleeves. "There are some things no amount of remorse can fix. Those are the things we all have to live with, Inwan included. His punishment wasn't half as severe as it should have been."

Etha sighed, reading just as clearly into Mathias's unspoken accusation as he'd intended for her to. "He would give his divinity all over again to bring Nessix back," she murmured, standing to walk up behind Mathias. "She is the reason he wanted to take up arms to begin with, and that is the reason I allowed him the might to do so."

Mathias's aching muscles tensed at Etha's embrace and he clenched his fist at her words. The faults of Inwan's past had resulted in his banishment, and it was that banishment that had rendered Elidae unguarded. Shand wouldn't have approached the island if he'd still stood guard, the demons would have never found their way here. If Inwan had just stayed true to his people, Nessix would still be *alive*. And if Mathias's dreams depicted any amount of truth, she should have lived a happy life, unburdened by the cruelty of leading men to war. Etha's forehead pressed against the middle of Mathias's back and her peace trickled through his system. Mathias closed his eyes and hung his head, only now realizing how much resentment corrupted him.

"Etha, I'm afraid to trust him," he said at last. "The Divine Council banished him for selfish misconduct, and I would smite him myself for his wrongs if you'd allow me." Mathias shook his head as Etha slipped her arms free from his torso and walked around to face him. He kept his steely gaze focused just above her head.

The goddess frowned at his bout of obstinacy. "I brought him home to Elidae for a reason. This nation needs her god again, and

I've no doubt that Inwan sees that. Not even I can undo what has been done, but that doesn't mean we can't work to try to fix the situation we currently have."

Mathias huffed irritably and shifted his glare up to the ceiling.

"Mathias, Inwan cannot bring Nessix back. I cannot bring Nessix back. Those are facts. But we can continue fighting for Elidae, just like she would have wanted."

He bit back his retort, appalled by the bitterness that tried to direct itself at Etha's words. Nessix had wanted much more than for her people to fight for Elidae. She had wanted Inwan to find his clemency and return to her. She had wanted to see the end of this war and suffering. She had wanted to be with *him*. Mathias pressed a hand against his eyes and drew a slow breath. There he went, trying to dwell on matters well out of his control again. He had to concentrate on the challenges he stood a chance on influencing before he could address those which seemed increasingly impossible.

"Fine." His eyes swept to the side, still avoiding Etha's tender gaze. "I will not turn him away, just as I didn't turn the peasants away when they thought they wanted to fight." He turned and plunked down in his chair, kicking the boots off his burning feet.

Etha produced a gentle smile at the opening Mathias offered her. "And look what became of those peasants."

The glower persisted inside Mathias, but he knew better than to continue this argument. Etha had deemed Inwan worthy of returning to Elidae and he needed to accept her judgement. Questioning her motives too often resulted in headaches and tonight, he preferred to avoid any more pain or complications.

Etha refrained from pressing the issue further as Mathias sorted through his wants and needs. If she knew only one thing about her paladin, it was that in his core, he hated nothing more than fighting with her. Even when doubt obscured every other viable path, he maintained his steadfast faith in her, trusting her to see him through. This devotion didn't thwart his displeasure in those tactics he disagreed with, but Mathias always caved to her will. She had spoken her word, and he delivered the response most appropriate for his current position. Etha released a blissful sigh.

"I have faith you'll find him every bit as useful as the civilian force," she said. "And I thank you for taking him in, regardless of your personal bias."

Her gaze seeped through Mathias's pointed avoidance, warming his core and coaxing his pulse to slow. Mind settling through Etha's invasive means, Mathias looked to her at last. He cracked a smile and shook his head at the stubborn glint in her eyes. The two of them could continue this debate all day long, but Mathias knew he stood no chance at winning.

"Forgive my delay in doing so, but I'd like to thank you for watching over the army while I was gone. Going after Shand had been reckless."

"You can thank me for watching over them, but Brant deserves the credit for rallying them." Her eyes shifted to the floor and her smile filtered away as she processed her thoughts on the matter.

Mathias reflected her frown. "He told me Nes is gone now. Does that mean he's not hearing her anymore?"

Etha pinched her lower lip and nodded. "I don't know which is worse, having him lose his mind to madness or lose his heart to loneliness. He seemed to find some sort of peace in his insanity."

"Will he be alright?"

She grimaced. "It's too early to tell. I imagine if he was going to snap completely, he'd have already done so. He's resting now, and I sent Sulik to keep an eye on him for the rest of the day. If we can see him through to sanity, he very well might prove to be Elidae's strongest general yet."

Worrying over that part of the future wouldn't help the immediate perils and Mathias sighed. "He won't be alright until I find Nes's soul, and I cannot allow myself to go looking for her until the demons are managed."

Etha wrinkled her nose. "You're still heading after that tunnel, aren't you?"

"It's the only way to stop them. Even if we neutralize Shand, the demons have a strong foothold. That tunnel has been my objective for too long now, and I have to see this through."

"So what's your plan this time?"

"That depends." The tension lifted from Mathias's shoulders as Etha kept her lingering reservations to herself. "Do you think Brant and Inwan can keep guard over the fortress in their current conditions?"

"I'm sure if Inwan felt cornered he'd find his way out, and I don't think it would take much to push Brant back into his violence."

Mathias's brows tugged closer to each other at Etha's choice of words, stomach unsettling. He needed Inwan to do more than protect himself, and tempting insanity out of Brant once again was one of the last things Mathias wanted to take responsibility for. Either way, his most viable option hinged on his ability to trust those two. "And are the demons preoccupied with Veed?"

Etha bit her lip and shot her gaze away from Mathias. "Veed's not the one facing them."

Mathias crossed his arms and jerked upright. It wasn't like Veed to miss a fight. "*Still?* So he signed his townships over as a loss?"

Etha shook her head. "His officers are holding their own for now." Both Etha's stomach and Mathias's lips twisted at the terrible outcomes Veed might have hoped for by acting in such a manner. "Do you think he's up to something?" the goddess asked.

Veed was *always* up to something, but Mathias never braved venturing deep enough into that man's train of thought to decipher what went on in that corrupt mind. The notion of leaving Brant behind now concerned Mathias; after the nature of the last encounter between Veed and the commander, Mathias legitimately worried over Brant's safety if he was left unsupervised. "I don't know," he said at last. "Would you give me updates if he shows signs of mobilizing?"

Etha tapped a finger against her pursed lips. "You're skating a fine line, my dear."

"I know," Mathias said. "And I don't mean to press my boundaries, but there's too much going on right now and I... Agh!" Mathias shook his head, pressing his hand to his temple. "Trying to stay on course is beginning to overwhelm me."

Etha sighed and walked up to him, coaxing his hand from his

head so she could rub his shoulders. "Then let's tend to those matters one at a time. You're right. The best course of action is to target the remaining tunnel."

"Do you think Shand will try to stop us?"

"I don't know." Etha's answer came too quickly and with an ominous uncertainty that dissatisfied Mathias. "She seems aware that she's overstepped her limits from confronting you earlier. She's gone to ground since then and could be anywhere."

That was far from the reassurance or guidance Mathias had hoped to hear. Shand overpowered him with a mere touch. What sort of damage could she deal average, mortal men? "I'll be alright, but I beg you to stay close to my force."

Etha's breathing grew shallow behind him and when no reply followed, Mathias turned to see if she was alright. He met troubled eyes sparking with a startling gleam of resolution, her lips tucked between her teeth. Mathias's heart caught in his throat.

"I will march among your force," Etha said. She held up a hand at the onset of Mathias's instant rebuttal. "And before you tell me it's too dangerous, do not forget the strength Shand used against you. I can be far more devastating if necessary, and you need me with you."

The idea of Etha maintaining her physical form while approaching the demons' realm threatened to purge Mathias's stomach, but he limited his argument to internal muttering. Etha had inserted herself too deep in this war to withdraw now. The demons knew she backed the flemans. Shand knew she backed the flemans. Whoever the fleman traitor was had to know she backed the flemans. And Mathias had to accept the fact that all of the opposing forces would conduct themselves with this knowledge in mind. He needed support now more than ever, and couldn't think of anybody he trusted more.

TWENTY-SIX

In the lofty realm of optimism, Mathias hoped the army could somehow sneak out before Brant caught word of their movement, but the number of soldiers mobilizing and the degree of nervous energy that accompanied their preparations made a ruckus loud enough to stir the dead. Trusting Sulik's judgment better than his own, Mathias signed command over to him with the promise of riding Ceraphlaks to catch up as soon as he dealt with Brant.

As Mathias predicted, Brant barked orders to unmindful ears as he stormed through the halls, his voice cracking and tone lacking adequate gusto to lead. The public display he made now that reality had silenced Nes's voice served his reputation even more poorly than his prior outbursts, and Mathias was relieved that Sulik had already led most of the army away.

"Commander," Mathias hailed. He strode toward Brant at a brisk pace, hoping to stop his display before he made it deeper into the remaining ranks. "Sulik and I have this campaign. I need you to safeguard the fortress while we're gone."

Brant jerked to an abrupt stop, eyes blank and mouth hanging open as his exhausted mind processed Mathias's words. The length of time he spent formulating a response should have validated how unfit he was to attempt engaging in combat, but his bittersweet recollection of Nessix, though her voice no longer called to him, reminded Brant of his duty. He blinked and when his eyes opened again, a perilous frenzy muddled his air of control.

"You can stay with the fortress," Brant said. "I've got more of a reason to be out there than you do."

Mathias held a deep breath, reserving his groan for himself. This would be a most unpleasant argument, one he dreaded inviting. "Your reason for wanting to engage right now is the reason I need you to stay here."

Brant scowled. His eyes were heavy from expelling too many tears and snatching too little sleep. His reactions to the most basic routine activities were sluggish and clumsy. He knew he stood a greater chance than usual of dying if he charged into battle like this, but maybe that was the point.

"And what are you going to do to try to stop me?" It comforted a small part of Brant's inner chaos to blow the dust off valid reasons to glare at Mathias again.

The paladin met Brant's challenge with a resigned calm he hoped to maintain. "I'll do whatever I have to. I hope it won't be anything more than speaking these words."

"I need to take the field."

"You need to recover and protect your fortress."

"I need to avenge Nessix."

Mathias sighed, the patience he clung to sifting through his grasp. "Brant, I will see to it you have plenty of chances to avenge her, and I swear to stay out of your way when that time comes. But right now, I need you to trust me."

"Just like how you needed Nes to trust you?"

Unclear whether or not Brant intended that as the cheap shot it felt like, Mathias winced and glanced away. "She hadn't trusted me," Mathias said, looking back at delirious eyes which suggested cruelty hadn't been Brant's aim. "Not when it mattered. And right now, it *does* matter. I'm asking you please, Brant, stay and protect the fortress."

Brant studied Mathias's sincerity and expectations. He'd gathered a great deal of experience on how this human worked and recognized that Mathias wasn't being completely honest with him now. Though they'd finally developed a rapport, Brant reflected

Mathias's halfhearted attempt in kind. "Alright," he said with a brief nod. "I'll stay."

Mathias's smile tugged against a grimace. That answer had come too easily to convey even a remote sense of credibility. Jumping into a debate over the matter ensured only a greater waste of time, time Mathias didn't have, and so he nodded and feigned appreciation. "Thank you, Commander. I'll try not to trouble you further."

The smugness of Brant's smile reinforced Mathias's suspicions, but he allowed the commander to think he won. There were more indirect ways to force Brant's compliance, and Mathias left to seek out Inwan. Given his reputation among the children gods, Mathias anticipated his request to be met with another argument, but it was one he needed to have. Keeping the fortress manned came second only to protecting Brant from his dangerous impulses.

The greater part of Inwan was still hung up on the horrors he'd seen when he ventured out to the battlefield. He knew his people were warriors and that battle carried with it specific dangers. He'd seen gruesome injuries and torturous ends to men he'd been fond of at the hands of ogres and horns of minotaur, but he'd never witnessed such maniacal slaughter as what demons conducted and enticed the flemans to reciprocate. After the first generation of settlers had cleared out the central lands of Elidae, there had been no epic wars to torture the island, no days where hundreds of men were reaped so casually.

Mathias encroached on these reflections, no more supportive than he'd been before, and Inwan kept his back to him. "You cannot and will not force me to stay behind," Inwan said. "I am a god—I am the flemans' god. I know you don't have faith in me, but they are my people and I will fight for them."

It was becoming increasingly difficult for Mathias to keep his inconvenienced grumbles to himself, and he tasted his disgust in the words that followed. "Inwan, I'm leaving you behind *because* I have faith in you."

Beyond the typical reservations which prevented the younger deities from questioning Mathias's authority, Inwan still didn't know how much of his strength he had at his disposal. Either way, he was committed to his cause. His heart refused the alternative. "Then let me lead the front."

Defenses worn from the exertion of restraining himself, Mathias allowed a laugh to slip from him at last. "Just because I said I have faith in you doesn't mean I'm willing to throw away the war."

Inwan's fists balled and his eyes lit with the first sign of divine fire Mathias considered remotely noteworthy. "You think I would—"

Mathias batted a disinterested hand in Inwan's direction and rolled his eyes. "I know very well that you'd give up your divinity all over again if it would fix the suffering. It's a common reaction from those who love their people. But all that would happen is you'd sacrifice your divinity, the demons would still survive, and your people would once again be without their god. Does that option suit you better?"

"You…" Fists trembling at his sides, Inwan fumed with resentment at the self-control required to converse with Etha's avatar. *This* was why his peers hated Mathias so much. A quiet chuckle rumbled in Inwan's throat and he shook his head. "I understand your position, Mathias, but you are still a man. I am a god."

"And we were both once average mortals struggling to survive in this world." Mathias sighed. This debate would take them in circles on whose might mattered more until the demons tramped their way to victory while the two of them bickered. "Where did you stumble across your god shard, anyway? Was it on the ship from Drailged?"

Inwan's guard faltered at his memories of mortality, those suppressed recollections of how uncertainty had plagued the refugees, of the pain inflicted by food supplies running low and disease threatening to sink their ships before the ocean could. So many tears shed, so much fear from brave men and women. Inwan's face melted in wistful resignation. "Somebody had to answer the prayers of the refugees," he said. "We *had* to reach Elidae. I couldn't stand back and let us all die."

Mathias bowed his head, finding an ounce of respect for Inwan at last. "What it comes down to is that where you spent time perfecting ways to spoil your people and yourself, I've spent nearly as long hunting demons. I am far more qualified to be on the field right now than you are, and you did not show up in time for me to feed you the knowledge you'd need."

Inwan frowned. He hadn't planned on losing this debate. "So what do you expect me to do while you march out and play hero?"

"I expect you to keep Brant safely in these walls and make sure he doesn't do anything more foolish than normal."

Inwan puffed bitterly and cast his glare aside. "We've been through this. He wants nothing to do with me."

"And right now, that doesn't get to be his choice. Whether or not he wants your help is irrelevant. He *needs* it." Mathias studied Inwan hard as the god's face twisted through various phases of rejection and denial. If this had been any other time, one with much less on the table, Mathias might have joked at how Inwan's reaction reflected a bitter breakup. Instead, Mathias focused on how close they crept to the war's turning point, for better or worse. "He is going to be the next general, and you know that. As you've mentioned several times now, you are a god. You are powerful. You have the strength to look past the fits he's thrown at you. Today, stay behind and protect Elidae's future in the way only her god can. Regain the faith of the lost. Your turn to take the field will come sooner than you're ready for."

Inwan's chin jutted forward and he crossed his arms. All he needed to do was stomp his feet or stick out his tongue and Mathias could have considered it an actual tantrum.

"You really think Brant will find faith in me?" Despite the bitterness of Inwan's tone, his stance lightened.

Mathias shrugged. "I don't think he ever lost it. Nessix never let him. He's hurt and he needs guidance. Guidance I can't give because I don't know him the way you do. Please, Inwan." Using such polite words with this god soured Mathias's mouth. "Keep Brant safe. If not for me, if not for Elidae or Brant, then do it for Nes."

That leverage sparked Inwan's sense of honor and his arms

dropped to his sides. He wanted his dignity back. He wanted his power and the love of his people. Watching over Brant and safeguarding the fortress were the first steps to take him there and Mathias was handing the opportunity to him graciously. Unaccustomed to bouts of humility or gratitude, Inwan hid behind fabricated pride which Mathias disregarded.

"I'll do it for Nes." Inwan jabbed a finger in Mathias's direction. "Not for you. But because she'd want it."

This time, Mathias swallowed his chuckle and lowered his head in a gesture which passed as appreciation. "Thank you. I'll be sure to report your compliance to Etha. She will be pleased."

Mathias left this conversation with a faint glow of hope, despite his misgivings regarding Brant and Inwan following through with their commitments the way he hoped. Regardless, Mathias had given it his best effort and needed to reach Sulik before the army got too far.

Etha waited for Mathias in his chamber, kicking her legs from where she dangled them over the side of his desk. When the door opened, she popped to her feet, searching Mathias with longing eyes. She'd trusted him to deliver instructions to Brant and Inwan, but had worried over the tact he'd use in the process. Concern etched tiny lines between Mathias's brows, expected given the weight of their current circumstances, but he gave her a calm smile that relieved the annoying flitter in her chest.

"So it went well?" she asked.

"Well enough." Mathias walked past Etha to his desk. He removed Nes's pendant and laid it on top then turned to begin donning his armor. "I'm still not sure I trust Brant to not chase after us, but you were right, as always. I believe Inwan will do everything in his power to stay here until further notice and that he's worried about Brant."

Etha smiled and immediately went to work assisting Mathias with his preparations. "Sulik's been making good ground. You're fortunate to have Ceraphlaks to help you catch up." When Mathias didn't respond, Etha quit handing him pieces of armor. "You're too distracted. What's on your mind?"

Mathias shook his head with a sigh, blinked, and then

retrieved the bracer from Etha's hands since she failed to offer it to him. "This feels too easy. Where have the attacks against us been? Why didn't Shand take the opportunity to take me when she had the chance? Something about this isn't right."

Thin lips tucking into a frown, Etha retrieved his pauldron. "Remember when you first faced the undead?"

He pulled the buckle of his bracers snug and chuckled. "Do I remember my resurrection? Yes, I do. That's the sort of thing that's hard to forget."

Etha shook her head. "Of course you remember that. I meant the war. That was one you didn't understand. Those were enemies that didn't make sense. You know demons and how they fight. This is where you shine and an enemy you know how to adapt to. Everything will be just fine."

"I do know the demons and how they fight," Mathias agreed. "And that's why I'm concerned right now. They're acting outside their established norms."

"Well," Etha said, patting Mathias on the chest as she walked past him to fetch Nes's pendant. She wouldn't let him go to battle without it. "You've surpassed the impossible enough times to prove that you—"

The instant Etha's fingers curled around the chain, an unearthly shriek reverberated off the walls, piercing through Mathias's heart and striking his ears so sharply they rang. She flung the pendant across the room and wrung her steaming hand close to her chest. Pain was a foreign concept to Etha, at least in the way mortals felt it, but her reaction to touching the pendant was so instant, so instinctual, and so intense that she couldn't stop it to save Mathias's life.

Just as Etha was unfamiliar with the sensation of pain, Mathias had never before seen physical harm affect her. Mentally and emotionally weak, yes, but never wounded in the way her agonized grimace and flawed flesh now suggested. Too shocked to move, both from Etha's sudden reaction and from the precious memento which catalyzed her drastic response, Mathias's heart pounded violently against his chest. His eyes stung.

"Nessix couldn't have... she..." His voice failed his feeble attempt to justify the apparent truth.

"No." Etha gasped past her heaving breath. "She couldn't."

"Nessix got that from Veed," Mathias murmured, blinking as the facts locked into place in his mind. "Son of a bitch, she got that from Veed!"

Squinting at Mathias through her agony and lashes, Etha choked as her paladin's alarm contorted into an abysmal wrath. She wished she could push the pain away.

Mathias wheeled from Etha and flung his armor stand to the ground with a roar. Pulling at his hair, he scanned the room blindly, scrambling to find calm. The longer he searched, the farther it drifted from his reach, and Mathias kicked the stand from where it had fallen on his sword belt. How had he been so stupid? Veed had practically spelled out every detail of his role in this war for him and Mathias had trusted him. Trusted *Veed*. Snatching his sword belt from the floor, Mathias strapped it to himself and spun to face Etha.

"Did this curse have anything at all to do with Nessix dying?"

Internal systems resuming enough function to permit her reply, Etha shook her head, still nursing her hand. "I doubt it would've done anything to her. It's very clearly meant to repel me, and I don't think I need to remind you of Nes's opinion of me."

Mathias struck a step forward and a growl of frustration shook his entire frame down to his clenched fists. Somehow, he'd been unable to predict Shand's involvement with the demons. He'd struggled over why the demons had quit targeting his force. And now, an oversight as careless as overlooking Veed's true nature had brought harm to Etha. To *Etha*! What had become of his instincts and sense? Mathias had faced countless opportunities to weed out the root of this entire war, but wasted them all with excuses for the lowest piece of filth he'd ever met.

Etha's soft gasp cut through the pounding in Mathias's ears. When his eyes rose to meet hers, she gasped again as she recognized the vindictive fury coursing through her gentle paladin.

"Mathias..." she begged. "Don't do something out of haste."

Disappointing Etha was Mathias's greatest fear, even greater than whatever the demons were doing to Nessix, but today, he would face that fear. "Oh, this isn't in haste," he swore. "It's been a long time coming."

Before Etha could speak a word to stop him, Mathias whisked himself through the channels of the divine plane. Etha pinched her eyes shut, wishing she had someone to pray to.

TWENTY-SEVEN

The door to the war chamber flew open to reveal a panting solider. Perturbed by the streak of insubordination running rampant through his otherwise obedient ranks, Veed speared the young man with a glare that promised a prompt demotion for the interruption.

"I thought I gave orders that I was not to be disturbed."

The soldier nodded, lines of worry etched across his forehead. "Yes, sir, you did. But it's—"

"Then you will leave me undisturbed."

Cringing in anticipation of a punishment more severe than a few strict words, the soldier took a single step back before sputtering, "Sir Sagewind is here."

The urgency of the report bordered terror and the soldier grimaced as though he was about to be ill. Veed's concern instantly shifted from reclaiming control over his army to what hubris Mathias had scrounged up to invade his fortress. The paladin had brought distress to these halls and the soldiers who manned them more than once, but never before thrust fear upon them. Veed stood to ask for clarification just as the soldier gagged against a brisk jerk to the back of his collar. He flew off his feet, flung backwards into the hallway. Mathias stepped forward in his place, a dagger clenched in a white-knuckled grip at his side.

"You have ten words to explain yourself."

Veed blinked at the sudden address, not quite soaking in the gravity of the situation. He knew better than to think he'd ever find remote camaraderie with Mathias, but a terrifying calm chilled the human's eyes, one Veed hadn't seen before. Even in the most chaotic settings, Mathias carried an annoying degree of warmth, but a frigid air of judgment choked out the compassion which Veed had once mocked. Assuming recent events had provided Mathias with more than he deserved to know, Veed frowned.

"What has gotten into you, Sagewind?"

"That was six."

A bolt of apprehension skated down Veed's spine, pulling him upright and snapping all of his battle sense to attention. He glanced at the nondescript dagger Mathias clutched in his hand and then to the empty scabbard at the human's hip. The color drained from Veed's face as he recalled the blessed blade's capabilities. He raised a hand and shook his head, heart rate leaping.

"I don't know what—"

Mathias believed in the law. He believed in fair trials and pleas for redemption. In most cases, he was willing to forgive. But he was too blinded by how far over the line Veed had crossed, too enraged by how many lies had been told. Mathias had given the vile man ten words to make things right, to beg for salvation, but the fool wasted them. Not that Mathias had been inclined to listen.

Mathias lunged at Veed, drawing his arm back to strike the defenseless man before him. Had Veed been a year or two less experienced, the attack might have taken him by surprise, but he saw Mathias's intentions at the last second and grasped a hold of his wrist as he struck. Their strength clashed against one another, evenly matched for the first couple heartbeats before a growl tore through Mathias and he drove his weight forward to slam Veed against the wall. Veed wrestled Mathias's arm to the side, twisting to stay out of the blade's reach and direct it away from himself in case Mathias ordered it to impale him. Against all codes of pride and inflated ego, Veed shouted for help.

Physically locked with his rival, Mathias maintained his calculated calm as reinforcements rounded the doorway, exclaiming

319

their horror at the bout raging within the chamber.

Mathias huffed a quick sigh. He liked to think none of Veed's soldiers knew of their general's treacherous connection to the war and that they didn't deserve a complimentary persecution. Mathias didn't want to fight these men, but as they rushed his direction with weapons drawn, he resigned himself to take the necessary action. Sweeping his arm downward, Mathias broke Veed's hold and spun to command a concussive force against the soldiers' attempts to intercept justice. Residually weakened from the pendant's curse and the energy depleted by teleporting to reach his destination, Mathias gave a quick shake of his head and blinked back a flicker of disorientation from that burst of divinity. He needed to save himself.

The soldiers' distraction provided Veed time to draw his sword, the blade radiating a gentle red, and as Mathias turned to face his opponent, he frowned. Veed had claimed to have cut ties with Shand, but that divine aura surrounding his blade sapped the faintest remnants of trust from Mathias. All magic originated in the divine realm, and Mathias refused to entertain the idea of Inwan lending Veed any of this might. Wary of the damage Shand's power could deal to him, Mathias erected a barrier of Etha's grace around himself.

"You should know better than this," Mathias said. "I'll give you one more chance. Ask for mercy, and it's yours."

Veed spat, surrendering to this inevitable fight. If the rumors were accurate—and he had no remaining reasons to discount them—Mathias couldn't be killed. He could, however, be neutralized and flung to the demons. "If this is how you want to play, then let's play."

The fleman darted forward, swinging his glowing blade. Having neglected to command his weapon back to its conventional size, Mathias blocked the strike with his vambrace. The power Veed wielded with what Mathias had always considered an ordinary blade cracked the sacred steel of Mathias's armor. It wouldn't hold up to a second blow. As Veed drew back for his next attack, Mathias realized the last oversight he'd ever make regarding this man. Veed didn't dabble with his art. He controlled it with a disturbing fluency.

Making note of the revelation but forbidding himself to dwell on it, Mathias ducked beneath Veed's elbow as it soared toward his face. He repelled from his opponent to allow his sword to stretch to a length more beneficial to serve him for this challenge. Mathias's eyes swirled with deep emerald storms, challenging whatever Veed hoped to accomplish. This bastard would regret every last perversion he'd cast across Elidae.

"You've been a cunning opponent," Mathias granted, emotionless save his vindictive frown. "You have been from the start. But this is not a game to be played. This is an execution."

At a clear disadvantage without the protection of his armor, Veed latched a hold on Mathias's willingness to continue speaking to grant him some amount of hope. If he could buy a bit more time, reinforcements would surely arrive, and Veed hadn't missed the waver in Mathias's constitution during his last divine display.

"An execution?" Veed asked. "That's not very just of you."

"Where's the injustice in it?" Mathias seethed. "You've taken my strength from me. You've tortured this land, deceived your men. For these sins, you seem to have been forgiven. But it is because of *you* that Nessix is dead. And there is no forgiveness for that."

Veed willingly accepted accusations tied to the crimes of his past, and as recent events had proven, he'd gotten better at voluntarily admitting them. But he'd never swallow the blame for wrongs which never belonged to him, least of all those as distorted as Mathias's claim. "I loved Nessix."

Those words struck Mathias in the gut and spurred him to a righteous frenzy, binding his justifications to charge down this reckless path. He'd waited months for an excuse to end Veed, and he wouldn't let anything—not honor, not common sense, not even Etha—stand in his way. Mathias rushed forward and pummeled his fist into Veed's unprotected abdomen.

Eyes flying wide, Veed gasped and dropped his sword as he doubled over. Mathias jerked his knee upward and toppled Veed over from a strike beneath the chin. Wheezing, Veed flailed one hand about for his sword as Mathias kicked it out of his reach.

Down the hall, the next wave of reinforcements rushed their way, shouting taut instructions to one another.

Mathias glared down at Veed, whose widened eyes, damp with tears of certainty, locked on his. Deep inside, a twisted part of Mathias delighted in Veed's acknowledgement of his pending death. "I told you once before that you would never again defile. And now, I will ensure it."

"I loved her!"

Mathias would hear no more. His blade sweetly sang the song of vengeance beating in his heart and with a single swing, he severed Veed's head free from his body.

Soldiers rushed into the room a moment too late, snarled curses catching in their throats as blood poured from their general's neck. They huddled closer to each other, gripping their weapons in unsteady hands. *Mathias* did this? The man who took pity on *demons* had slain Veed Astaldt? As a unit, they jumped as Mathias ripped his maddened gaze from his savage handiwork to look them over. Sense trickled back to him, urging him to sheathe his sword. These soldiers had nothing to do with this.

"You'll want to do something with that before it begins to smell," Mathias said. If he stayed much longer, these soldiers were bound to pull themselves from their stupor and rush him, and so Mathias salvaged the scraps of his energy to jump back to the peace of his room. Etha was now gone, but Mathias preferred as much. He never wanted her to see the beast he could become. Chest heaving with exhaustion and that rush of corrupt excitement, Mathias sank onto his bed and stared at his hands. He still had to deal with the demons. He still had to deal with Shand. But Veed was dead. And for now, that was enough.

* * * * *

Inwan was unaccustomed to waiting. The tedious practice of not acting on impulse brought a tickle of unrest to his skin, one which he couldn't quite scratch. Aware of Mathias's suspicions in regards to his reliability, Inwan busied his time trying to read a book that disinterested him, preoccupied with tracking Mathias up to his chamber and aware of Etha's presence alongside him. Inwan had no idea what had caused Mathias's abrupt departure from the fortress, but when Etha also whisked herself away, Inwan sprang to his feet to take advantage of this opening.

Let Mathias be Etha's favorite little snitch. If Inwan was quick, the paladin wouldn't even have to know he'd left.

Discarding his book for someone else to return to the shelf, Inwan bustled to the door. He tugged at his shirt to straighten the wrinkles from it, and gave himself a self-satisfied nod before reaching out for the door's handle. Inwan had never put much value in dread and concern, and though he didn't completely buy Mathias's excuse as to why he ought to stay behind, the pull of Brant's internal struggle tethered him to a rough construct of duty.

Elidae's future depended on Brant Maliroch and his lapse of a sound mind had become common, conversational knowledge by this point. He'd attempted to kill allies and enemies alike and proven unable to control himself when struck by one of his spurts of madness. The young man's grief had eviscerated him, compelling him to lash out without clarity or direction, but Inwan had known Brant since his youth. Brant wasn't a bad man and Inwan had absolute faith that once the war settled, Brant would once again find respect for him. And as unstable as Brant was in his current condition, Inwan knew Mathias had made the most responsible call. Inwan could not leave Brant alone and expect him to not seek out some sort of tragedy.

Heart racing at the thought of losing his valuable time while out of Mathias's sights, Inwan sniffed out the commander to where he looked out a window in the direction which Sulik had led the army. Brant didn't respond to Inwan's arrival, shoulders squared and hands gripping the bottom of the windowsill. One thumb dug absently against the stone.

"You want to follow them?" Inwan asked.

Senses dull in the void he'd fallen into, Brant didn't even blink at Inwan's question. "Do you?"

Inwan balanced his options, wondering one more time what consequences might await a blatant disregard to the White Paladin's orders. Inwan had already survived the greatest punishment a god could face, locked away while evil destroyed his people. Why did the thought of rebelling against Mathias even merit his concern? For the first time in centuries, logic beat out impulse, suggesting that there had been more to the paladin's instructions than a simple ego trip. If Inwan left, Nes's entire kingdom would be open to danger. He stared at Brant's back as the commander stood unmoving, and jumped at the hollow sound of Brant's voice.

"Sagewind made you stay here, too, didn't he?"

Brant's words ticked another mark for determination in Inwan's mind. He wouldn't admit that a man had given him orders, orders his pride had caved to. "He did, but it was to keep an eye on the people beneath us. Isn't that a worthy cause?"

Brant turned at last, his raddled eyes sweeping across Inwan's blank expression. "I don't intend to take anyone with me. I'll go by myself, appoint a captain to serve here in my stead. The people would be every bit as safe as they would be if I was still here. Maybe better off for it." He looked the shameful god up and down with every bit of scorn as he looked in on himself with, recognizing the hurt and regret which beat with each biological function that burdened Inwan. This was the god Brant had waited on for so long, the one prepared to stand up at last. His eyes solidified with acknowledgement and approval of Inwan's renewed acceptance of duty. "The damage you and I could do together…"

Inwan's lips twitched toward a frown. While Brant saw great appeal lurking within the power Inwan might hold, the god didn't recognize the same in Brant. Mathias had claimed Brant needed protection and guidance, and Inwan blew off the assessment as an excuse to demand compliance. Now, facing Brant's coldness, his lack of concern over his station and life, Inwan bent to the responsibility he'd volunteered for when he first bound himself to his god shard. The compassion he'd once invested in Nessix had a new place wrapped around Brant.

"You're ready to take your vengeance?" Inwan asked.

"I've been ready for it."

Inwan had witnessed Etha use her power against mortals dear to her in the past, and he'd seen his more immediate peers do the same. Besides bestowing his grace upon Nessix, the greatest extent

Inwan had ever interfered with his own people was limited to brief lapses of time and the occasional spilled secret. For that, he considered himself better than bad. He smiled at Brant.

"Then let's get you back to your chamber to gather your belongings."

Brant's eyes widened, the embers of hope stirring to life. Between Mathias and Sulik doting over him, Brant had all but relinquished the notion of ever taking the field again. "Didn't Sagewind order you to keep me here?"

"He did, but I don't answer to him."

The Brant from months ago, the one who still cared, might have seen through Inwan's motives, but this Brant's eyes burned with a renewed light. He nodded eagerly. "Yeah, let's go get my things together." His smile broadened and he laughed beside himself, slapping Inwan on the shoulder. "Let's end this, Inwan. You and me. Let's do it for Nes."

Inwan's response tangled in the lump in his throat as Brant spun and jogged down the hall. It was the first bout of positive energy he'd seen from Brant since his return. The god followed at a more casual pace, hanging close behind to avoid raising Brant's suspicion.

"Not even Mathias will be able to stop us now, not with you showing signs of your power again…"

Inwan allowed Brant to prattle on in his budding excitement. With the means he prepared to wield to subdue Brant, Inwan didn't have the heart to correct the commander's enthusiasm. He scratched the back of his neck.

"And with that power—" Laughter danced from Brant, a welcome sound under any other circumstances. "The demons don't stand a chance! They might have their goddess, but we've got a god of our own. One who has a reason to care. And—" Brant stopped himself and shook his head before mentioning Etha's role in their inevitable victory, unsure what had come over him. He looked over his shoulder, eyes glowing with hope for the first time in weeks. "We're ending this tonight, aren't we?"

Drawing on the deceit that had carried him this far, Inwan pressed out a smile and crossed his arms to keep from shaking. "If

I have any say in it, it will."

With an elated grin, Brant yanked open his chamber door and went inside, Inwan following quietly. The commander continued to rally himself with talk of their invulnerability until Inwan's lack of engagement whispered a warning at last. Brant's words tapered off and he turned to meet eyes that held a sorrow he couldn't quite name.

"What's—"

"I'm sorry, Brant."

Utilizing one of Etha's lessons at last, Inwan pressed two fingers against Brant's forehead and grabbed the man's arm to ease him to the ground as consciousness sifted away from him. Inwan stared down at what he'd done for a long, repentant moment, ashamed of himself for taking advantage of such a desperate soul. Committed to his course now more than ever, Inwan sighed and stepped into the pocket realm the children gods frequented to escape the grind of responsibility.

Just as he'd anticipated, Inwan found Shand tucked away in this hidden dimension, standing rigidly, the entirety of her concentration absorbed in one of the many scrywindows that poked up through the misty footing. Inwan remained silent, but followed her attention to where Mathias swept an arm toward a gathering of soldiers to repel them against the walls and shelves of Veed's war chamber. The paladin turned back to Veed, who glowed with Shand's aura.

There wasn't much of a scuffle to follow, and it panned out exactly the way any fight to the death against Mathias Sagewind did. What Inwan hadn't prepared to see, though, was the anxiety which constricted Shand. She wrung her hands at her chest, breath pulsing fast and shallow. When Veed hit the ground, she gasped, and when his head rolled from his shoulders, she raised a hand to her forehead and cursed sharply.

"I don't know what else you expected." A nostalgic corner of Inwan's mind bubbled with sorrow, as he'd shared more in common with Veed than he'd readily admit. The great deal of horror Veed's actions had brought to Elidae clipped that reminiscence short. If Brant and Mathias and even Sulik had spoken the truth, Veed hadn't been the honest man Inwan once knew for quite some time. If Veed truly had destroyed Nes in the capacities Inwan had been led to believe, he was pleased to see him tended to at last.

Shand gasped and spun, as she'd thought she'd had a private viewing. As soon as she recognized Inwan, she shoved her emotions behind a haughty laugh and smoothed out the skirt of her gown. "Inwan, my dear. Would you look at you! I'd heard Etha had let you out of your cage."

Inwan hesitated. He'd burned bridges with the majority of his peers years ago and wasn't sure how Shand would react to him taking a stand. With only a vague grasp of his current capabilities, he was reluctant to push Shand's limits in favor of longevity for both himself and his people. If memory served him right, and he hoped it did, Shand had been indifferent to his trial and subsequent sentence. Even if she'd bothered to establish a set band of followers for Inwan to exploit, she never invested much energy in the fates of the mortals she appointed herself over. Except, it seemed, for Veed. Inwan drew a deep breath and clenched his fists. Punishment served, he would no longer tolerate such disdain.

"This is my domain you're messing with, Shand," he said, pleased that reluctance stayed out of his voice. "Do you need a reminder of what happened to me for playing outside my grounds?"

Shand cracked a smile and hummed a gentle laugh. "Don't you think if it bothered Etha that much, she'd have locked me up by now?"

"If it didn't bother Etha, she wouldn't have sent Mathias." Inwan eyed his sister with repulsion, unable to break an opening through her tempered resolve, but cracks marred her contrived confidence. "And if you weren't afraid, you wouldn't be hiding here."

Among his peers, Inwan had gained the reputation of being a fool, but as Shand gazed into his clear eyes, she saw a startling part of herself in him. He might have been impulsive and selfish, but Inwan knew what he wanted. Shand willed her smile to broaden.

"Let me guess…" she murmured, tapping a finger to her lips.

If Inwan had been a simple mortal or she still had a good grasp on his capabilities, she'd have approached him, but as it was, she held her action. "You're here to let me do the *right* thing and leave?"

Inwan frowned. On the outside, Shand appeared collected and sure of herself, acting as though she held full and indisputable command over the situation. What she seemed to forget was that Inwan had once found himself lodged in a very similar place. He recognized a god on the cusp of losing control.

Shand mistook Inwan's silent reflections for apprehension and shook her head. "The offer's already been made, and by someone I've much more reason to be concerned over than you. I declined it then, and your whining won't make any difference now. Aren't you still on probation, anyway?"

"You're more afraid of Mathias than you are of me?"

"I never said I was afraid of either of you."

Inwan took his turn to laugh at Shand's flimsy defense. He narrowed his scheming eyes, prepared to pick up the slightest tell that might slip from her. "You can think little of me all you'd like, but while Mathias could only ask you to leave, I can ensure you do."

"And how are you going to manage that? Yell at me until I go? Stomp your feet until I tell you where the demons are hiding your little pet?"

Inwan's eyes darkened and his arms jerked with the desire to wring Shand's neck.

"I'm assuming Mathias did tell you all about that?"

It took substantial effort to deny Shand a reaction to her disregard for Nessix's life. "I will bring in whoever I must to banish you. You've destroyed my people."

Shand shook her head. "*I'm* not the one who started this whole mess. That's on someone else's shoulders."

"Veed is dead," Inwan said, "but retribution is still due in full as far as I'm concerned."

Shand internalized her relief. She realized with the most vivid clarity how close her plans stretched toward unravelling, but if Inwan still hadn't caught on to the corruption lurking within Elidae's populace, she had a bit more time to try and straighten matters in her favor. "Then take it from me," she challenged. "I dare you to try."

Inwan worked his jaw slowly, mulling over his prospects. He could walk across the realms once again. He'd proven himself capable of erecting substantial barriers. He knew he could manipulate the minds of mortals. But Mathias hadn't let him engage in combat yet, even against foes much less formidable than a full-fledged goddess. With just a pinch more faith in his ability to follow through, Inwan would be delighted to take Shand up on her offer. That tiny murmur of doubt shook him, though. He refused to risk leaving his children again.

"You aren't safe here, Shand," he said, "and you'd be wise to keep that in mind."

She narrowed her eyes above an unattractive snarl. "I'll believe it when someone's actually able to stop me."

Inwan cocked his head and seared as deeply into Shand as her defenses allowed. Of all of the talents his divinity allotted him, his ability to read a target's motives was among the most useful. He caught Shand's reluctance this time, the grain of fear he couldn't quite identify. "I think someone's already initialized that. I'm advising you of your best bet at survival."

Shand swallowed her gasp, glare hardening at Inwan's ominous warning. Her unwillingness to reply spoke as an adequate confession. Inwan had neither a want nor desire for further formalities. Creasing his lips in a stern frown, he whisked back to the mortal realm, leaving Shand alone to stew in her compounding dismay.

TWENTY-EIGHT

When Etha first created the mortal races, she'd sought to maintain connection with them by weaving life together with distinct threads of divinity. Few mortals were able to access these threads, and only those bearing such capabilities were able to manipulate divine energy. Carefully cutting one's own threads allowed the practitioner to tap into this divine power, resulting in magical talents. Time allowed damaged threads to mend themselves, but if too many were cut too soon, the soul would escape its shell, leaving the body to die.

The Divine Battle had disrupted the integrity of the most unfortunate mortals, coiling this elaborate matrix of divine essence into a single cord and twisting the soul within to distorted madness. It was the strength of this cord which made the demons so resilient to external damage, better able to hold themselves together when one of the threads snapped. Etha's greatest blessing, her careful design to bestow godliness to each of her creations, had opened the door to the demons' greatest strength.

Average men like Veed could only access these threads through trial and error of groping for their locations; it was a very real possibility that he hadn't even known the danger posed by severing them. Those who secured pacts with their gods, such as Mathias, could feel out their threads instinctively, and Etha's backing kept this particular example's much stronger than most. Mortal magic users could access their own threads, but a few individuals were born blessed with the ability to see and access the threads holding the lives of others together. On the surface, High Priestess Julianna Sagewind was one of those gifted few. In the hells, it was Annin.

His stomach churned about as he plucked at Nes's jumbled mess of loose ends, ignoring the terrified sobs of the priestess chained in the corner of the room. On a cot adjacent to where Annin worked, Kol lay on his stomach and resituated the fold of his wings. Again. Annin clenched his jaw and tunneled his attention on sorting through Nes's tattered threads. He concentrated a bit too hard.

Kol caught his comrade's reluctance and lifted himself up on his elbows. "You will carry out this order," he said. "We've been through this."

"We have," Annin agreed, keeping his eyes low to avoid the nervous pulse of Kol's threads. Outward vigor carried demons far in physical combat, but there were times when fear seeped past even the fiercest efforts. "That doesn't mean I think it's a good idea."

"Then let it be a bad idea. What's the worst thing that happens? I die?"

Annin heaved a sigh. Surviving the removal of as many threads as Kol needed to spare for this to work was unheard of, and Annin would have to find the balance between maintaining Nes's viability and Kol's chance of recovering from the damage he'd be taking. Approaching this misguided trial would have been easier if it was only Kol's head on the line for its inevitable failure.

"Lie back down," Annin muttered.

Kol eyed the oraku warily and followed the instruction without debate. Annin turned to fetch a small jar of soft yellow leaves from the table behind him. Beside that jar sat Nes's soul, swirling about in no less of a confused, uncertain heap as her threads, and Annin frowned. Most demons resented mortals for the obvious reasons, but Annin especially hated this Nessix Teradhel. No matter how many times Kol tried to tell him, he couldn't fathom what made her so special, why Kol so eagerly wanted to risk his life to bring her back. Then again, knowing these answers wasn't part of Annin's job. Turning from the table before he acted on the urge to shatter Nes's jar on the ground, Annin pulled out a generous pinch of the crumbled leaves.

"Take this," he grunted, depositing the medicinal component in Kol's open hand.

The alar glanced at it and knit his brows closer together. "What's it do?"

"It will dull the pain," Annin said. "I'll literally be cutting the threads out of you. You're aware of that, right?"

Kol shrugged and popped the dose into his mouth. Crushing the leaves between his teeth, he grimaced at the pungent flavor, swallowing rapidly as salivation charged in to attempt buffering the taste. "You've told me. Do what you have to."

Annin shook his head and turned to loosen the ropes that lowered Nessix's platform below Kol's level to allow gravity to feed her his blood. "You've heard the screams from the aranau we use?"

"Yes, but we kill them."

"We give them mercy."

Kol and Annin had worked together since the days of their mortal lives, and the alar often found comfort in his companion's cryptic nature. But in light of the situation Kol had placed himself in, he'd have preferred silence.

"You failed t'talk me outta this three times now." The sedative hit Kol faster than he'd anticipated. Embraced in warmth, his eyes drifted closed. "Fourth won' change me."

"Very well," Annin sighed and lanced a reed deep into Nes's torn jugular. He turned back to Kol and inserted the other end into his arm to begin a slow bleed. "Did you feel that?"

Kol's eyes fluttered open and he lolled his head toward his comrade. "Feel hmm?"

Annin swallowed his desire to try one last warning. He knew it wouldn't work. "Can you still understand me?"

"Mmm."

He nodded. "I'll cut each thread twice and remove the entire section once it's free."

Kol nodded. At least he thought he did. "Twice. Gotchya."

Annin drew a deep breath and braced himself to torture the man his mortal self had valued as a friend.

* * * * *

Renigan performed a mediocre job at best when it came to coordinating the troops, but mediocre sufficed quite nicely when the opposition planned to spare him. Instead of fretting over whether or not he'd survive this string of attacks, he got to worry about what would happen when he returned home to face Veed after his cunning general had stewed over the intelligence he'd stayed behind to gather. More troublesome, the fear which hindered Renigan's ability to breathe revolved around what would happen when Shand finally caught wind of his agreement with the demons. And—

His stewing concerns purged from his mind when the flap of his command tent swept open and a man dressed in armor bearing Veed's crest strode in without hesitation. Already flustered past his containable limit, Renigan shuffled his maps around, not sure what he meant to hide, only knowing he must. He raised paranoid eyes to his visitor, prepared to bark a reprimand when the other man cast back his cowl to reveal a luminous glower. Now, Renigan understood why his heart was racing.

"What are—" Renigan hustled from around the table to secure the tent flap once more. He spun to face his demonic intruder. "All of you really need to quit coming to see me unannounced and when I'm surrounded by people who don't need to know what's going on between us."

The demon, disinterested in Renigan's excitability, cast a calm glance through the tent's interior. "Why is that?"

"Because our cover will be blown if we're found. Do you have any idea what that would mean?"

The demon shrugged. "Doesn't have us bothered. There's enough of us to hold our own, otherwise we wouldn't be here to begin with. You should be more concerned about yourself."

Renigan spat. That was precisely what he was concerned

about, but he attempted to hide as much behind crossed arms, a dry snort, and the roll of his eyes. "And why would I be concerned about myself?" This sort of charade always came so naturally to Veed.

"You were supposed to ensure Veed was the one leading this front."

Renigan's scowl withered to something closer to a grimace as he plucked at excuses, grabbing the first one that came to him. "Well, yes. I tried to get him to come, encouraged him to take the lead since it had been so long since he'd been with the army, but he said he wanted to stay behind. As his commander and especially after the... actions taken against his power in his absence, I couldn't exactly argue with him, now could I?"

The demon narrowed his eyes and snapped his gaze to Renigan's. The fleman flinched. "And now, he's dead."

Renigan gasped, eyes wide. For as long as he'd fantasized about inheriting power, the news of Veed's death nauseated him. "He's— I thought you wanted him alive?" Renigan reached his arm behind him to grab for his stool before his knees gave out from beneath him.

"We did," the demon hissed. "It was Mathias who claimed him, not any of us. He was defeated in a matter of minutes. You do realize this poses a very unfortunate complication in our agreement, don't you?"

Most of Elidae's nobility had considered Mathias untrustworthy at some point and to varying extents, and Renigan hadn't been an exception. The paladin never hid his contempt for Veed and those who followed him, but to act out in this manner? It didn't add up from any angle. Veed had been so at ease when he returned to the fortress, hadn't expressed any concerns regarding Mathias whatsoever. And now Veed was *dead*?

"There must be some mistake..."

"I'd give it another hour or two before the formal report makes it to your camp. So tell me, so I may tell my superiors, what is your plan now?"

In brighter days, easier ones far away from insatiable demons and deities, Renigan would have gleefully slapped on his new title, wearing a distraught face to mollify the public. These days were about as far from bright as Renigan could imagine, and right now, he'd have gladly surrendered his station to have Veed alive.

Renigan knew his own limitations. He was a devious man and observant of details, but not the tactical mastermind Veed had been. Odds were good that the relations Veed had claimed to share with Nessix had spurred Mathias's deadly actions, but Renigan and Shand had also taken care to frame Veed as the nation's traitor. How long would it take Mathias to begin suspecting him? However long Veed had held out in his final battle against Mathias, Renigan was certain he'd be lucky to make it half as long.

"Should I take it that your silence means you don't have one?" the demon asked, barely glancing up from where he focused on picking at his nails.

Renigan sputtered a laugh and stood up, knees more trustworthy but head still spinning. "I've got a plan," he assured, expending the greatest extent of diplomacy he possessed to deliver the statement. "I'm still working out the specifics, but there's a plan, be sure of that."

The demon narrowed his eyes and gave a slight shake of his head. He believed that about as much as he believed Etha would open the heavens to his kin. "You will keep up with your end of the bargain. Do not forget the position you're in."

"I am a man of my word, if nothing else." Renigan threw out the most confident smile he had.

The demon frowned. Renigan had a lengthy record of the contrary, trailing all the way back to the day he first approached Shand to take Veed's place. "Clearly."

Renigan's expression faltered at the gruff reply, but before he found a fresh excuse to ramble on about, the demon sighed and pulled the cowl back over his head. He straightened, eyes hidden in the depths of his hood.

"We look forward to hearing all about this great plan you're brewing. Be quick about it. I don't think you need a reminder of the position we're all in at the moment."

Nearly choking on his tongue, Renigan nodded once and cleared his throat. "Of course. I suspect I'll have everything worked out within a day's time."

The demon inclined his chin to assess Renigan's flushed cheeks, then shook his head. This fleman had no idea the peril he'd lodged himself into. Freshly equipped with the most thorough report patience let him gather, the demon turned and left the tent just as casually as he'd entered it. Renigan leaned forward against the table, eyes wide and heart racing. He hadn't lied. He did have a plan. A big one. One which brought the burn of terrified tears to his eyes.

Few flemans understood the ways of magic, and Renigan was no exception. Part of submitting to Shand was the promise to access such wonders if he wanted to, just as she made sure Veed had carried them with him. As the need to protect himself threatened to suffocate Renigan where he stood, he'd never wanted to try anything so badly in his life.

The explanation of breaking threads and redirecting divine energy made no sense to Renigan and the effort to learn this art was too tedious for him, so he opted for the simpler method of evoking a god's might. Blood magic was rudimentary compared to tracing threads, but Renigan knew how to bleed. Shand had given him a shallow scrying bowl, just the size of his fist, and as he hadn't even entered combat, his veins pulsed with no shortage of blood. Trapped between the ire of a deranged goddess and the demons' suspicions, Renigan still wasn't convinced reaching out to Shand was his best option, but his only other one was suicide.

Pricking the tip of his thumb, he squeezed his blood into the bowl and held his breath. He'd never found the need—nor the desire—to summon his goddess before, and had no idea if his interpretation of magic would work. Part of him even hoped it wouldn't. Shand had kept relatively silent of late, a matter he hadn't dwelled on until now. In the span of time it took Renigan to draw his next breath, tiny ripples disturbed the surface of his blood, pulling together to reveal Shand's scowl.

"What?" she spat. If Renigan was smart, he'd take her anger as a warning. She had much more important matters to tend to than her pawn's whining.

Renigan flinched at the force of her words, wondering if

scrying carried the advantage of protecting him from physical retaliation. "Veed is dead, my lady."

"I know that," she snapped. "And it wasn't supposed to happen."

Renigan sucked in a deep breath and pinched his lips together. Was she going to blame him for this, too? Did nobody hold Mathias accountable for his actions? "But it did," he said, "and I can tell you that the demons are more unhappy about it than you are."

Her eyes flashed up to meet his, agitation reined in behind her thirst for information. "Why would they be?"

"How would I know? But they're holding me responsible and I would like to petition for your protection against whatever they plan to do to punish me for it."

Shand cocked her head, contemplation easing a hint of her rage. "They know who you are and know your place in my plans. What makes you think they'd come after you?"

Renigan averted his eyes and crammed his fear back down his throat. It didn't rest any easier in his belly. "My lady—" Considering he had summoned Shand to avoid an untimely death, he should have prepared his confession's delivery in advance. "The demons approached me on their own volition, not long before you ordered the hit on Nessix. They asked me to betray you in their favor, promised me the same things you did with the catch of being unshackled from you."

Shand drew her shoulders back, eyes dimming to a deep crimson in Renigan's blood. "You consider yourself shackled?"

Renigan couldn't decipher Shand's thoughts through the surface which allowed them to have this conversation. He cleared his throat. "The demons consider me shackled," he said. He knew Shand was too perceptive to swallow a flat-out lie, so he hid behind a grain of truth in hope of preserving his skewed sense of security.

"And what did you say to their offer?"

Renigan sweated beneath his armor and his eyes stung with uncertainty. He kept his hands beneath the level of the table to hide the fact that he couldn't stop his fingers from twitching. "I... I am ever loyal to you, my lady." He bowed his head with what he hoped passed for reverence. "And I told them I would work with them so I could keep an eye on their actions in case they were to try to threaten you."

His eyes sprang sheepishly to meet hers and Shand contemplated his claim. She knew Renigan was a tool, a relatively dull one at that. It was what made him so much easier to manipulate than Veed had been. It was what allowed her to control him through simple intimidation. It was what let her give him orders that he was too terrified to disobey. In his life, Renigan had sworn loyalty to the Teradhel family, to Veed, to Shand, all of these to try to gain a better position for himself. Shand had no doubt that he'd sworn loyalty to the demons and meant it with the same conviction he'd vowed to serve his previous lords.

Could this betrayal have been part of Shand's loss of control over the demons? Her eyes narrowed. No. Renigan only thought he was crafty. He wouldn't have been able to find a way to wield chaos as raw as the demons against her. Whatever they'd sworn to him was no more guaranteed than her own promises. Renigan was still being used, but he'd given Shand one vital piece of information. She now had the answer to one of her biggest problems. It was time for the flemans to meet their traitor.

"Renigan, my dear, thank you for telling me of this brewing deceit." The last word clicked smartly off her tongue, gaining a sharp wince from Renigan as he tried to interpret the degree of her honesty. "I will tend to this problem for you. All you have to worry about is keeping your troops alive. Do what you wish to the demons in your sights."

He blew his cluster of nerves out on a long sigh and Shand bit the inside of her cheek to keep from scowling at her pawn's simplicity. Wielding this fool's name ought to pull Inwan and Mathias both off her trail. Her pawn had exhausted his usefulness and she might as well dispose of him now. After taking a moment to compose her thoughts, she smiled at Renigan, a gesture he should have known better than to trust.

"Is that all you have for me?" she asked.

He grinned stupidly, assuming he'd finally escaped his danger. "It is, my lady."

Shand's smile bared her teeth. "Then stay safe, my dear. No matter who you've aligned yourself with, this war is dangerous."

She drained the blood from the bowl, forbidding Renigan the opportunity to respond. Mind racing over the fact that he'd just survived his confession, Renigan laughed at his good fortune. If only the poor fool knew. But then again, he never had.

TWENTY-NINE

Chaos erupted the day following Veed's execution. The men under Mathias, Brant especially, rejoiced the fact that they'd finally been relieved of the snake that was Veed, but struggled to accept that Mathias had been responsible for his death. Not only did his display of violence shock them, but Veed was now the second powerhead to die with direct ties to the paladin. While the general consensus agreed that Veed deserved his end several times over, it was no less alarming that it happened through the means which it had.

The men still present within Veed's fortress scrambled for order without their leader, already making preparations to overthrow Renigan's subsequent inheritance of power. The commander had previously proven he lacked the skill needed to uphold the title, but that left Veed's kingdom in an even more delicate political position. In the ensuing disorder, the soldiers flung themselves in every direction—some sought safety within the Teradhel ranks, some rallied to create a strike force against Mathias, others caved to how dangerous this war had become with allies slaying one another and sought to escape the scene entirely. Without Veed to lead them, this disciplined force was painfully lost.

Mathias had promptly vacated the scene and responsibility associated with it, and Inwan realized he was the only man willing and capable to take on the task of scrounging up some way to honor the fallen general. Several years ago, he'd taken an interest in Veed, entertained by the man's confidence and wit, and though he disagreed with the path Veed had chosen to travel in his final years of life, Inwan had learned that he cared about his people much more than he wanted to admit.

Amid the flourishing disorder, there hadn't been much time to coordinate elaborate means of disposing of Veed's body. Mathias's resounding opinion was to let the beast rot on the side of the road, but Inwan believed a man of Veed's tenacity deserved much more respect than that. Though he knew only a fraction of Veed's force would show for a proper funeral, he elected to conduct one anyway.

Giving up on coaxing compassion from Mathias on the matter, Inwan planned the service on his own, considering it his first gift back to his people. He carefully selected the site where Veed's remains would finally rest to form a point directly between Laes and Nes's graves, and negated the strident objections to his decision by wielding his restored divinity to create Veed's grave himself. A triangle now existed between the resting places of the two men and the girl they'd both given their lives to love. Despite the subtle uproar from Nes's troops, nobody but Brant had demanded a change of location, as not even Mathias could argue that Veed had at one time been important to the Teradhel family. At least Nessix no longer occupied her grave, and Laes would have preferred Veed to remain easy to find. The two of them had several matters to discuss in the afterlife.

There wasn't much Inwan could say at the funeral, as the Veed Mathias had slain was not the same one Inwan had known years ago. The service stayed short, interrupted only once when Inwan caught sight of a willowy woman in a black hood mingling through the crowd. When he was through with the limited address of what Veed could have been and after the ceiling of earth had been poured over the unfortunate general, Inwan dismissed the troops back to their duty.

They milled about in the way confused mourners do, tapering off until all that remained was Inwan, Shand, and the mound which sealed Veed away. Inwan gave the goddess ample time to approach him, but when she didn't, he folded under the pressure and strode forward.

"Did you come to pay your respects to your servant?" he called as he neared her.

Shand tilted her face upward to peer at Inwan from the depths of her hood. "I'm afraid I don't know what you mean."

Inwan frowned. The past day spent negotiating arrangements for Veed's burial between Etha and Mathias had tried his patience, and he had nothing left to tend to Shand's goading. "Veed is dead. You've lost your leverage. It's time for you to pack up and leave Elidae. Go back to whatever you were doing before."

She laughed quietly, just enough for her shoulders to shake, and threw Inwan a devious grin. "Oh, I'd wanted Veed," she admitted freely. "He'd have given me a much stronger foothold than I have now. But he was too smitten with that little tramp, just *refused* to hurt her. Well. Any more than he had by killing her father."

Inwan clenched his teeth at Shand's callousness. He'd loved Nessix and Laes, and he'd failed them in a way no god should ever fail his beloved people. Would things have been different if he'd been more diligent? Would Veed have still travelled down this same path?

Shand glided a step closer to Inwan and snuck a coy glance at the ground. "You're wondering if I'd have been bold enough to approach him in the first place if you'd been around, aren't you?" At the curl of Inwan's lip and the flash of his eyes, Shand continued. "I wouldn't have *dreamed* of coming to Elidae if you were still on watch. At one point, you really did have a decent amount of power. But you opened an appealing door, one I'm surprised nobody else wanted to take advantage of—"

"Nobody else is stupid enough to have tried," Inwan snapped. "I will tell you one more time. I have returned. This is my land and my people. Your insider is gone. Give it up, Shand."

She looked up at him again, the whimsy wiped from her face. "My insider is very much so still alive, and I've always been the type to finish what I start."

Fire churned in Inwan's core, promising to back him in whatever manner he'd require. He savored the warmth of it. "Are you taunting me?"

Shand's eyes narrowed and she shook her head. "Not at all. You want to know who betrayed the flemans?"

Inwan held his breath, having never imagined Shand would give up her source so easily. She smiled at his eagerness.

"His name is Renigan Falk, and he's the most pliable waste of life I've ever had the pleasure of wrapping my fingers around. Veed was too unruly and clever to fall for me, so I had to fish for an alternative."

"Renigan Falk." Inwan murmured the name firmly to commit it to memory. Despite any claims he'd made, he was not an all-knowing god. None of them were, save Etha, and this war had shown that even she could be deceived through proper measures. The flemans Inwan knew by name were limited to those he'd invested time in, and this Renigan had been well off his radar when Inwan had still been with his people. "How do I know you're being honest?"

Shand shrugged. "You don't. But I can promise if you went out to his front and put the heat on him, he'd bend like a cheap tavern whore. Tell him you'll provide him safety from me and the demons, and you'll get to use him however you'd like. In fact, I'll trade him to you for permission to stay and play just a bit longer."

Inwan growled. "You've given me what I need to know and now I have no reason to *allow* you to stay."

"Oh, I'm so very afraid of not having your permission! All I've seen you do is make holes in the ground to bury disgusting old men. That's not very powerful for a god, now is it?"

Inwan clutched to his composure, too close to regaining his influence to blow it now. He had a name. He had someone to hold accountable—someone who actually *was* accountable. Now he had to find who that was so he could tend to them in a way worthy of their treason.

Shand patted Inwan on the chest and touched his cheek. "Now run home, little god. Go and tell Etha's guard dog all about Renigan and the delightful games we played. I know you and

Mathias are *so* close these days."

When Inwan refused to react, Shand laughed and turned away, waving a nonchalant hand in farewell. She strode off from him, radiating arrogance and a distinct lack of fear. Inwan clenched his fist at his side, wondering yet again what all he'd recovered of his lost power. He couldn't risk an attack right now, not against Shand and her might, and so he wrestled down his impulse to charge after her.

He'd run home, alright, but it wouldn't be to talk to Mathias. The paladin had already chosen his path for vengeance and had apparently picked the wrong target. Besides, Inwan agreed that Mathias had deserved Veed more than anyone else had. As it was, Inwan knew someone much better suited for the job of interrogating Renigan. After Shand disappeared from sight, Inwan flashed back to the Teradhel fortress.

* * * * *

Months had passed since Brant last smiled, at least a genuine one not anchored in some sort of battle-fed madness. Still running high in the wake of Veed's death, his outlook had rebounded enthusiastically from the gloom that had held him down. It was a factor Inwan took deep into consideration, given the commander's propensity for hasty actions. This was the clearest Brant seemed to think since Inwan's homecoming. He hadn't heard the young man attempt to speak to Nessix over the past several days, though the renewed light in Brant's eyes still didn't quite speak of mental clarity. Either way, Inwan saw him as his only viable option and hunted him down in the mess hall.

"Brant, a word?"

Brant looked up from his meal, expression leveling at the sight of the god. "That depends," he said. "Do you intend to make a fool of me again?"

Inwan frowned. He should have known better than to expect courtesy from Brant. "I'd told Mathias that I'd keep an eye—"

"You are a *god*, Inwan." One of the benefits of having so little to live for was the fearlessness to question even this sort of might.

"Who gives a damn what Sagewind tells you?"

Inwan sighed and sat down across from Brant, pleased to note that neither personal grudges nor the habit of saving a spot for Nessix made Brant object to his action. Both were signs of improvement Inwan hoped would continue to flourish.

"What if I want to talk to you about something another god said?" Inwan asked.

Brant rolled his eyes and resumed eating. "I get enough of that from Sagewind."

Inwan straightened his position and darted his eyes through the sparsely occupied mess hall before leaning forward again. He beckoned Brant closer with the wave of his hand, a gesture the commander accepted after an peevish huff. "I spoke with Shand."

Brant stopped chewing and he forced himself to swallow a bite that wasn't quite ready to go down. "And what did she say?"

Inwan held up a finger and glanced away to think over the best way to explain himself. "Do not argue with me quite yet, but she said Veed wasn't the traitor—"

Brant disregarded the instruction and slapped the table, throwing his weight back from their hushed conversation. "Veed was the biggest piece—"

Inwan pushed himself to his feet and leaned over the table to grab Brant by the collar. A flare of divine authority stirred Inwan's hair and his hardened glare silenced Brant. Apparently, putting the young man out once had taught him a lesson he didn't need repeated.

"I'm not saying he didn't deserve to die," Inwan said, now that he'd gained Brant's compliance. "But I am saying he'd been honest when he told us he wasn't the one actively behind all of this."

Brant threw his gaze away from Inwan and calmed himself over a series of deep breaths before reaching up to pull his collar free. Inwan permitted the action and Brant settled into his seat. "Fine. Then who is?"

Inwan checked over the people in the room once more before leaning closer still. "Who is Renigan Falk?"

Brant's jaw dropped and he scattered his disbelief with a fierce shake of his head. *Renigan?* That couldn't be right in any stretch of the imagination. He had no real standing where it mattered, no real respect. How could he have been responsible for the downfall of the entire fleman nation?

"Well?" Inwan asked, this time with budding urgency. "Who is he?"

Brant blinked and stammered his response. "He's Veed's commander."

Inwan twisted his lips. That made sense. "Isn't he supposed to be leading one of the fronts right now?"

Brant looked up at Inwan, meeting the sly mischief he'd once known well. "He is. But if you're going to confront him, you're taking me with you."

"I really think this is something best tended to by me alone."

With a defiant shake of his head, Brant met Inwan's scheme with his own. "When you sat down, you didn't know who Renigan was, but I do. I'm willing to overlook how you stepped in my way to keep me from facing a goddess, but you will not stop me from facing a piece of shit mortal, do you understand?"

Godly pride instructed Inwan to correct Brant for his demands, but a quiet truth whispered that this was for the best. Nessix had been excused a generous share of obstinacy and even insults directed toward Inwan at times. Laes had been only slightly less bold. Mathias had assured Inwan that Brant was the future of Elidae, and whether or not Inwan wanted to be spoken down to by a mortal, he'd accept it from Brant. After all, the young man was trying just as hard as he was to adjust to life again.

"And whatever it is you plan to do to him, I will be involved in that, as well," Brant continued when Inwan didn't protest. "Sagewind should have given me Veed. He *owed* me Veed. I missed one shot and will not miss a second."

"Why are you so bent on this course of action?"

Brant looked down at his food, appetite lost amid shock and excitement. "For Nessix," he said. "Just like you. I'll do it for the people, also like you, but only because that's what she'd have done." He looked up at Inwan, a fresh mist of tears in his eyes. "Please don't take this from me."

Intuition and selfishness urged Inwan to do just that, but he truly wanted to help Brant. "Alright," he said. "Do you think you can meet me at the stables in two hours?"

Brant's heart fluttered as the chance for retribution grew increasingly near. "I'll wait for you, if you'd prefer."

Inwan sighed. What did dread feel like? "Very well." He stood and tugged on his shirt to straighten the unbecoming wrinkles from it. "Be discreet?"

Brant didn't need to be told twice. "Of course."

Inwan turned to leave the mess hall and Brant watched him disappear through the doors. He laughed to himself, accustomed by now to the pitying glances he received for his alleged insanity. Tension released, he covered his mouth with one hand. "It's almost over..." he murmured to the Nessix who was no longer there. "I'll fix this for you or die trying." Renewed, Brant resumed his meal, suspecting he'd need the energy later.

* * * * *

It took Mathias a full day to settle on the best way to tell Sulik what he'd done, as he still hadn't gotten used to disappointing his friend. Of course, Etha had informed Sulik the moment Veed's life flickered out, but she'd left delivering the details to Mathias. Sulik accepted both reports much more readily than Mathias had anticipated, and neither man made any further commotion about it. After all, poignant experience warned them about the dangers of losing focus on this mission.

The army pressed on by foot, well aware that the demons knew of their advance and objective. As individuals, the soldiers were worn from this war, ready to be through, and so tired of the consistent grind and losses dealt to them. As a whole, though, Mathias had never seen the Teradhel army so fit. Their need to put the war in the realm of history overshadowed their mountain of dread, and now that Mathias was free of his curses and Etha vowed to stay close, he suspected their victory celebration was at last close at hand. The war they suffered through would soon be through, and Mathias would be free to carry out his promise to find Nessix.

It didn't take long for Mathias to realize more than just

marching soldiers followed him and a wave of ease welled around him as he slowed his gait to allow Etha to catch up. She'd accepted his prayers, but this was the first time she'd approached Mathias since his rebellious actions. He timidly marched on, dreading the judgment she might carry. Etha allowed Mathias to gather his wits and when he glanced to his side, a smirk softened his brooding expression at Etha's chosen form of a gangly adolescent herald. Just because she said she'd stay with the army didn't mean she planned to stand out.

She walked beside Mathias, allowing him to bask in her peace until her prying mind insisted she break their silence. "Have you found even a bit of closure yet?"

"Closure?" Mathias asked. "Why would I need closure? An evil as wrong as Veed had to be righted. I did it for Nes. And for Laes. And everyone else he led into harm's way. I did all of Abaeloth a favor by removing him from the world. My only regret is that I hadn't done it sooner."

Etha grimaced. Apparently, word of Shand's confession hadn't yet reached Mathias. She had to tread carefully. "I can't offer you comfort for what Veed did to the noble family, but his soldiers knew his character and the dangers of war. You can't fault him for that."

"They expected his protection!" Mathias gripped the strap of his pack to keep from causing a scene by flailing his arms about in frustration. The indecency, the cursed pendants… why was Etha defending that repulsive man? "You can't possibly believe that plea of innocence he made."

Etha twisted her lips and grabbed one of her elbows, shifting a half step away from Mathias. "What else would you have me believe? The only thing divine about Veed was that curse he carried for denying Shand."

Mathias shook his head, the leap of his pulse driving tears to the backs of his eyes. "But you said yourself that he was protected—"

"I said whatever mortal was involved was protected," she corrected. "Veed was not. His vile nature limited itself to lust, but not of the caliber seen here."

Driven by the men marching behind him, Mathias commanded his legs to persist past their overwhelming urge to plant into the ground. "What does this mean?" he asked, the pounding in his ears prompting the question's delivery louder than he'd intended.

"It means…" Etha rubbed her brow, sneaking her eyes away from Mathias. There was no way he'd take what she had to say with the least bit of grace. Sucking in a deep breath, Etha spoke her next words quickly. "Your actions were only self-gratifying. Veed wasn't the one."

The revelation nearly jarred Mathias to a stop and Etha grabbed his arm to pull him along. His stomach churned, compromising the sturdiness of his knees. Mathias had slain an innocent man. That thought echoed through the core of his being, mocking him and all of the virtue he'd spent lifetimes trying to uphold. He'd slain an innocent man. His heart had run away with its own motives, and he'd been too weak to stop it. Some paladin he was! Some hero! Etha could have stopped him, could have reminded him who he was, but it wasn't her place to do so. Mathias could not pin this on anyone but himself, and he wasn't about to try. He, Mathias Sagewind, had slain an innocent man.

"So who is?" he whispered.

Etha snuck a glance at Mathias's pale face and unconsciously tightened her grip on his arm. "Shand just came clean to Inwan. She said she's been working with Renigan Falk."

Mathias flung his hands from his pack, balling them into fists. It made too much sense. Shand would have been able to locate Renigan easily from how close he was to Veed. The commander was no less crooked than his lord and cared more about the easy path to the top than anything else. This information was invaluable, but easily overshadowed by Mathias's preoccupation with his lapse of sound judgement.

Etha sighed and moved her hand to Mathias's back. "Veed's forces are in turmoil. Some are talking of a civil war. Most are too afraid to rally under Renigan and that's without even knowing what he actually is. This was not your best timed intervention."

Mathias groaned and grimaced at the twist in his gut. "You

349

don't have to remind me." He was no less a monster than Veed had been.

Etha frowned at his silent reflection and slid her hand to squeeze his shoulder. "He was far more a monster than you are," she said. "You did what you thought was right and followed your heart. He had hurt his people, hurt your Nessix. He was a bad man. Not evil, but certainly wicked enough to have earned justice."

Lip curled in disgust of his introspection, Mathias snuck a timid look at Etha. Where he'd been sure he'd find some degree of disappointment, he instead saw a placid calm, a peaceful ambience glowing about her unusual form. She truly supported the actions he'd taken and trusted he'd negotiate whatever consequences followed. Blowing out a deep breath, Mathias wiped the sweat from his brow.

"Nothing will erase what I did," he said at last. "I will never mourn Veed, but I'm pleased he had Inwan to grant him rest."

Etha closed her eyes with a soft smile, relieved to see Mathias choose to spare them both a debate. "You did a good thing, allowing Inwan that chance," she said. "That action was noted by Veed's army. It didn't do much to gain favor for you, but it did revitalize some faith in that old buffoon. I'm proud of you."

Warmth rose to Mathias's cheeks and eased his heart to a slower pace. While he wanted to bask in Etha's praise, there was one important matter to be dealt with first. "So what do we do about Renigan?"

Etha lowered her head and focused on moving forward. She knew of Inwan's current schemes, despite his efforts to hide them, but she supported what he hoped to accomplish. Informing Mathias would complicate matters for everyone, and so Etha kept her insight to herself. "For now, you only need to worry about this tunnel," she said. "Renigan will have his time, but throwing another problem on the table right now will overtax your army. You need to see this through."

He nodded. "I wasn't arguing that. I just can't figure out why I don't hate him the way I hated Veed."

Etha swept an inquisitive eye Mathias's way, longing to poke at him for admitting such a foul emotion as hatred, but one look at the disgust creased across his face wiped that curiosity from her. "You know how to fix the damage done to nations. You can mend bodies, but damage done at the level of the heart..." She crossed her arms to keep from grabbing his arm again. "Renigan betrayed the entire nation, but the people still have each other. Veed betrayed Nessix when she had nobody."

Mathias looked down and frowned. "I'd give anything to—"

Horns from the front lines spouted up in a disorganized fashion, their warning rippling back through the ranks. Mathias cast a quick glance at Etha, confused as to why she hadn't warned him of the danger ahead. The color drained from her cheeks and she shook her head slowly.

"Were they cloaked?" Mathias asked.

"They must have been," Etha murmured, brows furrowing in concentration.

Mathias scowled. That had to mean Shand was near. He squinted ahead to see if he could spot Sulik, but the commander was out of his line of sight. He turned to his herald. "Signify change of command to Commander Vakharan."

"Sir?" the young man asked.

"I've got some scouting to do; you'll be much safer if you stay with the army.

Licking his lips, the herald nodded and raised his horn, trilling out Mathias's order. The paladin turned from his ranks and marched against the flow of the diligent army, perseverance deafening him to the questions that popped up around him. Etha stayed close at his heels.

What are you doing, love...?

He didn't bother to spare a glance back at her. *I'm flushing Shand out. I beg you to stay with the army. She'll come much more readily if she sees me alone.*

Etha frowned and lengthened her stride to catch up to him. *Your shard of Affliction and my blessing can only take you so far against a god.*

And her god shard can only do so much against my shard of Affliction and your blessing. She's after me. She told me as much, but would she really target me in the middle of an army?

351

Etha's feet scuffed to a stop and Mathias paused to look back at her. He hadn't expected her to comply so readily. He met Etha's eyes and they steeled over with unwavering faith. *Be careful.*

Mathias closed his eyes and listened to the steady pounding of his heart, a heart which beat strong with divine grace. He was ready to face Shand, ready to end this war. Opening his eyes again, Mathias gave his goddess the charming smile that often meant he was up to so much mischief. *All I ask is that you listen for me and come when I call.*

Etha returned the gesture, though much less assured. *Just make sure you do.*

As Mathias hastened back toward the fortress, he had no fear of leaving the army behind despite not knowing the nature of their pending opposition. Historically, demons didn't coordinate large scale attacks as smoothly as their mortal adversaries, and they had their hands full managing three large fronts as it was. Mathias figured his allies would hold their own without him. Besides, Sulik was a competent leader and Etha had already proven her willingness to play dirty if necessity demanded it. He cast one more look over his shoulder to see clouds from combat rise up from the ground.

The sounds of distant battle picked at Mathias, begging him to go back to his army. He was much more experienced at fighting demons and the troops relied on his talents. Against the screams of discernment, Mathias stayed his course. Following impulse seldom worked in his favor and had been what ended Nes's life. He squared his stance and waited for Shand. He knew she'd come.

Mathias trained his eyes on the fortress, conscience struggling to pull his focus from the front he'd just left. A chill kissed the back of his neck, seeping down his arms to slowly penetrate the metal of his breastplate. He gasped and choked on a breath of frigid air as Affliction tracked the scent of malicious divinity. Mathias spun around, pulling his sword free.

Nessix staggered toward him, one hand reaching out, the other jammed against her neck. Blood oozed in a steady pulse from between her fingers and her breath came quick and shallow through parted lips.

"Mathias…" she whimpered. "Please…"

He sucked in a sharp gasp and shook his head. Insanity wasn't supposed to penetrate his blessings, not like this. Timid, Mathias reached out for Nes's soul, trying to draw on familiarity he could help, but it was no less distant than before. His sword shook in an unsteady grasp, primal instinct urging him to retreat as Nessix dragged herself closer.

Etha, I… Thoughts caught in a heap of desire and common sense, Mathias took a step back. "This isn't you," he told Nessix. It *couldn't* be her!

A sound that might have been meant to be his name pushed past Nes's uncoordinated lips, followed by a pathetic plea. "Help…"

He lowered his sword, sense born of Affliction screaming the truth to his deaf heart. The demons had Nes's body and Shand had told him that she'd been helping them perfect the blasphemy of necromancy. Nessix—*his* Nessix—was dead. But then again, if this was only a reanimation of her, she couldn't have been bleeding, not like this. Nessix stumbled and cried out, and Mathias dropped his sword, rushing to catch her and ease her to the ground.

Have you found Shand? Etha's voice answered at last.

I don't…

"I need you, Mathias."

Mathias couldn't tear his eyes from Nes's disoriented gaze as strength sapped from her feeble arms. He clutched her free hand, heart straining to conceive a way to make sense of this despite Affliction's firm guidance. Mathias's experience with the undead, while not as involved as his experience with demons, suggested this Nessix was not the danger he'd expected, and as her tears began to fall, he knew as much.

"Help me." Her fingers closed around his.

Mathias's breath caught in his throat and he raised her hand to his lips. "I don't know how…"

A frail smile softened the agony on Nes's face as she reached her bloodied hand to his empty one to guide it toward the wound that had already poured too much blood for her to have maintained consciousness. "Of course you can."

Mathias, have you found Shand?

Etha's words reached him clearly, but as he stared down into the hope and will to survive in Nes's eyes, all he could care about was her. Her breathing had slowed, but her eyes were no less clear as she pulled his hand to her bleeding neck. His fingers slipped over the wound. Her blood was cold.

The gasp Mathias tried to sound never came out and as Nessix's strength effortlessly raised her to a seated position, he froze, hand stuck pressed against her neck. Her smile broadened well past the impish grin he'd treasured. She splayed her bloodied fingers across Mathias's chest, eyes swirling about until they'd deepened into a menacing purple. Her laughter shook against his hand at her throat and Mathias couldn't move.

"To think, your heart is what put you in my grasp, and what's in that heart is the only thing keeping you alive. Oh, Mathias, love, you are an easy one to play."

Shand shook her head, casting the loose raven tresses into short silver strands and she shoved Mathias backwards to the ground. Swinging a leg over his waist, she pressed her palm against his breastplate. His armor had been given to him by Etha herself and was far more durable against divine threats than typical plate mail because of that, but Shand's unworldly strength did a fine job crushing him through its defenses. Mathias wheezed for breath and tried to twist his legs to shove Shand off of him, but the weight of her might held him immobile.

Shand leaned over him, her hair falling like a curtain around her face. "It's poetic, really. Nessix hadn't fought, either. She just fell to her knees and let the demons take her."

Mathias croaked an attempt at cursing Shand, struggling to pull his fingers into a fist. She pressed against his chest again and his ribs bent and groaned at the pressure. It had been ages since he'd had to wonder what it would be like to die again, and it was a sensation he didn't welcome.

The wind howled around them, ripping Shand's hair from its veil, and she growled before gathering her strength through her upper body for one last shove.

A leg swept through Mathias's field of vision, catching Shand

354

across the face, and the twisted goddess belted out a scream as she tumbled to the side. Mathias blinked at last, chest heaving as his body was now free to assess for internal damage, and he looked up to see Etha striding over him in Shand's direction. A distant roar of hooves and voices suggested she had backup on the way. Mathias pushed himself upright.

Through all of the ages and trials he'd served Etha, Mathias couldn't recall ever seeing her so illuminated with righteous beauty. Back in her preferred mortal form of a young woman, she now donned shining golden armor, lilies gracing the breastplate to put Mathias's to shame. Her helm was the head of a snarling fox, eyes alight with cunning and mischief. He couldn't clearly see her face behind it, but he didn't need to. The possessive energy radiating from Etha told him all he needed to know. He was lucky she knew him well enough to heed his silence as a call for help.

Shand wiped a glittering purple substance from her lip and hissed at Etha. "Tampering again, Mother?" She pulled herself to her feet, fists clenched.

"This is not fate," Etha said, her voice low and dark and deadly. "You will never again lay your hands on my servant."

Shand straightened, focus shifting away from Mathias and to the greater threat. "Or else what?"

"Do you dare to challenge me?" Etha asked.

"You know what," Shand said, reflecting on a new set of opportunities to exploit. Mathias was no longer the most important contender on the field, and the length of time Shand had spent playing on the mortal plane had inflated her confidence. "I *do* challenge you."

Mathias had made it to his knees and his mind timidly resumed wrapping around the burdens of reality once again. The sound of his army nearing grew increasingly distinct and he hauled himself to his feet. This wasn't going according to plan. At all.

Etha threw her tiny shoulders back and tipped her chin toward her shoulder to ensure her voice carried to Mathias. "Ceraphlaks will be here shortly. It is imperative you leave the field, Mathias."

Her words stunned Mathias and launched Shand into a bout

of haughty laughter. Mathias was Etha's shield; how could she ask him to abandon her in combat? Etha was all powerful, and Mathias steadfastly believed in the limitless nature of her might, but as he looked at Shand glowering in their direction, he faced the fact that even gods could bleed.

Mathias retrieved his sword and took a step toward Etha. "I will not—"

Etha did not face him again. "The army is backing me. That will have to be enough."

Mathias froze at her words and Ceraphlaks landed safely out of Shand's reach. *What are you doing?*

At this subtle sign of submission, Etha's shoulders relaxed to allow her to stretch out her arms. *There is only one way to destroy a god who is unwilling to obey me.*

Inside Mathias's chest, Affliction generated a dreadful passion, nearly doubling him over. The only time in Abaeloth's history when gods had been destroyed was at the conclusion of the Divine Battle. Etha couldn't possibly be considering such devastation again. Not after the lessons she'd learned. More importantly, did she have the time in the heat of combat to construct a weapon capable of such destruction?

No, she corrected, having risked a pinch of concentration to keep abreast of Mathias's concerns. *I don't. I need you to recover Affliction for me.*

He blinked, dumbfounded, and pressed his free hand against the burning Affliction's eagerness poured into his chest. Though Etha kept her attention focused on her target, Shand did spare a glance at Mathias's reaction. The evil goddess cocked her head.

"You and your pet planning something?" she asked. "Because I have no intention of backing down."

Mathias did his best to push aside his concern for Etha's safety under the imminent threat of an attack. *You destroyed Affliction.*

This is not the time or place, Etha snipped, her voice strained. *I couldn't destroy the spearhead so I buried it in the safety of my temple. Question me no more. Take Ceraphlaks, follow your shard, and bring me Affliction. Quickly!*

All this time, Mathias had assumed the entire weapon had

been shattered after serving its purpose, and his beloved goddess had allowed him to believe it. Though trapped on Elidae, it might as well have been destroyed. Had Etha allowed Inwan to reign over the island for this reason? To misdirect the flemans into blindly worshiping him to never know what Affliction was? It was a very real possibility, one Mathias prayed he'd have the opportunity to discuss with Etha in the future, but for now, he'd been given his orders and he would obey them.

Vowing not to disturb Etha any more than he had to, Mathias turned to mount Ceraphlaks. He had faced hordes of the undead. He'd escaped torture in the hells. He'd surpassed death at the hands of an army of demons. But the hardest challenge Mathias had ever faced was asking Ceraphlaks to turn and take wing away from the goddess who needed him now more than ever.

THIRTY

Traveling the spans of the divine realm was a new and unpleasant experience for Brant. Between the embrace of a god he still didn't completely trust and the flashes of eternity reaching out for him as they skated the distorted matrix of divine pathways, Brant would die content if he never had to use teleportation again. Regardless, he couldn't deny the method's efficiency and though his stomach twisted through the experience, his heart glowed with anticipation. The one benefit of traveling courtesy of Inwan's might was that they could escape the rules and restrictions which limited Mathias's abilities, freeing the pair to track an individual soul as opposed to needing familiarity with a unique location. It took Inwan little effort to sniff out Renigan with the help of Brant's insight.

The army was actively engaged against the demons, and Inwan made it no great secret that he'd arrived. Both sides of the field cringed as a flash announced the god's arrival, but neither Brant nor Inwan wasted time on concerns regarding the status of combat. Instead, they set their course to the exact spot Brant knew they'd find Renigan.

"Lurking in the back lines like the coward you are?" Brant shouted as soon as he caught sight of the man feigning distraction over a map. "Tell me, do the demons resent you as much as the flemans do?"

Brant made no attempt to hush his accusation and it gained instant attention from the surrounding troops. A few drew their weapons against Brant's aggression, his affiliation with Mathias making him a prime target for retribution, but they stopped at the sight of Inwan. Whether or not he had his powers limited, the god's wrath illuminated him with a frightening presence no mortal wanted to cross.

Renigan gagged on his shock, freezing in place as his glance darted between nearby soldiers. "I'm afraid I don't know what you're talking about, Maliroch." Last Renigan had heard, Brant's own army had labeled him insane. He wasn't supposed to have the mental capacity to make these connections.

Brant's lip curled and he squared his shoulders to charge when Inwan grabbed his arm in a firm grasp. "I think you should be more afraid that you know exactly what he's talking about," the god said.

Renigan shook a finger at Inwan, recoiling his arm quickly when it trembled beyond his control. "You are not fit to speak to me." He'd been under the impression that his talk with Shand had gone well. Could he count on her protection now? "After what you did to our people, Inwan? What gives you the right to judge me?"

"Sounds like a guilty conscience to me." Inwan strode two steps forward, dragging Brant behind him, and gripped Renigan's forearm in his free hand. "I've served my time for my sins." In a flash, he whisked the three of them away to the most secure location on all of Elidae, a room in Etha's temple. "And now, you get to serve yours."

Renigan cowered at the sudden action, wildly scanning the room for support that didn't exist as Inwan shoved him farther into the bare chamber. Still unaccustomed to such modes of travel, it took Brant a moment to gain his bearings. He'd grown up playing in this temple and was comfortable enough in this location to position himself between Renigan and the room's exit once Inwan freed his hold to step forward. This plan was working out better than Brant had imagined.

All of Brant's confusion and anger and pain boiled down to

one statement. "What happened to Nessix?"

Most flemans had never seen the inside of Etha's temple, and Renigan gasped for breath as he spun to face his aggressors. "How would I know?" he demanded. "Do you really think I spend my free time exploring the hells?"

"You wouldn't have the courage to tread those corridors," Inwan scoffed. "I'm amazed you had the gumption to involve yourself in Nes's murder to begin with. Brant asked a valid question. What happened to Nessix?"

Renigan's eyes darted above Brant's shoulder to the room's sole escape point. Brant stood fierce guard over the doorway, crouched over, arms poised to grapple and legs braced to spring. Renigan had witnessed Brant in hand to hand combat before and doubted his ability to get past his heated focus. Even if Renigan had a way to contact Shand, she'd proven less than diligent when it came to her concern for him. Between Inwan and Brant, Renigan knew he wasn't getting out of this, and so he buckled down on the truth to see where it would take him.

"Nessix was a tragedy," he said, "but it wasn't because of what *I* did. It started well before that. She'd always been a puppet for Laes and Veed, for you—" he flung a sneer toward Inwan. "In the end, all it took was a quick jerk on one little string, but getting her to that point cannot be put on me."

"Will Shand support that sort of blasphemy from you?" Inwan asked, grasping Brant's bicep before the commander shoved his way forward.

Renigan swallowed his reservations and prayed to someone other than his goddess that Shand would never catch wind of his next declaration. "Shand owes it to me."

Inwan belted out an uncontrollable laugh, the sound booming off the marble walls. Brant scowled at the outburst, failing to find even a pinch of humor in any of this, but Renigan shrank back in a defensive lump, tattling all about his uncertainty. "So what about the things you owe *me*?" Inwan asked.

Renigan's brows furrowed and he shifted another step away, wide eyes begging for another escape route to open. "What do I owe *you*?" he asked, nearly choking on his dry tongue. "What makes you think I'd owe you anything? Nessix had your blessing, Veed had your respect, and what did I receive?"

"Until today, I didn't even know who you were."

"Exactly," Renigan hissed. "Everything I got, I got through myself and Shand. I owe you nothing."

Inwan arched a brow and tentatively released his grip on Brant. "Have you overlooked what became of my country due to your stupidity?"

"I found a power worth following."

"You enslaved yourself to my bitch of a sister!"

"I am *not* her slave." Renigan's face burned and faint glimmers of light twinkled behind his eyelids when he blinked. "I am her head officer!"

If it wouldn't have been for how close Brant teetered on the edge of restraint, Inwan would have laughed at Renigan's futile attempts at trying to defend his devotion to Shand. How could anyone involved with her honestly believe she cared at all about their welfare? Shand had no regard for mortals, and if the demons weren't such seasoned weapons, she likely wouldn't have tolerated working with them, either. Inwan had every reason to hate Renigan for what he'd done, but his time in purgatory had taught him that sometimes the most effective punishment came from within oneself.

"Have you seen how she treats her officers?" Inwan asked. "Those are the people she keeps the closest eye on, and it doesn't seem like a very safe place to be."

Renigan's eyes darted away from Inwan, confirming he already knew that. Shand had treated him terribly, considering what all he'd sacrificed in her name, but she'd seemed at least interested in his safety during their last talk. Renigan had long ago quit trying to guess how the goddess worked, but held on to a feeble hope that she'd make an appearance on his behalf. "And how well do *you* know her? I *am* still alive. After nearly eleven years of serving her. All of your dear servants have already passed, if I recall correctly."

Inwan's eyes flashed and he straightened so briskly Renigan cringed, flinging his arms over his head. "Not all of them have passed," he said, clasping Brant on the shoulder. "And I'd like to think you'd note both my regard for him and his loyalty to me by the fact that he's maintained himself with nothing but faith that I'll let him have his turn at you when I'm through."

Color drained from Renigan's face as his hand inched toward his sword. The enjoyment Brant and Inwan received by soaking in his panic was short lived as the sound of demon horns filtered through the halls of the temple. Wicked hope shot through Renigan's desperation and he grinned. "Looks like you were wrong. My reinforcements are here."

Maintaining his firm glare on Renigan, Inwan didn't spare the concentration to try accurately accounting for what those horns implied, and he shoved his faith in Brant's obedience. "I promise I will not kill this wretch," he told the commander. "I will give you more than your fair share of opportunities to lay into him, but I need you to check what that ruckus is all about."

Brant's mind flowed more clearly than it had in months, and though he wanted to stay and peel the skin from the backs of Renigan's knees, he trusted Inwan. Nessix had.

Unbuckling his sword, Brant spun to exit the room, looking both ways down the hall to orientate himself. After all these years, neither the murals nor his memories had faded, and Brant closed his eyes to draw on the mental map he'd known as a child. He darted down the passage that led out of the temple.

The horns grew louder the longer Brant ran, pulling him faster. He turned a corner, squinting at the stream of daylight greeting him from the temple's entrance and he staggered against his momentum as he stepped outside. A unit of twenty or so demons chased Mathias, astride Ceraphlaks, toward the temple.

Brant didn't have time to worry over any reprimand Mathias might offer his insubordination, not with the flood of demons rushing his way. Even as a youth, Brant hadn't gotten the hang of praying, and so he wasn't sure how to do so now, but he invested his efforts on asking for guidance or, at the very least, for Inwan to get back to the fortress so Mathias wouldn't know they'd left it completely unguarded once this imminent skirmish was through. Drawing on his stalwart courage, Brant settled into his stance. Whatever was going on, he'd do his best to hold out.

* * * * *

When Mathias had left the Teradhel fortress, he'd done so with a healthy hope of Brant being restrained as he'd instructed. A nagging dread suggested that finding his unlikely reinforcement here meant Inwan couldn't be far away, but Mathias shoved his disappointment in the two of them aside to address later. There had been no siege bells, so in the best scenario, the fortress still stood safely. Mind already battered with ghastly premonitions, he refused to think of the alternative.

With his assailants close at his heels and committed to stopping him, Mathias leapt to the ground and glanced over his shoulder as they closed in. He made a quick assessment of Brant, relieved by the focus in the young man's eyes. "Think you can hold them off for me?"

"Will I have a choice?"

Mathias frowned. "I doubt you will for long."

Brant stretched his arms out and adjusted the grip on his sword. "How long do you need?"

"As long as you can give me, Commander."

Brant glanced at Mathias, surprised by the reluctance tarnishing the other man's expression. He didn't know why Mathias had been chased here by demons, but suspected there wouldn't be time for a greater explanation. "Whatever it is you need to get done, hurry."

"May the gods watch over you," Mathias said. He longed to call on Etha's grace to back Brant, but couldn't risk distracting her. Leaving Brant and Ceraphlaks to attempt to stall the oncoming demons, Mathias dashed into the temple.

He only had a vague idea of where he was going, racing his heart's tug to the throne room. Panting as he appraised the pristine chamber, Mathias scanned his surroundings briefly before rushing to the stairs he'd never thought to venture down in the past.

An immense divine power protested his descent, muddling his coherence the same way exhaustion claimed a man, and his stomach churned in discomfort. It was a simple ward, one designed to deter the curiosity of children and looters, but Mathias clamped down on his vow to Etha and pressed on. Affliction was a divine entity of its own, and the piece lodged in Mathias's heart loaned him the power to muscle through this barrier.

Mathias continued deeper, the hairs on the back of his neck trying to pull themselves erect through the dampness of his sweat. A foul, musty odor enhanced the roil in his gut and two steps later, he felt merciless eyes zero in on him. Holding his breath to keep from praying, Mathias banked on fragile hope that these unseen guardians would recognize him and abstain from intervening. May Etha herself help anything that tried to stop him now.

He hurried down the stairs, spiraling deeper than he thought the flight ought to lead him, and down into darkness. Gagging on the burn of bile, he kept a hand on the wall to stabilize himself from the invasive ailment, trusting there was an end to these stairs. Etha counted on him, and Mathias needed no other motivation. He turned one last corner, greeted by a dull, golden glow which illuminated the last two steps and a simple pedestal in a tiny room.

Mathias paused at the landing to catch his breath and survey the solid walls around him. The chamber was no wider than he was tall, and the only item in it was the frightful remains of the legendary god spear. A beautiful piece, it had maintained its splendor even through centuries of neglect. Ethereal words etched the length of the blade, but Mathias didn't dare read them. Affliction had been born of necessity to rip divinity from the gods, and in the glow of its terrible might, Mathias trembled.

Fixing the image before him into his mind, Mathias risked a single interruption to Etha. *Is this it?*

He held his breath as he waited for her delayed answer. *It's not complete, but should serve me well.*

Etha's response had been broken and distracted, ripping at Mathias's calm all over again. He'd achieved his objective, and his goddess needed him. Shoving past the fear and awe of this wondrous weapon, Mathias plunged his hand into Affliction's aura, cringing at the initial jolt that stole over him as he grasped it by what remained of the shaft. His heart raced, the spearhead's light beating in time with his pulse, and he dropped to his knees to gasp for breath. A great flare burst from the metal, blinding him as it investigated the nature of his energy. The flare dimmed to a gentle glow. Eyes wide, Mathias tested its balance.

It doesn't look like much, he told Etha, strain coursing through his thoughts. *It's awful light.*

Deceptive's what I prefer, Etha said. *Be quick and careful. Once Shand realizes what you hold, she'll stop at nothing to take it, and Affliction will corrupt to the level of its master.*

Mathias did not trouble Etha for elaboration. He'd been given his assignment, successfully fulfilled it, and now he had to return to Etha in time for it to make a difference. Mathias dashed back up the stairs, guided by Affliction's glow.

* * * * *

Brant used to pride himself on his effectiveness in combat, but that was long before the demons had torn him down so badly. They didn't waste their time playing with him the way they did with Mathias, throwing themselves at him in rapid succession. If he'd had a breath to spare for bitter reflections, Brant would have wished he'd never agreed to watch the paladin's back.

His strength sapped at an alarming rate, the time spent confined to the fortress stifling his full potential. The weight of his sword towed at his arm, and before he moved on to his third opponent, exhaustion forced him to wield it with both hands. Giving up couldn't be an option, especially now that the flemans had finally secured their position. Brant needed to keep these demons from interfering with Mathias's plan—whatever that was— and to trust that Inwan had Renigan under control.

A pair of demons targeted Brant, his courage shuddering as the beasts passed around him in a slow circle. Attention split between these two and the group standing by for their turn to strike, Brant narrowly caught one of the pair lunge forward, directing a spear at his face. Brant wasn't too worn to dodge a fatal blow, but the tip sliced across his forehead.

Vision distorted by blood, Brant grimaced through the pain. Adrenaline spiked, allowing him to grasp the spear's shaft. Before he had the chance to muscle it away, the demon gave his end a stout yank and pulled Brant off balance.

The commander staggered and failed to catch himself. As soon as his knee hit the ground, a demons' foot shoved him down on his back. Brant had barely made a dent in the offensive force clustered around him. If the sharp rasp of his own breathing hadn't been so loud, Brant would have heard Mathias shout his name over the pounding of his footsteps. Instead, all Brant could process was the desire to stay alive as a stocky demon hefted a great axe into the air above him.

Brant rolled as the axe fell. While he narrowly avoided a lethal blow to his neck, the axe caught his right arm just above the elbow. The limb severed on impact and screams of agony overpowered survival instincts as control of his physical functions fled him. His left hand clutched wildly at the wound, flailing about to locate a tangible part of the phantom limb, and panic flooded his senses. As the demons skittered about to organize their next strike, shock whispered its misleading peace to Brant. The last thought he managed to piece together was that he'd given Mathias a head start. Nessix would have been pleased.

* * * * *

Mathias hadn't seen Brant fall, but he did hear the commander's screams. Not wasting his breath to curse, he ran harder for the temple's exit, Affliction clasped in the vise of his grip. Brant would rather die than flee, and that thought did very little to put Mathias's mind at ease.

The exit came into sight, revealing Brant rolling on the ground, covered in blood and picking up more as he writhed in agony. Etha had ordered Mathias's haste, but Brant had shown a tremendous display of selflessness to buy him time, and as long as the young man still showed the will to live, Mathias had to attempt to rescue him.

Bursting into the daylight, Mathias wielded Affliction's spearhead like a dagger, brandishing it toward the demons poised to pounce on his commander. Still glowing with its lust for divine energy and radiating with the terror that had nearly rendered Mathias too afraid to touch it, the demons may not have recognized Affliction's significance, but they certainly registered its danger.

Never ones to balk at the concept of fear, the sight of Affliction in Mathias's hands sucked the demons' attention away from Brant's thrashing. Tuning out the anguished screams, Mathias sprang forward, trusting that this most sacred part of Affliction contained at least as much power as the tiny piece familiar to him. The weapon melded into Mathias's mind, consuming his instincts as he leapt over Brant's body to slam the blade into the first demon's gut. He spun to slash through a second's throat and by the time he turned to locate his third victim, the remaining demons scrambled from him, shoving each other out of the way to distance themselves from his devastating new toy. The power radiating from this awful weapon terrified Mathias, but he wouldn't dwell on his fears. Too many depended on him for that.

Ceraphlaks flew after the fleeing demons to track their departure until they'd distanced themselves to the point of no longer posing a threat. The chaos driving them from the scene suggested they didn't plan to return, but Mathias appreciated the support nonetheless. Panting from his exertion and from the residual ache radiating in his chest, Mathias knelt down and grabbed a hold of Brant's left shoulder to roll him onto his back. Brant drew his knees to his chest and attempted to roll over again, eyes pinched closed. Tears expedited the flow of blood down his cheeks. Even through this mask, the ashen paleness of death lingered close.

"Commander, can you hear me?" Mathias gripped Affliction tightly and glanced around to survey their surroundings. It seemed clear, at least for the immediate future. Ceraphlaks landed nearby, supporting that observation. "I need you to consent to my healing."

Brant sputtered a garbled reply, one which Mathias took the liberty of calling agreement. He cast a bleak look at the severed limb. Reconnecting Brant's arm would take much more power than Mathias could generate on his own. Brant already hated him, and if he did nothing at all, it wouldn't be long before the commander bled out. Drawing on his own life force, Mathias cupped his left hand over Brant's spurting stump and infused all of the strength he felt he could spare into the other man to initiate granulation.

The bleeding stanched and Brant's cries lost their delirious edge as he lay still, chest heaving. He swayed on the cusp of losing consciousness, but there was nothing else Mathias could afford to do right now.

"Keep patrolling the area," he told Ceraphlaks as he stood. "If any danger approaches, do whatever you must to lead it away from him."

The pegasus trotted over to Brant's side, delicate head raised high in the air, active ears surveying the area for danger. Mathias wanted to thank his old friend, wanted to give him a smile or a pat, but he was too disheartened to do so. This was not the way the war was supposed to end.

Unwilling to dwell any longer, unable to, Mathias enveloped himself in a veil of light, latched on to Etha's grace, and raced back to his goddess's side.

* * * * *

The chaos surging through the divine channels threatened to impede Mathias's journey, grabbing at him like thick spider webs, but he drove forward. Etha needed him. Forbidding himself from asking her about her current status, Mathias tried to reassure the grim beast inside himself that there was no way Shand posed a genuine threat to Etha. That internal monster, spinning whole spools of fear, warned Mathias not to discredit Shand's ambition. Besides that, what would happen when this fight resolved and the remaining god children were left to contemplate how Shand had stood against their mother? Mathias pressed the thought from his mind and doubled his efforts to reach his destination.

The sound of the battlefield struck Mathias before it came into view, the clash roaring much louder than he'd expected. When he'd left, it had only been the two goddesses and the small front of demons who chased after him, but now, the demons had driven the fleman force against the dueling deities. It was a perilous location for mortals.

The flash of Mathias's arrival stunned the battlefield, but did not hinder the progress of the two goddesses. The first time Mathias had rescued Shand, she'd been a mortal, beaten and run through by a crazed mage bent on uncovering the secrets of necromancy. At the time, Mathias's virtue and honor had insisted he save her, that his mercy would guide her off the dark path she travelled. She'd been the first person he healed after his resurrection, and as he stared at the vile goddess now, he wished he'd have left her to bleed out in the streets that day.

A thick, glistening ichor seeped from the lacerations across Shand's arms and face. Mathias had never seen a god bleed before, hadn't even known it was possible, and while seeing Shand's injuries startled him, he could hardly stand to look at Etha. Each wound flawing her pristine flesh streamed golden light glittering with her essence. As she swept in and out of Shand's range, those beams caressed the feuding armies around them, rejuvenating the flemans in their path and shriveling the most unfortunate demons to ash. Etha's grace blessed the field in an uninhibited cascade, but the determination she clenched down on rooted itself in exhaustion. This uncontrolled expenditure of energy was rapidly draining her.

The foolish bravery that had won Etha over in the past surged in Mathias's heart and he ran to aid his goddess.

Both divine women spun to face him, eyes zeroing in on the weapon clutched in his hands. For the first time in his life, Mathias was too overcome by Etha's power to move, and he was thankful she was close enough to grasp Affliction before Shand had the chance to move in. Etha's tiny hand wrapped around what Mathias had used as its hilt and she frowned.

"I am so sorry, my love."

Mathias gasped, fear of having done something wrong, of disappointing Etha, sucking the breath from him. He met her eyes, soaked in her sorrow, and then Etha slammed her free hand against his forehead.

A scream tore Mathias's throat raw as Etha extracted the viable life from him. He would recover. He had to. But right now,

Etha needed his strength in a way she never had before. In the final wisps of consciousness, Mathias saw each of Etha's wounds pull closed as the healing touch of her paladin's soul caressed them. She'd done what was necessary, a sacrifice he was honored to make, and as his world closed around him, Mathias almost smiled at the good he had done.

Lust engulfed Shand's gaze as she stared at Affliction. Mathias was so vulnerable right now with what Etha had sapped from him, and Shand's entire objective could be completed so simply if not for that enthralling chunk of metal in Etha's hands. She hungered for that spearhead, more than she'd hungered for power, more than she remembered hungering for her ascension in the first place. Fear never had a chance to strike her through the surge of awe and desire devouring her sensibilities. Etha stepped to the side, standing protectively over the body of her fallen son.

"You said you came here to lure Mathias away from me?" Etha asked, her typical warmth and charm flung aside. "As though you truly thought that could be done?"

Having robbed Mathias of all his strength and armed with a weapon capable of rending all of Abaeloth, Etha now held an indisputable advantage. Shand could run and she could hide, but it would be impossible to evade Etha for the rest of eternity. Obtaining Affliction was the last chance she had.

"You swore you'd never kill with Affliction again," Shand sneered, investing all of her hope in the idea that she'd be able to manipulate Etha's morals to trick her into dropping her guard. "And you don't break your laws."

Etha's brows arched, eyes hardening beneath them. All around her raged a war that never should have found this island, and Shand had been the one to bring it here. "You're right, Shand Heltsa," Etha said, "but I think I've already proven to care more about the integrity of my world than the laws I gave it. I crave order, and I will have it."

Etha's lips pressed in a thin line and she sprang forward, launching her tiny mass forward with speed defiant to reality. Shand had anticipated the debate to span at least a few more exchanges, but Etha's ambition to restore her vision of balance surpassed any inclination toward negotiation. By the time Shand registered how close Etha was, Etha had sank Affliction into Shand's abdomen.

Pain was a meddlesome sensation after having thrived so long without its inhibitions, and of course Affliction would be the first and only thing able to deliver it to Shand. The puncture itself sank in with little more than a firm pinch, the blade searing with holy energy that dulled the immediate agony of impalement. Shand's eyes launched wide and she wrapped her fingers around Etha's wrist, fingers digging into her mother's flesh, though she couldn't generate the strength to push her away.

"But... you... you *can't*...." A sputter of blood interrupted Shand's pitiful objection and her arms began to tremble.

"Kill you?" Etha asked. She hissed and narrowed her eyes. "I wouldn't dream of it."

Now came the pain as Affliction settled in Shand's core. Bolts of retribution shot through her system, burning her from the inside and roping the parts of her that made her divine. Etha had never extracted a god shard before, had never had the need to, and hadn't been certain if it could be done. The way she figured, if the process failed her, she could easily recruit an executioner to finish the job. Shand wailed against the pain as Affliction bound itself to her divinity, her eyes losing their brilliant glint as her hands fell helplessly away. Etha jerked Affliction free, severing Shand's link to the might she had so thoroughly abused, and pathetic sobs wrenched the mortal once-goddess as she doubled over and fell to her knees.

With Affliction vibrating an enthusiastic anthem in her left hand, Etha placed her right on the top of Shand's head and, against the vindictive urge proclaiming its authority in the deepest part of her being, she healed the cursed woman's physical damage. It was a filthy betrayal to the flemans and Mathias, but Shand still had a pivotal purpose on Abaeloth.

"What—" Shand's mind reeled in its search for comprehension, clawing for some hint of the power she'd taken for granted. The taste of weakness she'd suffered in the demons' realm paled to nothing in light of the gaping void mocking her now.

Hyperventilating, she reached her trembling fingers to pat at her prickling cheeks and cast bleary eyes to meet Etha's harsh scowl.

"I should throw you to the flemans," Etha stated evenly. "In fact, I'm tempted to see what Mathias wants to do with you after all you've done. I *am* awful fond of him, after all."

Tears rolled down Shand's cheeks as she shook her head, murmuring incoherent pleas that had no effect on Etha.

"But neither of them will deliver you the proper judgement," Etha said.

Shand held her breath, catching herself on weak arms as she toppled forward. "Then what…?"

Etha glanced over her shoulder to where Mathias lay crumbled in the dirt. She sighed. "I will escort you back to Zeal to face trial by the Council. I'm sure Mathias will be more than happy to testify against you."

The color drained from Shand's face and she wished for the first time in valid recollection that she hadn't been such a fool.

THIRTY-ONE

The demons had been quick to scatter upon Affliction's arrival to the field. Their retreat was encouraged faster still once Shand's fate became obvious, leaving the flemans to quake in terror and awe of the monumental bout that should have never come to pass. Etha entrusted Mathias's safety and recovery to Sulik's capable hands and escorted Shand and Affliction both back to Zeal. Inwan followed his mother's guidance at last and detained Renigan in a pocket realm well out of any vengeful fleman's reach.

Humbled by the perils of having faced Etha, the demons pulled themselves back to that last portal to regroup, allowing Elidae to creep out of hiding once more. The twisted fiends would continue to be a nuisance to this blessed land, but for now, the nation could breathe a sigh of relief.

Days after Mathias recovered from the sacrifice Etha had thrust upon him, he still struggled to gather the nerve to speak to Brant. The devastating events which had transpired outside the temple hung heavy on the paladin's mind, and though Sulik had assured him all would be well, Mathias didn't hold his breath, given Brant's opinion of him. Either way, Mathias knew words must be exchanged, if for no other reason than to confirm Brant was finally ready to accept the burden of General of the fleman army. Fending off a barrage of pessimistic speculations, Mathias sought out

Brant's location, following leads and instinct to the closed door of Nes's chamber.

He stared at the door for some time, negativity wriggling free and prodding him over thoughts better left sealed away. It shouldn't have been Brant who he was going to speak to at the end of this the war. It should have been Nessix, with all of her fire and enthusiasm. She'd have allowed herself to get lost in festivities this time, celebrating victory over the fiercest opponents her people had ever faced. He'd have done his job of seeing her through to her coveted brighter times, and he'd have been rewarded with her brilliant smile and gleaming eyes, her gratitude and affection.

Mathias closed his eyes and rolled his lips between his teeth, stuffing such sentiments aside for a more appropriate time when he could tuck himself away to reflect on them properly. Drawing in a deep breath past his grief, Mathias swallowed down the wad of regret in his throat, opened his eyes, and knocked on the door.

A bold order for his entry sounded from the other side and Mathias blinked. That hadn't been the sort of confidence he'd expected to hear from Brant after all of the suffering he'd so recently endured. After a brief gnaw on the inside of his cheek, Mathias opened the door.

The curtains had been cast back, illuminating the chamber with the day's hope and brightness. The room had been untouched from the last time Mathias had seen it, covers still rumpled from where Nessix had laid on the bed prior to her funeral, that same half-drained bottle of wine now powdered with dust on the corner of her desk. Brant stood calmly by the window, gaze cast out across the fields his cousin had contemplated with such tenderness. He didn't turn back to confirm Mathias's identity, and the paladin couldn't be sure if that was due to him already knowing or simply not caring. Brant had finally surrendered to wearing Nes's cape, though he kept it draped over his right shoulder, likely an attempt to obscure the fact that he no longer had that limb. Mathias refused to let himself avert his gaze.

"Am I interrupting something, General?" Mathias asked from the doorway, reluctant to enter as he wasn't yet convinced Brant welcomed his company.

Brant heaved a sigh and straightened with a jerk. He took his time to form his reply. "I'm not sure I'll ever get used to that title."

Mathias smiled that there hadn't been a fight put up about it this time. "You will," he assured, walking inside at the lack of warning in Brant's words. "But I'll ask you again. Had I interrupted anything?"

Brant turned his head to face Mathias, his expression placid. He looked over the man he'd spent so long hating, the man he'd hoped would fix Elidae's problems, and his jaded eyes softened. "Only my thoughts."

Mathias nodded and tested to see if he'd be allowed to approach closer. When Brant didn't pitch a fit, he walked up beside the other man to look out the window and across the fields of Elidae. "You'll be dealing with a lot of them now." He smirked. "I don't envy you that task."

With a sigh, Brant turned his eyes forward again. "I'm arranging for the caravans to start sending the civilians home," he said. "We're starting close by and as the army secures the more distant townships, they'll be released as well."

"A sound plan. I'm sure your cooks and maids here at the fortress will appreciate the decreased workload."

Brant's lips twitched at what could have developed into a smile, but he turned to face Mathias instead. "And what about you?"

Mathias would have thrown a clever quip if he'd been talking to Nessix, but he wasn't. He was talking to Brant Maliroch, the man who had wanted to see him dead up until the past few weeks. Securing his jest behind pursed lips, Mathias glanced away.

"So you're leaving us?" Brant asked. "Heading back home to Zeal?"

It took Mathias longer than he preferred to gather his wits and he looked to the broken man beside him. "I'm leaving and will secure reinforcements to assist in Elidae's protection in my stead. But I won't be going home. I made a promise to us both."

Brant frowned. "She wouldn't have let you leave, you know."

Mathias shifted his weight and scratched the back of his calf with his foot. "I don't believe she'd have been able to stop me."

Brant shook his head, eyes swelling with a rich remorse that pressed against Mathias's heart. "She had far more power than physical strength, you know. You—" He hesitated. Mathias had saved his life, and it had taken that for Brant to fully appreciate his worth. "You love her, Sagewind. You wouldn't have left her."

"And that is why I must leave now." Mathias cast his eyes to the ground and grasped an elbow. "There were times when she told me she had enough faith in your abilities to turn command over to you, and you've proven her judgement to be sound. All I ask is that you do not betray that trust."

Brant lowered his head, wishing he had a reason to hate Mathias all over again. "I've accepted my new position under the assumption that you will invest your energy in finding her. You've already given us so much, but I beg you… this one last thing."

It did them both good to feel a civil agreement pass between them at last, and ease trickled through the room. The war was over, Elidae had new faith and hope along with it. Mathias was prepared to quest for eternity to reclaim Nessix, and once he did, he would find Brant, living or dead, to reunite the cousins. Until that time, Mathias's heart would not venture far from Elidae.

"Will you and Sulik be able to hold down the fort for a couple days?" Mathias asked at last.

Brant furrowed his brow. "You really think it will only take a couple days to find Nes? After what you'd been dreading before?"

Mathias chuckled humorlessly and shook his head. "No, not for that. I do have to make a stop by Zeal. While I can't be here to guide your people through what's left, I've got an apprentice—"

"Sagewind, enough with your tricks…"

Mathias smiled and flicked a dismissive hand. "Not that kind. That's what Sulik's for. No, I think you'll like this one. A fine demon hunter. Able to teach your people a whole lot more than I did."

That sounded strange. Mathias had popped up, declaring himself the definitive authority on fighting demons. Did he really have this much faith in someone he'd trained? "So you suspect we haven't seen the last of the demons?"

"We still haven't tended to their last portal." Mathias paused at the delivery of that statement. Having failed at reaching it twice, he almost wondered if Elidae was meant to keep that cursed doorway. He shook his head. Brant didn't need to worry about the details of fate. "And after whatever it was Etha did to me, I'm not sure when I'd be able to tend to it. Between the officer I'm bringing and you, I've no doubt the demons will not cause the same trouble we just made it through."

Brant's expression remained dubious, but he didn't press the issue. "So did you come here just to check on me? To make sure I was sane?"

"I never doubted your sanity," Mathias said plainly. "The trials you faced have made you the general who's standing next to me now. You're going to be fine, Brant. We all will be." Mathias heaved an obnoxious sigh and fit a smile past his discomfort. "I'll let you get back to your thinking, General. I've got some travel plans of my own to tend to."

Brant smirked at Mathias as the paladin turned and left then shifted his gaze back out over his kingdom. "We did it, Nes," he murmured. "Just like you said."

* * * * *

"Fuck!"

Brant's sword clattered to the ground and he spun from Sulik who lowered his in exasperation.

"Maybe we should take a break," the older of the two suggested.

"No." Brant's voice was strict and out of patience. By habit, he reached for his fallen sword with the remainder of his missing arm and huffed his irritation as he retrieved it with his spent left hand. "We keep going."

"Things are quiet right now—"

"And they won't stay that way. Not with the other portal. Not with the unrest of Veed's men. Come on, Sulik. Come at me."

Sulik sighed and casually switched his sword to his off hand, drawing a glower from the younger man.

"Sulik…"

"Brant, you're still learning—"

"I told you to come *on*."

Sulik hefted a sigh and switched his sword over to his right hand as a throat cleared from the courtyard's entryway. Both men turned to see Mathias walking their way, his mischief only shining through in his eyes. Just behind him walked a woman and a gasp stuck in Brant's throat as his sword clattered from his weakened arm yet again.

He'd always been a bit of a player, not nearly as promiscuous as Veed, but well known around certain avenues. This was the first time that simply seeing a woman wiped all thoughts of casual flings far from his mind.

Her hair was a deep red, he'd guess roughly shoulder length, if she wouldn't have had it secured in a tidy knot at the nape of her neck. Her features were chiseled with a refined beauty reserved for someone far more prestigious than nobility. Mathias had said that the demon hunter he was bringing to watch over Elidae was well seasoned and possibly put his own skills to shame, but there was no evidence of a life on the field flawing this woman's smooth skin. Brant wasn't even able to take account of the arms she wore or how out of place that beautiful face looked framed in battered and tried armor. Instead, he stared at her enchanting green eyes, jaw slacked.

Sulik cleared his throat and repeated the address which had slid clear past Brant. "*General Maliroch.*"

Brant shook his head and retrieved his sword in a hurry, flushing as he struggled to return it to its sheath. He caught Mathias's glance, one accompanied by an irritating smile. It had been quite some time since Brant had considered the paladin a true nuisance, but right now, he'd have preferred to have been spared the other man's mischievous appraisal. *Great Inwan, have I really gotten that obvious?*

No matter how humorous Mathias might have wanted to find this situation, he was also well aware of how Sazrah's heritage affected Brant, though he hadn't expected such an experienced warrior to succumb so easily. "General, Commander," Mathias said, greeting the two flemans. "I'd like to introduce to you Sazrah the

Shade. She is the best demon hunter I've had the privilege to fight beside."

Sazrah smiled in the taut politeness of an adolescent standing by to listen to the exaggerations of a boastful parent, a gentle flush painting her cheeks at his words. "I am an efficient demon hunter," she corrected without a hint of the reluctance one might expect from someone contradicting Mathias. "I wouldn't say I'm the best."

"Efficient, see?" Mathias asked, jerking a thumb in Sazrah's direction. "That's the sort of thing you like to hear, right Brant?"

Brant's frown tightened as it became obvious Mathias was aiming to irritate him. "If she proves to be an asset, then yes."

Mathias grinned. "An asset..." He turned to Sulik. "Mind showing Sazrah around for me, Commander?"

Sulik swallowed his own humor and nodded. "If you'll come with me, Lady—"

"Sazrah's fine." She interrupted Sulik with a bold ease which Brant fought hard to ignore.

Sulik cleared his throat and clasped his hands behind his back, splitting a quick glance between those in his company. "Of course, Sazrah. If you'd come with me?"

The two walked off, leaving Mathias musing to himself and Brant back to fuming at the paladin. Old habits seemed unlikely to die quietly.

"You should have told me you were bringing a woman," Brant said.

Smirk broadening to an impish grin, Mathias glanced from where Sulik and Sazrah had left the courtyard and back to Brant. "And that matters?"

Brant cleared his throat. "Potentially."

Mathias slapped Brant on his left shoulder. "She's a good soldier, as I'm sure you'll see. Just..." He shook his head. "Good luck, General. She's willful enough to..." The humor faltered from Mathias's face and he let his hand fall back to his side. "She'll keep Elidae safe." He heaved a sigh. "I'd best get going. I've got a lot of ground to cover."

The abrupt change of subject struck Brant just as hard, and he bit down on the insides of his cheeks to keep the last of his raw emotions in check. Though he doubted it would ever disappear completely, the pain of having lost Nessix had finally begun to soften. "I'm trusting you, Sagewind."

Mathias lowered his eyes and nodded. "I'll be in touch."

A tense moment passed between the two of them, neither knowing what else to say, neither wanting to say anything at all. When it became apparent that Brant was content letting Mathias head down his new path, the paladin turned and walked back through the door. Brant watched this man, his hope, his comrade, stride away. One step, then another. A third, and he vanished in that flash of light. Brant stared at the afterimage, listening to the thump of his heart, then rubbed his forehead. Pulling himself back from the edge of despair, Brant sighed and left the courtyard to see how his new demon hunter was settling in.

* * * * *

Darkness whispered its uncertainties to her, suppressing the only sign of life behind the shrill ringing in her ears. Nessix clung to this trace of reality as muffled sounds beat their way through the auditory haze. Sharp cracks of lightning snapped through the air around her and thunder rumbled so deep it shook the ground against her back. Next came the stench, a disgustingly familiar aroma which scraped together some of her fondest memories. Battle.

There were no pounding hooves tramping around her or crashes of weapons. No war cries or blares of horns to distribute orders across the field. Instead came the haunting dissonance of grown men weeping in terror and anguish which razed Nes's courage, the blubbering of broken words she couldn't grasp. A strong hand took a hold of her arm and shook her, a more distinct—yet equally foreign—voice strained an urgent address. Nessix groaned at the force of a second shove and a crippling pain shot from her right hip, searing down her leg and up to her lungs. Nausea washed over her, receding into a chilly dizziness and her heart leapt as she identified the precursors to shock's fraudulent comfort. Trusting that this hand which tried to rouse her would see

380

her to safety, Nessix gathered her strength.

Eyes peering open, a piercing brightness bombarded her vision, crackling with bursts of light to compliment the raging discord in her ears. The voice called to her again, and Nessix turned her muddled attention to behold a man with half his face peeled off from lip to eye, the skin hanging from his lower jaw. Choking on a gasp, Nessix fought to pull her arm free. She attempted to push herself backward to distance herself from this horror, but as she braced her right heel into the ground to leverage a shove, the pain screamed louder, snatching away any whims related to fleeing. She writhed against the trembling ground beneath her, shrieking in agony.

The man reached forward and grasped her other arm. He leaned in front of her, speaking more words she couldn't understand. Flashes born in the distance raced closer toward them with each heartbeat, and when Nessix forced herself to level her teary gaze to meet that of this shredded man, she recognized the palpable terror in his glistening eyes.

He repeated his words and frantically gestured behind him. Nessix might not have understood what he said, but his message was clear. This stranger, no matter how grievous his wounds, was trying to help her. Gritting her teeth, Nessix nodded, the effort rattling bolts of agony through her head like a jar of loose marbles, and she clutched to her savior's arms as he hauled her to her feet.

Pain struck Nessix in hot waves as her broken hip released its hold on her right leg when she stood. Her body begged her to fall back to the ground and take the easy way out of this life, but the man held her close against his side. He waited for Nes's screams to subside to strained whimpers and began to drag them both away from the battlefield.

Another tremor shook the ground, this one more powerful and accompanied by a mournful groaning from Abaeloth's very soul. The man shouted again, panic slipping past that firm calm he'd commanded before. He tightened his arm around Nes's torso and tried to quicken their pace. Gasping and trembling, Nessix staggered along with him, pressing her face against his bloodied side as they ran as effectively as two broken warriors could.

Without knowing where she was, Nessix had no idea which direction meant safety. Anywhere was better than this field of certain death. A bolt of jagged light shot down twenty paces ahead of the pair and flung them back to where they'd started. Nessix struck her head on the ground, the ringing returning as she shoved her dazed self upright to find the faceless man lying in a mangled heap nearby. His body seized with violent spasms much stronger than a man on the brink of death, and as Nessix watched on in horror, a second bolt struck ten feet from her, splintering a vein of light into her chest.

Pressure crushed down around Nes's lungs, squeezing the air from her as she gagged for breath. She clawed at her throat, pulled at her hair, wheezed for all she was worth as tears squeezed from her eyes. Another bolt passed above her and she heard her companion scream again. As Nessix's vision began to dim and her hands lost the strength to keep tearing for freedom, the pressure lifted.

The battlefield might have shown her mercy, but the darkness of the hells maintained its suffocating embrace, and with a desperate gasp, Nessix's eyes flew open.

The Afflicted Saga

Defilement

Tale of the Fallen: Book III

DEMONS HAVE MADE A NEW LEGEND…

The room was small, barely large enough for a pair of bunks, though this one contained only one simple cot. Thin streaks of blood swept across the top and Kol's brows furrowed at the thought of Nessix being handled so carelessly without his oversight. There were no other access points besides the door which Kol stood in, but Nessix was nowhere to be seen. Kol's mind still crept along with his recovery, preventing him from acting or even thinking to ask Annin if he was sure Nessix had been secured in this room.

Kol took a step forward and the door instantly slammed shut behind him. Before he had the chance to jump at the sudden sound, rough fibers of rope wrapped around his neck, followed briskly by a pair of nimble legs latching around his waist. Nessix made no sound as she struck, her breathing controlled and even, unfazed by this act of violence. Her heart beat steady against Kol's back with the confidence he expected from such a well-forged weapon. For a moment, he was so swept up by Nessix's effectiveness that he nearly forgot to fight back. Unlike Nessix, however, he couldn't afford to be neutralized.

His wings wouldn't allow him to effectively crush Nessix by slamming her against a wall or the floor, so he reached over his shoulders to grope for her wrists. One hand grasped the tail of the rope—close enough to buy him an extra breath—and the one that brushed against warm flesh was instantly pierced by Nessix's teeth. Kol didn't have the time to marvel at how little hesitation Nessix used to counter his defense as her teeth threatened to sever the tendons in his hand.

He howled at the injury and snarled with determination. He'd hoped to win Nessix over without undue force, but it seemed she liked to do things the hard way. Sucking in a deep breath, Kol released his hold on the rope and it dug into his throat once more. This time, Nessix began to saw its rough edges against the thin flesh of his neck, and Kol drew his dagger at last.

Four fingers still functioning, he grasped a hold of Nessix's ankle to make sure he didn't misjudge her location and plunged his knife into her calf. A scream tore from her, ringing in Kol's ears, and Nes's entire body cringed against his back. Kol gave her credit for her tenacity as she continued clinging to him, but his attack had momentarily weakened her enough for him to grab her ankle and pull her from his back.

Before Nessix had the chance to recoil, Kol made sure to rip his dagger free from her leg. It would have done him no good at all to let her be armed with anything more substantial than a piece of rope.

"Do you need assistance?" Annin's bored voice drifted casually from the other side of the closed door, expressing a distinct lack of surprise that Kol had encountered difficulty.

Kol glared at the door. "We're fine," he seethed, casting his gaze back toward Nessix as she hunched over her injury. "Just in need of a little training."

"Am I free to address the lords, then?"

Through the perils of physical assault, Kol's heart rate had only climbed an inch. The thought of announcing to Grell and the other inoga that Nessix was alive nearly shot it straight from his chest. Having shown enough weakness to Annin and unwilling to divulge it to Nessix, Kol bit down on the inevitable.

"Tell them what they need to know. I'll be by as soon as I'm through here."

Annin never gave Kol a verbal response, but he seldom did after receiving orders he didn't particularly want. The lack of reply didn't bother Kol, as he was focused intently on Nessix as she pushed herself away from him, hands clasped around her bleeding calf. Kol allowed her to seek this distance from him, in no rush to force her submission. After all, they had the rest of his life to work on that. He wiped his blade clean on the leg of his pants and shoved it back in its sheath.

Nessix kept her eyes pinned on Kol, her jaw rigid. She didn't pulse with the fear Kol expected from past trials, though given her illustrious past, that couldn't completely surprise him. Rather, her eyes bore an eerie loneliness, as if she felt betrayed by the very mechanics of life. It was a feeling Kol knew far too well.

"That wasn't a very smart move, you know," the demon said, crossing his arms as he studied Nessix's deepening glower.

She refused to answer him, though Kol gave her adequate time to do so.

Kol sighed and strode past her, smirking as she flinched away from him. He flicked his wings back and sat on the edge of the cot. "Do you know who I am?"

Silence still, not even a nod to allude to compliance.

"Your reaction to seeing me suggests you must at least know *what* I am." He narrowed his eyes in careful consideration. The past few months Kol had spent bonding with Nessix's soul had led him to believe that she'd been more aware of her circumstances. Was she playing him now, or had he misjudged her reactions due to his own aspirations? "Do you remember nothing about me at all?"

Nessix lifted the heel of her palm from her wound and grimaced before pressing it down again. "I am dead."

Kol cocked his head. "Are you? Do you recall how that came to be?"

Nessix ventured a fleeting glance at Kol's wily orange eyes. "You…" Her tone was bold and firm, riddled with no more fear than her daring assault had been, but that uncertain void in her eyes glowed of something else entirely.

"I what?" Kol asked.

"You killed me." The confidence in her voice shrank away at her statement. This demon had slaughtered Nessix Teradhel, leaving Elidae to struggle alone without her general. *No, she* thought. *Not alone. They still have Mathias.* Nes's eyes closed, her brows tipping in a melancholy relief, the faintest smile touching her trembling lips.

Kol raised a brow. Happiness was one reaction he'd never witnessed from an akhuerai realizing what had happened to them. "And it was an honor to do so."

A clipped chuckle beat its way free from Nes's chest and she opened her eyes. Feisty courage swirled about her now, deepening her eyes and raising her smile to a degree that bristled Kol. "I suppose it would be an honor for one of you pathetic beasts to be slain by Mathias Sagewind."

Kol blinked and straightened, his resentment of Nes's arrogance shuffled aside. "I wasn't—" He clamped his mouth shut and wrapped his fingers around the edge of the cot as he leaned forward. "What do you mean?"

Nessix's smile flashed her teeth, wicked validation illuminating her face. "I am dead," Nessix repeated, "and this is the afterlife. I never imagined my heaven to be like this, but if you're here, Mathias couldn't have spared you. He destroyed you, and that's enough for me."

Kol erupted with laughter at Nes's determined claim, unable to witness her flicker of indignant confusion through the tears in his eyes. He covered his mouth with a hand, straightening his behavior with a drawn-out, mirthful groan. "Oh, Nessix, you *are* a gem."

She frowned at Kol's reaction, face contorted in rage over how little her declaration concerned him.

"Does your leg hurt?" Kol asked, wiping the dampness of tears from his lower eyelids.

Nessix's eyes narrowed and she shifted her grip on her calf to apply more pressure to the wound.

"Do you think pain is something that registers when you're dead?"

She didn't answer him this time, either, at least not with spoken words. Instead, she looked down at her leg as the pain dulled toward numbness, stared at the coating of blood which painted her hands. Nessix had no idea whether or not pain like this could affect a soul, but her general understanding was that bleeding was a very mortal response. A quiet gasp parted her lips and frightened eyes darted up to Kol's laughing orange gaze. The demon stood and took a step closer to her before crouching down, just as he had before he'd killed her.

"This is not your heaven, Nessix, and you and I are both very much so alive."

The fire dulled from Nes's eyes, the rate of her breathing picking up as instinct flailed between the need to run or fight and the terror of not knowing how to do either. "How… how did…?"

Kol smiled with a hum of satisfaction, pleased to see how readily Nessix was accepting her fate. "I brought you here, brought you back." He reached forward to cup the back of her head in one hand, leaned forward, and kissed the top of her head. "You are destined for great things, Nessix. Do not think of disappointing me."

He stood and crossed his arms, delighting in the confusion tumbling about his treasure's fractured soul. This was exactly where he wanted her, and as long as she remained timid and subdued, introducing her to Grell should go off without a problem.

"Let that breathe," Kol said at last, nodding toward Nessix's injured leg. "It'll heal faster that way."

Kol strode to the door and pulled it open, hesitating briefly as he exited. "Do not greet me like that ever again," he said over his shoulder. "I do not like the idea of hurting you. I am your only ally down here. Do not make me regret that."

Nessix hadn't watched Kol reach the door, too stunned to follow his movement, and she didn't respond to his warning. The door fell shut with a dull thud followed by a lock thumping into place. Nessix drew her knees up to her chest, willing herself not to cry.

ABOUT THE AUTHOR

A lover of literary adventure and notorious breaker of writing rules, Katika Schneider's been an obsessive writer for most of her life. She started out writing for herself before surrendering to her characters' demands, and began pursuing publication in 2014. She's a firm believer that everyone has a story to tell.

Holding her degree in Animal Science, Kat planned on attending veterinary school until incisions started making her faint. She lives with her husband and their abundant family of critters.